HE WAS DRESSED AS A PIRATE . . .

. . . complete with golden hoop in one ear, a bandanna securing dark waving hair, and a rapier at his side. He bowed before her. "Excuse me," came his low voice from behind a black satin mask. "The orchestra will next play a fandango—a Spanish dance of some passion. I would be honored to have you as my partner."

Rebecca's heart nearly stopped. She gave the pirate a careful look. Yes, she saw it now, even through the elaborate disguise. "Captain Caldwell—I warned you. . . ."

Throbbing guitars and the sensuous rhythms of a native drum drowned out her heated protest.

Blaine swept her into his arms and moved across the ballroom floor. He held Rebecca firmly against his body, locked in a demanding embrace as he slowly circled the room. Her toes barely touched the floor as he maneuvered her among the dancers, then swept through the French doors and onto the veranda beyond.

"Let me go!" she flashed, balling her fists against his shoulders. "How dare you drag me outside!"

His mouth came down hard on hers, searing her lips, forcing them into submission.

She started to pummel him, but he gripped her wrists and pinned her arms to her sides. She felt her resistance melting before the explosion of her own desire. All rational thought gone, she curved against him, feeling his arms slip around her, her body pulsing with liquid heat, with sensations she'd never experienced. . . .

Books by Krista Janssen

Wind Rose
Ride the Wind
Creole Cavalier

Published by POCKET BOOKS

For orders other than by individual consumers, Pocket Books grants a discount on the purchase of **10 or more** copies of single titles for special markets or premium use. For further details, please write to the Vice-President of Special Markets, Pocket Books, 1230 Avenue of the Americas, New York, NY 10020.

For information on how individual consumers can place orders, please write to Mail Order Department, Paramount Publishing, 200 Old Tappan Road, Old Tappan, NJ 07675.

CREOLE CAVALIER

KRISTA JANSSEN

POCKET BOOKS
New York London Toronto Sydney Tokyo Singapore

This book is a work of fiction. Names, characters, places and incidents are products of the author's imagination or are used fictitiously. Any resemblance to actual events or locales or persons, living or dead, is entirely coincidental.

An *Original* Publication of POCKET BOOKS

POCKET BOOKS, a division of Simon & Schuster Inc.
1230 Avenue of the Americas, New York, NY 10020

ISBN: 0-671-87464-0

First Pocket Books printing December 1994

10 9 8 7 6 5 4 3 2 1

Cover art by Alessandro Biffignandi

Printed in the U.S.A.

For my editor,
Denise Silvestro

My deepest thanks, Denise, for your enthusiasm, for your encouragement and expertise, and especially for your faith in me from the very first.

CREOLE CAVALIER

1

Tennessee
May 1814

It was a turkey, all right—fat, dumb and delicious—rare these days in the woods near the settlements.

Rebecca stood as still as one of the towering oaks surrounding her. Her boots became one with the leaf-strewn forest floor. Barely breathing, she lowered the butt of the long-rifle to rest on her toe and pulled a bullet from the pouch. Then she extracted a small scrap of cotton that had been soaked in grease. She wrapped the bullet, placed it into the small bore and used her hickory rod to send it down the barrel—all within thirty seconds and without making a sound. Still she chastised herself for not having her weapon ready. Until this minute, her search for food had bagged only one squirrel and a handful of wild berries. Now that she was nearly home, she had a turkey sitting pretty as you please on a low branch just a hundred yards away. At this distance, she couldn't miss.

Taking aim, she held her breath and slowly squeezed the trigger. A blast, a jolt, and she saw the bird crash to earth in a flurry of feathers. Thank goodness, there would be plenty of food on the table for a day or two.

The shadows were growing long in the late steamy afternoon as she approached the cabin she shared with her mother in Morgan's Landing. She was sweating with the effort of climbing through the brambles in the woods near the house. There was no smoke curling from the chimney to welcome her—nor had there been since her mother had taken to her bed eight days ago.

She increased her pace as she crossed the newly planted garden, balancing the long-rifle in one hand and hauling the plump turkey in the other. If her mother was worse, she would walk the mile to their nearest neighbors, the MacGregors, to see if Mrs. MacGregor had any more of that bitter concoction she'd brewed up to lower a person's fever. No one knew where this disease came from or how to effect a cure. A few remedies were tried, but in the end, whatever happened would be up to God—and maybe the patient's own will to live.

Her mother had always been a strong woman, Rebecca thought as she hurried up the path. She had been widowed and alone when she arrived in Morgan's Landing seventeen years ago, and in the early stages of pregnancy. She had never remarried, and until lately, Rebecca had never questioned her decision to remain single. But a man would have been a great help around the place all these years—and surely her mother had missed having a husband's love and protection and companionship. She'd always seemed happy, though, and said she never regretted her decision to leave Scotland. She claimed that whatever hardships she found here, none were as terrible as the persecution of the Coventers and the campaign of terror against the clans in her homeland. Here in America, the Scots had been free to organize their presbytery and worship as they pleased. The land belonged to the people—and it was a giving land if a body was willing to work to bring it to harvest.

"Mama?" Rebecca called. "Mama, look. I shot a turkey—not a big one, but we'll have meat for supper."

She placed her gun by the door and plopped the bird onto the rough-hewn table in the middle of the room that served as parlor and kitchen. Pushing back the drapery separating the two rooms of the cabin, she looked toward the bed.

Her mother appeared to be dozing under her light quilt, her head propped on a goose-down pillow. Even from here, Rebecca could see how pale she was in the soft light filtering through the single dusty windowpane.

"Mama?" she called softly. "Are you asleep? I'm back. Can I fetch you a drink of water?"

The figure on the bed stirred. "Rebecca—honey? I'm glad ye're home. Come sit awhile. I . . . I need to talk to ye, lass."

"Surely, Mama. I'll just wash up and light the fire under the kettle. Then after we visit, I'll start supper."

A few minutes later, she pulled up a chair beside the bed and grasped her mother's thin hand. It was plain her mother was much worse today. After supper, she'd scoot over to the MacGregors and get the medicine.

Rebecca stroked her mother's heated forearm. "What do you want to talk about, Mama?"

Elizabeth Gordon moved up on the pillow and managed a smile. Her skin was like yellow parchment, weathered and lined. Her blue eyes were sunken into their sockets and her prematurely white hair was matted around her ears and neck. All traces of her early youth and beauty had been erased by years of struggle and hardship. She reached to grasp her daughter's hand. "Becca, honey, I've had a good life. I wouldn't change a bit of it. And I have no fear of death."

A cold fist turned in Rebecca's stomach. "Now, Mama, don't talk about dying," she said with forced lightness in her tone. "It's just a passing spell . . . like that one you had last fall. Just think of getting well and going with me to the fair in Nashville."

She saw the smile fade from her mother's lips. Oh, she did look much worse today. But surely she couldn't really be dying. Why, she was not yet fifty.

"Listen, my darling," came the raspy voice. "I have loved thee dearly, have I not?"

"Yes, Mama. Always—just like I love you."

"I've taught ye all I know—to read and write and cipher—and education is a most important thing."

"Yes'm."

"But I've been sorely worried this past year, seeing how ye've grown into such a fine girl, such a bonnie lass, and so quick to learn your lessons."

"You see me with eyes of love, that's all. And why should you be worried?"

"'Tis plain ye're not like the other folks in Morgan's

Landing. They're good folks, but . . . but ye're . . . well, cut from a different cloth. I've seen the look in your eye lately. Ye're restless, Becca. Ye want more, and you deserve more than the life I've had here. 'Tis time ye thought about leaving Tennessee, especially now that I . . ."

Rebecca shook her head. "It's your fever, Mama. You just imagine such things. You've worked so hard to make us a home here. I wouldn't leave . . ."

"Listen to me, daughter. Though it's in God's hands, I believe my time is short. I have to think of your future. And . . . and I must tell ye . . . tell ye . . ." Elizabeth's eyes filled with rare tears but her voice gained strength. "Now I must tell ye something very hard . . . hard for me to speak about."

"Don't tire yourself, Mama," Rebecca suggested tenderly. "Rest and I'll start supper. We'll talk later."

"I've got to say it while I have the courage—and pray when I'm done ye'll understand. Ye see, child, for years I've lived a lie."

"A lie? But you're the most honest soul in Tennessee. Everyone knows that."

"I've tried to be a good woman—and I think I have been since I left New Orleans to come upriver to make our home."

"Of course you have. Some folks claim you're a saint, the way you help the sick, and work in the church, and—"

"Not a saint, child. Not even close. I thought I would never tell ye what happened, but . . . I have to now. I have to tell ye about your birth."

"I don't understand."

"Just listen and I'll explain. It began when Allan and I left Scotland to make our home in America. Our son, Gilbert, was just sixteen, but already he'd joined the Highlanders regiment and left home for good. Ye know the story of how Allan died on the ship and I arrived in New Orleans, a widow with hardly a penny to my name."

"I know, Mama. You were pregnant too. It was a terrible time."

Elizabeth's eyes were red-rimmed spheres in her gaunt face. Every word was labored. "Nay, Rebecca. I wasn't yet pregnant. And the time I spent in New Orleans was the most beautiful of my life."

For a long moment, Rebecca struggled to comprehend what her mother was saying. Finally, she whispered, "But then how . . . when was I conceived? And who . . ." The question stuck in her throat. She'd always honored the memory of her father, taken pride in the Scottish heritage of the Gordons. What was her mother trying to tell her? She felt a vise tightening around her chest, slowing her heartbeat and choking off her breath.

"What I'm saying, my darling Rebecca, is that Allan Gordon was not your father."

The words hung in the air between them, echoing in the heavy silence long after the sound had faded away.

Rebecca felt them like a physical blow. It was as if a part of her very being had been torn away; the very foundation of all she believed in was falling into an abyss under her feet. Through tight lips, her voice almost imperceptible, she asked, "Then who . . . who am I?"

Her mother squeezed her hand. "Ye're my precious daughter . . . and the daughter of a man I loved beyond all reason or sanity. I worshipped him, put him above God and everything I'd been taught was right. I loved him then and I've never stopped. And my sin to bear, darling Rebecca, is that I've never been sorry it happened. I may pay with my immortal soul, but I've known the greatest joy a human can have on this earth—and I have ye."

Rebecca was trembling now, her head spinning, sweat trickling along her spine. She stared at her mother's stricken face, but felt as if she were looking at a stranger. She couldn't think clearly. It was as if she'd been dragged from her own body and put into someone else's, someone she didn't know at all. And her own mother, whose hand she gripped tightly, was unknown to her.

Elizabeth pushed to one elbow. "Condemn me if you will, daughter. That also is part of my cross to bear. I never told ye because I wanted to spare ye pain—and myself too. I didn't want ye hurt, or to feel shame because ye were born . . . out of wedlock."

The full implication of what she was hearing washed over

Rebecca like a black tide. Out of wedlock. Illegitimate. She, who had been baptized Rebecca Anne Gordon, who had been confirmed in the Church, who had taken great pride in her Scottish roots—she was a bastard, not a Gordon at all, and her mother had conceived her in sin. She was beyond tears. It was a nightmare. Something important inside her was broken, and she couldn't think how to fix it.

"At least let me explain how it happened," Elizabeth gently pleaded. "Let me tell ye about your father—your real father."

Her throat was so thick, she could only nod.

"His name was Etienne Dufour," Elizabeth began, her words husky with effort. "He was French Creole, a fine gentleman, and he came to me when I was so lost and alone. I had just arrived in New Orleans and found work in a restaurant near the square." Her eyes became dreamy and distant as she relaxed against her pillow. "Why, Louisiana wasn't even part of the United States then. The day I arrived at the levee there was a misty rain—not like a Highland shower, but like the air was full of tiny drops of water swirling around with nowhere to go. After a time, the ship's captain took me to an inn near the wharf. I had enough coins for two nights' lodging and a bite to eat."

Rebecca tried to concentrate. Somehow she must force herself to listen despite her sense of unreality and growing feeling of despair.

Her mother went on. "I remember lying in bed my first night in the New World and listening to the wind and the rain and crying until my pillow was as damp as the stormy night air." For several seconds, her gaze looked beyond Rebecca into that faraway time. Her lips trembled with the memory.

Rebecca brushed her hand over her eyes. Listen, she urged herself. You must accept the truth. You must learn who you are, what you are, or you might live your whole life knowing only half the truth.

Taking a deep breath, Elizabeth continued. "Next morning was bright and fresh and sweet-smelling as any in a Scottish spring. And I was still young and strong and had money for breakfast. I walked to a little market and had coffee so rich and delicious it warmed me to my toes. I figured I could get a job. I could earn my own passage upriver. The man at the levee told me how much it would cost and said that keel boats made the trip to Natchez. Then I could go by boat or wagon on to Morgan's Landing where my uncle James MacGregor lived. Right then and there, I made up my mind to do it."

Rebecca could see her mother was no longer aware of her, or of the tiny room in their cabin in the woods. She had drifted away in time and was living in the past.

"I took a job at the coffeehouse on Bourbon Street. I served the patrons ten hours a day, six days a week—made enough to pay for my room and had plenty to eat where I worked. Except for being lonely and grieving over Allan, I did pretty well. I'd never seen folks like those who came into that place. Elegant, I can tell you. As elegant as any in London or maybe even Paris. And all speaking French and Spanish like in a foreign country. It wasn't a big city—just a few thousand souls. It belonged to Spain then, but I saw two dukes of France ride by on fine horses. Why, it took my breath to see it. And then . . . then . . ." Her voice fell.

Drawn now into the story, Rebecca waited for her mother to continue. It was like hearing a tale when she was a child, only this tale was not pretend; it was real and it was her own legacy. She felt her heartbeat returning to normal. Her earlier shock and fear was replaced by a strange calm, an acceptance, even curiosity.

"Then I met Etienne," Elizabeth said softly. "He came to the coffeehouse and he always asked me to attend his table. He was the most handsome man I'd ever seen—and very rich. Different from Allan." She sighed deeply. "I loved Allan because we were alike; we grew up in the Highlands together, and we shared our dream of coming to America. But Etienne was . . . was as beautiful, yes as beautiful as any man could be—dark and smooth with skin like ivory and hair like a blackhawk's wing, and eyes like deep brown pools, sort of sleepy looking and ever so wise. Sometimes he would catch my hand and speak to me in French. I couldn't understand the words, but their sound sent shivers along my back and made my heart jump right out of my breast."

"Etienne Dufour," Rebecca murmured. So that was her father's name. How odd it sounded on her tongue. It was smooth like silk, and mysterious. She was French. Well, half-French. The thought caught at her, wrapped around her, fascinated her. She felt as if she were being reborn at this very moment.

"One day, he asked me to go walking along the levee. He did speak English, you see, as well as other languages, and he said his people were called French Creole and were something like royalty in the New World. He said Louisiana had belonged to the Spanish Bourbons and then Napoleon, but he expected before long it would be a country all its own—and he might even be a king if that happened. Me—out walking with a king. Why, I was so thrilled to make such a friend. It was so romantic. . . ." For a time, she was silent. Then, "I fell in love, of course. And he loved me. He told me so, over and over. He said we could marry, eventually. I knew he was worried though. He was from a different world, and he was Roman Catholic. That worried me too, but still . . . I . . ."

"It's all right, Mama," Rebecca said, and knew she really meant it. She had been wrong to think her mother had fallen from grace. After all, her mother had loved this man and they had talked of marriage. How could she sit in judgment on her mother when she herself had never had such feelings nor been so sorely tempted. "It's all right," she repeated. "What happened then?"

"Etienne was very good to me. He gave me a fine apartment with a little balcony above the street. I could stand there at night and see the lamps come on. New ones had just been installed all over the Vieux Carré—that's what the center of town was called. I felt like a princess in a fairy tale. He bought me clothes and flowers and made me quit my job at the coffeehouse. He came almost every night. All day, I just sat on my balcony in the warm, thick sunshine and dreamed of being in love—counting the hours till he would come back. He said he was a businessman, and I thought that sounded grand. He introduced me to his business partner and we had an elegant dinner at a nice restaurant. Oh, I was so happy . . . happier than I'd ever been. And that was when ye were conceived, Rebecca." She turned to look at her, forcing her gaze back into the present. "But then, everything changed."

Rebecca held her breath. Now she would learn the truth. She closed her eyes, feeling her former fear seep into her enchantment. Something had gone wrong. Something terrible had happened. She waited, aware now of darkness creeping into the room, the air cooler, the call of an owl outside the window.

"He left for a business trip, a brief one, he said. That's when I got the letter."

"He . . . wrote to you?" She hung on every word her mother said.

"His business partner whom I'd met, Mr. Laurens, brought it to me. He was a kind man, very smart and rich too. I could tell he was sad and felt very sorry for me. He didn't know I was pregnant, of course."

"Did . . . did Mr. Dufour know?" She felt the breath stop in her throat as she awaited her mother's answer to this question.

"Oh no. I never told him. I wasn't far along . . . and I wanted to be certain. I thought he would propose as soon as he returned from his trip. Then I would tell him. I didn't want him to think he had to marry me."

Rebecca was swept with feeling. Why, her mother was a wonderful person, a real woman, brave and sensitive, capable of so much love, even if it meant risking a broken heart. Never had she loved her more. "I see," she said, fighting tears. "Then, he never knew . . . about me."

"No, he never knew," Elizabeth whispered.

"But what did the letter say?" she asked, though she could guess its contents.

"That he couldn't marry me. That his family would never accept someone of my class, my background, my religion. He said he would always love me, but marriage was impossible. He had sent some money, enough for me to go to my relatives in Tennessee. His friend, Mr. Laurens, gave me the money. It was generous . . . really . . ."

Rebecca covered her lips to hide their trembling. She felt moisture on her cheeks—and the beginning of resentment in her heart. How could anyone treat an innocent woman, a wonderful lady, in such a way? The beauty and romance of the story dissolved into anger and disappointment. Allan Gordon had at least been a man of honor. Her own father had betrayed and abandoned her mother, all the while claiming he loved her. Shame uncoiled inside her. For the first time in her life, she felt guilty over her heritage.

"I was nigh onto killed," Elizabeth went on. "I thought about taking my life. But I knew that was a sin, and I had to think of my baby. *My* baby. Ye, Rebecca. Thank God I lived—for your sake."

Rebecca forced her thoughts back to her mother. "You were very brave, Mama." She couldn't keep the bitterness from her tone, but her mother seemed not to notice.

Elizabeth struggled to sit up. "Can you . . . will ye be able . . . to forgive me," she choked.

Rebecca scooted onto the bed and wrapped her arms around the shrunken shoulders. "There's nothing to forgive. I love you . . . and I know you did the best you could." For a time, she held her mother close, giving them both a chance to regain control of their emotions. She almost hated Etienne Dufour, and yet, that man was her father. She wanted to know about him—everything her mother could tell her. Clearing her throat, she eased her once more into the pillows. "Tell me more about Mr. Dufour . . . about my father."

"He is dead," Elizabeth said weakly. "I have more to tell ye, my darling. I wrote to Etienne a few months ago. And now my letter has been answered." She pulled a wrinkled envelope from beneath her pillow.

Dead. So her father was dead. Oddly, this news didn't touch her heart. It was as if she'd been informed about some stranger's passing. "I see," she said, accepting the envelope. "Then who wrote to you?"

"Mr. Guy Laurens answered my letter. I had informed Etienne that he had a daughter, and I asked for his help."

Rebecca gasped. "You asked my father for help? But why, after all these years? Mother, we don't need help from anyone!"

"I thought a long time about it, darling. I've been feeling poorly. But besides that, I wanted more for ye than what I've had. Ye have good blood, Rebecca. Your Scottish blood is strong. Be proud of that. But your French blood is noble. Ye might have been a king's daughter if . . . if things had been different."

"Oh, Mama, this is America. I don't want to be anything but what I am."

"I know, child, but there's no future for ye in Morgan's Landing. Ye could marry one of the MacGregor boys. Lindsey is struck dumb with love for you. But I don't want you to live as I have, struggling, growing old before your time."

In her deepest heart, Rebecca had to agree. But she'd never allowed herself to think such thoughts, or dream false dreams. "I . . . I can't live in New Orleans."

"Perhaps not, not since Etienne is gone. Ye couldn't be alone in that city. It is full of rich, handsome men who charm innocent girls and break their hearts. But ye can go to Scotland. Your brother has a comfortable home there and can provide a dowry for ye. Ye can marry a landowner and have a good life. Things are better now in Scotland. Ye can keep our faith and raise a family in safety."

"Scotland!" Rebecca was stunned. "Leave America?" She'd never considered such a thing.

"I know ye're surprised, Becca, but it's the only way, especially now. Mr. Laurens has sent a ticket for ye to travel to New Orleans. He said he is in charge of Etienne's estate and feels responsible for looking after ye. He sent a bit of money too. It's there in the envelope. He said ye can stay with a lady friend of his until the war is over and then ye can sail to Scotland. He's a fine man, darling, and I'm sure he can be trusted."

Speechless, Rebecca shook her head and glanced into the envelope. Sure enough, there were several gold coins inside with the letter.

Her mother continued. "There is only one thing Mr. Laurens insisted on. I hate to talk about it, but he said I must." When she saw Rebecca was unable to respond, she went on. "He said ye must tell absolutely no one about being Etienne Dufour's daughter. He said that would be extremely . . . well, extremely embarrassing to Dufour's family and to his too. Oh, I'm so sorry to hurt ye, child." She raised her head and faced Rebecca with tears spilling down her cheeks. "I didn't want ye to know . . . anyone ever to know . . . about your birth."

New resolve drove into Rebecca's heart. Her mother

might be ashamed; the rich Dufours and Laurenses might be ashamed. But she herself would never feel shame over something that wasn't her fault at all. She was created in love and that was the most important thing. And she had good blood. Her mother had said so. Her voice was sharp and clear as she slipped the envelope into her pocket. "I will respect Mr. Lauren's request—if ever I go to New Orleans. For now, I've heard enough, and you've exhausted yourself with all this talking. You must rest, Mother, and get well. We'll go together to Nashville in July and you can see me in the shooting match like we've planned. After that, we'll talk about New Orleans. Maybe we could visit there next fall. We can use the money I win in Nashville, and we'll meet Mr. Laurens and return his coins to him. And, Mother, if you really want to leave Morgan's Landing and return to Scotland, we can talk about that too. As soon as you're able. I would like to see more of the world. And I'd love to meet my brother, Gilbert." She leaned over and kissed her mother's cheek. It was flushed and bright now with fever. Her earlier worries renewed, Rebecca stood up. "I'll fix a bite to eat, Mama. Then I'm going to Mrs. MacGregor's to get some medicine for you."

"Wait, my darling. Before ye go, I have a favor to ask."

"Of course . . . anything you say." She felt her courage melt at the sight of her mother's upturned face.

"In the bottom of my bureau drawer is the letter from Etienne. I've kept it all these years, but never read it again. I'd like to hear it now. Would ye . . . read it to me . . . please, sweetheart. I'll just lie real still and listen. Then you can put it back."

Rebecca's heart raced unexpectedly at the thought of seeing the fateful letter, a letter in her own father's handwriting. She moved to the bureau and opened the drawer. Far at the back behind her mother's few petticoats and stockings, she found a folded piece of paper. It crackled with age when she opened it, but she could see it was fine paper and the handwriting was in beautiful though faded script.

Coughing to clear the tightness in her throat, she returned to the bed and sat down. She saw her mother close her eyes and a smile touch the corners of her lips. Softly she began to read:

"My dearest Elizabeth,

"It is with deepest sorrow and regret that I find I must write you this letter. I have asked our dear and trusted friend, Mr. Guy Laurens, to deliver it to you in person. I hope you will rely on his strength and understanding to comfort you at this time.

"Sadly, I must end our beautiful and memorable relationship, though it tears out my heart to do so. Never have I known such happiness. I have lived for the delight of your presence. You are not only beautiful and wise and strong, but a woman of wit and kindness like I've found in no other soul."

Rebecca had to pause to dab at her eyes. The writing was becoming blurred and she could see where the ink had been blurred before, long years ago, by another's tears.

"Au revoir, cherie. My heart is broken, but I cannot force you into a life which could only mean pain for both of us. I live in a society where background, education and class is more important than life itself. I would leave New Orleans, but I dare not because of business responsibilities to my mother and my family. I know you would never be comfortable in my world. I would change it if I could, but generations of breeding have made it thus, and I must accept it. And then, of course, our religious beliefs, so strongly felt by each of us, are bound to tear us apart as the years go by. I pray you will take up the course you have abandoned for my sake. In that regard, I have asked Mr. Laurens to give you this. . . ."

She couldn't continue. Her eyes were overflowing and she could imagine the rest. She looked up to see her mother was sleeping peacefully, the smile still on her lips. Carefully she pulled the quilt up under her chin. "Rest, my dear mother," she whispered. "Sleep and dream of Etienne—and your walks in New Orleans—and all the wonderful things you did when you were young and in love. I'll bring you a supper tray when you awake."

She folded the letter and put it back in its place deep in the drawer. It was all she had of her father, all she would ever have. She was sorry now he was dead. She wished she could have known him. She closed the drawer and slipped out to the kitchen. Her heart was so full, her feelings such a jumble that she would have liked to sit on the front porch and gaze into the night. But there was supper to prepare, a turkey to pluck and put in the springhouse, and then the walk to the MacGregors' to get her mother's medicine. It was better to stay busy, she decided as she lit a candle and swung the kettle into place over the kindling. The pragmatic Scottish side of her told her that work would chase away pain and confusion. For now, she would let that side of her legacy prevail.

2

A pistol shot split the air; the stocky blood-bay horse leaped forward and galloped full speed down the quarter-mile track.

"Excellent," shouted the man holding the timing watch at the end of the track. "Did you see that, sir?"

"I certainly did. He looks fit enough to conquer the field tomorrow. What do you think, Caldwell?"

Blaine Caldwell took his foot from the bottom railing and nodded to the imposing figure at his side. "Looks fast, General. Mighty fast. I'd like to see him run in New Orleans."

"Someday, Caldwell, when this blamed war is done and Louisiana secure." He turned back to his trainer. "Cool him down, Elliot. Have him at the track early. Come along, Captain Caldwell. You haven't met Mrs. Jackson. We'll have refreshment at the house—then get down to business."

Blaine walked shoulder to shoulder beside Andrew Jackson, matching the general's long stride and admiring his energy and vitality. Only two days ago, Jackson had arrived from Mobile to spend a few days at his plantation home near Nashville. He'd had little time to rest since last March when he had concluded a savage battle against the Creek

Indians. Soon after, the United States government had placed him in charge of the seventh military district, which included Tennessee, Louisiana and the Mississippi Territory. If the treaty with the Creeks was signed, Jackson could then direct his attention to the war against England. The British were poking along the eastern coastline like a lion looking for a weak spot in its prey. A hastily formed United States militia badly needed Jackson's fiery leadership. Blaine strode beside Jackson along the path from the stables to the front of the two-story house of Hermitage Plantation.

"Just pull up a chair there, Caldwell. We'll have a breeze off the river. Excuse me, I'll see if Mrs. Jackson is about. The children keep her occupied these days."

After Jackson disappeared into the house, Blaine took a seat and gazed across the green lawn toward the distant river. It was a beautiful spot, he thought. As attractive as the plantations along the Mississippi. His summons to the Hermitage had been quite a surprise. For the past two years, he had been conducting his own private war against the British, slipping past their blockade, delivering messages to Washington and hauling secret caches of gold to supporters in foreign ports. He appeared to New Orleans society as an enterprising businessman, a man with expensive tastes and the means to satisfy them, a man with little interest in the ebb and flow of American politics. But he had secretly made child's play of passing through the English net closing along U.S. shores. Three years ago, the British had illegally boarded one of his trading ships and impressed several of his best crew members into their navy. That dastardly act had ended his neutrality and he'd thrown his personal efforts and considerable fortune into preventing the English from retaking their American colonies. He'd worked quietly without involving himself in the official military efforts of the young country. For a partner, he had enlisted the help of his old friend, the notorious buccaneer Jean Lafitte.

How much did Andrew Jackson know of his clandestine activities? Obviously he knew something, thus the urgent request to rendezvous in Nashville. Blaine warned himself to be on guard and let the general do the talking.

"Getting damned hot already," said Jackson as he emerged from the house and pulled up a chair opposite

Blaine. "Typical July though. Mrs. Jackson offers her regrets, but she's tending a feverish baby."

"Oh? Nothing serious, I hope." Like everyone else, Blaine knew the story of how Jackson had decimated the Creek nation, then rescued one small Indian baby and brought him home for his wife to raise.

"No, Lincoyer is sturdy as a hickory stump. Just a touch of summer hives. Here, have some cool tea."

An impeccably groomed black slave placed a tray on the table. He poured tea from a pewter pitcher into tall glass mugs, then bowed himself away.

"Care for a cheroot?" Jackson offered.

"Thank you. Do enjoy them," said Blaine, accepting the cigar.

"If we had time, I'd show you my plans for the new house. I know how much store you Louisiana French put in a proper home. As soon as the war's over, I'll start construction on the knoll overlooking the property. I want Mrs. Jackson to have the finest house in the territory."

Blaine nodded and sipped his tea. "You're a fortunate man, General. Both your plantation and your wife are famous for their beauty."

"I understand you're a single man, Caldwell."

"I've not had your luck as yet."

"You're young and there are some advantages to being single in wartime. It's hard to be away for so long from the place most dear to one's heart. And it's hard on my wife. My stay here is for only a few weeks, less if I'm needed back with my troops."

Blaine leaned forward. "Do you expect the Creeks to sign the treaty?"

"Of course they'll sign. They have few warriors left, so they have no choice."

Blaine drew on his cigar without responding. He had great respect for the natives living in and around New Orleans. He disagreed with Jackson's methods while at the same time he admired the man's courage and dedication.

When Blaine made no comment, Jackson continued. "The Indian wars are hopefully behind us. But the British under that fanatic Cochrane are posing a great danger. Now that Napoleon is in their hands, they can turn their full attention to fighting us. Do you realize how quickly we could lose all we gained in the War for Independence?"

"I pray that won't happen."

Jackson studied him for a moment, his eyes penetrating above his beaklike nose. "You answered my summons to come to Nashville, Captain Caldwell. I assume that means you're willing to work for me in the American cause."

Blaine hesitated. Some of his exploits against the English bordered on piracy. Would the general condemn such methods? Jackson had the power to arrest him on the spot and requisition his ships. Finally he said, "Of course. But why have you chosen me?"

"I know what you've been up to lately. But have no fear—your recent activities are known to very few. You can be assured I would do nothing to jeopardize your efforts."

Blaine held Jackson's gaze. He was certain the general spoke the truth. Still, traps had been baited by many innocent appearing souls. He chose his words carefully. "May I ask your source of information?"

"I was taken into confidence by one of your own cousins."

"My cousin? My only relatives are in Virginia."

"Well, as you know, I recently purchased an outstanding racehorse from a Virginia breeder."

"I've heard of Truxton, General. A fine horse. His fame has spread to New Orleans."

Looking pleased, Jackson puffed on his cheroot. "While in Virginia, I visited the Caldwell plantation near Williamsburg. I met your cousin Charles. He explained how his father and yours arrived in Virginia as young cavaliers seeking their fortune. His father stayed in the colony while yours traveled to New Orleans to engage in shipping and then married a French Creole lady of wealth and beauty. Sadly both men are now deceased."

Blaine nodded. "The story is accurate. And I do visit Charles on occasion."

"You have an intriguing heritage, Captain: half-English cavalier and half-Creole businessman. And yet your loyalty is to the United States. If I can count on that loyalty, you could be of enormous use in the cause of freedom."

Blaine decided to put his trust in the general. "You can

count on it, sir. In spite of my English roots, I abhor what's happening now. Shortly before the war, I was pirated by an English admiral. The son of a bitch impressed five of my best seamen. When I reached for my pistol, he shot me—missed my vitals, but put me down for a time. It's time free Americans disposed of the redcoats once and for all."

"Well said. Then you're willing to help, even at great risk and expense?"

"I am, sir."

"Then I'll explain my dilemma. I must shortly return to Mobile to rejoin my troops. The British are threatening Mobile Bay. It is in my mind, however, that were I the British, I would sorely love to take possession of New Orleans. To hold that port would cripple American commerce the full length of the Mississippi. And it's well known that the citizens of your fair city are disinclined to take up arms. In fact, their indifference to which flag flies from their statehouse is surprising."

"True, but in our defense, I must point out we've been traded from Spain to France to America in little more than a decade—and no one bothered to ask our opinion on the matter."

Jackson chuckled. "The spoil of powerful governments. And all the while the citizens continue to plant and harvest and thrive beyond the dreams of most. I've been to New Orleans and I find the place delightful. Despite heat and swamps and a penchant for revelry, it is still a city of rare charm."

Blaine nodded his agreement. "You must come again soon. I'd be pleased to have you as my guest at Dominique Hall."

"I may be there sooner than you think." Jackson put down his glass. "If my instincts are right—and by gawd, they usually are—the English will fake a move to Mobile, then head directly for the mouth of the Mississippi. I must have some warning if I'm to arrive in time to defend the city. This means I need someone who can discover the British plans and send me word at once. In other words, Captain, I want you to spy for me—for the United States—in the cause of freedom for our great land."

Blaine smiled and released a whiff of smoke between his lips. "Spy? I fear that's a tame word for what I've been doing lately. What you ask should be fairly simple."

"But there is one difference, Captain Caldwell. As a privateer, or even a pirate, you could be captured and punished and still survive. But if you're caught *spying* for the American cause, you'll be promptly shot. And I doubt if your sacrifice will even be noted in Washington. Of course, you'll be paid nothing. Although I can probably round up a few gold pieces to pay some expenses."

"Forget that. If the United States rids itself of the English threat, I'll build a shipping business comparable to any in the world. Financially I have everything to gain. And, I might add, I'll have revenge for being nearly murdered on my own ship."

Jackson leaned back and crossed his legs. "Excellent. We understand each other completely. Do you have access to British Admiral Cochrane?"

"I saw Cochrane in Bermuda three months ago."

"Well, I'll be damned. You've more guts than I realized, Caldwell. You're saying you just sailed into Bermuda and had a visit with the redcoats?"

"In a manner of speaking. I have relatives at Hamilton Bay. Paid them a social call, then attended a formal dinner honoring the British admiral. I can tell you, sir, the man's a rare son of a bitch. Hates Americans. Says they're like spaniels—must be drubbed into good manners. It's his goal to restore all the land southwest of the Chesapeake to Great Britain—if not the whole bloody country."

Jackson cackled and slapped his knee. "A bite like that would choke the English like a fox swallowing a buffalo."

"He also has unique ideas for recruiting men. He's convinced that the blacks will rush to fight under his banner against their former masters. Says they're fine horsemen—with training could be the cossacks of the English forces."

"Cossacks? That's a sight I'd pay good coin to see. My guess is the Negroes are a helluva lot smarter than that. They'd just as soon stay where they are as spill their blood for the British. The man's a fool, it's plain to see."

"Not entirely. He'll have better luck recruiting what's left of the Creeks. And they're fighters to be reckoned with."

"Hellfire. The Creeks. I've already sent them sky-winding."

"That's exactly why the remaining warriors will support the British."

"Hm." Jackson ran long slender fingers through his shaggy mop of hair. "No doubt, no doubt. Well, we'll have to make do with what we have. If it comes to a battle at New Orleans, we may have to rely on what Creoles we can muster, some free blacks and some militia from Tennessee and Kentucky. I'd put my sharpshooters up against the best marksmen in the world."

"Good. Then I'll do my best to stay cozy with the English commanders. If they arrive off our coast as you predict, I'll slip the blockade and feed them a morsel or two of false information. Maybe I can learn their plan of attack."

"Excellent. In the meantime, I hope you're comfortable in Nashville. I regret I have no guest accommodations at the Hermitage."

"Quite comfortable. I'm staying at an inn near town center."

"You'll attend the fair to celebrate Independence Day—be my guest at the races. The little quarter horse you saw this morning is sure to win. I'd recommend a sizeable bet on his nose."

"Of course. And I appreciate the tip." Blaine stubbed out the remains of his cigar. "If you'll excuse me, General Jackson, I should be on my way and leave you to your family."

"Very well, Captain. We'll meet again at the fair. And our little agreement will be the best kept secret in the territory."

Seven miles out of Nashville, the campground near Clover Bottom Fairground was filled to overflowing. Tents were raised haphazardly across the open field and wagons had been pushed into position to offer shade from the fierce summer sun. Youngsters dashed about adding to the din of fiddle and pipe, drum and banjo, and frequent firing of guns by reckless celebrants. Smoke from a hundred cookfires scented the air with roasting meat, bacon, coffee and rabbit stew. Cakes and pies of every description were set out to cool while similar pastries were carried to the big tent nearby for the bake-off competition. By midmorning, the entire area was a frenzy of activity. Sack races for the older children were under way at one side of the field. A sawing contest occupied many of the men, and the twelve fine American-bred quarter racing horses were being paraded in the paddock near the racetrack.

Every able body in Nashville was in attendance and hundreds of visitors had traveled from as far away as Knoxville and Memphis. One proud horseman had brought a lean stallion all the way from Charleston, West Virginia.

Rebecca climbed onto the paddock rail to get a better look at the shiny-coated, high-rumped, barrel-chested sprinters. Could the MacGregors' horse, Piper, outrun all these wonderful animals—one of which was owned by Andrew Jackson himself? For a moment she had doubts, but then Lindsey MacGregor walked Piper by and her confidence was restored. Piper had far outdistanced all the competition around Morgan's Landing.

"Good boy, Piper," she called. "You can do it." The animal turned his head toward her familiar voice. "You'll show 'em," she cried excitedly.

Lindsey waved back at her, then continued leading Piper around the crowded paddock.

A smattering of applause caused her to look around. General Jackson and his guests were approaching the area. She stepped off the rail and tried to see him, but her view was blocked by the crowd.

She took off her tam and smoothed back her hair. She had just come from the dancing contest and was still damp with perspiration under her light wool skirt and knee-high socks. A glance at her shoes proved she had definitely soiled the black slippers that had been ordered last year from a shop in Atlanta. Her mother had given them to her on her seventeenth birthday. The memory sent a stab of pain through her heart. She still missed her mother terribly. Only two months ago, Elizabeth Gordon had been laid to rest in the churchyard in Morgan's Landing. Rebecca had longed to win the dance contest in her mother's honor, but she'd lost even though she'd done her best to twirl and step in proper time to the skirl of the pipes and cadence of the drums. A girl from Murfreesboro with auburn locks bouncing around her shoulders had taken the grand prize. Rebecca supposed she would never be a really good dancer, but she had an excellent chance to win the shooting contest coming up soon.

The people standing between her and General Jackson parted enough for her to get a good view of the most famous man in Tennessee. He was quite impressive, she decided. Not exactly handsome, but rugged and imposing with a strong chin and deep blue eyes. He was a military hero, an Indian fighter, a politician already well known in Washington. But today he was a horse-owner just like the other eleven—just like the MacGregors of Morgan's Landing, she thought proudly while listening to the comments of the general and his friends.

"Star Boy looks mighty good, General. I believe our money is safely invested."

"He's ready, I promise you, Mr. Caldwell. Hm—look at the dark bay. Never saw such a powerful rump before. That's where the quick start comes from, you know. The start is crucial in the quarter mile."

Rebecca perked up her ears as the general and the tall man by his side moved near her.

The man said, "Doesn't have the legs of your Star Boy. Looks a bit stiff in his hock action. Wouldn't worry about him, General. Besides, I hear he's from some little farming community in the hill country. Probably used for plowing except once a year on the Fourth of July."

She glared at the stranger who had dared insult Piper in such a rude manner. "His legs, sir?" she blurted. "His legs are perfect. Pulling a plow is good for muscle and stamina." When a hush fell around her, she felt slow heat rise in her cheeks. A sidelong glance showed everyone within hearing was staring at her.

"I—I beg your pardon," she stammered. Why, even Andrew Jackson was giving her a surprised smile. "You see, Piper is . . . partly mine . . . well, not exactly . . . only I ride him a lot and he's mighty fast. He—he's beaten every racer in the valley."

The tall man was inching toward her. His elegant wide-brimmed hat shadowed his face, but she could see his lips firmly set. Obviously he was a close friend of General

Jackson's. And she had snapped at him, corrected his observation as if he were some ignorant cotton picker. She felt like running, but for some reason, the feet in dancing slippers that had moved so blithely an hour ago were planted like stumps in the hay-strewn earth of the paddock.

"Pardon me, young lady," came a low voice from the shadow of the hat. "Certainly I meant no insult to your fine animal."

"Your . . . apology is accepted, sir," she surprised herself by saying.

The man moved closer. In the background, Jackson was laughing and moving on through the crowd. To her enormous relief, the curious eyes turned their attention to the next horse being paraded in the ring.

But the stranger lingered. "I apologize," he said, "but I do not change my opinion. He has poor leg confirmation—at least for a racing horse. For a draft horse perhaps . . ."

"Draft horse?" she snapped. Why, the insult was dreadful. Putting one hand on her hip, she shook her finger toward him. "You've never seen Piper run. His legs are sound and stronger than any of these other horses, I'll wager."

The man tipped back his hat just a bit. The sudden play of light revealed a visage so surprising that her breath stopped in her throat. Hair the color of vintage brandy curled damply above eyes as green as rye grass in spring. He was much younger than his low-pitched, rather officious voice had indicated—less than thirty she guessed, and his skin was a rich golden brown, obviously darkened by long hours under the sun. All in all, he was the most handsome man she'd ever seen, but not a bit dandified despite his clean-shaven elegance and impeccable suit cut from pearl gray linen, a cravat gathered above a ruffled shirtfront. He was gazing down at her with a look not entirely unfriendly. After the first moment of appreciation of his good looks, her former annoyance returned. He had virtually nullified his apology by issuing a second insult to her beloved Piper. And he had followed his rude words by approaching her as if he dared her to contradict him.

"Once my stallion is on the track, I believe you'll change your opinion, sir," she said, tilting her chin defiantly.

"Perhaps. But then it's too late to change my wager."

"Wager?"

"I assume you feel strongly enough about your animal to place a bet on him. Otherwise your touts are hollow words thrown to the winds."

"I mean every word. That is, I'm absolutely certain Piper is going to win."

"Then you have made a wager?"

"No . . . well, not yet. It's still several hours until the race."

"Of course. Plenty of time to make a decision."

Was he making fun of her? His lips appeared to twitch a bit at the corners. "I must add to my gambling money first," she explained, though why she felt compelled to explain anything to this overbearing stranger escaped her.

"And how do you intend to do that, miss . . . ah . . . mistress . . ."

"Gordon. I intend to win the shooting contest. It begins within the hour. Excuse me, I must change from my dance costume."

"A pity—Miss Gordon," he said, his eyes twinkling now with restrained enjoyment. "I missed your dancing, I'm afraid. Your costume is the most becoming I've seen today. May I assume you're a Gordon of the Aberdeen Gordons?"

"Why, yes. You know Aberdeen, sir?" she asked with sudden animation.

"I visited there some years ago. When I was a student in London, I enjoyed an outing to the Highlands. Forgive me." He reached for her hand. "I'm Captain Blaine Caldwell." Lightly, he brushed her fingertips with his lips.

For several seconds, she was awestruck into silence. This man had kissed her hand as if she were a fine lady. She'd thought hand-kissing existed only in books of fantasy. "You're a . . . captain?" she asked inanely.

"Of a ship. Of several actually. I have a small fleet—an export business in New Orleans. But don't let me detain you. I will, however, make a point to see the shooting match."

"I do expect to win," she stated.

"It's unusual, is it not, for a lady to win a sharpshooter match?"

"It's never been done here in Nashville, Captain. Not until today."

His sudden grin was completely disarming. "Then I'll be sure to be there. If you win, we'll plan a celebration. Would you like that?"

Celebration? What on earth did he have in mind. For a moment, she felt like scurrying away like a frightened rabbit. But she quickly overcame her shyness, and returned his gaze. "We can talk about it afterward, I suppose. I'm . . . with my friends from home, you see."

He nodded. "Why, of course. I should have expected that. But still, I'd enjoy a share in your victory."

My, she would like that too, she admitted silently. But she'd never seen such a fine gentleman, never visited with one—and certainly never *celebrated* with one. "I . . . I better go now," she said lamely.

"Au revoir, Mistress Gordon. I will see you again soon."

Abruptly, she turned away. Her emotions were so unsettled, she almost lost her way to her tent. Was that French he'd spoken? He was from Louisiana, after all. Don't be a simpleton, she chided herself. He's a man of wealth and position, a captain with a ship—no, several ships. He's toying with you as he would a child. He must enjoy knowing how he dazzles you with his charm and manners, his London education, his voice with its strangely stirring accent.

She ducked inside the tent she shared with one of the MacDougal girls, removed her plaid skirt, cotton blouse, socks and muddied slippers. She put on her breeches and homespun shirt secured at the waist by a leather belt. Shooting could be dirty business and she needed her pockets for extra bullets. She'd use the metal rod today since silence was not important. Concentrate, Rebecca, she told herself. Those green eyes that had so intrigued her could cause a miss—and then no New Orleans—no Scotland, and probably a marriage bed with Lindsey MacGregor. She must win the prize money if she were to pay back Mr. Laurens and sail abroad. She pulled on her worn everyday boots, tied her hair back with a red bandanna, drew her rifle from its case beneath her pallet and headed for the firing range.

3

Blaine made his way across the field toward the firing range. He had removed his coat, but felt sweat gluing his fine silk shirt to his spine and gathering in droplets along his forehead beneath his wide-brimmed hat. For a moment, he considered turning back to rejoin Jackson's party at the general store where they'd gone for cooling drinks and protection from the midday sun. But then he remembered the young lady's face when he had promised to watch her shoot in the competition. There was something about her that intrigued him, more than just a pretty young girl with a vivacious manner and winning smile. He had seen her before. No, that was impossible. She was a country lass who'd probably never been five miles from home. But still he couldn't overcome the feeling her face was familiar. She resembled the creamy-skinned beauties of New Orleans more than the girls of Scottish heritage from the Tennessee hills. And there was something more—a definite tilt of her nose and curve of her full lips, the way her dusky hair met in a slight widow's peak at the center of her forehead. Her look was distinctive—and he'd seen it somewhere. He had an immediate attraction to her. It was worth a little sweat to take a closer look at petite Miss Gordon—of the Aberdeen Gordons.

A sizeable crowd had encircled the contestants waiting to fire at the target set up beneath a distant stand of oaks. Blaine eased his way along until he could get a good look at the proceedings.

He spotted Rebecca Gordon, who was next in line to compete. Tipping back his hat a bit, he studied her. Her clothing was nothing short of shabby. She had secured her thickly curling hair with a scarf at the nape of her neck. Her breeches fitted rather snugly and the sleeves of her homespun shirt were rolled to her elbows. Why would her appearance be causing undeniable stirrings deep inside him? Hell, he had known women of remarkable beauty, dressed in the finest Paris gowns, who moved him far less than this simple little sprite, clad like a brown sparrow, her nose slightly burned from the sun and her fingernails chipped and uneven. When he'd held her hand, he had felt the calluses along her palm which must have come from heavy work, maybe even work in the fields like the plantation slaves. Odd that the look she'd given him when his lips brushed her fingertips had caused such a tug at his heart. She was like a child opening her first Christmas gift—expectant, surprised, but totally lacking in guile of any kind. But to his amusement, the moment the kiss was ended, the girl had resumed her spirited defense of the horse. If she was innocent of guile, she was also a lass with plenty of spunk.

He wiped a rivulet of sweat from his brow. The announcer was calling her name. He saw her step forward carrying a long-rifle almost as big as she. As the onlookers grew silent, she skillfully loaded the rifle, then lifted it to her shoulder. He wished somehow he could capture the way she looked at that moment: her booted feet firmly planted, her full young breasts pressing against the fabric of her man's shirt belted at her slender waist, her bare forearms smooth and creamy along the wooden rifle stock, her hair gleaming darkly in the sun as she pressed her cheek against the weapon and sighted down the barrel. Yes, little Miss Gordon stirred him most remarkably.

Rebecca had never been so nervous in all her life. Of course, she'd never competed against so many riflemen—

and another woman too. There were thirty in all. The noise of the crowd was distracting; three howling youngsters were dashing helter-skelter among the waiting contestants.

When she heard her name, she stepped to the firing line and took aim at a bucket placed on a stool exactly one hundred yards away. Her hands were clammy and the bucket seemed to be jumping around in some crazy dance. Nonsense, she chided herself. She never missed a target at a hundred yards. For a moment, she closed her eyes and tried to shut out all the noise and hullabaloo surrounding her. When she looked again, the bucket was steady in her sights and she felt herself grow calm.

She squeezed the trigger. The explosion jolted her, but she stayed steady on her feet. When she heard the sudden applause, she knew the target was down.

"Very good, Miss Gordon," said the announcer. "Please stay for the second round."

Smiling, she stepped aside and looked across the crowd for a familiar face. There was Lindsey MacGregor grinning and waving his encouragement. She continued searching. Admit it, she thought to herself, you're wondering if he's here—the green-eyed stranger who promised . . . There—on the left. She dropped her eyes at once, but it was too late to avoid his gaze. Yes, he was here, and he was definitely watching her. The knowledge both thrilled and unnerved her. She must get hold of herself. The target was being moved to two hundred yards and she would need her best skill. She had done it before, once or twice. Her rifle was amazingly accurate at this distance; if she missed, she would have only herself to blame.

Despite her efforts to stop herself, she lifted her eyes again toward the captain. She saw his coat over his arm and smoke curling from the cigar he held between his fingers. As she looked, he gave her a slight nod and one side of his mouth crooked upward. It was a secret half-smile that crossed the distance between them and found its way to her heart.

Quickly, she looked away and moistened her lips. Concentrate, you silly girl, she commanded. You'll lose it all: the money, the trip to New Orleans—and all your dreams for the future. All lost because of a stranger's smile.

The other contestants each took a turn—and missed. She would be last. If she missed, the target would be moved closer until someone could be declared winner.

When her turn came, she stepped forward and jammed the gun butt firmly into her shoulder. Before her nerves could fail her, she firmly squeezed the trigger. Far beyond the rifle barrel, she saw the distant target jerk upward and splinter in the air. The crowd erupted in wild cheering and applause.

She had won.

Her cry of delight was lost in the shouts of the throng around her. Holding the rifle high with both hands, she grinned and acknowledged her accolades. In moments, her friend Lindsey ran forward to embrace her and lift her off her feet.

The contest official appeared as Lindsey released her. She was given the winner's pouch as the yells and clapping continued unabated.

"A woman!" someone called. "A woman—first time ever!"

"Must be one of them hill country gals," another shouted.

She didn't care what they said. She was proud of being a girl and proud of being from Morgan's Landing. Why, if she hadn't learned to shoot to put food on the table, she wouldn't be standing here a rich woman.

"Congratulations, Miss Gordon," came a smooth, low voice at her elbow. "I owe you that celebration."

Extracting herself from Lindsey's grip, she turned to look up at Captain Caldwell. "Thank you, sir. But you don't owe me anything. I was pretty lucky, I guess."

"Takes more than luck, I'd say. Skill and practice, more likely."

She knew she was blushing, but there was no help for it. "I promised to win, didn't I? And now my horse will win too."

"Could be," he said pleasantly. "May I guide you to the track? It isn't long till the horses will be at the post."

"All right, Captain. It's important I place a sizeable bet."

Taking her arm, he maneuvered her along, smiling at the way she balanced her rifle safely on her hip.

After a few steps, she turned back to call to Lindsey, "Meet you at the winner's circle."

Biting her lip in excitement, she did her best to appear nonchalant as she strolled along, achingly aware of the handsome man beside her and of the feel of his hand touching her elbow. Was this what it was like to be a fine lady protected by a powerful gentleman with polished manners? She supposed so, though she surely didn't look the part. She should have at least given her gun to Lindsey, but it was too late now.

Wordlessly, they crossed the fairgrounds and entered the area where the grandstand had been erected for the quarter horse race.

"Are you quite certain you want to place the bet?" the captain asked as they approached the wagering desk. "General Jackson is running a fine stallion."

The feeling that he was offering her his protection lingered as she looked up into his disturbing green eyes. Something in his gaze penetrated her deepest being, and she forgot her drab attire as she absorbed his warmth. For a moment, she felt almost pretty. A tingle ran along her backbone, but at the same time, she felt a little frightened. She had been boldly stared at plenty of times, today especially as she'd ambled around the fairgrounds. But the captain's eyes were those of a caring friend, like someone she'd known for years and who could see through to her heart. They held admiration, and understanding, and a dash of challenge and mystery. She sensed she could trust this man with her life . . . or could she? Didn't the captain exactly match her mother's description of the type of man she should beware of: handsome, rich, charming, a manipulative sort who could quickly break an innocent girl's heart? Trying to figure it out caused her to stand there staring up at him as if she'd lost her wits.

"Pardon me, ma'am," said the man behind the betting table. "Did you plan to make a wager? The horses are on the track and we're closing down the betting."

"Oh . . . yes," she quickly responded. She pulled out the pouch and placed it on the counter.

The man emptied it loudly and his eyebrows lifted. "Well now, you must be pretty sure of winning. Which horse will it be?"

"Piper," she said with a great show of confidence. She

gave the captain a sidelong glance. "Piper—to win," she said defiantly.

Caldwell leaned near. "Are you sure, Miss Gordon? It's not too late to change your mind. After all, one gold piece would prove your faith in your animal."

She answered by tossing her head and pushing the coins toward the man at the table. "I say Piper will win. I'll bet it all."

"Very well," Caldwell responded, smiling. "You said you'd win the shooting match and so you did. You're a lady of your word, it appears." He turned to the table. "Five hundred on Piper—to win." He produced the coins from a pocket in his coat.

The attendant gaped at the money. "But . . . but, sir, you just bet on Star Boy. They can't both win."

"Enter the wager," Blaine said firmly. He took his receipt and guided Rebecca into the stands. "Shall we watch the race from Jackson's box, Miss Gordon? I'd be honored to have the company of the best shot in Tennessee."

She took his arm and held her head high. She knew people were staring, but she didn't care a flip.

Sudden shyness overtook her, however, when they arrived at Jackson's private box overlooking the track. She acknowledged the captain's introduction, once more aware of her dusty breeches and boots, her plain shirt and rolled-up sleeves, her tousled hair and burning cheeks, and especially of the awkwardness of greeting the general and the beautifully gowned ladies while balancing a rifle instead of a parasol.

But Andrew Jackson was completely charming with his informal manner and expression. "Is that a fact?" he was saying. "Beat all the sharpshooters? Well, well, that surely is a surprise. I'll know where to look for help if the redcoats come calling." He chuckled and winked at Caldwell. It was obvious the two men were on excellent terms.

"Miss Rebecca Gordon," Jackson continued. "Well, young lady, I'd suggest you place a bet on my horse, Star Boy. This looks like your lucky day."

She returned his smile. "My luck rides with the stallion from Morgan's Landing, General Jackson—Piper, by name."

Jackson threw back his head and guffawed. "Now aren't you the feisty one," he finally said with a grin. "I don't expect there's a chance of his winning, but I'll not argue with the best shooter in Tennessee—not when she's holding her gun at her side. Will you and the captain join me in my box for the running?"

She looked at Blaine. "I—I'd prefer to watch from the finish line, General. But the captain may stay here—if he likes."

Caldwell was watching her with undisguised pleasure. "No, if Miss Gordon wishes to go to the railing, we'll go at once."

She was more than pleased. It would have been hard to tear herself from Captain Caldwell's side, but she knew she would be most uncomfortable watching the race with this elegant party—especially if Piper did win, after all. And if Piper lost, and all her dreams evaporated as well, she would be better off to bear her disappointment alone. But now, with Captain Caldwell to keep her company, she would feel she had a friend, whichever way the race should end.

Blaine ushered her down the wooden steps and assisted her to stand by the rail close to the finish line. Not that she needed his assistance, he thought. He'd never met a more self-assured young woman, completely feminine, but quite capable of taking care of herself. It continued to amaze him how pretty and refined she seemed despite her rough, masculine clothing. Put her in a gown of lace and silk, give her hair a good brushing, give those slender hands a rest from manual labor—and she'd put to shame any woman of his acquaintance. Not that he would ever consider such a tyke for a serious liaison. A tumble perhaps—but when he finally took a wife, she'd naturally be a lady from one of New Orleans's best families, or so he'd always assumed. Still, little Miss Gordon had the looks of a French coquette, despite her Scottish temper. Quite a rare and intriguing combination, he admitted.

"Miss Gordon," he said, leaning near. "I have a proposition for you since you're a gambling woman."

"Yes?" she replied, not taking her eyes from the horses parading to the post.

"A little wager between us. If your horse wins, I'll treat you to dinner at my hotel in town."

"And if not?"

"But you've assured me he will. I've staked my last dollar on him."

Her eyes were dancing when she looked up at him. "Then we'll celebrate together. I'll gladly accept."

No other words were possible in the screaming and shouting as the packed crowd rose to its feet.

Twelve horses raced at top speed straight down the track toward the finish line. For the first few seconds, they were shoulder to shoulder, nose to nose, with hooves pounding the beaten earth.

Then two inched forward, their nostrils flaring, their muscles straining.

"Piper and Star Boy," called Blaine.

"Piper!" screamed Rebecca. "Run, boy, run!"

At the finish, it was Piper's nose that edged ahead.

Without a thought, Rebecca threw herself into Blaine's embrace, almost dropping her rifle in the process. She was laughing and crying at the same time, all thought gone but the thrill of the moment.

"Careful there," he said, laughing with her. "Don't shoot off my toes if you expect us to celebrate over dinner."

Releasing him, she looked up with eyes as blue as the sky and sparkling with happy tears. "Oh, Captain," she said coyly, "you know my gun's not loaded. Come now, let's go to the winner's circle."

He shook his head. "Nay, lass. You go without me. This is a time for you and your friends to share. I'd better give my condolences to the general. Will you meet me here in two hours? I'll arrange a carriage to take us to town."

"Of course, I'll be here. But I promise to leave my gun in my tent and . . . and to wear a proper dress."

Her girlish face, alight with unrestrained joy and so free of vanity, reached all the way to his heart. The memory of her lithe body against him moments ago started again that pressure in his loins.

"Go now, enjoy yourself," he murmured. "I'll collect my winnings." Shaking his head in amazement, he watched her duck under the rail, still cradling the long-rifle, and run toward the winner's circle.

He made his way back to Jackson's box, where the general had arranged for refreshments to be served: sandwiches, small cakes, cider, and whiskey for the gentlemen.

Immediately Jackson broke from his companions and approached him. "Captain . . . a private word, if you please."

"Certainly. Sorry about Star Boy. He—"

"Never mind. He'll win another day."

The general took his arm and walked him out of earshot of the others. "Thank God you returned," he said, scowling.

"I never left. As you know I watched the race from the finish line. What's wrong, sir?"

"I thought you might leave with the young lady. I've just received word that the British brig, *Sophia,* is headed for Grande Isle near the mouth of the Mississippi."

"That's Lafitte's island at Barataria Bay."

"Exactly. The captain of the *Sophia* is carrying a packet to Lafitte—a personal letter from the British urging Lafitte and the citizens of Louisiana to join with them in putting down—and I quote—American usurpation of this country."

"Lafitte won't accept, General. I assure you, he is loyal to the United States."

"Ah, but that isn't all. He's also been offered the rank of captain in the British navy and thirty thousand dollars in gold."

"Mon dieu. The British obviously value him more than the Americans. When I left New Orleans, Governor Claibourne had arrested Lafitte's brother and imprisoned him."

"That's the worst part. The British have also offered to free his brother—one way or the other."

"Damnation. I can't guarantee Jean would refuse that. Has the offer reached him yet?"

"No. My information came from my sources in the Bahamas. The *Sophia* had other duties first, but is expected at Grande Isle within two to four weeks."

"Then I must leave at once. I'll talk to Jean. Surely he can be persuaded to remain loyal to the American cause."

"I'm counting on that, Caldwell. This could mean keeping or losing New Orleans, and you know how disastrous it would be if the United States lost its port on the Mississippi."

"I do, sir."

"I've a good horse waiting. Leave immediately. Ride through the backwoods to a settlement called Payton. My people there will escort you to the Mississippi, where you can take the steamboat downstream to New Orleans. Time is critical. And for God's sake, do or say whatever is necessary to keep Lafitte from leading Louisiana into revolt against the States."

"I'll do my best, General. Ah . . . I would ask a small favor, however. I had arranged to meet Miss Gordon at the track finish line. I'd hate to leave her standing alone for long, and she might think my disappearance odd. Could you send her a message . . . offer my regrets."

"Naturally. Don't worry a moment. Go now. Good luck, Captain Caldwell. Much depends on you."

Blaine strode briskly toward the stable where the horse would be waiting. He was sure if he reached Lafitte in time, he could convince him not to join the British. Lafitte was popular enough to raise a small army of his own or influence the indifferent Creoles to avoid any sort of serious defense against the English. Either event could be calamitous. Blaine figured, with luck, he could arrive in New Orleans in two weeks. He was familiar with the steamboat, the *New Orleans,* and trusted it would make good speed south on the Mississippi. He would take time only to stop by his hotel and change before riding west on the river road. Damn, he hated to miss his rendezvous with the Gordon lass, but there were plenty of attractive women—and only one City of New Orleans.

Rebecca waited at the finish line at exactly the spot she'd left Captain Caldwell. She had rushed to her tent, bathed her face, put on her calico dress and tried to polish her slippers. She had brushed her hair till it glistened with blue-black highlights and tied a ribbon to confine its fractious curls. She had no powder to dust her shiny nose and cheeks, but that couldn't be helped. Captain Caldwell had invited her to dinner even though she had looked a terrible mess. Surely he wouldn't be too disappointed with her present appearance.

She opened her small pouch bag and removed a tiny mirror. Why, she was so nervous, her hands were trembling. In the bottom of the pouch were her winnings for the day. She wouldn't dare leave them behind in her tent. Glancing in the mirror, she thought of the MacGregors' stern faces when she'd told them she was going to have dinner in town with a gentleman. They'd lectured her, and Lindsey had gone into a childish pout, but after all, she was not their daughter and could do as she pleased.

She waited, wondering if she'd misjudged the time. Having no timepiece made it difficult to be exact, so she had arrived plenty early just in case. The grandstand was deserted now. The track stretched mutely in the late afternoon sun. A wisp of wind kicked up dust and there was the distant smell of the stable and paddock. From across the fields, cooking smoke was rising, mixing with the dust of wagons leaving for home.

She waited, tapping her fingers on the railing in time with the rapid beat of her pulse. What a grand time she would have in the company of Captain Caldwell, she thought, tightening her lips to keep them from lifting into a silly grin. For several minutes, she passed the time practicing what she would say, how she would act, how she would manage to hide the fact that it was her first dinner in a real hotel, and that her escort was a man whose looks and manners made her heart flip-flop every time she looked his way.

The sun became a fiery ball and dipped toward the west.

It soon became apparent he wasn't coming. It must be seven by now. She scanned the horizon. An ache grew beneath her rib cage as she watched the handful of workers sweeping the grandstand and heard the distant popping of fireworks near the campgrounds. No, he wasn't coming. Smoothing back her hair, she held tightly to her pouch and chastised herself for feeling so terribly disappointed. So, this was her first lesson in dealing with a real gentleman. She had been stupidly naive to think he would actually take her in a carriage to a restaurant in town. Why would he, after all? Maybe he had only felt a momentary sense of obligation because she had told him Piper would win, thereby enriching his pocketbook considerably. She would be wise to remember her mother's warning in dealing with rich, handsome men such as he.

Leaning one elbow on the rail, she gazed at the approaching evening. She assured herself it was quite fortunate that she would have no further encounter with the captain. She had found him far too attractive and might possibly have become seriously infatuated. That would certainly lead to further heartache. Of course, it would be embarrassing to explain to Lindsey MacGregor why the dinner didn't take place. She'd have to take a heap of teasing, for sure.

She rattled the coins in her purse as she walked slowly toward the campground. It doesn't really matter, she told herself. She had her winnings and it had been a glorious day. Tomorrow she would return home, and in a day or two take the barge to Payton, then on to Natchez. She would go to New Orleans, and as soon as the war ended, travel on to Scotland. There she would meet her brother, Gilbert, who would take her under his wing. Why, in no time at all, she would forget all about the devious Captain Caldwell.

4

The distant roll of thunder signaled the retreat of the summer squall which had drenched the barge traveling downriver from Morgan's Landing to Payton. The tiny village was the last stop for the boat before it reached its destination at the burgeoning community of Natchez.

Rebecca crept out from under the barge roof and followed the boatman's directions to the inn a few paces from the jetty. Slender shafts of late-day sun filtered beneath low-hanging clouds that engulfed the nearby green hills in rolling mist. The loneliness and depression that had haunted her since she'd left home six days ago persisted despite her best efforts at optimism.

She entered the rustic hotel and placed her pouch bag on the floor by the desk, then waited politely for the attendant to acknowledge her.

Finally he looked up from his writing. "Need a room, miss?"

"Yes, sir. I just arrived on the packet." She placed one of her gold coins on the counter. "For one night only. I'll be traveling on to Natchez at first light tomorrow—on the boat, of course."

He stared at the coin. "Surely, miss. Ah . . . got one room left . . . upstairs . . . number four. You'll find it clean enough, I reckon. Pot's under the bed." He scooped up the coin.

"Thank you. I'll go right up," she said. "Oh, do you have any food available?"

The innkeeper smiled broadly. After all, he had just collected ten times the usual fare for one night's lodging. "Supper's over. We only set a few tables 'twix five and six. There's some biscuits left in the kitchen out back. Probably a slice or two of ham in the box. Help yourself, young lady."

"I'll do that," she replied, and hurried up the short flight of stairs and along the hall to room number four. She bolted the door behind her and surveyed the tiny enclosure. It seemed quite small for the cost of an entire gold piece, but at least a snack was included.

She placed her satchel on the narrow bed and took out her cloak. She would go for a walk in the nearby woods. After sitting in the cramped barge the past eighteen hours, she felt the need to stretch her legs.

Within minutes, she left the room and made her way through the deserted parlor to the kitchen. No one was about, so she helped herself to ham and biscuits, added a hunk of cheese, and wrapped the food in a clean cloth before tucking it into her pocket. She had nothing to drink, but perhaps she would find a spring in the woods near town.

As she strolled past the shuttered storefronts on the village's only street, she breathed deeply of the rain-scented air. Apparently the heavy showers and approaching evening had chased everyone indoors. The only sounds were the birds calling their final song of the day, and the distant thunking of an axe against timber.

She entered the fringe of the forest and discovered a leaf-strewn path leading beneath stands of stately oak and walnut trees whose leaves made a cool, shady bower. She pulled up her hood as protection against the dripping caused by the breezes rustling overhanging branches. The respite from the July heat was most invigorating, she thought. She doubted if New Orleans would be half so pleasant. Well, perhaps she wouldn't have to stay there for very long. Mrs. MacGregor had said the politicians were meeting in a city called Brussels to discuss a peace settlement with England. If the war ended soon, she'd sail at once for the British Isles and then travel on to Scotland. Of course, she would need to pay a polite visit to Mr. Guy Laurens. She was eager to repay him for the ticket he'd provided for her passage on the steamboat. She didn't want to be indebted to anyone when she left the country of her birth. She had given the cabin in Morgan's Landing to her dearest friends, the MacGregors. The house was in good condition and the garden in full summer production. She admitted it had been hard to leave, especially to say her last good-bye at the cemetery in the churchyard. At the river landing, she had given Lindsey a hug and a kiss—and her prized possession, the long-rifle. He would soon get over his boyish crush, she was sure.

"Gilbert," she whispered her brother's name. "I do hope I can find you. I pray you're back safely from the war in France." Her one concern was that she might arrive in Aberdeen and find no trace of Gilbert Gordon or his family. "Nay, he'll be there," she reassured herself. And if he was away, she'd find Gordon relatives in abundance.

The sound of gurgling attracted her and she left the trail to find the source. Pushing aside branches, she discovered a tiny brook, its water pure and sweet as it hurried toward the river. A perfect spot for her picnic.

The dying sun's rays slanting through the treetops dappled the forest floor, giving a faint watery glow to the secluded glen. It was like sitting in the midst of a rainbow-colored bubble, she thought as she settled onto a fallen log by the stream. She would eat here, then return to the inn for a good night's rest. Maybe that was all she needed to lift her drooping spirits. Biting into the biscuit, she told herself that traveling was quite a fine thing to do. One could see strange and fascinating sights, have new and wondrous experiences, enjoy the present moment while anticipating adventures over the next horizon.

She spread out one corner of her cloak and placed the ham and cheese on the open napkin. Then she leaned over the brook and cupped her hands to capture a cool drink. When she turned back to her meal, she was amazed to discover the ham had completely disappeared.

She looked overhead for a bandit bird, but saw none. She squinted into the brush, but saw no living creature. Yet she was positive she had placed the ham in just that spot. At that moment, a dark head with spikey ears, large brown eyes and short wirey whiskers appeared above a tuft of nearby grass.

"My goodness," she said in surprise. The animal instantly disappeared.

It looked like a dog . . . a very small dog. "Come here, puppy," she encouraged. "Come now. I won't hurt you."

Getting to her knees, she offered the piece of cheese. "Look here, little pup. I'll gladly share." She whistled softly.

Sure enough, the head reappeared, followed by a thin, stringy body with a bedraggled tail behind.

"Oh, poor thing," she crooned. "You look half-starved. Here, you can have all of it."

The puppy crept forward and gobbled the cheese she extended. Then it lay down on her cloak and gazed up at her with soulful eyes. It was wet and trembling and its paws were caked with mud.

She shook her head. "Now, aren't you a pitiful sight. And after I gave you all my supper. Don't you have a home, little one?"

At the sound of her voice, the pup managed a weak wag of its tail.

"Now, don't start begging. You can't be my dog. I'm just passing through your town and have no way to take you with me."

The puppy wagged its tail more vigorously and inched closer.

"Oh, I suppose I can at least warm you a bit and take you as far as the village." She picked up the dog and wrapped it in her cloak. "A boy, huh? And skinny as a stick. I don't recognize your breed, but I reckon you're a little of this and that. Some folks are like that too, so don't worry one bit about it. You must be a couple of months old, I'd guess."

The puppy settled in her arms and began licking her thumb. The undercurrent of loneliness she'd felt over the past days eased a bit. "Oh, you're a clever one, aren't you. I suppose . . . well, you're mighty small. If I had a box, maybe I could take you to New Orleans and find you a proper home."

The puppy's eyelids began to droop as it rested in her lap. For a time, she sat in silence, holding the sleepy animal and listening to the sounds of the stream and the wind in the leaves.

She started to rise when she heard voices. It sounded like two men were walking along the path just beyond her view.

She squatted in the grass and held the pup close. Hopefully they wouldn't see her. After all, she had her small fortune in gold tied to the pouch at her waist. She had no weapon and knew the dangers a woman could encounter when alone in the woods.

"So, you talked to Old Hickory himself?" came a voice.

"I did. He said I'd find someone in Payton who could take a message south after showing me a shortcut west."

"That would be Jarvis."

"Well, where is the man? I've been cooling my heels since yesterday at that ramshackle hut calling itself an inn. I need a fresh horse and a good tracker to get there in time."

Rebecca stifled a gasp with one hand. She would know that voice anywhere. It was definitely Captain Caldwell—her captain of the Nashville Fair. He was absolutely the last person she wanted to see—and he must be staying at the inn in Payton.

The men stopped just beyond the trees and one lighted a cheroot. The fragrant aroma brought back the memory of how the captain had looked when she'd seen him at the shooting match. Strange how the memory stirred bittersweet feelings deep inside her.

"Jarvis is at the stable. That's why I came looking for you. He's got your horse saddled and will guide you through the forests. Once you get close to town, he'll head south. But why don't you take the packet? It docked an hour ago and leaves for Natchez at daybreak."

She held her breath. Surely nothing could be worse than sharing that cramped boat with the bold and unreliable Captain Caldwell.

"Don't want to chance being seen this close to Jackson," replied Caldwell. "Secrecy is most important, as you know."

She sighed with relief and listened closely.

"And you met with British Admiral Cochrane?"

"I did. I was a guest at his home in Bermuda twelve weeks ago."

She frowned and concentrated on the smooth, low voice. What was the captain talking about? Could he be a friend of the English in the midst of their war against the United States? Why, that would be treason.

"Excellent," said the other man. "I can see why you've kept your visit to Jackson a secret. How does it feel to be a spy?"

Spy! The word seared her brain.

"Seems natural enough. I'm glad to do anything to help."

"When will you slip back to the redcoats?"

"As soon as I've talked to Lafitte. The British offered him thirty thousand pounds to raise an army to fight the Yankees."

"Gol-durn, I'm glad he's in our camp."

"I'll confirm that as soon as possible. Let's get back to Payton. I'll pay that wretched innkeeper his due and head for the stable."

The stub of a cigar flew just beyond Rebecca's head and landed with a sizzle in the brook. The serenity of the spot was definitely shattered.

Crouching in the brush with the pup under her cloak, she waited until the footsteps faded away. This new revelation was stunning. She had believed Captain Caldwell was a charming manipulator with dishonest intentions. Now she knew he was far more dangerous; he was a traitor and a spy. If only she could return upriver, she would warn General Jackson. But the packet wouldn't return east for a week or more, and the journey upstream would take even longer. And she wouldn't dare travel alone across country. No, she would have to let Jackson do without her assistance for now. Surely such a great man would soon discover the villain's treachery on his own. In the meantime, she would avoid the inn until she was sure it was safe to return without being discovered by wicked Captain Caldwell.

"No, ma'am, you can't come aboard with a dog. Rules are rules."

"But I already have my ticket," Rebecca pleaded. "I must get to New Orleans. You see, I've left everything behind—my home, my friends, I have no family. . . ."

The stern-faced boatman pointed to the box sitting by her feet. "You'll have to leave *that* behind if you're going on this steamboat."

"But, sir, I promise the pup won't be any bother. He's very small. Please." She was growing frantic. Her stomach was churning. She hadn't eaten in twenty-four hours and she'd had no real sleep the past three nights, ever since she had obtained her new puppy at Payton.

An hour ago, just as the sun was rising, she had left the barge and made her way along the docks to the steamboat *New Orleans.* Her spirits lifted when she saw the beautiful ship, whitewashed and gleaming, with rows of little windows and the pilot's cabin commanding a view of boat and river. But when she attempted to board, this rude crewman had refused to accept her ticket.

She had a new idea. "Gold, sir. I have gold to pay." Her voice brightened. "I'll buy an extra ticket for my dog. And . . . of course, there'll be another coin just for you."

The man's hesitation gave her hope.

"Look," she said, opening the pouch at her belt. "Ten dollar gold pieces. One for the puppy's ticket—and one for you."

But the crewman shook his head. "I'd like to oblige, miss, but I'd be found out for sure, and I'd lose my job. Single women stay together in the aft cabin so you couldn't hide the pup. No, you'll have to decide—the boat or the dog." He crossed his arms to close the discussion.

Unwanted tears sprang to her eyes. She absolutely had to get to New Orleans, but my goodness, she'd already let the puppy take hold of her heart. What could she do? She was tired and hungry, and her gold seemed worthless.

Angrily she swiped at her tears. "Very well. I suppose I'll have to find the pup a home before I leave Natchez."

"You'd better hurry. We sail in an hour. The engineer's already busy in the engine room."

She picked up her belongings and walked away from the dock. Would it be possible to find a good home for the dog in so short a time? The thought sent an ache twisting through her heart and the tears began anew.

The pup's insistent scratching could no longer be ignored.

She found a grassy area beneath a stand of cottonwoods and released him from the box. For a moment, he seemed reluctant to leave her side, but then scampered away to tend to his needs.

She sat on the box and buried her head in her hands. She was feeling woozy from fatigue, hunger and heartache.

Blaine saw it all. He had arrived in Natchez sometime around midnight and caught a few hours of sleep in the stable where he would leave his mount. At dawn, he had taken time to freshen up and change clothes in the blacksmith's shack, then arrived at the dock only minutes ahead of Rebecca.

The moment he spotted her, he stepped into the shadow of a stack of crates. His feelings at seeing her again had run the gamut from surprised pleasure tempered by concern for the secrecy of his mission, to annoyance at the boatman's stance, to sympathy for the girl's obvious suffering. The sight of that ragtag little lady pleading for herself and her dog, observing her obstinacy, her prideful battle with her tears, hell, it would melt the heart of a granite boulder. It certainly melted his.

When she scooped up her belongings, he followed at a discreet distance. It gave him time to weigh the risks of revealing his presence to anyone who had seen him with Jackson. But the girl was no doubt ignorant of political affairs and certainly had no connections to the British. What harm could it do to offer his assistance? The steamboat captain was an old and trusted friend and would surely bend the rules if properly approached.

He stopped to watch when she opened the crate to release the source of her difficulty—a scrawny black pup with few redeeming qualities that he could see. But when she sank onto the box and looked about to faint, he made up his mind.

"Good morning, Miss Gordon. What a pleasant coincidence to find you here."

She jumped to her feet. At once, she began to topple forward.

He caught her before she hit the ground. In seconds, her eyes opened and she looked up at him. Her face registered shock and she grew rigid in his embrace.

A sudden yapping and puppyish growling interrupted the moment.

"Damnation," Blaine muttered, trying to free the edge of his pant leg from the creature's determined bite.

"Oh, dear," she scolded from her place in Blaine's arms. "No! Stop this instant. Oh my, is he biting you?" she asked with real concern.

"No. Just the fabric. I can be grateful, however, he's no bigger than he is."

The puppy sat on his haunches at the sound of its mistress's voice, but kept his eyes fixed on Blaine.

"A fierce protector, you are," Blaine noted. "I can see I underrated you entirely."

"I saved him from starving," Rebecca said, staring again at Blaine as if she'd seen a ghost.

"Well, he's a peppery little mutt. And from the size of those paws, he'll one day be a protector worth his feed. Speaking of starving, when did the two of you last eat?"

She squirmed nervously. "A while, I guess. I'm fine now, Captain. Please put me down. I must search for a home for the pup."

He kept her firmly in his grasp as he cautiously reached down and picked up the dog.

"What are you doing?" she demanded.

"Solving your problem—if you'll remain quiet." Carrying her while she held the animal, he strode back to the dock and confronted the startled boatman.

"I'm going to occupy the private cabin. And don't be concerned about the dog. I'll explain to your captain."

The man stared wide-eyed. "But . . . the lady . . . she has to stay with the others in the aft cabin. It's the rule."

"What rule?"

"Well, single women in the aft—men of quality and married couples in the private cabin—single men forward. That's the rule."

"Are you suggesting we are not married?"

"I . . . why, I didn't think you were together . . . I mean . . ."

"Do we *look* like we're together?"

"Yes sir, I mean, *you're* quality, sir, that's plain . . . but . . ."

"Then, are you suggesting my wife would not be quality as well?" He felt Rebecca stiffen, but at least she held her tongue.

The boatman's eyebrows popped into his hairline.

A glance showed Miss Gordon's eyes equally amazed. Blaine gave her a quick wink. "We'll board now," he said sharply to the boatman. "I'll retrieve Mrs. Caldwell's belongings before we sail."

"Mrs. . . . Mrs. . . ." Rebecca stuttered.

Without further ado, he marched up the gangplank. "It's all right, my dear," he said loudly. "I know you're angry, but all newlyweds have these little spats. Everything will be fine when we reach New Orleans. Of course, we'll have to add some new dresses to your wardrobe."

She was gaping silently at him when they reached the cabin door.

Leaning his shoulder against the door, he shoved it open and marched inside. None too gently, he plopped her down on the bed and stared at her as if she were a child who required a firm hand. "There, Miss Gordon . . . or Mrs. Caldwell, whichever is most convenient. Stay put till I return. I need to collect your knapsack and round up some victuals before we sail. I doubt if the cook will serve us before luncheon."

She laid aside the puppy and scooted off the bed to face him with hands on hips. "I don't know why you've been so accommodating, Captain Caldwell, but I could make a few guesses—none of which are the slightest bit proper. I'm grateful to be aboard with the pup, but I have no intention of remaining in this cabin, and certainly will not use your name, even for the brief journey down the Mississippi."

He grinned which only added to her indignation.

"I'm leaving at once," she announced crisply, and turned to pick up the dog.

He put his hand on her shoulder. "Use your head, my girl. It's quite pretty, but surely not beyond the capacity of clever thought. Stay here for now. I'll get your things and soon we'll be steaming downriver. At least you and"—he gave the dog a resigned look—"you and that animal will be making your way to New Orleans. The ship is practically empty of passengers, I noticed. Three or four tradesmen are lounging at the forward deck and a matron and her daughter are headed aft. You look exhausted." His voice held more compassion. "After all, you did me a great favor in Nashville by giving me a tip on a winning horse. I wasn't able to treat you to the proposed dinner. Allow me to repay you by helping you through this . . . ah . . . crisis."

Heaving a sigh, she sank down on the bed. Already the pup had jumped to the floor and was exploring the cabin. It was attractively furnished with thick carpet, a maple bed and dressing table, and lined with windows viewing both sides of the river.

"I . . . I suppose . . ." she began. "Yes, I suppose I could rest here a few hours. I would like to wash up a bit."

"Good. I'll get your things and be back within the half hour."

True to his word, he was back within a short time. He found her sound asleep on the bed with the puppy curled up beside her. What a pair, he thought. It was a toss-up as to which was the scruffiest. At least the girl had possibilities. As for the dog . . . a mixed breed mistake, if he ever saw one.

As if answering his thoughts, the dog raised to its feet and uttered a low growl.

But Blaine was prepared. He quieted him with a meaty bone, then laid a basket of fresh fruit and newly baked scones beside Rebecca's satchel on the dressing table. Quietly, he slipped back out the door.

Rebecca awoke with a start. It took a moment for the fuzziness to clear from her brain, but then she remembered everything. She relaxed on a pillow and contemplated this startling turn of events. It seemed fate kept thrusting her upon the mysterious Captain Caldwell. Oh, she knew he was a spy and totally untrustworthy, but he did have the most fascinating emerald eyes, crinkling at the corners when he gave her that knowing grin. Tarnation, he was attractive. And he treated her so nicely—as if he really cared what happened to her. For a moment, she allowed herself to imagine what it would be like if he truly was her beau—and she was in love—how heavenly—if only . . . *no!* She stopped her impossible daydreaming. She mustn't let herself be fooled. Whatever else he was, he was definitely a traitor to the country she loved. Although she was prepared to leave the United States, she would have died before betraying it to the enemy. Idly, she wondered what his first name could be. Where was his home? Perhaps New Orleans, if he had a fleet of ships.

Suddenly remembering the puppy, she sat up. There he was beside the bed with . . . yes, with a sizeable bone well-chewed. Her cheeks flushed as she realized the captain had been here while she slept. And there was her traveling bag, and food as well.

She slipped off the bed and pulled up the chair of the dresser.

The pup followed and took up a spot to beg.

"Oh no, not this meal. We'll see about your food later. Well . . ." She slipped him a morsel. "You need a name, puppy, if you're going to stay with me. Let's see. The captain said you were a peppery sort. Pepper. Yes, that does seem to fit. You're small and full of spice and mischief. So, Pepper it will be."

Suddenly she felt the boat rock beneath her. "Oh, we're moving," she cried, and ran to the window. "Why, Natchez is already out of sight—and look at the river and the shore beyond. My, it's lovely."

The midday sun turned the water into a broad ribbon of silver silk, bordered by deep green forests on either side. The movement of the ship was like a gentle glide, punctuated by occasional bumps as the twin paddle wheels dug their way through the current. The pace was brisk heading downstream—no need to raise the sails at the fore and aft of the vessel.

After absorbing the panorama for some time, she left the window and sat back on the chair. She made short work of the balance of her meal, thinking with every bite that she was succumbing to a traitor's wiles.

With her hunger assuaged, she took a good look in the mirror before her. The sight horrified her. Quickly, she located fresh water in the lavabo and began to tidy herself. She put on the calico dress, clean though badly rumpled, replaced her traveling boots with her slippers, and brushed the dark waves of her hair until they glistened. In sudden annoyance, she dropped her brush to the dresser top. It had just occurred to her that she seemed to be spending a good deal of time attempting to look pretty for that deceitful Captain Caldwell. With a toss of her head, she left the cabin, where Pepper contentedly chewed his bone.

The sunlight reflecting off the water was dazzling. For a time, she stood at the rail and gazed at the passing scenery. There were other, smaller boats on the river, she noticed. Most were flattopped barges laden with cotton for southern ports.

From the smokestack came a low-pitched throaty warning to a craft that was coming too close. The *New Orleans* was obviously the queen of the Mississippi.

Shading her eyes, Rebecca gazed upward. From the pilot's cabin, Captain Caldwell was looking down at her. As she watched, he climbed down the steps and headed toward her. For a moment, she had the urge to flee, but after all, where was there to hide on a ship?

"I see you're rested," he said pleasantly. "And you've put on quite a pretty dress. I'm enchanted, cherie." Lifting her hand, he brushed her fingertips with his lips.

She remembered how thrilled she had been the first time he had greeted her in this way. She would not be fooled again by his honeyed words and courtly manner. Quickly, she pulled away her hand and clasped it behind her.

"Yes, I feel much better," she replied, though her tone was distinctly cool. "Thank you for your assistance . . . and for the food."

"And the pup?"

"Oh, your bone has him quite busy. I will need some . . . ah . . . papers to spread for his training. The carpets are beautiful . . . well . . . he is a puppy, after all."

"Yes, I'd thought of that. You'll find scrap paper in the wardrobe."

"Thank you. I do, however, plan to move in with the ladies as soon as possible. Does the ship's captain know about the pup?"

"I explained the circumstances. And there's no need for you to move. You'll be more comfortable in a cabin of your own. And every night, I'll be leaving the ship with the crew."

"Oh? You mean the ship docks every night?"

"It ties up by the bank to allow the crew to bring on wood.

I'll share quarters with the men when we return aboard. In other words, you won't be disturbed in any way."

She wasn't sure what she had expected, but this announcement took her by surprise. "Oh. Then I'll truly have the cabin to myself? Just Pepper and I?"

"Pepper?"

"I've named the dog Pepper."

"Good choice. Yes, the cabin will be exclusively yours."

For a brief moment, she felt guilty at having displaced him from the delightful accommodations which must be his usual quarters. But he had virtually forced it upon her, she reminded herself. "It is kind of you," she felt obliged to say.

"Of course, I had to explain to my friend, the captain, that my *wife* and I were quarreling. I told him she had thrown me out on my ear—ordered me to chop wood and leave her alone."

His teasing grin was irresistible. Before she knew it, she was returning his smile. "One must learn to live with one's lies, I suppose." She caught her breath at the audacity of her words. She must remember she was speaking to an English spy.

He threw back his head and laughed. The sunlight highlighted his thick brandy-colored hair; an errant shock curled over his forehead giving him an unexpectedly boyish appeal. Her heart skipped a beat, but she hastily recovered. "I must apologize for any embarrassment I've caused you," she said sharply to conceal her emotions.

"I don't embarrass easily," he replied, taking her elbow. "Come. We'll stroll along the deck. I assume this is your first steamboat journey."

As soon as possible she removed herself from his grasp. "It is. It's all very interesting."

"I agree. This could be the most interesting trip I myself have made. Tell me, Miss Gordon, why are you making this excursion downriver—completely unchaperoned?"

"My mother recently passed away. I'm staying with . . . with friends in New Orleans till after the war. Then I'm going to Scotland to live with my brother."

"Friends in New Orleans? Um, anyone of my acquaintance?"

"I have no idea. How could I?"

"What I'm asking is the *name* of your friends." He smiled indulgently.

She considered carefully before she answered. Her personal life was none of his concern. But she decided this bit of information would do no harm. "My friend is Mr. Guy Laurens. Actually, I haven't met him, but he was a close acquaintance of my fath—" Tarnation, she'd almost let it slip. Maybe he hadn't noticed. "It was he who sent me the ticket for the boat."

He stopped walking.

She looked up at him, wondering why he had suddenly tensed.

His brow furrowed as he turned and put his hands on her shoulders and gave her an intense look. He scrutinized her for so long, she became exceedingly uneasy.

"What's the matter?" she asked.

"It's just there's such a resemblance to someone. I can't quite recall." He dropped his hands and relaxed his expression. "You are quite a lovely young lady. The dress is most becoming."

Flattery again, she thought, but enjoyed it just the same. "Do you know Mr. Laurens?"

His lips tightened as he gazed beyond her toward the horizon. "I do. I wouldn't want to speak ill of your friend, but I must honestly say, the man is no friend of mine."

"Is that so?" So here was more proof of the captain's treasonable activities. No one, certainly not a nice man like Mr. Laurens, would befriend a traitor. No doubt the captain's secret was known by a few important people in New Orleans.

"I'm sure you keep busy with your own affairs," she said coolly.

"Let's just say that Guy Laurens and I move in different circles."

She considered that for a moment. City folks did have an interesting way of expressing themselves. "Different circles. I'm sure I understand," she stated.

His look clouded. "I'd suggest you beware of the man."

"Beware? But he was kind enough to invite me to New

Orleans. He's made arrangements for me to stay with a lady friend of his. He described her completely and I'm looking forward to staying at her house."

"Now, who would that be?"

"Miss Josephine Laclair. She lives near the riverfront, and she will meet me when the boat arrives."

He started to reply, then clamped his lips. Watching him, she could swear he was struggling for words, a difficulty he'd never had before. He reached into his shirt pocket and removed a silver case. From it, he took a cigar and spent the next moments attempting to light it in the breeze. That accomplished, he drew on it at length until the end glowed a bright orange. Smoke from the cigar veiled his eyes when he finally asked, "You say he described Josephine Laclair in detail? He told you about her . . . establishment?"

A warning sounded in her head. His attempt to appear casual didn't ring true. Already she had revealed too much to this man who was completely untrustworthy. She must end this conversation and return to her cabin. "I know all I need to know," she said curtly. "Now, if you'll excuse me, I must see about Pepper. The papers, you know."

His eyes glittered like green frost; his lips were no longer teasing. "I see. Forgive me if I'm . . . disappointed."

"Disappointed? I don't know what you're talking about. Besides, it really doesn't concern you, does it?"

"Of course not. Only that your innocent facade is very convincing, and, I might add, very appealing."

She was confused. What did he mean by innocent facade? And why was he disappointed? Then it all became clear. He was disappointed that she was innocent. In addition, he was disappointed she was under the protection of Guy Laurens and Miss Laclair. He must have ensconced her in his beautiful cabin with every intention of taking advantage of her. Why, she had suspected that from the beginning, and now he was telling her right out that he was disappointed she was not a loose woman. "You're very bold, Captain Caldwell. I realize my roots are not . . . not quality like the boatman said. But my mother was a good woman and my father was . . . an important man."

"I'm sure that's true. We have no control over our

beginnings, Rebecca, but we do control our destiny. Are you certain you want the life you'll find at Josephine's?"

"As I told you, sir, I intend to travel on to Scotland after the war. I'll only be at the lady's house for a short time."

"And Guy Laurens explained about Miss Josie?"

"He did. I'll be her guest or work for her if that becomes necessary to supplement my traveling expenses. Do you know her . . . or does she also move in a different circle?"

"Yes, I know her." His eyes became limpid as he surveyed her from beyond a new curl of smoke. "It appears I misjudged you, or I should say *underestimated* you, Miss Gordon. If you're determined to follow your chosen path, I see no reason to wait until you're established on Rue de Bourbon. Would you dine at my table tonight? There's a small room near your cabin where guests are served. Food is quite good, as a rule."

She knew she was not highly educated or as worldly-wise as Captain Caldwell, but she would not let him get the better of her. His moods seemed to change swiftly and she didn't understand them. But if she was going to eat in the ship's dining room, it may as well be with him. Perhaps she could figure out his sudden air of mystery and double-talk before the meal was over. "Yes, I suppose so," she said loftily.

"I believe dinner is at half-past six," he said, guiding her back along the deck to her door. "I'll look forward to it." He bowed slightly and strode away toward the pilothouse.

5

Blaine was angry—and he didn't know why. Standing on the deck outside the pilothouse, he gazed unseeing at the passing scenery. Rebecca Gordon had gotten under his skin, that was certain. He didn't know whether he wanted to kiss her or shake her till her teeth rattled. He could have sworn she was an innocent little country girl, unsophisticated and unaware of the ways of the world. Hell, he'd been about to offer his protection, look after the imp as if she were a younger sister—or even his daughter.

Dammit, Caldwell, he cursed silently. Quit deceiving yourself. Admit your feelings for her are not those of a protector. You'd love to bed the lady. You're fascinated with her combination of womanly beauty and childlike vulnerability.

It appeared, however, he had underestimated the complexities of the young lady's background. He was certain she had been about to say "father" when she'd suddenly clamped her lips. And she'd said her father was a man of importance. No man of importance would have a daughter traveling alone on a steamboat or headed for a whorehouse in New Orleans. More than likely she was one of the illegitimate little urchins who drifted into New Orleans as soon as they could escape from the backwoods. He knew

Guy Laurens had placed more than one ambitious girl at Miss Josie's for his private indulgence. The bastard had even brought in a few virgins and offered their first tumble at a high price, the proceeds to be shared by both Josie and himself. The girls were willing enough, so no one questioned the practice.

He exhaled cigar smoke between his lips. Personally he detested Laurens—always had. The man had gone through his wife's money in a few short years, and only survived financially when he took over control of the estate of his deceased partner, Etienne Dufour. Dufour had been a popular and respected member of the community sixteen or seventeen years ago until his mysterious death at the hands of some brigand. There had even been hints that Laurens had played a part in Dufour's murder.

And now the villain was delivering little Miss Gordon into a life of prostitution. Laurens would take great pleasure in it, especially since the girl was most definitely attractive and probably a virgin.

Bloody hell, the idea of Laurens selling that winsome girl into white slavery turned Blaine's stomach. Hold on now, he ordered. Don't forget the girl seems quite willing to go along with the plan. And with her face and figure, and tidied up a bit, she'd make a killing at Josie's—maybe become some rich man's mistress—if she gave up that business about going to Scotland.

The thought of her willingness infuriated him further. How could she do such a thing? She was bright and spunky and . . . well, a considerable cut above the women he'd known at Josie's. Oh, they had been beauties, all right, and appeared to enjoy their work. He'd never before questioned their beginnings—never cared where they came from or if they enjoyed their work—or asked what their future plans might be. Most of the especially pretty and intelligent girls moved on to occupy private dwellings provided by a wealthy protector. He'd heard it said these mistresses generally received as much attention as the gent's wives—and were more content.

Turning his back to the view, he leaned against the rail. So that would be the fate of Rebecca Gordon. He knew it, and obviously so did she. Guy must have promised her a good income, more than enough to eventually travel to Scotland if that was her choice. He could understand how that would appeal to a poor little chit from the Tennessee hills. Yes, that must be the answer. She'd made it clear she intended to work at Josie's and then use her money to reestablish herself in Scotland. No one there would be the wiser, and she would attract a husband with ease. Clever girl, he decided. But dammit, it riled him beyond all reason to think about it.

A new idea crept into his mind. Why not make Rebecca his own mistress—exclusively? He'd never had one, never had time or inclination. His off and on courtship with Sonja Delgado needed resolving. She was pressing for marriage and he'd almost decided to go ahead with it. Dominique Hall needed a woman, and he wanted children. He'd soon be twenty-eight, past time to settle down and start a family. The huge house was empty and quiet as a tomb with only himself to occupy its vast elegance. He spent little time there, preferring to be at sea with his shipping fleet or at Barataria with Jean Lafitte and his motley gang of privateers. Lately, his involvement with the war had occupied him entirely.

Yes, it was a helluva good idea. He'd take an apartment in the Vieux Carré. He could pay Rebecca more than she'd ever earn at Josie's—and he'd have a lively companion to ease his loneliness. He could keep her happy for a time, he was sure. Later, if she really was determined to go to Scotland, he could pay for her passage or send her on one of his ships. At least she wouldn't be pawed over and sullied by all the hotbloods doing business at Josephine's whorehouse.

As for Sonja, he would ask for her hand as soon as the war was over. Her family was more prestigious than his own, and almost as wealthy, though some of the Creole fortunes had waned since Louisiana became a part of the United States. Two women in his life? Why not? Now all that was left was to convince little Miss Rebecca Gordon to share his bed. That shouldn't be too difficult. He'd never had much trouble convincing a pretty girl to indulge in a romp.

"Pepper—no, no, no," Rebecca scolded the pup. Oh, dear. Too late. She reached for the paper and tidied up. Well, accidents were bound to happen. Especially when the poor creature was so confined.

It was early afternoon and she was growing restless sitting in the cabin and playing with the dog.

Opening her traveling bag, she drew out a long rope and called Pepper over. "We'll walk on the deck—maybe meet some other folks," she explained as she made a loop and placed it over the pup's head. "Not too tight. There. After all, we have several days ahead of us. We'll have to find a way to occupy our time."

Being careful not to look toward the forward deck, she left the cabin and strolled aft, pausing for a time to watch the giant wooden paddle wheel at the port side thrusting its way in a mighty circle, splashing below and moving the ship forward with powerful steam-driven strokes. They swept past a levee on the far shore where nearly naked children jumped up and down and yelled at the passing boat. In answer, the pilot gave them a brief and friendly toot of the ship's whistle. Their delighted cries carried across the water on the summer breeze.

Nice to grow up on the Mississippi, Rebecca thought, waving back at the children. Her own creek at Morgan's Landing had once seemed enormous, but compared to this broad, shining river, it was merely a pleasant backwater stream.

She continued walking toward the back of the boat, letting Pepper have a little more slack as he pulled and bounded and tested the rope held by his mistress.

"Oh, a puppy," came a child's voice. "Look, it's a black puppy."

Rebecca smiled as a shabbily dressed little girl, about the age of eight, scurried forward, then halted and clasped her hands before her. "Oh, isn't it cute. Will it bite? May I pet it . . . please?"

Pepper was doing his best to leap into the child's arms. His tail wagged frantically and his tongue lolled below his chin whiskers as he tugged on the rope.

"He likes you," said Rebecca. "You may pet him, but don't let him tear your dress." She knelt near the child on the planks while the pup cavorted between them.

"Shandy, what are you doing?" came a scolding female voice. "What is this? A puppy on board?"

Rebecca jumped up. She'd almost forgotten the rule about dogs on the boat. "Hello," she said, giving the approaching woman a bright smile. "Is this your daughter? She's mighty cute. She and my pup have just made friends."

The woman was also poorly garbed, her homespun dress threadbare and stained from long wear. "I'm Martha Thatcher. This here is Shannon Kildaire. She ain't mine. I'm taking her to New Orleans so she kin make her way."

"Make her way?" Rebecca said astounded. "Why, she's just a child. Where are her parents?"

The Thatcher lady looked uneasy. Before answering, she twisted one bony finger through a stand of stringy mushroom-colored hair. "Don't rightly know, I s'pose. I'm fetching her from Memphis to New Orleans to keep her out of the pokey."

"You mean—jail?"

The little girl continued to pet the dog, ignoring the discussion concerning her.

"Jail. Yes'm. She's light-fingered and slippery as they come."

Rebecca frowned down at the child. She was almost pretty with eyes the color of amber glass and naturally curly blond hair. A missing front tooth and a sprinkling of freckles gave her an innocent look belying her dubious reputation. "Then . . . she has no family? No home?"

"I don't know 'cause she won't say. I was traveling to New Orleans for my employer when she convinced me to take her along. Said she was an orphan and in a heap of trouble. The captain let her ride without a ticket if I promised to look after her."

Rebecca put out her hand. "Hello, Shannon. I'm Rebecca Gor—ah . . . Caldwell." She remembered her subterfuge in the nick of time. "Just call me Rebecca."

Shannon sprang to her feet and took the extended hand. Her eyes held a look wise beyond her years. "Pleased ta meetcha. I'd like to play with the puppy if it's all right, ma'am. In our cabin, I mean, so the rope can come off. He doesn't like it, I can tell."

"Of course you can," Rebecca agreed. "That is, if Martha will allow it."

"Sure, as long as the captain don't object. You kin come too, Rebecca. We'll make some tea. It looks like we're the only women aboard the *Orleans.*"

Happy for the distraction, Rebecca followed Martha into the aft cabin. It was spacious enough, but contained four bunks and much simpler furnishings than her own private cabin. On a table in the middle of the room was a partially unwound bolt of blue silk and a sizeable sewing basket.

"I was about to stitch a new dress," Martha explained. "One needs to find busywork on these voyages."

"Oh, what lovely fabric," Rebecca exclaimed. Almost reverently, she touched the delicate silk, the rich azure of a summer sky just before sunrise. The look of it was in startling contrast to Martha Thatcher's shabby attire.

Martha noticed her surprise. "My employer owns a dress shop in Memphis. I'm a good seamstress and I'll sell this garment in New Orleans for a tidy sum. Then I'll buy some cloth and go back upriver."

"Oh, I see."

"Do you sew?" Martha inquired. "I have some leftover material and extra buttons and a piece of lace I have no use for."

"Yes, I do sew," Rebecca answered enthusiastically. "My mother was a wonderful seamstress, but we never had real silk like this."

"Then it's settled. You kin let Shandy play with your pup, and you and I kin each sew a dress."

"I'll pay you, of course." Rebecca popped open the pouch and laid out a coin. "How much is it? I believe I have enough."

"Thank ye, I'm much obliged. The silk is special—come from London before the war. And I kin use the extra money in New Orleans."

Rebecca was delighted. Pulling up a chair, she smoothed out the fabric. "Tell me, where do you stay in New Orleans, and what will happen to Shandy?"

"I have a cousin who works in a shop. I won't stay long—just until the ship heads north. My employer sends me twiced a year—trusts me, she does—with the money and all."

Rebecca smiled across at her. "Yes, I can see she does. But what about the child? Surely she can't run loose in the streets."

"Not my business. She was loose enough in Memphis. I'm just doing her the favor of getting her away from the law. Made her promise to behave on the trip, I can tell ye."

Rebecca shook her head. She had mustered all her courage to undertake her own journey to New Orleans. It was unthinkable such a youngster would blithely leave home without ways and means to survive.

Martha passed her the scissors. "We'd best get busy. It's only a few hours till dinner is served. If we work fast, we kin finish our dresses before we reach New Orleans."

The afternoon passed swiftly. Rebecca worked skillfully with needle and thread, taking care with her measuring so she wouldn't waste a single inch of the exquisite material. The thought of meeting Mrs. Josephine Laclair in a dress made of this elegant blue fabric was like a dream come true.

She let the talkative Martha Thatcher dominate the conversation. That was better, she decided, than risking exposing the truth of her own identity. How she wished Captain Caldwell had never invented the tale of their being newlyweds. She disliked lying and was poor at it. One lie required another, she'd always discovered. Besides, she enjoyed hearing Martha prattle on and on about her job, her rascally husband, the joys of being childless, and the amazing sights in New Orleans.

"Oh, it's a sinful place, I kin tell you, Rebecca. You must avoid certain parts of the Vieux Carré. One neighborhood is known as The Swamps. Murderers, cutthroats, thieves, the dregs of foreign shores, folks practicing black magic. You mustn't go there a'tall." She rambled on. "Now, there's other parts of the city that are pretty enough to take your breath away. The Creoles—that's the old families of French or Spanish extraction—they're mostly rich with fine carriages and slaves to do their bidding at the wave of a fan. No one of their class, not men nor women, do any work that I know of. Some own big plantations up along the river or on the lakeshore."

"Well, what do they do with their time?" Rebecca wondered.

"Oh, they do mostly sinful things—play cards all day, dance all night. Oh, yes, they love to dance. The Creole ladies have fancy dress balls. Most of the houses have upstairs ballrooms. And the men . . ." She lowered her voice. "They go to some dances wearing masks so no one will recognize them. Dances called Quadroon Balls, where free ladies of color entertain them. Married men too. Their wives know, but can't say a word. And if you're a Yankee, don't try making friends with them. The Creoles are as clannish as any people on earth."

It was more fascinating than Rebecca had imagined. She couldn't wait to see for herself. She ventured, "I'll be staying with a friend of my mother. She's a great lady, I understand. That's why I'm so happy to have this new dress."

"You *and your husband* will be guests of the lady?"

Drats, she'd slipped up again. Completely forgot she was supposed to be a married woman. "Oh, yes . . . Captain Caldwell and I," she corrected.

Martha rested her needle and leaned near. "You say your mother's deceased?"

"Yes. In late May."

"Then let me give you a piece of advice. I'm not quite old enough to be your real mother, but I've had a bushel of experience . . . being married five years like I have."

"Why, of course, Martha."

"Well, I couldn't help noticing you and your husband seem to be having a problem. When I inquired from a crewman—thinking you and I might get acquainted soon—he said you were newlyweds who'd had quite a spat."

Rebecca was horrified. Ship gossip seemed to fly faster than a bullet. "Well . . . yes . . . you could say that."

Martha nodded knowingly. "Is it the usual problem—like most newlyweds?"

"I . . . I suppose so," she answered, not at all certain what the "usual problem" might be.

"Well, I figured 'twas. It was the same with Mr. Thatcher

and me in the beginning. It's just something you have to accept if you want to keep your husband satisfied and out of mischief."

The light dawned in Rebecca's head. She felt her cheeks turn pink under Martha's gaze.

"Don't be embarrassed, girl. We kin talk about it and maybe that will help. It only hurts the first time. Just keep the room dark and pretend you're somewhere else—on a picnic or a walk in the woods. It doesn't last long, now does it? Then your husband will be so grateful, he'll treat you like a queen—for a while anyway. And who knows, you might soon start a baby. Then you'll have eight or nine months with a good excuse to sleep alone."

Rebecca swallowed hard. She had grown up on a farm and knew all about sex. But never had she discussed the matter unless it had to do with breeding the sow or encouraging the stallion to perform when required. "Thank you," she murmured, then cut her eyes toward Shannon and the pup lying stretched out on one of the bunks.

"I'll say no more," Martha said, placing a finger over her lips. "But remember my words. You're a good-lookin' woman, Rebecca. That gives you a powerful weapon I never had. Use it when you need to. Pleasure your husband. But never let him forget how much he owes you for the privilege." She picked up her needle and slid it through the silk. "We ladies must stick together," she observed. "Our men have wars, and have to make a living, and worry aplenty. But we women have strength—and the courage and the power to get what we want if we use our heads a mite. God passes things around, and we must make the most of whatever He gives us."

6

Beautiful? No. Rebecca thought it was very nice of Martha to compliment her like that, but she was sure it was a white lie. She could see in the mirror—and *passably pretty* was the best she could hope for. Anyway, that was the description she'd overheard a couple of years ago when Lindsey MacGregor and Roe Jameson were smoking pipes behind the well house. Of course, she'd grown up some since then. But beautiful? No, Martha Thatcher was just being polite.

Rebecca was sitting cross-legged on the bed in her cabin, trying to make a decision. She had been in a stew ever since Martha's comments about the problems of the marriage bed. It seemed her rightful punishment to be embarrassed beyond words. She had gone along with Captain Caldwell's story when she should have had the gumption to defy him. No wonder he expected favors—though he acted like a perfect gentleman. Why, everyone knew a spy was expert at pretending all sorts of things.

Leaning back in the pillows, she made her decision. She would not go to the dining room for dinner. Hopefully she could manage a snack later from the cook in the galley. But she could not sit through an entire meal talking with the captain as if she were his wife, especially under the maternal eye of Martha Thatcher, who was sure to be at a nearby table. Besides it would do Captain Caldwell good to know she was not at his beck and call. He probably thought that just because he was a rich gentleman, he could have whatever he wanted—including her. Well, she'd show him. In fact, she would have liked to move in with Martha and Shandy if she could, but that would require some sort of explanation to Martha, which would mean more lies. She felt guilty enough for the ones she'd already told.

That decision made, she clasped her hands behind her head and stretched out her legs beside a snoozing Pepper. The ship was very still now, having tied up in a bend of the river for the evening.

She must have dozed because she abruptly became aware of a knocking on her door. She scooted off the bed and opened it. Standing outside, balancing a tray with a covered platter, two goblets and a bottle of wine, stood Blaine Caldwell.

"I hope you're not ill," he said with a suggestion of a smile.

"No," she answered crisply. "I'm just resting a bit. I guess I was more tired than I realized after last week's journey."

He eased by her into the cabin.

Humph, she thought, *he acted as if the place were his.* She was about to ask him to leave, when Pepper began leaping around his ankles, his paws paddling the air and his tail wagging merrily.

Chuckling, Blaine placed the tray and wine on a small table and reached down to pet the dog. "Well, Pepper, you like me better now, it appears. Here, I have a treat for you." He produced a bone from his pocket and placed it into Pepper's eager mouth.

What could she do? Sighing, she took a chair at the table and peeked under the silver cover. The sight and smell of freshly grilled chicken, mustard greens, tiny new potatoes and gravy, and sweet potato pie made her mouth water, reminding her she'd had nothing but Martha's tea since her snack at midmorning.

The captain pulled up a chair opposite her and poured wine into the goblets.

As hungry as she was, she was tempted to refuse the meal. Why, the man had marched in here and laid out the dinner without even a by your leave. It was as if they truly were husband and wife. Maybe it would have been better, after all, if she had gone to the dining room. There, at least, she wouldn't be trapped by circumstances—alone with this . . . this traitor. She picked at her food while he watched in silence.

"You've eaten, I suppose," she said to break the awkward moment.

"I have—when it was plain my dinner companion had abandoned me. I suppose you're having your revenge for my missing our dinner engagement in Nashville. If so, we're even now. An eye for an eye, a tooth for a tooth, as they say."

She hadn't thought of that, but she wished she had. She met his eyes as if revenge had indeed been her purpose.

"Fair enough," he said. "I've paid my penalty. But you need some meat on your bones, little lass. I want you to eat every bite I've set before you."

"I appreciate your interest, Captain, but I've looked after myself for quite some time. I expect to continue doing so."

"I have no doubt," he said, shaking his head. "Damned if you aren't an uppity young lady. Are all Tennessee women so independent?"

"I wouldn't know." She washed down a bite of chicken with a large swallow of wine. It was a delicious drink, she thought—far better than the berry wine or the homemade brew from her valley. She wasn't used to spirits, so she must be careful not to overindulge.

"Rebecca." Blaine put down his goblet and leaned forward. "I would truly like to be your friend. I'm sure you think you know what you're doing, where you're headed, what life's all about, but I'm older than you and know a bit more about the world. I'd like you to reconsider your plans for your future."

"I have considered all that is necessary," she stated firmly. "And my decision is made. I'll stay at Miss Laclair's until the war is over, then I'll be off to Scotland."

"You would leave the country of your birth so easily?"

She gazed at him over the lip of the crystal glass. He was so very attractive, and seemed so . . . so gentlemanly, so protective. Something deep inside urged her to trust him, but after what she'd overheard, knowing what she did about him, she had proof enough of his treachery. It was just that here, in the glow of the candles with the fading sun casting long shadows obliquely through the narrow windows, watching the play of light on his smooth, tanned skin and chiseled features, with his very nearness sending tiny waves of pleasure along her spine, she found it difficult not to believe he had her best interests at heart. Maybe it was the wine that was causing those warm, tingly feelings in the pit of her stomach.

"*I* love this country," she said, noticing her voice had lost some of its frigid tone.

"Then stay," he suggested, his eyes searching hers, forcing her to look into their depths. "Stay in New Orleans. Don't go to Josie's."

She spilled a few drops of wine onto the table. Why, the man must think she had no sense at all. "But . . . I have to . . . I want to . . . really, Captain, I have no choice."

"I'm offering you a choice. Surely you understand my meaning."

She replaced her goblet so sharply that the wine sprayed over the rim. His implication was clear. He apparently wanted her to become his mistress. "I do understand. You . . . you're insulting. I must ask you to leave at once." She stood and squared her shoulders. "Please don't interfere in my life again. I've told you I can take care of myself."

Frowning, he shoved back his chair. "Forgive me," he said quietly. "I assure you it was not my intention to offend you."

She couldn't stop her tongue. "I've lived in the hill country, 'tis true. But I know about men like you. I know what you expect to gain with your wealth and courtly charm."

His look of consternation changed to one of wry amusement. "That's quite a display of temper. Am I to understand you're refusing the offer of my protection?"

"You understand perfectly," she snapped.

"Then I must tell you, I don't lightly take no for an answer. For now, I will accept your decision. I must leave, at any rate. The crew will be going ashore before dark to fell a tree or two for the ship's boiler."

"Good," she said relieved. "I'm certain they'll be glad to have an extra hand."

Cocking an eyebrow, he stopped to look at her from the doorway. "Chopping wood is not my usual way to pass a pleasant summer's eve. You're a hard taskmaster, Rebecca Gordon. You drive a man to all sorts of mad behavior."

"Leave my cabin, sir," she ordered haughtily.

Instead, he moved toward her.

She didn't flinch. Defiantly, she held her position by the table.

"I think we'll say a proper farewell," he said huskily.

When he slipped his arm around her waist, she stiffened, but made no effort to escape. She wondered why her righteous indignation didn't turn into staunch resistance. It occurred to her she should even be fearful. But she wasn't afraid of him. Quite the contrary. She had the most annoying urge to return his embrace.

He tipped her chin back and covered her lips. The kiss was gentle and lingering, but it sent streaks of fire racing through her body, almost stopping her breath. With her eyes closed, she absorbed his overwhelming masculine presence, the feel of his arms enfolding her, his strength, his latent passion held carefully in check. It was the first real kiss of her life—and she couldn't deny the thrill of it.

Her hands were resting lightly on his shoulders when he eased away.

"Good-bye, my dear," he said as if speaking fondly to a child.

Good-bye? For the moment, she had forgotten she'd ordered him to leave—and rightly so. Quickly, she removed her hands and backed away. "Yes. Good-bye," she answered with studied indifference.

As soon as he was gone, she sank heavily into her chair. The kiss had been a revelation, while at the same time, it created confusion. Her attraction to the captain was shockingly real, but why had her body betrayed her mind so completely?

She heard the crew noisily leaving the ship. For a while, she picked at the food left on her plate. For the first time since she could remember, she felt she had lost control of her feelings and her thoughts. Is this what her mother had experienced all those years ago in New Orleans: this awakening of passion, this deceiving sense of security, this unexplainable sense of longing? Yes, she had sent the captain packing, but even now, she wished to see him again—to have him look at her in that special way that sent her heart bounding in crazy rhythm. She must have taken leave of her senses, she decided. She would avoid him as much as possible or she might succumb again to his seductive wiles.

As soon as she had eaten and fed the scraps to Pepper, she carried the tray back to the galley. The moon was barely visible beyond dark, scudding clouds above the river. The ship seemed deserted with only a light in the pilothouse and another aft where Martha Thatcher was staying. Leaning on the rail, she listened to the music of the frogs and crickets and the distant sounds of hatchets bringing down a tree in the woods. Two, perhaps three more nights and she would be in New Orleans, and in the safe care of Guy Laurens and Miss Josephine Laclair.

A sudden bolt of lightning startled her from her reverie. It was closely followed by another and then an ominous roll of thunder. The moon disappeared and large drops of water splattered around her. Gusts of wind ruffled the black expanse of river, and the ship rocked slightly, stretching the heavy ropes securing it to the shore.

As she headed toward her cabin, she noticed the pilot making his way briskly to the upper deck.

Hurrying inside, she was greeted with Pepper's nervous yapping. She picked him up and reassured him. "It's all right now. Just a summer squall." Wind lifted the lace curtains from the windows; rain splashed noisily onto the low cabin roof. She rushed to close the shutters against the torrent.

Sitting on the bed, she cuddled the dog in her arms. Never had she been in a storm while on the water. Was there danger? The ship groaned and creaked as the gale intensified. She thought of the logging crew on shore—and of Blaine Caldwell. At the very least, they were getting a good soaking.

Even as she considered their plight, she heard cursing and

hoots of laughter as the men clambered across the gangplank and regained the ship. A loud knock on her door brought her to her feet.

"Come in," she answered, knowing full well who was demanding entry.

Dripping wet, Blaine Caldwell burst into the room. Not only was he sopping, but he was bare to the waist and carrying his dripping shirt in one hand.

He shouldered the door shut and faced her. His hair was clinging to his forehead and curling along his ears. Rivulets ran down his shoulders, streaking his well-muscled chest and arms. His expression was half-apologetic and half-amused. Looking down at her, he said, "I'm sorry to disturb you again, Miss Gordon, but my change of clothing is in that wardrobe. I did expect to occupy this cabin, as you know. I might add that it's just been pointed out to me by several crewmen that my *wife* must certainly be concerned about my safety."

The sight of his gleaming wet and magnificent physique left her breathless. The remembrance of his lips covering hers, his powerful arms holding her against his length, sent unbidden desire coursing through her deepest recesses. "Oh . . . I see," she said tightly. "Then of course, you must dry yourself and change your clothes. I'll wait outside."

She put down the dog and started to walk by Blaine when he caught her arm and turned her toward him. "It's raining like hell," he reminded her.

"I'm aware of that," she said, though she was far more aware of his powerful body and the strength of his hands gripping her shoulders.

He stopped her words with a fierce kiss. His arms encircled her, pressing her against his hard body. She felt the heated moisture of his chest penetrate her bodice. For a moment, she placed her hands defensively against him, then gradually slid them around his shoulders.

His lips demanded a response and she was incapable of resistance. She was forced to stand on tiptoe as his arms curled around her back. Binding her hands over the wet strands along his nape, she gave herself up to the fiery intensity of his embrace. She was lost in the rain-washed scent of him; her ears were pounding, and she felt the pulse-beat in his neck while sensuously his tongue teased her lips apart and explored the inner recesses of her mouth.

Suddenly, he released her. She was almost as wet as he. Gently, he stroked her cheek and smoothed back loose curls from her forehead. He was breathing deeply, his bare chest only inches from her lips.

As if entranced, she gazed up at him while he traced her tingling lips with his fingertips.

"You're a woman to be reckoned with, ma cherie," he said softly. "If in some ways, you're still a child, I suspect that will soon be a thing of the past."

She wasn't a child. His annoying implication, laden with suggestive meaning, shocked her into action. She spun away and marched out of the cabin. Outside, the storm had subsided, leaving only a heavy mist falling like a silvery shower between the river and the intermittent moonlight. She walked to the farthest point of the stern deck and breathed deeply, fighting to calm her raging emotions.

Behind her, she heard her cabin door open and close. She heard Blaine's footsteps striding away toward the forward cabin where the crew was quartered. Her fingers fluttered to her lips which still tingled from his kiss. She had succumbed to him, allowed his liberties, thrilled to the power of his masculinity. She still trembled from the force that had engulfed her. If he hadn't called her a child, something dreadful might have happened. From now on, she must keep her distance, ignore him—somehow. She must protect her heart at all costs from Captain Blaine Caldwell.

7

For the next two days, Rebecca saw Blaine only from a distance. He had moved in with the crew and took his meals with them as well. He often spent time with the captain and the pilot, occasionally manning the wheel himself.

Every afternoon, when the boat had been secured for the night, he would go ashore to chop wood with the men. She couldn't help wondering how a gentleman of wealth would fare under such circumstances. The crew of the *New Orleans* appeared to accept him as one of their own. At least, he never came again to her cabin or made any attempt to talk to her.

As for herself, she spent her days with Mrs. Thatcher, working diligently on her dress and keeping her lips sealed regarding her identity. She explained to Martha that her husband, Captain Caldwell, had vacated their cabin by his own choice, that he was taking this opportunity to learn the workings at every level of the first steamboat ever to ply a regular route on the Mississippi. Though it was apparent Martha doubted certain aspects of the story, Rebecca declined to enlighten her.

On July 12, the *New Orleans* landed two miles above Baton Rouge and eased near the shore to drop anchor. As usual, six crewmen and Blaine Caldwell took to the woods to obtain fuel for the final leg of the journey.

Shortly after dinner, Rebecca retired to her cabin. She slept fitfully, plagued by disturbing dreams and bouts of insomnia. Once, she jerked awake in a cold sweat over some already forgotten nightmare. Rising just before dawn, she lit her candles and pulled the nearly completed blue dress over her head. Today she would stay alone in her cabin away from Martha's chitchat, and sew the lace around the neck and sleeves. Then the dress would be finished—just in time for tomorrow's arrival in New Orleans. She assumed the steamboat's arrival would be well advertised, and either Mr. Laurens or Miss Laclair would be on hand to welcome her.

Distant shouts caught her attention. People were running along the deck. It was much too early for such commotion, she thought. Going outside, she peered through the first pink light of dawn. The smokestack was raising steam; the two paddle wheels at port and starboard were rotating, churning the water into a murky caldron, but the *New Orleans* wasn't moving an inch.

As she watched, the crew and even the cook crowded down the steps toward the boiler room. Something was definitely amiss.

Within minutes, the ship's captain and the pilot emerged and crossed to the port bow to stare over the side.

Rebecca stayed out of the way and strained her ears to hear their comments. She only caught snatches, but it became apparent that the *Orleans* had either run aground or was impaled on something invisible beneath the hull.

At that moment, Martha Thatcher arrived at her elbow. "I declare, isn't that the limit!" she exclaimed. She was garbed in a blue cotton nightshift, flowered robe and lace nightcap. "I do hope Shandy doesn't awaken."

"Is there any real danger?" asked Rebecca.

"More likely just the nuisance of a delay. Why, two years ago this boat survived the earthquake in New Madrid."

"I remember that. We felt it all the way to Morgan's Landing in Tennessee."

"I thought the Lord in His wisdom was shaking the earth to bits. It was the *Orleans*'s maiden voyage down the

Mississippi. The steamboat was shaken up plenty, but made it on downriver. I'd say it's a sturdy craft."

No sooner had she finished her reassuring observation than the boat began to slowly revolve in place, until the stern faced downstream while the bow faced north. There it hung motionless fifty yards offshore while the river flowed around it.

This brought the captain running ahead of his pilot to inspect the starboard side. He yelled over his shoulder, "Get Caldwell over here!"

Rebecca felt her heart skip at the sight of Blaine Caldwell striding forward to consult with his fellow captain. His clothes were rumpled and he had a day's growth of beard, but his impressive physique and his confident stride gave him a dominating presence. She felt better knowing he was lending his assistance.

Again the boiler ejected an enormous blast of steam from the smokestack. The paddle wheels dug through the water. The stern began to swing around until it had turned 180 degrees and traded places once again with the bow. It was like a top spinning slowly in place.

"Damnation!" cried the *Orleans* captain. "It's hung up dead center. The river fell during the night. Never seen anything like it."

"I suggest you shut down the boiler," Caldwell said. "Wait for the river to rise."

"Hell no!" shouted the captain. "We're behind schedule now."

"Better to be late than put the boat on the bottom," Caldwell observed.

"Well, we'll have one more go at it. Blake," he called, "drop the starboard anchor. That will stabilize the ship. We'll heave to and try to break loose from the sandbar—or whatever's down there holding us."

"Excuse me," Blaine interjected. "You asked my opinion, now I'm giving it. It might not be a sandbar. It could be a tree stump. You could tear the bottom right out of this vessel."

"No stumps this far out. I appreciate your advice, but I'll give it one more try. If we don't get free, we'll have to stay till the river rises, I reckon." The captain marched back into the boiler room to issue his orders.

"Well, it's quite exciting," Rebecca said to Martha. "But I do hope we're not delayed."

Mrs. Thatcher viewed her in the brightening morning. "My, you're wearing your new dress. It certainly does look pretty."

A masculine voice came from behind Rebecca's shoulder. "May I add my compliments on your attire—*Mrs. Caldwell?*"

She whirled to look up at Blaine. As before, his eyes were teasing—and tinged with admiration.

"Oh . . . Captain. Thank you. I've been sewing these past few days."

He nodded appreciatively. "You're a talented lady, in more ways than I realized. 'Tis plain my choice of wife was a wise one."

Lifting her chin to face him, she said crisply, "Your choice seemed a bit *hasty* at the time."

Mrs. Thatcher cleared her throat. "Excuse me. I believe I'll check on Shandy."

"Oh, I'm sorry, Martha." Rebecca suddenly remembered the lady's presence. "May I introduce Captain Caldwell. Captain, this is Mrs. Thatcher."

Blaine bowed over Martha's hand. "It's a pleasure, ma'am."

"Do you think there's any danger, Captain?" Martha asked while holding the neck of her robe in sudden awareness of her dishabille.

"Probably not. Though I'd rather stay put than force the boat—"

He was interrupted by a deafening blast of steam from the whistle. The boat rocked and creaked; the stern shifted a few feet toward the port side.

"Oh, lord, he's done it now!" Blaine snapped.

Abruptly Rebecca and Martha were thrown against the railing. The deck beneath their feet had shifted to a precarious angle.

Blaine rushed toward the boiler room.

Martha screamed as the boat listed, allowing water to wash over the planking. Several large crates stored on the cabin roof broke their bindings and crashed downward. One struck Martha a glancing blow and sent her sprawling.

Rebecca fell to her knees as water washed around her.

Two members of the crew dashed to the longboat and tore away its ropes. "Over here!" a man yelled. "Passengers here! We'll get ashore!"

Rebecca crouched on the wooden deck as the ship tipped at a sickening angle above the river. What once had seemed as steady and safe as land itself had become a topsy-turvy world with boxes and debris sliding and banging in wild disarray.

The ship's whistle screeched a frantic distress signal.

"The hull's split below," came a shout. "Abandon ship! Abandon ship!"

Stunned at the suddenness of the disaster, Rebecca was momentarily disoriented. Just beyond her, she saw a crate of chickens slide into the river and break apart. Inanely, she wondered if the chickens could swim. After all, shore was fifty yards away.

"Get in the boat, lady." A man pulled her roughly to her feet. "Hurry now. The *Orleans* is sinking for sure."

Her head cleared and she gazed around. One paddle wheel was partially out of the water, but still revolving as if in a desperate effort to save itself. The pilothouse was silhouetted against the rising sun at a crazy angle. Black smoke poured from the boiler room, and the sound of the whistle had been replaced by frantic shouts from the captain and crew. The scene was like a hellish nightmare.

She let herself be led to the longboat before she remembered. "Pepper," she cried. "Wait—my dog . . . and my coins! They're in my cabin! Let me go!"

A hand grabbed her wet skirt. "Help! Help me, Rebecca —please."

The choking voice was Martha Thatcher's. She was lying in the boat, her forehead and cheek streaked with blood. Her eyes rolled in absolute panic as she clung to Rebecca.

"Let me go, Martha! I have to get back to my cabin. Let go, I say. You're safe now." Rebecca's voice was shrill above the din made by cries and the incessant clanging of the ship's bell.

"It's Shandy! I can't find her! I think she's asleep in the cabin."

Waves of alarm swept through Rebecca. "Maybe one of the men has gone for her," she shouted near Martha's ear.

"I don't know," Martha cried. "I was out cold. You're the first person I've talked to. I wish you'd look for her. The tyke was already scar't of the river—can't swim a lick, she claims."

One man was trying to retrieve the longboat's oars from under a seat; another was holding the prow to keep the craft from swamping in the whirlpools of the churning river. Rebecca couldn't be sure if anyone had gone for the child. A quick look around showed several swimmers heading for shore.

Tripping over her sopping skirts, she stumbled, half running, half crawling, along the slippery deck toward the ship's stern. It was an uphill struggle as she used the broken railing and whatever handholds she could find to make her way. At least for the moment, the vessel had stopped moving, its hull speared as it hung partially immersed in the river's current.

When she reached the aft cabin, she found the door open. On hands and knees, she inched her way forward.

A moan from under the cot started her heart racing. "Shannon honey, come here. Hurry, pumpkin. It's your friend, Rebecca."

"No . . . no, don't make me. I can't swim."

"Shannon Kildaire, come here this minute. You don't have to swim; there's a nice little boat to take us ashore."

After a pause, the girl slid through inches of water to land in Rebecca's arms.

For one short breath, Rebecca grasped her tightly, then reversed her position and scooted back out the door.

The return trip to the longboat was more difficult. Now she had only one hand to grasp whatever protrusions were available. Her clothes were soaked as the swirling water reached for her like fingers of doom. At least Shannon was small and clinging to her neck with all her might.

"That's a good girl, sweetie. Hold tight and you'll soon be with Martha."

Her brave words were swallowed in a scream as the ship

suddenly jerked, listing even farther into the whirlpool around it.

"Hang on—I'm coming," ordered a masculine voice.

At the far end of the deck, Blaine was making his way toward her, half crouching, clinging to the battered railing, his boots swamped by the rushing tide.

"Blaine!" she called. "Take Shannon!"

She slid along the wet boards, holding Shannon before her, until she reached his outstretched hand. "The longboat," she gasped.

Blaine lifted the child and placed her into waiting hands. "Now you," he commanded.

The boat heaved again, tearing her grasp from the piece of broken planking. She slipped into his embrace and clung to him with all her remaining strength.

He muttered something but she couldn't hear if it was a curse or a prayer. But the words "brave lass" reached her ears.

In moments he was forcing her away from him. "Let go, Rebecca. Come now. Here's the boat."

Biting her lip, she looked up into his face, her every sense heightened by a tumult of fear and desire. "Come with me," she begged.

His look was sardonic, almost amused. "Soon, Mrs. Caldwell. Now, in you go." He swept her over the railing and into the arms of a muscular crewman.

"Blaine," she cried. "It's sinking. Come—" Her plea went unfinished as she was plunked into the bottom of the longboat.

"Get going!" the crewman ordered from behind her. "Row like hell. We don't want to be pulled under if it sinks."

Rebecca eased herself onto a plank seat and tried to control her nerves. She was wet through and through, and her fingers were scraped and bleeding. A glance showed Shannon clinging to Martha Thatcher. The two were glassy-eyed with fear. The only sound was a roaring in her ears. The four men strained at the oars, forcing the boat away from the doomed *New Orleans.*

Burying her face in her hands, she thanked God for their lives. She was shaking with a hard chill; the journey toward shore seemed endless. Now that Shannon was safe, she thought miserably of her own loss—especially of Pepper. She looked back at the steamship. Only one paddle wheel was still visible above the water, like a clawing hand, desperate in death. Then it too disappeared. Men were bobbing like corks between ship and shore. Several had latched onto floating debris and were kicking against the river's current. Fortunately, the Mississippi here was broad and slow-moving with a minimum of undertow.

What had happened to Blaine Caldwell? Again her heart cramped with fear. Surely he would manage to survive. He was strong, and there had been ample warning for everyone to escape the sinking vessel—unless he'd been injured or trapped in the boiler room. She clutched the gunwales and prayed. It was all she could do for now.

The longboat slid through a marshy area along the riverbank, then eased onto solid turf.

The men tugged the small craft ashore and assisted the ladies to climb out.

In a voice choked with emotion, Martha put one arm around Rebecca and whispered, "You saved Shandy's life, Rebecca. It was a mighty brave thing."

Rebecca embraced both Martha and Shannon in one wide hug. "Don't cry, Martha. Just thank the Lord."

"Over here—everyone here," came a call from a few yards away. The captain was waving the scattered survivors together.

Rebecca, Martha and Shannon joined the group.

Climbing onto a tree stump, the captain addressed the crew and passengers of the ill-fated steamship. "Praise God. Almost everyone is accounted for. Only two men are missing, but they could be downriver, carried by the current."

Rebecca made a quick search of the soaked and breathless group. Blaine Caldwell was not among them.

"Excuse me, sir," she called. "Is Captain Caldwell one of the missing?"

"He is. Last I saw of him was in the boiler room."

"Oh, he left there," a crewman offered. "Don't think he was drowned."

Martha's arm tightened around her. "Oh dear, Rebecca, I've been so scar't, I forgot all about your husband."

Rebecca couldn't stop shaking. She was beginning to feel light-headed.

"Listen, everyone," the captain continued. "We're just two miles north of Baton Rouge. And there's a cabin beyond those trees. I'd like some volunteers to help search for Caldwell and Blake. The ladies can shelter in the cabin. We've had a tragedy, but we're alive and we'll soon be taken care of."

Alive, Rebecca thought as she slogged along with the others toward the clearing. Yes, she was alive, but at the moment, her heart felt like a chunk of lead. Captain Caldwell was missing, maybe dead. Pepper was almost certainly drowned, poor little pup, and she'd lost her gold, which was all she had to make her way in the world. Maybe she should have gone to the bottom of the river with the *New Orleans.*

The cabin was deserted, but it offered some protection. She entered with Martha and Shannon and took stock of the shelter.

Abruptly Martha announced, "You kin stay here if you like; I'm going home."

"Home? You mean . . . to Memphis?"

"No reason now to go to New Orleans. I've got friends along the river and I kin stop off with them on my way. I'm leaving as soon as I dry out my clothes."

Rebecca looked at Shannon. "But . . . what about her?"

"I told you, she's not my responsibility."

"Do you . . . do you want to go back to Memphis," Rebecca asked the solemn-faced child.

The bedraggled girl gave her a brittle look. "No'm. Cain't go back. I'll go with you to New Orleans."

"But . . . well, yes, I suppose you can. At least we can travel on together—when we have some means."

"I won't be no trouble. I'll just skedaddle when we get there." Her eyes narrowed in defiance. "I've been on my own since I was five. Done okay too."

"We won't argue, Shannon, but it's thanks to Martha you're not behind bars. If you go with me, you'll have to give me the same promise you gave her—to behave yourself."

Shannon paused as if reluctant to acquiesce to authority. Then she lowered her eyes and muttered, "You saved me from the river, ma'am. I'll do what you say—until we get where we're going."

Feeling a rush of sympathy for the waif, Rebecca slipped an arm around her. She hadn't realized the girl was shivering. "Then we're agreed," she said gently. "Now, help me build a fire and we'll dry our clothes. We're going to get along fine, Shannon, just fine."

"Call me Shandy," the girl suggested as she crossed to the hearth.

Rebecca spent the next hour with Martha and Shannon crouching near the fireplace in the cabin. Shannon undressed for the drying process, but neither lady considered disrobing with so many men in the vicinity. It was well past dawn when Shannon pulled on her dry clothes and headed outside to see what was happening.

"I'm leaving now," announced Martha. "It's been nice to make your acquaintance, Rebecca. You were brave to help Shannon. Guess you've got her on your hands for a spell."

"I don't mind. She'll keep me company. I just don't know what I'll do with her when we get to New Orleans."

"Turn her loose. She's scrappy enough to get along. Oh, I'm sorry you ruined your dress. It was mighty pretty."

"We didn't drown, Martha. That's the main thing."

"Good-bye . . . good luck, now."

Rebecca followed Martha to the door and watched her disappear into the trees in the direction of the river road.

With a sigh, she leaned against the cabin stoop. She wondered how long the wait would be. After the captain's brave speech, his mood had turned black, and he had announced he would dry himself by walking briskly down the road to Baton Rouge. A crewman had joined him while three other men began a search of the riverbank.

Within a few minutes, Shannon came running. "Hey, Mrs. Caldwell, here comes one of the crew."

Sure enough, Blake, the missing crew member, stumbled into the clearing, none the worse for having been carried downriver by his floating plank. He reported that he hadn't seen Blaine Caldwell.

Her mood bleak, Rebecca settled on the edge of the porch in a patch of sun and watched Shannon's restless play with a collection of rocks and twigs.

Shortly before eleven, two wagons and a carriage pulled into the clearing near the cabin. The captain of the *New Orleans* emerged.

Still feeling a bit weak-kneed and quite despondent, Rebecca joined the survivors.

"Everyone climb aboard," came the order. "The folks in Baton Rouge are making arrangements for all of us."

She barely looked up as she crossed to the conveyance.

"Oh, Mrs. Caldwell, if you please," requested the captain.

Her eyes widened in surprise. He was holding the carriage door with one hand, while in the other, he clutched a squirming bundle of fur.

"Pepper!" she cried happily. Taking the puppy, she squeezed it so hard, it whimpered in complaint.

The captain led her beyond the hearing of the others. "Mr. Caldwell is just fine," he said before she had time to ask. "Now, miss, you and I both know that Caldwell is not a married man."

Limp with relief, she answered, "Yes . . . yes, I know. He just sort of made that up so I could have his cabin . . . and the pup. But where is he?"

"He rescued your dog, then hung onto a box which floated within a quarter mile of Baton Rouge. He merely swam ashore. He was on his way here when I encountered him on the road."

"But . . . why didn't he come? I must thank him. I . . ."

"He was in a mighty big rush to get to New Orleans. He wanted me to explain to you how he saved the pup, but he said to tell you he lost your coins in the river."

The lump in her throat was enormous. "He's . . . all right?"

"He turned south on the river road. Said he would see you in New Orleans."

Tears blurred her vision. Blaming them on her weakened condition, she turned away to hide them. "Thank you, sir. And thank you for delivering my dog."

Some time later, tucked into bed at a rustic inn in Baton Rouge, she thought sleepily of Blaine Caldwell. He was a man she could love, she admitted—if only she didn't already distrust him so completely.

8

Steamboat *New Orleans* Sinks! No Loss of Life in Tragedy, screamed the headlines in both the French and American newspapers of New Orleans the third week in July.

The day was sodden and overcast when the flat-bottom boat carrying the survivors came alongside the levee in the river port city. Beyond the wharf area stretched the Place d'Armes, an expansive square bounded by the cathedral property and government buildings. Surrounding the central square was the gracious Vieux Carré, the "old town," a charming blend of French and West Indian architecture suited to the lifestyle of the southern clime.

But on this afternoon, New Orleans was hidden from view like a teasing child hiding behind a drawn curtain. Swirling mist veiled the landscape, obscuring the structures and creating a chill in the air despite the warm temperature.

Rebecca's mood was a mixture of anticipation and anxiety bordering on fear. Holding Pepper in her arms, she waited on the dock with Shannon beside her while the other passengers hurried away with friends and relatives. Her tattered blue frock hardly gave her the appearance she had hoped for at this important moment.

She was startled when Shannon took hold of her hand.

"'Bye, Mrs. Caldwell. Thanks." Without another word,

the little girl scampered along the levee and disappeared in the fog.

"Shandy!" Rebecca called after her. "Wait, Shannon, don't go!"

With a sinking heart, she knew her cries were futile. Shannon Kildaire was a wild creature with a will of her own. Not once during the journey had the child opened up to reveal her past. It was as if Shannon had come out of nowhere, and now had plunged back into her private world of mystery. Looking in her hand, Rebecca found a smooth river rock, onyx black with delicate pink veins. The simple gift moved her deeply.

Awash with sudden loneliness, she hugged Pepper and strolled along the deserted dock. If only Captain Caldwell hadn't made such disparaging remarks about Guy Laurens. If only she knew someone she could trust. If only she were not penniless with no personal resources whatever. She had dreamed of this moment for weeks, and now that her dream was reality, it was a dreary and uncertain venture into the unknown. For the first time, she thought longingly of the security of her home in Morgan's Landing.

She stood in the gloom, surrounded by stacks of cotton bales and crates of produce, observed by the occasional passing stevedores, whose stares she ignored. Even Pepper was lethargic. She hoped his dunking in the river, along with short rations, hadn't caused him to be sick.

From beyond the heavy fog, she heard a carriage approach, the wheels and the horses hooves clattering on the stones below the level of the dock. She strained her eyes to see who was coming. Someone was climbing the steps—someone who appeared like an ethereal vision draped in shimmering gold.

Pepper growled.

"Shh," she whispered.

The draped personage walked up to her and pushed back her hood. "Pardon, mademoiselle, are you Rebecca Gordon, by chance?" came the low voice with a trace of a French accent.

Rebecca gazed in awe at the stunning woman. This had to be the grand Miss Josephine Laclair. And what a sight she was. She was large in stature and had most unusual coloring.

Her skin was a rich butter-brown, her cheeks crimson and her full lips vermillion red. Her hair was piled high above her round face and was as golden as the coins Rebecca had lost beneath the Mississippi. Her amber eyes were catlike beneath lids glistening with violet cream. Enormous golden hoops dangled from her ears, and a comb encrusted with jewels perched atop her elaborate coiffure. Her silver embroidered brocade cloak swept from her broad shoulders to the ground, creating the effect of a shimmering tent.

"Yes, I'm Rebecca Gordon. Would you be Madame Laclair?"

"Oui, ma petite cherie. What a poor little waif."

Rebecca was enveloped in a hug that nearly squeezed the breath out of her. The heavy scent of lilacs was suffocating.

"My, my, come along with me, child. And bring that poor half-starved pup with you. Just let Miss Josie take care of everything."

Rebecca was only too happy to comply. It seemed years since she'd left Tennessee, and her spirits were as bleak as the weather. It was all she could do to keep from breaking into tears as she climbed into the coach. Still, she must find the strength to explain. "Forgive me, Miss . . . Madame . . ."

"Call me Miss Josie. Everyone does."

"Miss Josie. I must tell you that I lost everything in the shipwreck. I had gold to pay for my keep. Plenty of it. But now . . ."

"Don't you worry, honey. Mr. Laurens wants you to have anything you need. I promise to take very good care of you."

Rebecca sensed the woman was speaking from the heart. "You're a good friend of Guy Laurens?"

There was an odd pause before Josie answered. "We are business associates. I thought he explained to you."

"Only that you were friends—and you would help me."

"I see." Her voice took on a new quality.

Uncertainty gnawed on Rebecca. "You . . . will help me? You don't mind? I don't want to be any trouble."

Again Josie gave her a squeeze. "You'll be no trouble a'tall, child."

Rebecca couldn't resist taking a gamble. "Mr. Laurens wrote to my mother. He was her friend, you see. She also knew a Mr. Etienne Dufour—but not very well," she added hastily.

She felt Miss Josie's eyes on her.

"Monsier Dufour was a close friend of mine. I knew him very well. In fact you might say we had a very special friendship. He helped me start my . . . ah . . . my business, you see. Since his death, his estate has been managed by Mr. Laurens. He holds the mortgage on my property."

"That's interesting." She tried to sound casual. "Was Mr. Dufour married? Did he have children?" Rebecca knew she was taking a chance, but she couldn't resist asking.

"No. He died so young. He visited me often and I held him in great affection. Once when he was in his cups a bit, he said he'd loved a lady—a sprightly young widow from Scotland. Said he wanted her near him, offered her a good life, but she refused him and ran away. It wasn't long after that that he was killed."

Rebecca sank against the plush cushion. So her father had been killed. How had it happened? She wanted desperately to inquire further, but she must not appear overly concerned. What's more, someone had lied to her. She couldn't believe her mother would lie while on her deathbed, even to keep her daughter from knowing some awful truth. No, it seemed more likely that Etienne Dufour had lied to Miss Josephine to hold on to her affection. And he had pulled the wool over Mr. Laurens's eyes too. She disliked her father more and more. Feeling the need to say something further, she commented in a low voice, "We are both lucky, I guess, to have Mr. Laurens help us out when we need it."

"Hmm." Josie leaned back in her seat and studied Rebecca's face. Her large eyes were soft and caring despite the harsh look of her paint and powder. For a time, she seemed lost in thought. The only sounds were the clip-clopping of the horses as the coach made its way along deserted, rain-swept streets.

Rebecca cleared her throat. "I . . . I hope it's all right if I keep my dog. He's small and already trained to go to a paper. But of course . . ."

"Why certainly. He looks like . . . well . . . my, look at those paws. I doubt if he remains small for long."

Rebecca studied the scruffy pup in her lap. "I don't know

what his breeding is. I found him in the woods when I was on my way here."

"I've seen one other dog resembling him," Josie noted. "A hound breed, that one. Irish, his owner told me and I declare, he was quite the largest dog I've seen before or since."

"Oh, dear, really? I suppose we'll just have to wait and see."

"Here we are. We'll bundle you right inside and into a hot tub. And I'll have Marie give the pup a bath in the washhouse out back. Then we'll take another look at the two of you to see what we've come up with."

Feeling better, Rebecca returned Josie's contagious smile and stepped out of the coach.

She was totally unprepared, however, for the sight of the interior of Josie's three-story house.

The immense parlor was modeled after the Hall of Mirrors of Versailles near Paris. The wide curving stairway swept upward where it appeared to end in Heaven itself. The ceiling was cerulean blue and decorated with plump cherubs dancing in a circle of innocent glee. The furnishings were French Empire, gilded and cushioned in gold and blue velvet. Matching tables were equally ornate and held multi-tiered candelabra created from Venetian glass.

Rebecca caught her breath at the opulence. She had tried to imagine Josephine Laclair's elegant home, but this was a palace fit for a queen.

At this hour, the parlor was empty except for a grizzled Negro man seated at a hand-painted pianoforte in one corner. He stood and nodded at the two ladies.

"That's Mr. Dubee," explained Josie. "He's the finest musician in New Orleans, I can tell you. Later you can hear him play, but now, upstairs you go. I've prepared a suite and ordered a bath. Come, cherie. I'll help you myself with your toilette."

Rebecca's first hours at Miss Josie's were overwhelming. She came to the conclusion the house was more like a grand hotel than a private residence. One clue was the doors opening off the hall which had numbers to identify them. Either this was a hotel or a boarding house for the very rich.

As soon as she had a soak in the exquisite porcelain tub in her suite, followed by a meal that was four times what she could eat, she had snuggled down between the silken sheets of her bed and slept soundly through the night and until midmorning of the next day.

She was awakened by the rich aroma of coffee mingled with the fragrance of lilac perfume. Miss Josie was smiling at her from a chair near her bed.

"Morning, Rebecca. My, you're looking better already. I've brought café au lait and muffins hot from the oven. Oh, and look who's here to greet you."

Pepper jumped atop the bed and wiggled into Rebecca's arms. His wiry coat was gleaming; he wore a new soft red leather collar, and he definitely effused a new fragrance.

She laughed as the pink rough tongue scoured her cheek. "Why, Miss Josie, he smells like—like a lilac bush in full bloom."

"I did give him a squirt of my perfume," Josie said, grinning. "Wanted him to feel at home. And you should see that pup eat. I've ordered scraps from the market to be sent daily."

Holding the dog, Rebecca gazed with fresh eyes at her lavish accommodations. The canopy over her bed, the plush rugs, the wall hangings, all were in shades of fuchsia pink and ruby red accented with gold. It was so beautiful, she could hardly believe it was real. A satin chair, the size of a single bed, occupied one corner beside a huge ivory-colored wardrobe. On it was spread a dress of violet silk. Beside the dress was a pair of matching slippers.

"I put away your poor raggedy dress," Josie explained, seeing Rebecca's amazed look. "And your shoes and undergarments too. They were just a terrible mess."

Rebecca nodded, thinking of the hours she'd spent sewing the blue gown—and how she had planned to impress Miss Laclair with its loveliness. The idea now seemed foolishly naive.

Josie rose. "Eat your breakfast, my dear. You're as thin as a toothpick. I'll send Mimi to help you dress. You'll have a visitor at teatime today."

"Oh?"

"Monsier Laurens is quite eager to see you. After all, he did make all the arrangements."

"Oh, yes, of course. I'm looking forward to meeting him." She tossed back the sheet and swung her legs off the bed. "Thank you for everything, Miss Josie. When you have time, I'd like to speak to you about employment. I do hope there's something I can do here to earn my keep."

Josie stared at her in silence. Then she murmured, "Petite cherie, you can earn as much as you like . . . but . . . well, we'll see. Later on, we'll decide."

Mimi proved to be a delightful imp about the age of ten, an Acadian child from the bayou whose happy prattle was completely unintelligible to Rebecca. Still, through giggles and hand signals, the two managed to freshen and dress Rebecca in her new finery.

Rebecca was just revolving in front of the mirrored wall of her room when Josie returned.

"C'est superbe! You look divine, cherie."

Rebecca continued to find Josephine Laclair's appearance startling to say the least. Today, with sunlight pouring through the French doors, the large-bosomed matron was even more colorful and dramatic. Her lavish hairdo, which had seemed golden yesterday, looked positively flame-colored today. Her plump face was heavily made-up, but traces of youthful beauty were still evident. That she carried African blood, there was no doubt. But the features of white ancestors appeared to dominate. This morning her dress was a simple design cut from a West Indian fabric splashed with overblown blossoms of royal blue and chartreuse. A wide band of matching cloth encircled her head without concealing her curls. Strands of beads draped from her neck; diamonds dangled from her earlobes, bouncing as she nodded her head in enthusiastic approval of the vision before her.

"Yes, the violet dress was a good choice. We'll pick some real violets from the patio to twine in your hair. And what hair it is, my dear. Pulled back like that, it emphasizes the peak at your forehead and the tilt of your nose. Mr. Laurens will be pleased."

Uncomfortable with Josie's detailed appraisal, Rebecca asked, "He will be here for tea?"

"I sent a message to his home this morning. He had asked me to let him know the minute you arrived."

"And his wife? Will she come too?"

Josie seemed not to hear.

"Excuse me, Miss Josie, I was just wondering about *Mrs.* Laurens."

"Yes, I understand. But . . . it's unlikely . . . quite unlikely Mrs. Laurens will come. You'll meet her at the proper time, I expect. For now, come downstairs to the parlor. We've opened the doors to the garden—so refreshing after yesterday's shower."

Josephine continued to talk as she guided Rebecca down the elegant, carpeted stairway. "The paintings are originals from Paris. Only the best artists. The marble in the entry is from Carrara—that's in Italy."

"It truly is a wonder, Miss Josie—the most beautiful hotel I've ever seen. Well, honestly, it's only the second one I've ever seen, but it's a far sight better than the first."

Again there was silence from Josie.

Rebecca entered the parlor which she'd only glimpsed last night. Its gilded opulence was more astonishing in the full light of day. "Oh." She sighed. "It's like a dream—a castle—maybe even like Heaven."

"Linger awhile, dear. I must check my kitchen staff and go over some papers in my office. None of the other girls . . . ah . . . guests will be down before tea. Please make yourself at home. When I return, we'll have a nice long visit. I think Monsieur Laurens has not quite made clear some important details of your visit. I must say, he has rather misled us both."

"Oh?" Rebecca's brows knitted. "Why, I'd surely like to know all about that," she said. "Yes, if there's any misunderstanding, we must have a talk right away."

Josie patted her arm and smiled. "Don't worry, ma petite. Everything will be just fine. I'll be back shortly." She hurried from the room, leaving a trail of scented lilacs.

For several minutes, Rebecca stood in the middle of the high-ceilinged room and gazed in awe at her surroundings. She supposed this was what paradise looked like if a soul got past the pearly gates. An ornate seven-foot-high grandfather clock bonged the quarter hour as she looked at the luxurious furnishings. From beyond a double set of open doors came the song of birds enjoying the sparkling afternoon sun from treetops in the garden.

She strolled outside into the patio and circled the brick walkway, taking note of the riot of climbing vines and shrubs and flowers in full summer bloom. She recognized the roses and geraniums and honeysuckle, but many others were unfamiliar. She had stopped to inspect a particularly fragrant white blossom when she sensed someone was behind her.

"Gardenia," came the masculine voice. "Lovely—but its loveliness pales beside you—Mrs. Caldwell."

She spun around to face Blaine Caldwell. His look was guarded and yet surprisingly intimate. It was the look of an old friend who had committed some mischief—but who wasn't quite ready to ask for forgiveness.

"Why, Captain. I . . . I didn't expect . . ." She collected herself and extended her hand. "I'm happy to see you. I've been wanting to thank you for saving Pepper."

He grasped her hand, but did not give her his usual bow. Instead he kept her hand firmly in his and carefully scrutinized her from the top of her head to the tips of her slippers peaking from beneath her skirts.

She felt herself blush as his eyes lingered on the daring décolleté of the Empire style bodice of her gown. Never had her breasts been so exposed. She knew her mother would have certainly disapproved, but after all, she could hardly refuse to wear the dress Josephine had provided.

"You are happy here?" he asked in a low voice.

My, he had the devil's own charm, she thought. "I only just arrived," she said, masking her admiration. "But Miss Laclair has been very kind—and this is the most beautiful place I've ever seen."

His green eyes were shuttered. "Miss Josie has explained . . . everything?"

"Explained? Well, we haven't had much time to talk. I still must arrange the terms of my employment."

He released her hand and took a deep breath. A shadow crossed his face. "I see."

She couldn't help thinking he must surely be the most attractive man in New Orleans—or anywhere for that matter. Maybe it was the combination of his intense emerald eyes and swarthy skin-tones, or the way his dark hair was tinged with auburn highlights where his sideburns followed the line of his sculptured cheekbones. Or maybe it was his mouth, yes, his lips were fascinating, especially when one corner crooked into the suggestion of a smile—like now.

"I made myself a promise, Rebecca Gordon. It has to do with a certain highly valued prize. I'll speak to Miss Josie. Whatever the price, I intend to be the first."

"You do speak in riddles, Captain."

His smile widened, but the amusement didn't reflect in his heavy-lidded eyes. "Come. I'll show you the ballroom. Adjoining it is a suite Josie reserves for me when I'm . . . a guest here."

She put her hand through the crook of his arm. The linen of his coat was smooth and cool to her touch. His equally fine breeches fit snugly over his hips and along his calves to just above his shoe tops. He was a quality gentleman from head to toe. What harm could it do to allow him to escort her on a tour of Josie's hotel? No one knew he was a spy. And he had done her the enormous favor of saving her dog.

He led her up two flights of stairs, pushed open a pair of gilded doors and stepped back as she entered the largest and most magnificent room she had ever seen. The room had a subtle golden life of its own, even with the banks of French doors closed along its perimeter and the floor-to-ceiling windows darkened by jalousies.

The floor was inlaid wood, polished to crystal smoothness. The walls were covered with creamy brocade satin interspersed with gold and silver threads. Mirrors in ornate frames graced the walls and ceiling and a half-dozen crystal chandeliers hung suspended, waiting for the candles to be lit. There were no furnishings, but at one end of the room was a raised dais with a tall carved music box in its center. The effect was one of sleeping beauty, waiting only for the proper moment to come alive with gaiety and splendor.

Gripping Blaine's arm, Rebecca walked around the room, awed by the overwhelming magic of it. She had the urge to lift her arms and twirl across the gleaming floor.

"We have the room to ourselves," he noted. "One moment and we'll have music, if you like."

"Oh, could we?" she effused.

He stepped upon the dais and cranked the arm of the box. When he stopped, the tinkling musical notes began, playing a popular French folk melody.

It was an incredible moment. Rebecca closed her eyes, raised her arms and revolved in place, losing herself in the exquisite ambience—and then his arms closed around her.

It happened so quickly and felt so natural, she relaxed in his gentle embrace. He led her smoothly across the floor, turning slowly as the music continued, one hand around her waist, the other holding her right hand extended.

Turning, turning, caught up in an enchanted spell of wonder, she laid back her head and let laughter bubble from deep within her.

He lifted her slightly and feather-kissed her ear with his tongue.

The music stopped. Supporting her back, he lowered his head and pressed his lips softly just above the cleft between her swelling breasts. It was only for one breath, but it sent delicious tingles spiraling through every part of her body.

Her arms went around his neck as she leaned against him, momentarily off balance both physically and emotionally.

Reaching beneath her knees, he scooped her up and strode across the ballroom and out the door.

She forced herself to come to her senses. "Where are we going? Captain . . . if you please . . ."

His quick kiss interrupted the speech she was attempting to formulate.

He carried her across the hall and through a single door into a lavishly appointed bedroom. He crossed the room and without comment laid her across the satin coverlet and stretched out beside her.

She squirmed, but one strong arm kept her on the bed. His lips covered hers in a kiss that was both demanding and harsh.

She twisted her head away, but his heated lips trailed the tender skin of her neck and brushed the half-moons of her breasts.

The sensation was maddening. She felt desire coursing through her even as her mind screamed a warning that this must stop.

Placing her hands on his shoulders, she pushed with all her strength.

Immediately, he released her.

She rolled to one side and sat up. Through gasps of indignation, she managed, "How dare you. If this treatment continues, I have every right to . . . to shoot you."

His eyebrows raised. "Shoot me? You're certainly capable, I can attest. But after all, you've accepted Josie's offer. Damned if I understand your resistance. Your virginity can only be given once and I—"

She whacked him across the cheek as hard as she could.

"Damnation, woman," he muttered, and got off the bed to gaze down at her. "What did you expect in a place like Josie's? I had hoped to make your first time at least special . . . and pleasant. One minute, I think you like the idea—the next, I seem to offend you. We need to get this settled, once and for all."

Sitting on the bed, her dress tangled around her knees, her hair awry, she gaped up at him in confusion. What in heaven's name was he talking about? Her first time? A place like this? Her virginity? The truth seeped in like mud coating a pure-white pearl. This place. Miss Josie's. This was no fine lady's hotel, not a palace of wealth and sophistication. Even in Morgan's Landing, she'd heard tales of whorehouses—and the kind of women who lived in them.

She flung off the bed and ran from the room. Her feet barely touched the stairs as she dashed into her own suite and slammed the door. She saw no bolt, so she turned her back and put all her weight against it, planting her feet to add further leverage.

Her cheeks were on fire. Fury and embarrassment far outweighed any other emotions. Of course, the captain wouldn't have raped her, but she had had a close call, just the same. The more she considered it, the more guilty she felt. Why, she had invited his attentions—dressed herself like a harlot and allowed his intimate caresses—and worse, she'd *enjoyed* them. He must have had no hesitation over undoing her chastity. He was a man who was used to getting what he wanted. And—she reminded herself forcefully—he was also a British spy. That remembrance gave her a sudden surge of power. Why, his secret was worse than her own.

She moved from the door and opened the wardrobe. The remains of her blue silk, hand made dress lay piled in one corner. Grabbing it, she gave it a shake and laid it across a chair. Furiously, she began unbuttoning the bodice of her violet dress. If the captain made another attempt to force himself on her, she had the power to stop him. She knew what he was up to, and she could expose his dirty dealings if he persisted in pursuing her. The only problem now was getting out of this perfumed house of decadence and finding Mr. Laurens. It was plain that Guy Laurens didn't understand what Miss Josie was doing in her house. He must think she ran a respectable hotel. The lady had a very kind manner, she admitted as she tossed aside the seductive gown, and she must have fooled Guy Laurens entirely. After all, Mr. Laurens was a married man and wouldn't know about places like this . . . unlike . . . unlike that rascally Blaine Caldwell.

Pepper. She must fetch him from the kitchen. She hoped the Laurens family wouldn't mind taking in the two of them. She had no choice but to walk to Mr. Laurens's home since she couldn't hire a carriage. Hopefully it wasn't too far and she could ask directions on the way. But if she had to walk all the way home to Tennessee, she wouldn't spend one more minute in this bawdy house of Josephine Laclair's.

9

Even as Rebecca was being waltzed around the upstairs ballroom by Captain Caldwell, Guy Laurens was seated opposite Josephine Laclair in Josie's private study.

"You saw her?" Josie asked across a cup of steaming coffee.

"I did. A short time ago. But she didn't see me," Guy explained. "She was standing in your parlor in a violet dress. Mon Dieu, I've never seen such an exquisite girl."

"Exquisite, yes. And the image of her father."

"What . . . what do you mean?"

"Did you think I'd forgotten what Etienne Dufour looked like?"

"Sacré bleu," Guy growled. "So now you know who her father was. I'm sure you can understand my reason for bringing her to New Orleans."

"I can guess. But why don't you tell me?"

"I owed it to my old friend. No one knew the Scottish whore was pregnant. A few months ago she wrote that she was dying and asked for help. She wanted her daughter to travel to Scotland. So I'm doing everyone a favor."

Josie's voice was frigid. "Rebecca's mother wasn't a whore. I know a bit about that unfortunate lady. I saw her once, and Etienne talked of her constantly. She was a foreigner, a sweet naive widow—quite pretty—and she left Etienne with an aching heart when she jilted him and went upriver. She had plenty of spirit and pride, and I see the same qualities in her daughter."

"Etienne was a fool. Every woman has a price. He just didn't offer the woman what she wanted."

"What she wanted was marriage. When she considered their class differences and the religious problem, she broke off the relationship for his sake and went on to Tennessee. He told me about her letter."

"Humph. Well, that's past history. His bastard child is living proof that the saintly Etienne Dufour was not without sin. I find that most gratifying."

"Why is that, monsieur? Is it because you were always jealous of his popularity in the town?"

"You forget yourself, madame. Quadroon prostitutes do not insult their best customers."

"Rarely do I feel the inclination. But Etienne was good to me. He arranged my loan on this house, made my education possible and kept me exclusively as his mistress for five years. Why, my mother was a slave when Etienne Dufour bought me at auction and gave me my freedom. Say or do whatever you please, Monsieur Laurens, but do not defile the memory of Mr. Dufour."

"You loved him. Everyone knows that, Josephine. But you've never liked me despite the fact I've spent a fortune at your establishment."

"My feelings for you are of no importance, one way or the other. What is important is the future of Etienne's daughter. She is not the usual ragtag from the country."

"As I have seen with my own eyes."

"It's more than her beauty that is exceptional. The girl is intelligent. She has a certain air—class and grace—and she's as innocent as a newborn lamb."

"No doubt. When I sent for her, I didn't expect her to be so . . . to look so . . ."

"So like her father?"

"Hell, most of these by-blows are eager and happy to go to work for you. I thought she could stay here awhile and then I'd see her off to Scotland. It's what her mother wanted. Well, Scotland, anyway."

"Oh? I expected you to leave her with me—to train."

"I've changed my mind. Naturally I'll pay you for your trouble."

Josephine placed her cup on the coffee table. "I would like to have her. Not to put her with the other girls, but to develop her . . . for some other purpose. I'll pay you a fair price, if you would consider selling her." Her voice was laden with contempt.

"She is *not* for sale," he snapped. "I arranged for her to come to New Orleans, and I will decide her fate." He pulled several gold coins from his vest pocket. "This should cover your cost. I'm taking her to my apartment on Royal Street."

Josie rose to glare down at him. "And what about her inheritance?"

Guy paled. "What inheritance?"

"As Etienne's daughter, she's entitled to something—morally, if not legally."

"Morally?" he shouted, coming to his feet. "You talk about morals? *You?* Don't be absurd."

"I can't stop you from taking her, but if harm comes to her or I hear she's unhappy, I have ways to take revenge. It's the least I can do for my dear friend, Etienne."

"Don't threaten me, woman. Remember I hold your mortgage, and that document *is* legal. You free blacks will get your comeuppance one of these days. If the English win the war, you'll be picking cotton soon enough."

Josie's face was livid. Her diamond earrings danced around her cheeks. "The Spaniards outlawed slavery. I wish to God they had never traded New Orleans to the French!"

"Don't fret, my dear. Your people will fare no better under American rule." He slapped the coins to the tabletop. "I'm taking her immediately. I'll see if she's in her room." He walked briskly outside and climbed the stairs.

Without knocking, he flung open the door to Rebecca's suite.

She was on her knees looking under the bed for her slippers.

"Pardon, mademoiselle." He bowed from the waist. "Allow me to introduce myself."

With a nervous scream, Rebecca leaped to her feet and faced the stranger.

Startled by her reaction and confused over the change in her appearance since he'd first seen her, he was momentarily speechless.

"Get out," she ordered. "Get out at once. I'm not . . . what you think."

He shook his head. "And what *do* I think? Do your talents include mind reading, my dear?"

His answer came from a man filling the door behind him. "It doesn't take a mind reader to know what *you're* thinking, Laurens. Leave the girl alone."

Guy swung around to face Blaine Caldwell.

"Laurens?" Rebecca gasped. "Are you Mr. Guy Laurens?"

With a satisfied smirk toward Caldwell, Guy again made a deep bow. "At your service, my dear."

To Guy's surprise, the disheveled girl threw herself into his arms. She clung to him as if hiding from the devil himself.

Guy embraced her protectively and gave Blaine a derisive smile. Patting her shoulder, he said soothingly, "There, there, cherie. It's obvious your coming here was a terrible mistake. If I'd known you would be exposed to nouveau riche Americans and privateers, I'd never have allowed it—not even for one night."

She buried her face in her hands. "I'm sorry . . . so embarrassed," she stammered. "My mother would be so ashamed." She looked up with stricken eyes. "But I assure you, nothing happened here. Absolutely nothing." She gave Blaine a withering look.

Guy kept his arm possessively around her. "Don't be upset, ma petite. Miss Josie promised me she would look after you, but I see she had a lax moment. She will hear of my displeasure."

"Dammit, Laurens . . ." Blaine began.

"Watch your language, monsieur. This is not the deck of a pirate ship. These are innocent young ears." Guy placed both hands along Rebecca's cheeks and smiled reassuringly into her eyes.

"I'd like to leave, sir," Rebecca said. "I was just about to walk to your home."

"That would have been a mistake . . . ah . . . it's dangerous for a lady to walk abroad alone and make calls unannounced. But I will certainly take you away from here at once."

"I'm sorry my dress is in such a state, but—"

"Don't worry your pretty head, dear. I have a charming town house you can call your own. Tomorrow the dressmaker will come to measure you for an entire new wardrobe."

"Laurens, just hold on a minute," Blaine growled. "What the hell are you planning?"

"Planning? Why, to take excellent care of this innocent girl. And it is none of your business, Caldwell. It's obvious you've annoyed the young lady beyond her endurance."

"She hasn't the slightest idea what's going on here. You know that as well as I do. As for my interest in her, we became friends when we were en route here on the *New Orleans*. It's important to me she is not misled."

Rebecca turned to glare at him. "We are *not* friends, Captain. You saved my dog and that's all. I'll repay you for that, somehow. But we will *never, never* be friends."

Blaine's brows knitted. "I hope I can persuade you otherwise. Certainly I owe you an apology; that's why I came to your room just now."

"It's not just your recent behavior. Under the circumstances, your mistake can be excused. It's . . . it's . . . you're . . ." She glanced obliquely toward Guy. "Oh, never mind. I accept your apology. I don't want to cause trouble. I just want to leave here."

"I understand and I bow to your wishes," Blaine said between tight lips. "Good luck, Miss Gordon. I think you're going to need it." He walked from the room and disappeared down the stairs.

"Complete oaf," observed Guy. "His Yankee father married into a Creole family and immediately put on the airs of a gentleman. Rest assured, you'll never be bothered by him again."

Recovering her composure, Rebecca stepped back to take a good look at Laurens. "I'm happy to meet you, sir," she said politely.

Guy bent over her hand. "The pleasure is entirely mine. Now what's this about a dog?"

"Pepper. I'll have to get him from the kitchen, if you don't mind."

"I suppose not." He offered her his arm and led her downstairs. Looking at that delicately lovely face, those large trusting eyes, that tumble of dark ash-colored hair, that blossoming young body beneath the tattered dress, he knew he had gotten the girl out of here just in time. Her looks were unique, and anyone who'd known Etienne Dufour could easily see the strong resemblance. What rotten luck Blaine Caldwell had seen her first. Caldwell had been a boy when Dufour was alive, but the Caldwells and Dufours had been close family friends. Certainly Blaine would remember what Dufour looked like. And that bitch, Josie, had already guessed the girl might be entitled to Dufour's money. In fact, as Etienne Dufour's only living heir, Rebecca could lay claim to all of it, taking control of the estate completely out of his hands. Dammit, he should have met the girl at the wharf and taken her straight to his town house. But he had figured if she worked at Josie's while waiting for a ship to Scotland, she'd have no chance to claim any of Dufour's estate, even if she went to court. No judge would take a fortune from a respected businessman and put it in the hands of a whore who was illegitimate. Well, it was too late now. He'd stash her at his town house and keep her busy and under close scrutiny until this idiotic war was over and he could get her out of the country.

Blaine stormed into Josie's study.

Startled, she looked up from her Louis XIV desk, where she had been penning a letter.

Exerting as much self-control as possible, he said, "Pardon the intrusion, Josie, but I require a word with you." It was with effort he calmed his temper and concealed his anger and frustration.

"Why, Captain Caldwell, it's always good to see you. It's been a long time. I'll order fresh coffee sent in."

"No, I'm not staying. But I must tell you I have just made a colossal fool of myself. I'm here to get some answers."

"Oh? You do appear upset. It's not like you, Captain."

"I want to know about Rebecca Gordon—what she's doing here—and what hold Guy Laurens has on her."

"My goodness, you've met her already? She only just arrived."

"I met her on the *Orleans* before it sank. And I have reason to believe she's an innocent girl about to be badly misused."

"Hmm. If you'll please close the door and sit down, we can discuss the lady. I'll gladly tell you what I know, but I want strict privacy in this matter."

Blaine complied and took a seat on the elegantly tufted armchair.

Josie studied him briefly, then asked, "When did you last see Miss Gordon?"

"Five minutes ago. She's with Guy Laurens now. He's taking her to his house in town."

"Does the girl remind you of anyone?"

"Yes, but I can't decide who. She certainly looks more Creole than Scottish."

"She's both. She's the illegitimate daughter of Etienne Dufour."

"My God."

"Please, Mr. Caldwell, you must never breathe a word of this, to her or to anyone else. I'm risking everything to tell you, and I only do so because you've been a trusted friend for years."

"Dufour. Yes, I see it now. Does she know?"

"I'm certain she does. She questioned me about him right away."

"My memory also includes how generous Etienne was to you, and your devotion to him was well-known. Is this the way you repay his kindness?"

Josie was silent for a moment. "As a matter of fact, you echo my own concerns for the girl. I dislike Guy Laurens, and I don't trust him. But there's little we can do. He sent for Rebecca and paid her passage. I think he'll send her to Scotland as soon as possible. Apparently that's what she wants, as well."

That idea upset him even more. Burying his feelings, he shouted, "I don't give a damn what he plans for her future. What I want to know is—if you'll forgive me—why did he have her delivered here instead of welcoming her into his home? You have the finest and most lavish brothel in Louisiana, Josie, but it *is* a brothel."

"I knew nothing about the girl until she arrived last night, except that she was illegitimate and lived in poverty in Tennessee. Also, that after her mother died, she had no place to go. It has been my experience in the past that attractive young girls in such a situation have been eager to join my establishment. They do very well for themselves. Money opens many doors, Captain. And can close some, as well."

"I have no quarrel with a girl making such a choice for herself. But I don't believe Rebecca Gordon has made that choice. Oh, I admit I did at first. In fact, I . . ." For a moment, he hesitated in his tirade.

"You what?"

"Oh, hell. I thought as long as she was planning to work here, I'd introduce her to lovemaking. I even thought about making her my mistress."

"You, Captain Caldwell?" she said, mildly amused. "I declare, I never thought I'd see the day."

"Never mind the lecture. The girl is as charming as she is beautiful. I didn't realize how truly lovely she is until today, though I think the violet dress was a bit on the garish side for such a lass."

"I can see you're fond of her. Does she return your feelings?"

He shook his head. "That's the peculiar part. Not that I expected her to fall into my arms. But most of the time, she acts like I'm poison. One minute, she's friendly, the next she treats me like I'm a black-hearted villain."

"Um. A rare experience for you, I'm sure."

"Enough barbs, Josie. I just want to know the truth. A short time ago, I danced with her in the upstairs ballroom. She seemed happy enough about that. Naturally, I thought she was willing to allow me to take her to bed. I intended to be her first lover—then see where that would lead."

"Captain Caldwell! You know the rules here. You should have consulted me first."

"I know your price for a virgin, Josephine. I would have paid it, and more. What's strange is that I wanted to possess her, but I didn't want to believe she intended to be a . . . a prostitute. To be honest, I was almost relieved when she slapped the hell out of me for carrying her to bed."

Josie laughed. "I knew she had spirit."

"The blow opened my eyes to a lot of things. First, I don't think she had any idea she was in a whorehouse. Second, she proved she is not going to be seduced until she's good and ready. But most disturbing, is that she's willing to put herself into the hands of Guy Laurens. Of course, she has no idea what a rake he is."

"Be that as it may, there's nothing we can do under the circumstances. From what you've told me, you don't hold her trust. That's most unfortunate. I have no choice but to let Monsieur Laurens take her away. I had already decided to protect the girl's innocence until I could determine her true wishes. She would have been safe enough here for the time being. As it is, I've only been able to threaten Laurens if any harm comes to her. I do have ways, you know, of sullying a man's reputation."

"Good for you, Josie," Blaine said more kindly. "But I doubt if he cares a bit about his reputation. He's a scoundrel and a philanderer. Only his heritage and his money gain him acceptance in New Orleans society. Even his poor wife knows what a lout he is. Still, you did what you could for the girl and I thank you for it, though I doubt she does at the moment."

"Captain Caldwell," her voice softened, "I believe you're truly smitten with the young lady."

"God's blood, Josie, I barely know her," he said more fiercely than necessary. He pushed back his chair. "You're right about one thing, though. For now, we're helpless to protect her. Where is Lauren's little prison?"

"On Royal, near St. Ann. He's had plenty of other girls there before her. Keeps a discreet staff on the premises. Eventually the girls seem to drift on or disappear upriver. I do think he pays well."

"Damnation," muttered Blaine. Josie was right. He'd let Rebecca Gordon get under his skin far too much. He'd have to cool off considerably and get back to the business at hand. There was a war in progress, and tonight he would rendezvous with Jean Lafitte. "Merci, Josephine," he said in a controlled tone. "I would appreciate you letting me know how she fares. Time will tell the tale, I suppose. Au revoir, madame."

10

"If the dog becomes a nuisance, he'll have to go," said Guy, eyeing the pup in Rebecca's lap.

Rebecca took her eyes from the panorama beyond the carriage window. "You don't keep a pet? For your children . . . or your wife?"

"I have no children. And my wife would never allow an animal in the house."

"Oh." Rebecca stroked the pup's head.

The elegant carriage traveled the brick and cobbled streets from Josephine's neighborhood toward the exclusive area occupied by the first families of New Orleans. It was a short drive and a lovely scene in the bright, rain-washed sunshine tinting gold the Vieux Carré's old-world style and charm. As they clopped up Bourbon Street, Rebecca peered at the unique three-story clapboard and stucco homes opening directly off the flagstone sidewalks. They traveled along Chartres to give her a closer look at the cathedral dominating the square.

"That's the marketplace, Rebecca," Guy pointed out. "You'll find the world's treasures at your fingertips."

"Even with the British blockade?"

"The privateers get through. The Lafitte brothers, Jean

and Pierre, keep us well supplied with European and West Indian goods. Of course, Governor Claibourne—that self-righteous American bigot who took charge when America bought Louisiana—calls the Lafittes smugglers and pirates. Pierre is locked up in the Cabildo at this very moment."

The name Lafitte triggered her memory. She thought of Blaine Caldwell's comments about Lafitte's value to "our side." No doubt Captain Caldwell was working with Lafitte against the United States cause. It seemed odd that Mr. Laurens would disparage Caldwell while extolling the heroic efforts of the Lafittes. But then, the Lafitte brothers were French—and that was plainly a most important virtue to Mr. Laurens.

Her mind wandered from the scenery as Blaine's face filled her thoughts. She was lucky to have escaped his clutches, she supposed. The fact that she had thoroughly enjoyed his advances was quite annoying. He had proven himself completely villainous, and she was fortunate to have Guy Laurens as her guardian.

Looking at the profile of the pale-skinned man so stylishly dressed, she speculated about what he was really like. He appeared to be in his early forties. His blond hair was thinning and tinged with gray. His nose was straight and his face retained a trace of former good looks. But his jowls were paunchy and his eyes puffed and shadowed. His hand covering a gold-tipped walking stick was pasty white and soft. Even the massive ruby ring could not make the hand attractive.

Catching her look, he lowered his eyelids and gave her an intimate smile. "My dear child. You have nothing to fear ever again. You must put yourself totally in my hands."

"Of course," she responded softly.

"You know I was considerably younger than your father —God rest his soul."

"I'd like to know more about my father, if you don't mind, Mr. Laurens."

He smiled indulgently. "It's not necessary to address me as Mister. I want you to think of me as a devoted friend. Please call me Guy."

She nodded politely. "Miss Laclair said my father was

killed. She didn't say when or how that happened. I . . . was wondering . . ."

"Of course you were wondering." He covered her hand with his. "A tragic affair. You must be brave as I tell you, then we'll never speak of it again. Agreed?"

"Yes." She disliked the feel of his moist palm on her hand, but she forced herself to hold still. She must have an answer to her question.

"Your father was murdered by a gang of villains during a trip downriver visiting friends. He was returning alone on horseback rather late one evening when it happened. He was shot through the heart and robbed of his valuables. There were plenty of ruffians roaming the woods in those days—still are in some areas. That was in 1797. It was a memorable year, I swear. Etienne had just turned thirty and I had just married. Two wonderful celebrations—and then tragedy." His voice was heavy with remorse.

So he had died the year she was born. "I see." She wasn't surprised at the news. Except for . . . "Thirty? And he hadn't married?"

"He was too busy. So much was happening in those days, the city booming after the American War of Independence. Louisiana purchased from the French. There were fortunes to be made, and Etienne set himself about it. So did I, of course. We worked hand in glove to build our export business—and invested in real estate and construction. When poor Etienne died, I was forced to take on all the responsibility alone." He shook his head. "A terrible loss. His widowed mother died soon after of heartbreak. He was her only son, you see, and no one to carry on his name."

She could see he was deeply grieved. "I . . . I wanted to thank you, Mr. . . . Guy, for your kindness to *my* mother. She spoke highly of you."

He patted her hand. "Poor woman. Etienne misled her, I fear. But for a time he was quite taken with her. I'm sure you understand how these things happen—when a man is single, wealthy, and has a roving eye. He had courted my own sister for a time. I had hoped . . . but then all was lost."

"Oh, you have a sister? I'm looking forward to meeting your family." His abrupt look of concern startled her. He removed his hand. Her heart sinking, she realized she'd made a stupid mistake. How would Guy Laurens explain her to his family—or to anyone for that matter? "Oh, I suppose no one knows about me."

"Not exactly," he said. "Seclusion is best for now. But don't fret, my dear, I'll see that you're well cared for."

"I do hope I won't be a burden. I have skills, you know. Especially sewing. I made this dress, though it was ruined when the boat sank. I'm a fair cook too, and I have knowledge of healing herbs . . . if you have them here. And—"

"No, no, cherie," he said, flashing yellowed teeth. "You will not be treated like a poor orphan from the country. I can see you're in for many pleasant surprises. You'll have your own house, a staff of servants. You'll have a lovely wardrobe of dresses and ball gowns copied from the latest Paris fashions. Why, you'll bloom like a summer rose, dear girl. I assume you have some basic education."

"Of course," she said proudly. "You won't have any reason to be ashamed of me, sir."

"Look there." He gestured beyond the window. "That building on St. Peter Street is the opera house. We have a new theater soon to open at Bourbon and Royal. You'll meet John Davis, an entrepreneur who owns several of our finest ballrooms. Dancing is an immensely popular pastime in New Orleans."

"Oh, dear. I must warn you, I'm not much good at that. I've tried a time or two, but . . ."

"Not to worry, darling child." He patted her knee despite a suspicious glare from Pepper. "You'll have the finest instruction in whatever graces you're lacking. I assure you, Etienne Dufour's daughter will have the best of everything New Orleans has to offer. Eventually I'll take you out to a few places—and then, of course, as soon as this damnable war is over, we'll arrange your passage to Scotland."

This was much more than she'd expected. Her highest hopes had been to find respectable employment in an inn or a shop until she could save enough money to travel on. "How . . . how will I pay for all that?" she wondered aloud.

He cackled. "Pay? My dear friend's child—pay? No, my

adorable innocent. I will provide everything you need. It is the least I can do. And in time, I hope to win more than your gratitude—your respect and your affection."

"Oh, I'm very grateful," she hastened. "You paid my passage. And Miss Josephine was nice . . . except . . ."

"Let me explain, dear, about Josephine. You're not worldly enough to understand that men of power and wealth have many friends at various levels of society. Miss Josie was especially close to your father. When she heard you were coming, she insisted on meeting you, offering you some female assistance until I could make preparations at your new residence. It was only a warm bath and a bed for one night."

"Well, she did treat me most kindly. In fact, I liked her right away. It's too bad she's . . . well . . ."

"I know. But Josephine is a wealthy woman now, though of course she doesn't mingle in polite society. I must again apologize, however, for her momentary lapse—to allow that lecher Caldwell access to your person—a shocking event." He drew her hand to his lips. "Will you forgive me, my dear," he murmured above her fingertips.

"It's quite all right," she agreed. "I'm afraid I was not very careful since I thought Captain Caldwell was my friend . . . after we met on the boat."

"I understand. But frankly, I am curious about what he was doing in the north."

Be careful, she warned herself. Later she might decide to reveal all she knew about the captain. But spying was a serious matter, and she must be careful about making such a charge. "Business, I expect. He didn't say. But he did save my dog from drowning. I was grateful for that."

Guy's glance toward Pepper didn't hold much sympathy. But he said pleasantly, "How fortunate. Still, he was a rascal to expect you to repay him by allowing special privileges. It's no wonder he terrified you."

She looked out the window to hide her flushed cheeks. It hadn't been like that at all, but she had no obligation to explain things to Mr. Laurens. "Yes. I suppose he's quite an evil man."

The carriage jolted to a stop.

"Ah, mademoiselle, here we are. Your new home. Allow me."

She was astounded as she alighted from the conveyance and entered the two-story whitewashed town house. Although it was infinitely smaller than Miss Josie's, it had the same lavish decor and furnishings, and a parlor with tall windows enclosed by jalousies and framed with brocade draperies. She spotted a small garden beyond the French doors.

"You can put the dog outside for the moment. Later we'll tour the kitchen and meet the servants," said Guy. "Come upstairs. There is a fine view overlooking the street and garden."

She felt like a princess in a fairy tale as she climbed the winding stairway. At the top was a hallway leading to two bedrooms with an adjoining door. A hand-painted porcelain woodstove stood in one corner of the boudoir, and double doors opened beyond the canopied bed onto a gallery above the central patio. That this sumptuous house would be hers was beyond her wildest dreams.

Guy crossed his arms and looked at her with satisfaction. "I can tell it pleases you," he observed.

"My gracious, why wouldn't it? I didn't expect to have my own house . . . I mean, I thought . . ."

"Fine. It's settled then. Come downstairs and meet Pearl. She always takes care of my . . . rather, she'll be your personal maid and manage the house for you. You might enjoy an outing to the market in the morning. She can show you what produce is best so you can plan meals. I don't believe you'll need a carriage of your own right away. Later, perhaps, when you're better acquainted with the city. Some areas should be avoided by upper-class ladies. Pearl will arrange for a dressmaker, but in the meantime, there are several new frocks in the armoire. You'll need shoes and bonnets—all from Paris, of course."

This was too much. Rebecca could barely absorb it all. If she had suddenly landed on the moon, she couldn't have been more astonished.

When they returned to the parlor, Guy abruptly bowed and murmured, *"Je vous felicite.* Remember you are Creole

French, the finest race on earth, the best of the Old World blended with the best of the New. You will rise to your new station like a bubble in rare vintage wine. I will be your mentor—your protector—your dearest, most trusted friend." He leaned near and kissed her cheek, then quickly pecked her other cheek.

She started to draw back, but he caught her shoulders and gave her a mildly condescending smile. "It's a tradition. You'll soon learn that kissing and dancing . . . and a few other delights are acceptable and most enjoyable. Now, I must go to my home across town. Pearl must be out doing errands. I have business matters that require my attention, but tomorrow evening we'll dine here. Au revoir, Rebecca."

He swept from the room before she could respond. Standing in the half-light of the drawing room, she had an overwhelming sense of unreality. Everything was happening so fast she could hardly absorb it all. Guy Laurens was nice enough, and generous beyond belief. But something about him made her uneasy. Maybe it was the tone of his voice, a tone a person would use with an ignorant child. Of course, she supposed she was ignorant in his eyes. But she wasn't a child. And the way he looked at her hinted that he knew that too. She wasn't acquainted with high society manners, but she'd found his familiar behavior uncomfortable—and not as innocent as he wanted her to believe. She looked again at her luxurious surroundings. She'd just have to be on guard as she was with the amorous bucks back home. And she'd enjoy herself and learn all she could about being a lady.

To her chagrin, Blaine Caldwell again intruded on her thoughts. She had a momentary vision of meeting him again someday—after she was elegant and refined. She would love to thumb her nose at him at some fancy party. It would be her revenge for the way he'd treated her like . . . like a whore.

The silver water of Barataria Bay lay still as sculptured marble, ringed by the olive green shoreline of the mainland. Resting at anchor near the island of Grande Isle was the schooner, *Carolina,* the flagship of Jean Lafitte.

On this steamy afternoon, there was no breeze at all to stir the moss dripping from the intermittent stands of cypress dotting the island like bristles on an old man's cheek.

In a clearing between vegetation and the water's lip, two men faced each other, their swords poised and glinting in the sunlight. They were sweating beneath their blousy shirts, their brows furrowed in intense concentration as they eyed each other, each watching for a tiny opening in his opponent's defenses—an opening that could bring swift death at the thrust of a superbly honed weapon.

In a lightning movement, the stockier of the two men lunged forward, his sword penetrating his foe's territory until its tip quivered against the bare flesh above the open neck of the shirt. No blood was drawn as for one breathless moment, the fencers held their stance like statues in a Roman loggia.

"Touché, my friend," snapped the taller man, blithely ignoring the point tickling his Adam's apple. "A clever move," he added, then stood at attention and saluted the victor with a sweep of his weapon.

Laughter and applause erupted from a dozen onlookers who were lounging in the shade of trees along the narrow beach. A lady in a well-worn dress, with tousled hair the color of ripe raspberries, rushed to throw her arms around the neck of the loser and press her body invitingly against his muscular thigh. She moved snakelike along his hip and placed one bare foot on the toe of his boot.

"Pobrecito," she crooned. "Poor Nikki—come along and I will mend your broken spirit."

For a moment, he hugged her to him, then with a half-smile ruffled her hair and moved away. "Not now, *querida.* I have business with Jean. I've delayed too long already, but I had to answer his challenge at once." He grinned at his mustachioed opponent, who had struck a cocky pose of victory.

The girl swung her hips and snapped her fingers under his nose. "Don't come begging later, Blaine Dominique. It's rare I make such an offer to one who is vanquished."

Blaine lightly swatted her enticing behind, then turned his attention to Lafitte. "Hell, Jean, you saw that hole in the sand behind my foot. Do you call that a fair fight?"

"Of course, mon ami. All I needed was a flicker of your

eyelash to signal my attack. Besides, you're sluggish today. Your decadent life of indolence and luxury is taking its toll."

The two walked side by side into the trees and took chairs at opposite sides of a rough plank table. Mugs of rich brew were promptly delivered by a shirtless black, and both men drank deeply beneath the verdant emerald canopy.

Blaine finished first and thunked his pewter mug on the table. "Indolence and luxury," he echoed. "I'll have you know I've spent the past month in constant toil and deprivation. I traveled to Tennessee and back, hacking my way along forest trails from the back of a nag fit only for plowing. I chopped firewood with the crew of the *Orleans* till the damn ship sank—then swam half the length of the Mississippi with a struggling mongrel pup under my arm."

"Belonging to the lady you described?" Jean queried as he wiped his mouth with the back of his wrist.

"The same," said Blaine. "I thought the rescue would earn me some show of appreciation from the lass, but I misjudged her from the start."

"Is this true? You, who are the finest judge of women in the Americas—besides me, of course." He selected a cigar from a silver tray. "Smoke?"

With a mirthless laugh, Blaine shook his head. "I concede another victory to Lafitte."

"Ah, but how can you laugh at such a tragedy?"

"Hell, Jean, what else can I do? I acted like an idiot."

"But matters of the heart should always be taken seriously. And, mon ami, your laughter has a hollow sound."

"Forget I mentioned it," he muttered. "I deserved her slap for being so stupid—assuming far too much. My primary concern is that the naive young woman has fallen prey to that bastard, Laurens."

"I'll kidnap her for you," Jean offered with a sly grin. "Perhaps all she needs is a few days alone with you to become better acquainted. Given time, I've never seen you fail to win the lady of your choice. Now as for me . . ." The dark-eyed French privateer blew smoke through rounded lips, creating a nearly perfect ring. "I prefer to move more quickly. I have no time or inclination for lengthy courtships."

"Wouldn't work. I had her to myself on the *Orleans*. Why,

I delivered her meals, made friends with her dog, even hinted I'd install her as my mistress. Still, she was as cool as yesterday's pudding."

"Unbelievable," quipped Lafitte. "How could she resist you?"

"Of course, I realize now she never intended to stay at Josie's. But she not only resisted, but found me most disagreeable. There was just that one moment . . ."

"When you danced with her?"

"Aye. She was like a bright little imp in my arms—quicksilver and a violet bird's wing—a silken ribbon of laughter."

"You wax poetic, my friend. I'd like to meet the lady who can inspire such a description from a pragmatist like you."

"Maybe you will, in time—unless she disappears like several of Laurens's other women. But enough of Rebecca Gordon. We need to formulate some plan to get information for Jackson. He's been made military commander of the district and must be kept informed of British movement."

Lafitte nodded. "Shouldn't be too difficult. Between the two of us, we have vessels strung all the way from New Orleans to the West Indies. If Cochrane and his fleet rendezvous in Jamaica, then sail west, we'll have plenty of advance warning."

"Jean, you know how much we appreciate your loyalty to the American cause. I myself assured General Jackson that you are completely trustworthy. But damned if I understand why you've chosen our side. Governor Claibourne still imprisons your brother; he calls you a pirate and a ruthless scalawag; he threatens to destroy your compound here at Grande Isle. That's enough to drive any man into the arms of the enemy. And now there are rumors of the redcoat's offer to pay you thirty thousand dollars cash."

"The offer hasn't been made yet."

"Then you're still thinking of accepting it?"

Smiling wryly, Lafitte fingered his tankard. "I should, I suppose. It's considerably more than I'll get from the poverty-stricken Yankees."

"Jean . . . I . . ."

Lafitte laughed deep in his throat. "Don't worry, my old friend. I have no intention of accepting the offer. I have a great fondness for the people of New Orleans. And you, Blaine, have never failed me—whether we fight or play. This is my home now. There comes a time when a man wants to feel he has roots—loose ones perhaps, but a place to call one's own. New Orleans is part of the United States now. My future and that of this young country have become intertwined."

"Now who's waxing poetic?" Blaine noted with a relieved smile. "And let me assure you, I intend to do everything I can to get Pierre out of prison."

"I appreciate that. He hasn't been the same since that stroke four years ago. I worry about his being confined."

Blaine sat back in his chair. "I plan to slip the blockade the day after tomorrow. There's a chance of intercepting my frigate en route from the Indies and getting information on the redcoats' troop movement. Now that Wellington has Bonaparte in hand, those British regiments will be free to join the war against the United States. I'm afraid Jackson would be hard-pressed to defend New Orleans against such a sizeable force."

"A good idea." Lafitte suddenly grinned. "While you're away doing a bit of spying, perhaps I'll call on the mysterious Mistress Gordon."

"Why not?" Blaine replied with studied nonchalance. "I'd rather see her in your arms than those of Guy Laurens."

Lafitte chuckled knowingly and tilted his head to send another smoke ring toward the sky.

11

"Tarnation!" Rebecca stood in the center of her boudoir and tugged at the white kid glove stretched above her elbow. Beads of sweat dotted her forehead and moisture trickled under the ringlets dangling about her neck. Her dance lesson had gone poorly again today, and she took out her frustration on the clinging glove.

"Come off there, you useless creature." She addressed the glove as if it were alive. "What good are you, anyway? Except maybe to hide dirty fingernails—and I don't have those anymore. Why, I never saw such a nonsensical idea in my life as snow-white gloves fit for nothing. You make my hands feel like they're wrapped up and ready for winter storage. I can't bend my fingers or feel anything that touches them." She extended both arms. "One, two, three, step; one, two, three, charmed; one, two, three—oh, it's enough to give a body the vapors."

After a concentrated effort, she stripped off the gloves and threw them onto the dressing table beside the hair ribbons and jewel case. "Humph, the only sillier fashion are these two-part sleeves that run from underarm to knuckles. Sleeves should be long in winter, short in summer, not both at the same time. Guess this dress will have to be washed and ironed right away. It does seem a waste of time to get all gussied up for a gaggle of teachers. A few weeks ago, I had two gentlemen fussing over me. Since then, I've been stashed away with nothing to do but learn a batch of useless nonsense—this fork, that spoon, keep your eyes lowered, don't say *tarnation*—TARNATION!" she shouted.

She kicked off her slippers, then walked through the open doors onto the gallery overlooking the giant live oak and carefully manicured garden below. She had been told not to help care for the flowers and shrubs, a task she would have readily enjoyed. She had concluded her only basic talents—shooting, sewing and gardening—were neither desirable nor proper for a lady of New Orleans society.

Sitting on a bench, she let the fragrant coolness rise from below to caress her. This was her favorite spot, although the past four weeks she had seen many amazing sights in the town. She had visited the Cathedral of St. Louis, strolled along narrow streets lined with fascinating shops and restaurants, and toured the immense market where produce and goods from all around the world were offered for sale. Pearl was always her silent chaperone. It was too bad the mulatto girl wasn't more talkative, but she acted as if every word she spoke were absolute torture. Pearl kept to herself in the servants' quarters unless she was needed for some specific task, and then she performed it efficiently without comment.

What was more odd was Guy Laurens's total disappearance from the scene. He had come for dinner that first night, then left his new ward to her lesson masters for nearly a month. Notes of encouragement and bouquets of flowers had arrived frequently, but he'd not bothered to come in person to check her progress. Rebecca supposed he had a great deal of business to attend to.

She leaned her elbows on the wrought iron railing and peered below. There lay Pepper in his favorite spot in one corner of the flower bed. She was lonely for company, but she wouldn't disturb the sleeping dog. My, he had grown lately. Must be the rich table scraps and meaty bones she brought from the market. He had once played around her ankles, but now he stood closer to knee level.

She mused as the sweetly scented breeze rustled the leaves just beyond the balcony. What could have happened to

Blaine Caldwell? Her best efforts to dismiss him from her thoughts had failed. His face appeared at unexpected moments during the day; at night the memory of his lips on hers, of his arms around her, the way he smiled and saw through to her heart, invaded her last waking moments and flowed into her dreams. She still reddened at the thought that he had believed her to be a prostitute. It was plain his only interest had been in taking her to bed. Her rebuff at Miss Josie's must have dampened his interest once and for all. Just as well, she thought, thumping her fingers on the railing. He was too attractive, by half, and had nearly caused her to forget the warning about gents of his class. Yes, it was good he was out of her life completely.

She picked up a book she'd left on the bench and ruffled the pages. It was a play by an Englishman named Shakespeare loaned to her by her instructor from the College of Orleans. The tutor had warned her of its occasional violence and suggestive dialogue. He promised her that as soon as her French improved, she would have a better selection of reading material. She wanted to tell him that her conquering of the French language would probably equal that of her dancing. She found the words beautiful, but difficult to mimic. Besides, as soon as she traveled to Scotland, she'd have no use for French.

Scotland. How long would she have to bide her time in New Orleans before she could continue her journey? Sometimes Scotland and her brother, Gilbert, seemed like a fading dream of childhood days gone by.

"Pardon, mademoiselle, you have a message."

Startled from her reverie, she turned to see her catlike maid extending a sealed envelope.

"Oh . . . merci . . . thank you, Pearl." It was probably another note from Guy. She carefully opened the note and gazed at the lovely script. As she read, her amazement grew. The note was from Josephine Laclair and was an invitation to tea—at a house near the esplanade owned under the name Beatrice Morgan. Josie explained she had important matters to discuss, and she would send a closed carriage at three o'clock so the visit could be a secret between them.

The idea of a clandestine meeting was too much to resist.

Rebecca looked at Pearl who stood with folded hands. "Is there a messenger waiting for a reply?"

"Yes, miss."

"Tell him, please, I'll be ready at three."

"If you're going out, Miss Rebecca, I'll go with you."

"No need, Pearl. I won't be gone long—not long enough to be missed. I have no lessons scheduled for this afternoon."

Disapproval was evident in Pearl's face, but she nodded and said simply, "Very well, miss."

Rebecca was almost giddy with the excitement of dressing up and going calling—even if her hostess was the most infamous madam in the Vieux Carré. She hadn't realized until now how desperately lonely she had been since her arrival in New Orleans. After all, Miss Josie had been kind to her in the beginning, even adopted a maternal air. Surely there was no harm in thanking her in person for her earlier hospitality.

As she rode through the sun-dappled streets, she decided her lessons had been of some value after all. She knew that her dress with its stylish Empire waistline and long tapered sleeves puffed at the shoulders and her straw hat with its high crown and wide brim secured under her chin with a bright ribbon were in the latest Paris fashion. If she didn't speak French, at least she had new knowledge of the world, its history and current events. And she was armed with table manners fit for a duchess. Yes, the outing was already lifting her spirits—and how intriguing to know Miss Josie had a separate residence under a secret name.

The house was a one-story unimposing clapboard set back a few yards from the banquette in the new style of the Americans. This allowed for a tiny front garden and one tall willow tree shading the veranda.

The door opened as soon as Rebecca stepped out of the carriage.

"I'm so pleased," effused a demurely attired Josephine. "Come in at once so no one will recognize you."

"I'm not concerned about being recognized, Miss Josie. It was good of you to invite me, and I'm quite unknown in New Orleans, at any rate."

The two were soon seated in the parlor before a laden tea table. Heavy silver pots offered both tea and rich dark coffee; silver trays displayed finger sandwiches and petit fours.

Rebecca laid aside her tasseled purse and accepted a cup of tea laced with sugar and frothy milk.

"How have you fared this past month?" Josie asked pleasantly.

"Very well, thank you. You might say I've been to school. Tutors have come daily to Monsieur Laurens's house to instruct me." She glanced at her pinky finger to see if it was at the proper angle. It was.

"Has Monsieur taken you to the opera? The theater?"

"Oh, not yet. In fact, I haven't seen Mr. Laurens since the first day I arrived at his town house."

Josie's face relaxed into a pleased smile. She nodded and took a large swallow from her cup. "Oh, yes, I suppose he's been busy of late. The war effort and all."

"If he's a patriot for the American cause, I'm not aware of it. But we haven't discussed politics. He seems more French than anything else."

"Excellent observation, my dear. But then that's not unusual in Louisiana. The United States obtained this country just a few years ago, you know."

"Oh, I wasn't being critical. In fact, Mr. Laurens has been very generous. It's just that I can't see him riding into battle or becoming excited over political matters."

"Hm. He does have a quality of indolence about him."

"Indolence?"

"Laziness."

"Yes, he does at that. His eyes seem about to close even when he's speaking."

Josie chuckled. "They surely do. But don't you misjudge him. He's sly as a fox. I'm just happy to see you faring so well after all this time. You look stunning—and you've developed grace and charm. Of course, those attributes were there all along. It just took a bit of polishing to make them shine."

Rebecca set down her cup. "I mustn't stay too long, Miss Josie. You mentioned important matters."

Josie smiled warmly. "The most important matter was to

discover if you're well treated. I'm satisfied on that point. The other matter concerns Captain Blaine Caldwell."

"Cap . . . Captain Caldwell? Oh, yes," she said archly. "What possible interest could I have in that gentleman?"

"He is truly concerned about you, Rebecca dear. He wants to see you—alone, if possible. He's just returned from the Indies . . . a mission of some secrecy."

"I understand exactly what you're saying. I *know* what Blaine Caldwell is—and I do not intend to see him again."

"You know what he is?" Josie's brows lifted.

"A spy." There, she'd said it. Since Josie was obviously his friend, she must know it already.

"Oh. Well, yes, he could be described that way. I'm rather surprised he told you about it."

"He didn't. I overheard him talking one night in Tennessee, right after he visited Andrew Jackson."

"And you disapprove?"

"Why, of course." Rebecca was on guard at once. If Josie approved, she could be in league with him. She smiled sweetly. "But I never involve myself in such matters. The war will soon be over, I'm sure. Then I'll be on my way to Scotland to join my brother."

A peculiar look crossed Josie's face. She hesitated, then said, "I see. Nevertheless, I'm convinced the captain does care for you. He urged me to arrange a rendezvous."

"My last meeting with Blaine Caldwell was very unpleasant, as you know. Besides, it would anger Monsieur Laurens and place me at risk. I owe him my loyalty, and I won't break his trust."

"Umph." Josie looked disgusted. "You've still got a few things to learn, so it seems." Then her voice became more gentle. "Do be on guard, ma petite. Mr. Laurens has a reputation as a devious man. No, don't be angry with me. I'm only telling you what I've learned through many years."

Rebecca rose from her chair. "I appreciate your concern. I really must go now."

Josie accompanied her to the door. "Don't worry, child. Your visit today will be our secret. You're not to tell your Mr. Laurens. Just remember, I'm your friend. I'll be here if you ever need me."

After a polite farewell, Rebecca rode home in the carriage,

unfortunately more depressed than ever. The two people she had liked best in New Orleans could not be trusted. Blaine Caldwell was a British spy, and Josie's judgment was questionable since she'd befriended a man who was a traitor to his country. Rebecca didn't want to believe the vague warning about Guy. After all, if she couldn't put faith in her father's close friend, then no one could be trusted at all.

She arrived home shortly after four o'clock and hurried inside.

Waiting beside the fireplace, a brandy goblet in his hand and fire in his eyes, was Guy Laurens.

She caught her breath, then collected herself. "Oh . . . Guy. You surprised me. It's been so long since you've visited."

He put his drink on the mantel and approached her. "No doubt I did, little miss. I've been waiting almost an hour. I demand an immediate explanation of your absence."

Refusing to be intimidated, she took her time untying the ribbons of her bonnet. "I've been to tea with a friend. If I had known you were coming, I would have made a point to be here."

"Did I not order you to take Pearl whenever you went out? I've provided for your every need for weeks, and now you have deliberately disobeyed me."

"Disobeyed?" she questioned, her own temper rising. "I value my independence, sir. I'll not trade it for . . . for luxuries—though naturally I appreciate your generosity."

Taken aback by her defiance, he hesitated. "Everything has a price, Rebecca," he said tightly. "I can see you've learned your lessons well. You look quite . . . different than when you arrived—speak differently too. A vast improvement, I might add. I've left you in peace and comfort, given you complete freedom to come and go—only chaperoned by Pearl. I am most annoyed."

"Then I apologize for having upset you. It was not intentional," she said acidly.

"Very well. But don't let it happen again. Now, where did you go for tea? I wasn't aware you had any acquaintances in New Orleans—except for Blaine Caldwell." He spat the name.

So that was it. She realized now that Guy had suspected

she had rendezvoused with the captain. She could set his mind at ease about that possibility, but she musn't cause trouble for Josie. She would have to fib and make the best of it. "I do have another acquaintance: Martha Thatcher from Memphis. We met on the *Orleans*. She's visiting friends here and sent a carriage for me." She prayed he wouldn't ask for details.

He studied her briefly, then nodded and moved back to retrieve his brandy. "Very well. Next time, have her call on you here."

"She's leaving for Memphis right away. I won't see her again."

His look softened. He finished his drink and said, "I apologize for my anger. It's just that I feel responsible for your safety and well-being." Crossing to her, he clasped her hand and pressed it to his lips.

Relieved at her narrow escape, she allowed the kiss to linger. Still, she disliked his touch, his fawning manner. She couldn't understand why she found him vaguely repellent. After all, he was attractive and well-bred. He had shown her kindness and generosity. Was she allowing the negative remarks by Josie and Blaine Caldwell to color her feelings? Withdrawing her hand, she remarked, "I understand your concern, Guy. Now that we've both apologized, we can have a proper visit. I'll serve tea, if you like. I can display my new social skills."

He smiled insipidly. "No, I must be going. Actually I came to invite you to your first public engagement. Your tutors have praised your accomplishments, and I've decided to escort you to a masked ball on Saturday evening. It's quite a large affair, perhaps Governor Claibourne himself will attend."

"My, that would be wonderful," she said with true enthusiasm. "Oh, where will I find a mask?"

"I've brought a costume for you. Pearl took it upstairs. It's a duplicate of a gown worn by Empress Josephine at Napoleon's court a few years ago. The jeweled demimask is quite elaborate and beautiful. I'll call at eight. Make certain you're ready."

"Yes, of course," she replied, some of her excitement clouded by his officious attitude.

"Au revoir, Rebecca. Until tomorrow's eve." He strode from the room.

A masked ball, she thought happily. At last she would be introduced to society—meet all the fine ladies and gents. She hurried upstairs to take a look at her costume. Maybe she had misjudged Guy after all. He was justified to concern himself with her whereabouts. In the future, she would try not to alarm him. Josie was not entirely wrong, though. Guy did have a jealous nature and a nasty temper. If he continued to badger her, she would simply move out and find a new situation. No one, whether captain or powerful Creole gentleman, was going to order her about as if she were a mindless guinea hen.

12

Blaine cantered his stallion along the path leading to the front entrance of Dominique Hall. It was good to be home after weeks at sea. The grassy lane was bordered by rows of lilac bushes and ornamental orange trees, creating a shady bower from the street to the hitching post below the wide steps. The distance was short by plantation standards, but Dominique Hall had been one of the first homes in the area built back from the street to make room for formal front gardens. The mansion was convenient to town, yet close enough to the river to allow the upstairs rooms to capture the view and refreshing southeast breezes. Classic revival in design, built of stuccoed brick painted in creamy beige with white trim, the house had become the prototype for the stately homes of the newly arriving Americans with wealth and a distinctive taste for luxury.

On this steamy afternoon, Blaine had just completed a successful tour of his orchards and stables. It was always a relief when he returned from a lengthy voyage to find his ancestral home in good order.

He swung from the saddle and left the horse to be led away by his overseer. He entered the cool study off the entry and rang for his majordomo.

"Any message from Miss Laclair while I was away,

George?" he asked of the liveried mulatto who hurried to answer his summons.

"Yes, sir. She sent her house girl two days ago, and she gave me a message for you. I'll tell you exactly what she said."

"Yes?"

"She said the lady of your mutual acquaintance had come to call. She is doing well and has not been harmed in any way. Miss Laclair said the lady would not agree to meet you, but there is a ball on Saturday. Miss Laclair suggested you go there because the lady might be attending since it's the first big party in the quarters this season." George took a deep breath after his careful recitation.

"Excellent report. Any other messages?"

"Yes, sir. Captain Lafitte is waiting in the garden."

"Jean?" Blaine headed for the door. "Mon Dieu, he shouldn't be here. Claibourne would love to pop him into the same cell with Pierre. Serve us brandy, George."

He walked briskly through the central hall and out into the secluded courtyard at the rear of the house.

"Jean! What are you doing here? You took a helluva risk."

Lafitte remained in his place, leaning against the trunk of a centuries-old oak. "As you know, mon ami, I slip in and out at will like a river rat. And I have news that required a firsthand report."

"Let's hear it. I've ordered brandy."

"Merci. The summer's heat seems never to end." He took a seat on the arm of an elaborate wrought iron chair. "I came to tell you the British brig, *Sophia,* is anchored off Grande Isle. Lieutenant Colonel Nicholls came to me as we expected and made a handsome offer—the rank of captain and thirty thousand dollars in gold. He also guaranteed to rescue Pierre from prison. In return, I and my Baratarians will join in the British attack."

"Hm. Then Jackson's sources were correct from the beginning. What was your response?"

"I declined—politely, of course."

"Dammit, Jean, the Americans don't deserve you. But I'm sure as hell glad you've chosen this course. We must remain loyal to the United States. It's the only way to hold on to freedom and prosperity for future generations."

"I agree. That's why I came to warn you about the brigantine's approach. You can carry the message to Governor Claibourne."

"And so I will. Ah . . . our drinks. Here's to you, Jean Lafitte, and to your friendship and courage."

After the toast and a few comradely swallows, Lafitte asked casually, "What news do you have of your lady, Mademoiselle Gordon? I cannot believe you've forgotten her."

"No," Blaine said with a hint of frustration. "One bit of good news: Josie just sent a message that she had a visit from Rebecca. The girl said that Laurens hasn't been near her since she arrived at his town house. In other words, he hasn't bedded her as yet."

"Josie said that?"

"Not in those exact words, but I caught her meaning. Laurens must be toying with Rebecca like a cat with a canary."

"What do you plan to do?"

"I have evidence that Laurens may be selling information to the British—so far just a rumor. If I could get proof, I could have him arrested or at least deported. The problem is I want the girl out of his clutches immediately—before he causes her real harm."

"If I can help, my friend, just say the word."

"Thank you, but first we must do something about your brother rotting in the Cabildo. There's a costume ball in the quarters on Saturday. Every important Creole in New Orleans will be there with his lady or mistress."

"No wives, I presume."

"Of course not. They never attend parties where there are guests of mixed blood."

Jean smiled sardonically. "Does keep the gentlemen busy—scurrying from ball to ball—keeping wives and light-o-loves apart and happy. I understand the Yankees disparage the practice."

Blaine grinned across the rim of his goblet. "The Americans may come around eventually. As for Saturday's event, I have a plan."

* * *

The upstairs ballroom of the Charles Hotel was the most popular public dancing parlor in New Orleans. The dance floor was immense, and an elegant saloon offering every kind of liquid refreshment was incorporated into the area.

But on October 3, the evening of the Grand Masque Ball, the Charles Ballroom was closed to the public. The usual banjoes, mouth-harps and tamborines had been replaced by a harpsichord, four guitars and five violins. Guests would be admitted by invitation only.

The word was circulating that the governor himself would make a brief appearance as proof that although Americans might look askance at so much ribald revelry, they would not outlaw the popular pastime—especially with the threat of war hanging over the city.

Rebecca arrived on the arm of Guy Laurens. The dance had been in progress for several hours and was expected to continue until dawn.

Just before entering the glittering ballroom, she had the sudden urge to turn and flee. If her old friends from Morgan's Landing could see her now, she was certain they'd tease her unmercifully over the way their tomboyish pal was "gussied up."

Her dress was something to behold. It was created from white satin and embroidered throughout with golden thread. The bodice was cut so low and wide that she felt one deep breath might cause her bosom to pop right out and reveal all—and she was expected to *dance* in this shimmering gown. Tiny gathers under her breasts caused the skirt to flow straight to the hem, which brushed the tips of her flat-heeled silver slippers. Her arms, however, were demurely hidden by the "extra" sleeves attached under the puffed shoulders of the dress. Pearl had spent nearly three hours designing the Grecian style hairdo with tiny ringlets around her face and nape. Tiny diamond and pearl earrings dangled from her earlobes. To complete her spectacular ensemble, she wore a white satin demimask with feathery plumes attached near her temples and arching over her coiffure. She had laughed at her reflection in the mirror, and could only hope that the other ladies present would be as outrageously attired.

What's more, it had taken all her willpower not to collapse in giggles at her first sight of Guy Laurens. It was hard to believe he would appear in public wearing a pale blue satin suit and knee hose tied with blue ribbons, high-heeled slippers and a wreath of laurel banded around his forehead above a blue satin half-mask. He was serious, though. His solemn eyes peering through the slits and the haughty tilt of his lips indicated his appearance was not a joke, but a matter of pride, if not outright vanity.

"People say I resemble Bonaparte himself," he had pointed out upon his arrival. "But naturally I remind admirers that my own ancestors are of purest French blood, while the emperor was merely a Corsican. Still, the man had a flair for fashion."

Rebecca thought to herself that if Bonaparte looked anything like Guy, his appearance surely contributed to his downfall. Still, she was eager for the evening to begin. Conquering her worry over her daring costume, she took pride in the fact she was at last making an appearance in society. She floated beside Guy as if she had been born into elegance and sophistication. Her graceful carriage and slight smile belied her inner excitement and nervousness.

The stringed orchestra began a quadrille, a dance she'd recently attempted to master. Seated at a private table for two, she watched in fascination as the participants circled the room. She was relieved to see all the other guests wearing masks and costumes, many even more garish than hers or Guy's.

Guy rose and bowed before her. "Honor me, mademoiselle, if you please." Aware of dozens of eyes following her, she took his arm and joined him on the dance floor.

The music was like a heavenly chorus, and the stirring rhythms made it easier to follow the steps. With her feet hidden under her gown, she could make a mistake or two and no one would be the wiser.

She was surprised when a man tapped Guy on the shoulder and she was handed over to a new partner. She managed to control her nerves and smile up at the hidden face of the man dressed in shepherd's garb. Her next partner was a king in royal robes, and the following, an Arabian prince. My, this was great fun after all, she decided. She shouldn't have been so nervous in the beginning. And she must remember her pledge to be more agreeable to Mr. Laurens. If not for him, she wouldn't be having such a delightful evening.

At the close of the quadrille, Guy guided her to her seat and left her alone to visit with friends he'd spotted across the room. Waiting for his return, she thought of his unfortunate wife who never attended dances. Mrs. Laurens didn't care for them at all, he'd said. No wonder he was glad to have someone else to join him in the fun.

Suddenly a man appeared before her. Tall with broad shoulders and tapered hips, he was dressed as a pirate, complete with a golden hoop in one ear, a bandanna securing dark waving hair, and a rapier at his side. He bowed and addressed her. "Excuse me," came his low voice from behind a black satin mask. "The orchestra will next play a fandango—a Spanish dance of some passion. I would be honored to have you as my partner."

Quickly she looked toward Guy, but he was deep in conversation. Was it proper for her to dance with this stranger without Guy's permission? Well, why not? She was his guest, not his possession. She took the pirate's hand and accompanied him to the dance floor.

Looking up at the striking visage with black sideburns, mustache and pointed beard, she gave him an amused smile. Then she said gaily, "Forgive me, Sir Pirate, but I must warn you—I've never danced a fandango—not even in my classes. You'll have a poor partner, I fear."

"It shouldn't be too great a challenge for one who excels at the Highland fling."

Her heart nearly stopped. She gave the pirate a careful look. Yes, she saw it now, even through the elaborate disguise. "Captain Caldwell, I warned you . . ."

Throbbing guitars and the sensuous rhythms of a native drum drowned out her heated protest.

The captain swept her into his arms and moved across the nearly empty floor. Gradually a few other couples joined in, each interpreting the dramatic music in an individual way. One couple clad as gypsies were especially adept, the dark-skinned lady even clicking castanets to add to the Latin beat.

Blaine held Rebecca firmly against his body, locked in a demanding embrace as he slowly circled the room.

She felt his muscles contract beneath her touch and his thighs press her hips as he carried her against his body. She wanted to struggle free, but she was reluctant to create a scene—and the music—and his fierce embrace—were playing havoc with her senses.

Her toes barely touched the floor as he maneuvered her among the dancers, then swept through the French doors and onto the veranda beyond.

"Let me go!" she flashed, balling her fists against his shoulders. "How dare you drag me outside. Mr. Laurens will—"

His mouth came down hard on hers, searing her lips, forcing them into submission.

She started to pummel him, but he gripped her wrists and pinned her arms to her sides. She felt her resistance melting before the explosion of her own desire. All rational thought gone, she curved against him, feeling his arms slip around her, her body pulsing with liquid heat, with sensations she'd never experienced.

His lips, his tongue, brushed the delicate skin below her ear, then flamed across her bare shoulder until they found the flaring half-moon of her breasts.

A sigh escaped her throat as she moved her hands to his shoulders, giving herself up to the enchantment of the moment, the distant throb of drums, the night scented with jasmine and honeysuckle, the power of the man embracing her.

The fandango ended in a final fury of triumphant guitars. Reality returned like a glaring flood of light. Gasping, she pushed away and made an attempt to recover her former angry indignation.

"You . . . you . . ." she sputtered. "Haven't you forced yourself on me enough for one lifetime, Captain? This is . . . scandalous."

"Well, I'll be damned," he said, a teasing lilt in his voice. "If it isn't little Rebecca Gordon. Couldn't tell with all that finery. Scandalous, eh? Sounds like you've enlarged your vocabulary this past month."

"You're no gentleman, Captain Caldwell. Yes, I've learned a great deal lately. But I already knew about men like you."

He whipped off his mask. His eyes no longer held mirth, but were heavy with annoyance. "It's a great mystery why you have taken such a dislike to me, Rebecca. I would swear your kiss revealed otherwise. But whatever you think of me, the point is I want to get you away from Guy Laurens. He may be your guardian, but he can't be trusted. I figured he would bring you here tonight, even though this is no place for an innocent girl to be on display."

"But I wanted to come. And it's a wonderful party."

He cupped her chin with his hand. With the other, he untied her mask and lifted it away. For a moment, he gazed down at her. "Holy saints, Rebecca, you are completely unaware of your mind-drugging beauty. And you're as innocent as a rosebud in spring. For some reason, I feel compelled to look after you. Maybe because I first saw you with a dirty face and homespun breeches, not much more than an urchin defeating the best sharpshooters in Tennessee. So whether you like it or not, I'm taking you out of Laurens's reach. If you want to go to Scotland, so be it. I'll take you on my own ship—and we'll leave tomorrow."

His statement took her completely by surprise. "Tomorrow? You must be insane."

"I would take you out of here tonight, but I have something most urgent to attend to before midnight."

"I can't possibly just up and leave New Orleans. Besides, Mr. Laurens has made me quite comfortable . . . and there's the blockade. The British have the bay well guarded."

"That won't be a problem. I run the blockade with ease."

A warning sounded in her brain. Was this further proof of his traitorous maneuvering? "With ease, you say? I see. But I have no money to pay for such a journey. And *I* would feel quite cowardly to leave my country in its hour of need."

This remark brought a smile to his lips. "And what do you plan to do for your country, Rebecca?"

Lifting her chin, she said sharply, "Anything asked of me. I certainly would never betray the United States."

"Um." He studied her as if weighing some new thought. "You're certain you want to go to Scotland?"

"Yes, of course."

"I remember you as a gambling woman, Miss Gordon. I'll make you a wager. If you win, we leave within the week."

"Wager?" What now, she thought, eyeing him suspiciously.

"You've heard that Governor Claibourne will make an appearance tonight."

"Yes. I've heard."

"Do you intend to engage him in conversation now that you're so worldly-wise?"

"I suppose you think I can't manage that?" she snapped.

"I'm inclined to doubt it. It's easier to put on a pretty dress than to converse with a governor."

"I'm not afraid to talk to anyone. I got along fine with Andrew Jackson, didn't I?"

"But that was Tennessee. This is New Orleans."

Oh, the captain was so annoying. "I'll prove it if you care to watch. As soon as he arrives, I'll walk right up and say hello. You'll lose your bet, Captain Caldwell, and owe me a trip to Scotland."

Abruptly, a masculine laugh rolled from behind the nearest lilac bush. A short man, dressed in the uniform of the Louisiana militia, emerged from behind it. "A lady of such exquisite beauty, mon ami, shouldn't be allowed out of New Orleans. I myself would be devastated."

"Hell, Jean, stay out of sight. It's risky—"

"Damn the risk," Lafitte said, swinging onto the veranda to join them. "By the saints, you never told me she looked like this." He made a low bow over her hand. "Jean Lafitte at your service, mademoiselle. I would risk more than death to bask in your charms."

So this was the famous pirate who was Blaine Caldwell's friend and partner. Stay calm, she urged herself. She smiled insipidly. "Delighted to meet you, sir. But your uniform surprised me. You and the captain must have switched your identities."

"Quite so," answered Lafitte.

Blaine leaned near. "Tonight, Empress Josephine, no one is exactly who they seem."

"That's true." She laughed uneasily. "Now, do you intend to watch me chat with the governor?"

"I would like to see it, but Jean and I must leave at once. I do have friends here, however, who will report to me all that transpires. I might also recommend that you say nothing to Mr. Laurens about our meeting here. No doubt he's frantically searching for you by now. You must assure him you've been alone on the veranda for a breath of air. Agreed?"

"Agreed," she answered.

"Claibourne is due here within the hour. If you engage him in conversation, say, for five minutes, you win our wager. I promise to take you to Scotland as soon as my ship is ready."

"That will be as easy as eating apple pie. Did you know that the governor was chosen by President Madison," she announced, proud of her newly gained knowledge of world events.

"Yes, and since that is the case, you might like to converse with him about . . . well, about your passionate patriotism, I expect."

"So, that's all? You want me to visit with Governor Claibourne for a few minutes? That is enough to earn my passage to the British Isles?"

"I guarantee it."

"Then I will do it."

"You haven't asked what your penalty will be if you fail."

"I won't fail such a simple task, but what did you have in mind?"

"I'll know how you fared by tomorrow morning. If you fail, I will arrive at your door in my carriage and take you to new lodgings, under my protection."

She laughed at the idea. "Your protection? You do have absurd notions, sir. I'd be better protected by a Tennessee weasel. The bet is on. Good night, Captain Caldwell—and Mr. Lafitte." She retrieved her mask and walked majestically back into the ballroom. Could she do as they asked? She was pretty sure she could. Talking to folks had never been a problem for her. She figured if she had the nerve to go to a party in this outlandish garb, with Napoleon Bonaparte as her escort, she could say hello to the governor.

She quickly discovered the captain was at least wrong about one observation. Guy hadn't missed her at all. He had been busy fortifying himself for the dancing with an ample amount of whiskey. She mumbled some explanation about her absence as he led her at once into a Virginia reel. Her own mood had mellowed considerably. Though she followed along as best she could, even smiled from time to time, she couldn't tear her thoughts from the feel of Blaine Caldwell's lips, his embrace, the way he started her heart racing beyond control. For the first time, she truly understood how her mother must have felt when under the spell of Etienne Dufour. But she would not have *her* heart broken. No matter what, she was determined to resist the captain's deadly charm.

As anticipated, Governor Claibourne arrived at ten o'clock sharp. He was not in costume or mask, but was elegantly dressed and accompanied by an entourage of his personal staff. Like any skillful politician, he moved around the room with ease, stopping to shake hands with the voters of his state.

If she was going to win her wager with the captain, she must make her move at once. She turned to Guy. "Excuse me, sir, I'd like to meet the governor, please."

"What? Oh, of course, my dear, though you must listen politely and make no comment. It isn't seemly, you know, for ladies to involve themselves in talk of politics or war." He tapped her chin with one finger. "Just look beautiful—as indeed you do."

When she joined Claibourne's circle, she did exactly as she'd been told. She smiled inanely as the governor carried on about the importance of support from every man in New Orleans, whether he be upper-class Creole or ordinary American citizen. He said the threat from the redcoats was ominous; the bastards had burned Washington and were threatening to reclaim the upstart colonies if they had to destroy everything in their path.

As he expounded, his eyes drifted over her, pausing far too long on the swooping neckline of her dress. Whether he was disapproving or admiring, she couldn't decide.

He talked on. "Flying high after whipping Napoleon," he declared. "Claims there's not a worthy leader among us since George Washington."

She leaned near Guy and softly inquired. "Do you know the time?"

"Almost half-past ten."

She wondered if she'd done a proper job to win the bet. No, it was probably required of her to speak. "Excuse me, Governor, do you expect General Jackson to arrive soon? I'd put him up against any Englishman in the field."

The gathering hushed and all eyes fell on her.

"Rebecca," Laurens hissed. "I told you—"

The governor's voice boomed. "Why, my dear little lady, that's an excellent question. General Jackson should arrive in New Orleans before Christmas."

"But that's two months away. And I've heard there are English ships already approaching."

Along with embarrassed coughs, several men chuckled.

"Now don't worry your pretty head about such things, missy. I have everything under control. Pierre Lafitte is in prison and I expect to snare his rascally brother before this night is over. Which reminds me, I must return to the prison to make certain my orders are carried out. Lafitte is to be brought to the courtyard for whipping at precisely ten-thirty. With luck, I'll trick his brother Jean into some careless behavior." He removed his timepiece. "Oh, oh, I'm late. Good evening, friends. Continue your dancing."

Rebecca beamed in triumph. She had engaged the governor in conversation. And Blaine thought she couldn't do it. The governor had even complimented her astute question. Why, he stayed long enough to talk to her and . . . She felt the blood drain from her face. So that was it. She'd been duped into distracting the governor at the precise moment he intended to capture the infamous scoundrel she'd just encountered in this very house. How dare they trick her into such a traitorous act! She should have known Blaine Caldwell couldn't be trusted. Why, he had no intention of taking her to Scotland. She must do something at once to foil his plans.

She tugged Laurens to one side as Governor Claibourne hurried from the ballroom. "Guy, listen to me. I know you'll be furious with me when I tell you what has happened, but maybe it isn't too late."

She could see he was already greatly annoyed by her unladylike comments of a few moments ago. He might be inclined to throttle her when he heard what she'd done. But she had no choice and would just have to pay the consequences later. "A short time ago, a man in a pirate costume danced with me," she began. "I didn't know at first it was Blaine Caldwell."

"Caldwell—here? Damn him. Did he molest you?"

"Please pay attention. We talked privately after the dance—and he . . . ah . . . said he was meeting Jean Lafitte very soon. I'm sure they were up to mischief. You heard what the governor said. I'm absolutely certain Captain Caldwell has gone with Lafitte to rescue Pierre."

Guy's brow furrowed as the news registered. Then he smirked down at her. "Dear Rebecca, you've redeemed yourself. This could be the chance I've been looking for for years. I'll overtake the governor and give the warning."

"I'm going with you."

"No—well, yes, I suppose you must. I have no time to deposit you at home."

She locked her arm through his as they rushed from the room.

Blaine and Jean Lafitte hurried along darkened alleys until they reached the square with its softly glowing lamps. At this hour, there were few people abroad—only a handful of revelers on their way to the second party of the evening, and a few drifters from the waterfront saloons.

Blaine was elated over the events at the masked ball. He had taken a chance when he had forced Rebecca into his arms. But the gamble had paid off. Her resistance had quickly dissolved and her kiss had proved she had strong feelings for him after all. Not only was her innocence a thin veneer over simmering sensuality, but she was attracted to him in the same way he was attracted to her. They were kindred spirits and would make a fabulous match if he could gain her trust. The only problem was his own feelings were getting beyond control. Her unique looks set his blood on fire, but more than that, his heart was getting involved.

This was an entirely new experience for him and he'd better be on guard. He had no doubt she'd talk to Claibourne tonight. That distraction should buy him and Jean the few minutes they needed to pull off the rescue, and she'd never be the wiser. Then, of course, he'd arrange to take her aboard ship and sail east. Two things would be accomplished. He'd get her away from Laurens, and he'd have a chance to further his own relationship with her. Maybe they'd never reach Scotland. Maybe they would go to the Indies instead—or even return to Louisiana where he would arrange for her to become his mistress after all. Or . . . no, he wouldn't think of marriage. At least, not now.

The Cabildo loomed ahead, its Hispanic-Moresque facade ominous in the subtle blue glow of the moonless night.

With their backs to the concrete wall, Blaine and Jean edged their way toward the gate. Beyond the gate, the inner court was lighted by a roaring bonfire built for tonight's scheduled flogging.

Jean stopped to listen for any nearby activity. His band of twenty rugged mates would soon be on the scene. He whispered, "I still don't understand why the governor chose this hour of the night."

"A wily move," answered Blaine. "He knows how popular the Lafitte brothers are in Louisiana. A public daylight flogging would bring out sympathizers in force. This way, he can bait his trap for you and your men without interference."

"His ploy will fail," Lafitte said with total confidence.

"Of course. Claiborne's played into our hands."

"You mean into your lady friend's hands. We only need the extra few minutes while the governor's delayed at the ball."

"I believe Rebecca will do as I ask. It will be easy for her and she'll never know what she's done."

Lafitte's voice fell. "My men are here."

Blaine had seen and heard nothing, but he trusted Lafitte's jungle instinct. "Let's go, then—and good luck, mon ami."

Lafitte clapped him on the shoulder. "Your risk is greater than mine. I won't forget this, Caldwell. Take care." Turning, Lafitte marched boldly into the firelight and approached the guard at the immense iron gate. Smartly outfitted in the blue coat and white pants of the American navy, his face shadowed by a black bicorne hat with gold braid, he cut an impressive figure. "I've come to witness the flogging," he announced with no trace of his French accent. "Open the gate. Governor Claibourne is right behind me."

The guard snapped to attention and saluted. Without hesitation, he unlocked the crossbar and shoved open the gate.

At that moment, Blaine dashed forward, followed closely by Lafitte's well-armed Baratarians. They rushed into the courtyard where half a dozen soldiers stood with Pierre Lafitte in their midst. The guards appeared to be waiting for someone—no doubt their American governor.

The startled soldiers were quickly surrounded and held at gunpoint. In near silence, Jean removed Pierre's bonds and hurried with him toward the opening.

Blaine waited until both Lafittes were safely outside. He held his pistol ready, but to his relief no resistance was offered from the troops. The stealth and quickness of the maneuver was like a rat slipping the cheese from the trap before it could be sprung. Blaine smiled to himself. It appeared Claibourne's dalliance with the stunning Rebecca had cost him his bait.

He was backing toward the gate, covering the escape of Lafitte and his men when he heard a clatter of wheels on flagstone breaking through the night.

A soldier shouted, "He's getting away. There comes Claibourne."

A lieutenant shouted, "Draw your arms!"

Blaine spun on his heels, but the guard at the gate was pushing it closed. Blaine knew he could shoot the man and still escape, but he had no intention of injuring or killing one of his countrymen. He had known this all along—and prayed that his bluff would be sufficient. Until now, it had worked to perfection. He tossed his pistol to the stones and held out his hands in surrender. Immediately he was surrounded and his arms clamped behind him. A suddenly emboldened soldier powered a fist into his jaw.

The blow staggered him. Pain shot through his skull and he tasted blood from his torn lip. His anger was tempered by the knowledge that the soldiers would be in deep trouble with their governor. They had let the chicken fly the coop.

Governor Claibourne, his face livid, marched into the courtyard.

Blaine pulled himself up as best he could considering that four men clutched his arms and shoulders. Two others had pistols aimed at his head. He would also be in considerable hot water with the American government, but he knew better than anyone that Lafitte and his men were loyal to the United States and would be invaluable in the coming encounter. He figured if he were imprisoned, it was likely to be a brief stay in the Cabildo—and better he than the seriously ill Pierre Lafitte.

But the sight he saw next was as stunning as it was disappointing. Entering the courtyard, her exquisite costume concealed by a flowing cape, was Rebecca Gordon. She was gripping Guy Laurens's arm as if her life depended on it.

Blaine held her round-eyed gaze, completely ignoring the furious condemnation by the governor. She was pale and tight-lipped as she looked at him. She seemed almost in a trance.

Frowning, Blaine allowed the governor's acid remarks to penetrate his brain.

"I'm shocked—absolutely shocked. I thought you were a loyal American, Caldwell. Now this—entering my compound—threatening my men—and letting loose a known pirate and smuggler whose brother I've been trying to capture for months. It's very close to traitorous conduct, sir. And you, a captain in the American navy. Why, I almost didn't believe Mr. Laurens when he told me. If it hadn't been for him and his lady, you might have gotten clean away." He shook his fist under Blaine's nose. "Tomorrow there'll be a price on Lafitte's head. That damned pirate will feel the wrath of the United States, or my name isn't William C. Claibourne."

Blaine's heart sank. So she had betrayed him. That realization caused more pain than the blow to his jaw. The fact that she also appeared completely miserable was little compensation. Why had she done it? It must have been Laurens's influence—or else he'd misjudged the feeling she expressed in her kiss. But Laurens disliked Americans; that was common knowledge. Why would he help Claibourne unless there was something—or someone—he hated even more? Looking at the satisfied face of the Frenchman, he knew he'd found his answer. Laurens despised him, and now the man was afraid of losing control of Rebecca.

Claibourne's blustery tirade continued, but Blaine heard no more of it. His eyes captured Rebecca's in a questioning look. He had challenged her, but she had betrayed him. Why? He had assumed she was a loyal American, but she did have Scottish roots, after all. She wanted to leave the United States, so she said. Dammit, he shouldn't have counted on her naivete. The truth was, she was far more clever than he'd guessed, and he'd been foolish enough to nearly lose his heart to the little vixen.

He drew himself up and gave Claibourne a hard look. The windbag should shut up and get this over with. Pierre and Jean Lafitte were safely away and Claibourne's rantings wouldn't change anything.

"Take him below," ordered a breathless Claibourne. "The lowest dungeon in the place. If it was up to me, I'd have him flogged in Lafitte's place and hung at sunrise."

From the corner of his eye, Blaine saw Rebecca sway against Laurens. She looked near fainting, but he hardened his heart. If the thought of his swinging from a gibbet made her sick, it served her right.

The soldiers jerked him roughly around and marched him into the dank gloom of the prison.

Rebecca's head was splitting and her heart felt like lead as she crouched in the far corner of Guy's coach and tried to think. As they made their way in the gloom, she watched Guy gulping long draughts from a silver flask. Between drinks, he eyed her with relish, his bright eyes and pleased smile revealing his satisfaction with her.

She worked up the courage to question him. "I wish you would explain what's going on, Guy. I didn't expect Captain Caldwell to be arrested and . . . maybe hanged. He was only helping Jean Lafitte's brother. I mean . . . you said you didn't like Claibourne or the Americans, but do you hate Blaine Caldwell enough to cause his death?"

His voice slurred, Guy replied, "Of course I hate Caldwell. The Lafitte brothers had their chance, but showed their black hearts. They're pirates and cutthroats—and Caldwell is no better."

She had no idea what he meant by the Lafittes "having their chance." And she could see Guy was too far in his cups to give her sensible answers. She would just have to find out for herself what was going on.

The carriage arrived at the town house and Guy emerged, then pulled her out after him. What a fool he appeared tottering up the steps, his thin legs wobbling and his laurel wreath drooping over one ear. At the top of the steps, he forced her into his arms, his liquored breath coming hot and heavy. She turned her face to avoid his disgusting kiss.

He was too drunk to keep his hold on her. With a muttered farewell, he staggered back to the coach and ordered the driver to take him home.

She closed the door and leaned against it. She was in a turmoil of confusion. One moment, she had responded to the captain's kiss, the next she was answering his challenge to speak to the governor. It had seemed more like fun than anything dangerous. But it *had* been dangerous. She should be pleased that she'd arranged the capture of a British spy. But she felt more like a rotten scoundrel. To make things worse, she wanted to believe in Guy Laurens, but his unseemly behavior tonight did nothing to win her trust or affection. She felt truly alone and didn't know whom she could trust. To add to her despair, she may have caused Blaine's death tonight. If he was hanged, it would be on her conscience forever. Rebecca's head was spinning and she didn't know what to do. But right now she was too tired to do anything. After she had some rest, and her mind was clear of the effects of wine, she would find out what would happen to Blaine Caldwell.

13

"Sit down, Pearl," Rebecca ordered in a nervous whisper. "We can see the proceedings from here."

"I'm scared, Miss Rebecca. I think Mr. Laurens is going to whip me for sure."

"No, I'll take the responsibility. I couldn't come to the Cabildo alone."

"I don't think ladies come here a'tall. This is trouble, miss. Can't we leave now?"

"Don't worry. This is just a hearing room where any American can get a fair trial. With all these other folks, no one will notice us."

"Mr. Laurens will be lookin' for us. He'll skin me—and you too, most likely. He doesn't allow his girls—"

"His *girls?* What do you mean?" Rebecca asked sharply. "Oh, never mind—there's the judge coming in." She gave Pearl a hard look. "But we *will* discuss it later. I'm going to get some straight answers today if I have to rattle some teeth to do it."

"But Mr. Laurens . . ."

"Forget him. He was reeling drunk when he brought me home last night. I'm sure he won't be abroad before noon."

Pearl shrank into her chair and pulled her hood close around her face.

Looking past the dozen or so spectators, Rebecca waited for the accused to be brought forth. Her nerves were screaming; her head ached and her eyes were burning from a miserable, sleepless night. She had tossed in her bed until dawn, going over and over the events of the evening. When she closed her eyes, she saw Blaine's face, dark with disappointment and laden with condemnation, as he stood pinioned by guards, blood seeping from his damaged lip. Yes, she had betrayed him. But after all, he had tricked her into helping a criminal to escape. He must surely be a spy for the British, and spies were usually shot if they were caught. Why hadn't she thought of that last night? Didn't Claibourne represent the United States? Why would the governor want to imprison the Lafitte brothers if they were loyal citizens? In the beginning, the entire affair had seemed a game of wits between Blaine and her. He had used her to advance his scheme, but she had outsmarted him and nearly thwarted his plan. But then, seeing him helpless and in pain because of her had torn her heart to shreds.

Worst of all, though, was the possibility she had caused Blaine's capture and imprisonment—maybe even his death. Her good sense told her he deserved to be punished for his escapade, but her heart was in agony at the prospect. If only she had stayed out of the entire situation. But no, she had been so stuck on herself after one month of being "uplifted," she had interfered and caused this dangerous predicament for a man who had done nothing more to her than enflame her with his kisses. She tried to remind herself that he was a spy, but that fact did nothing to ease her misery.

The judge's gavel interrupted her thoughts. Two guards escorted Captain Caldwell to the stand at the front of the room. He looked haggard, she thought, his eyes sunken, his lip swollen. A night's growth along his chin replaced the fake mustache and beard of his pirate's disguise. But he appeared confident, and he looked amazingly attractive with his shirt slashed to the waist, and his hips and muscular legs encased in form-fitting pants and buccaneer style leather boots. His bandanna and gold earring were gone, and his hair curled loosely around his ears and neck. When a small sigh escaped her lips, she glimpsed a troubled stare from Pearl.

The judge made a lengthy speech about Caldwell's misdeeds. When he asked if the accused had anything to say, Blaine merely replied no.

The judge continued. "The sentence for the crime of aiding a criminal to escape is fifty lashes and five years at hard labor."

The courtroom buzzed with excitement.

Rebecca covered her mouth to keep from crying out. This couldn't be happening. Wasn't he to have a trial—a jury trial as guaranteed by the new constitution? He was only guilty of helping a friend, and no one had been hurt. After all, she alone knew he was a spy.

The judge pounded on his desk to restore order. "Citizens, I'm not finished."

A hush fell across the room.

"I was about to announce that due to unusual circumstances—the fact that the accused is a hero of the present war effort and has no previous record of villainy—the punishment has been reduced to ten lashes and a fine of twenty thousand dollars to be paid at once into the coffers of the governor for use in the protection of the city."

Applause and shouts of approval erupted from the onlookers.

Rebecca was dizzy with relief. She signaled Pearl to slip out of the courtroom. Twenty thousand dollars was a great deal of money, and the whipping made her stomach turn, but at least he would not be imprisoned. And what was that the judge had said about his being a hero of the war effort? Was it possible that she was mistaken about his spying for the British? Or was he so clever that he could appear to be fighting for the United States while working for the enemy?

Before they could escape the building, they were caught up in the crowd pushing toward the inner courtyard.

She heard a man's voice. "He can afford it. His bank account won't feel a thing."

"His pampered flesh will, I reckon," came the reply.

"Ah, Caldwell's a good man. Different from most of the Creoles. A friendly sort. Claibourne's a fool to go after the Lafittes, anyhow. Why, they supply most of the goods we have these days."

She was bumped against Pearl as the spectators carried them through the hall and out into the sunlight.

Another man chuckled. "Still, I don't mind seeing one of them high and mighties take a beating now and then. Remind 'em they ain't no different under the skin than a black slave."

When she realized what was about to happen, she tried to escape. It was too late. The courtyard was being closed off and the guards were leading Blaine to the whipping post on a platform where all could see.

She clasped Pearl's arm. "Oh no. I don't want to see this." But there was no escape through the crowd. She looked again at Blaine, who was stripped to the waist and being bound to the post.

"Jesus, no," she choked. She knew floggings were common punishment, but she'd never witnessed one. And this beating was largely her fault. Blaine was neither a slave nor even a criminal. He was a man of wealth and education and culture. If she was wrong about his being a spy, she would never forgive herself for her stupidity. And even if she were right and he was evil through and through, she would never want to be the cause of his suffering. Why, it had broken her heart to spank Pepper for misbehaving. And now she'd caused a man who had once done her a great favor to endure torture and disgrace. The captain would hate her forever, and he would always bear scars to remind him of what she'd done.

She clenched her hands and stiffened her spine. He was making no protest and there was nothing she could do. Looking at his lithe back, the taut muscles flowing beneath his smooth bronze skin, she felt tears sting into her eyes.

The whip cracked through the air and cut into his flesh.

The spectators released their collective breath.

Another stroke. Blaine flinched slightly as a bloody red line appeared across his shoulders.

Rebecca's throat was tight as she fought for control. She had to admire his courage. As for herself, she agonized at every stroke and bit into her lip to keep from screaming.

The whipping continued at a steady pace until ten strokes were counted. Blaine showed no sign of weakness though his back was etched with bloody stripes.

As the guards cut his bonds, a smattering of applause

broke from the onlookers. Blaine Caldwell had lived up to his heroic reputation.

Her hands clammy, her knees weak, Rebecca clasped Pearl to keep from stumbling. The mulatto girl showed no signs of emotion.

"We've got to get out of here," Rebecca whispered frantically. Tugging on Pearl, she pushed her way toward the door, only to be blocked by the guards accompanying Blaine.

To her horror, she saw he had spotted her. He was soaked with sweat and carrying his crumpled pirate's shirt over his arm. Hesitating for a split second, his eyes held hers.

His look sent misery and guilt stabbing through her deepest core. Had he been furious, she would have understood. But his face held the hurt confusion of a youngster who had been unfairly disciplined by a parent. It was a fleeting moment, but she would be haunted by it for the rest of her days.

Then he was gone—back into the building, no doubt to settle his fine.

In a daze, she walked out of the Cabildo and hailed a carriage. Only when inside did she bury her head in her hands and sob in an agony of remorse.

For five days Rebecca heard nothing at all from Guy Laurens. She wanted to confront him, to demand he move her to other quarters or allow her to look for work. If only she were on her way to Scotland. But she had ruined her chance to go on Blaine Caldwell's ship, so she would have to wait for the war to end. Rebecca spent much of her time escaping the humidity and heat of the town by puttering in the garden in defiance of Guy's orders, and teaching Pepper to "sit" and "roll over." Her impatience grew with every passing day and her regret over her part in Blaine Caldwell's punishment made happiness or contentment impossible.

At last a note arrived from Guy announcing he would call in late morning and escort her to a local sporting event which he thought she would enjoy. Normally she would have relished the experience, but her mood was far too bleak to allow her to enjoy anything so frivolous. She hoped she would have a chance during the outing to announce her plans to leave his town house as soon as possible. His response should give her a good idea of what was really in his mind.

Guy was buoyant when he arrived. He presented her with a bouquet of fresh-cut roses and showered her with compliments in both French and English. He pinned a corsage of rosebuds onto her simple checked gingham frock, and seemed completely unaware of her cool manner and the pointed way she addressed him as "Mr. Laurens."

Tying her bonnet, she followed him outside. Today he had provided an open-air carriage and it was impossible not to enjoy the sparkling morning. As they were carried toward the edge of town, she tried to find a way to bring up the subject of her leaving. But he was intent on doing all the talking and finally mentioned the name that had been on her mind constantly for days.

"It's a disgrace the way the town has taken sides with Caldwell. He should be stewing in prison instead of walking the streets like a damned hero. And after the risk I took to see that he was apprehended. No doubt, he greased a few palms along the way to freedom."

"Tell me," she ventured, "is Jean Lafitte on the side of the British? I assume he must be."

"Not at all. Oh, the Yankees feared he might throw in with the English. I'm sure he was offered a tidy sum by the royalists. In my opinion, he's a fool not to take their offer."

"*You* would side with the British?" She kept her voice casual.

"Oh . . . well, no. That would be traitorous, wouldn't it. No, but I do expect the English to win the war. That view is confidential, of course."

For a moment, she considered his comment. She now understood his earlier remark about the Lafittes "missing their chance." Maybe it had been a drunken remark, but more and more she thought Laurens favored a British victory. "But why does Claibourne hate Jean Lafitte if Lafitte is supporting our cause?"

"Claibourne's a puritanical ass. He wants to make a name for himself by cleaning out the pirate's nest at Barataria. Lafitte, of course, is so popular with the local citizenry, he could take over the territory, if he liked."

"If you dislike Claibourne so, why did you want to help him keep Lafitte from escaping?"

"Personally I've come to hate Lafitte. He's completely untrustworthy even though he claims loyalty to the United States. And I would love to see Blaine Caldwell hanged from the tallest tree."

"Why? Do you think the captain is a spy?"

"A spy? For whom?"

"Why, for the British, of cour—" The new thought that sailed into her head stopped her speech. That the redcoats had spies seemed natural—but the Americans . . . could Blaine be a spy for the *Yankees?*

"Tell me, Rebecca, do you have reason to believe Caldwell is a spy? If so, you should warn me at once. You showed courage before in coming to me to reveal his clandestine activities. I would be especially grateful if you did so once again."

She merely shook her head. It was all she could do to conceal her feelings at that moment. Indications were that Blaine was a spy. Why, even Josie had said so—but it had never occurred to her he could be spying for the United States. If so, his visit with Andrew Jackson made sudden sense—and his friendship with Lafitte was quite justifiable. Her elation at the possibility was tempered by even more guilt at what she'd done to him. She'd scorned him, insulted him and been the cause of his being arrested, whipped and fined. She was consumed with inner turmoil when they drew up to the playing field that had been cleared from the surrounding swamp.

A huge crowd was gathered, some fans seated on a collection of wooden benches while others encircled the immense grassy field.

Feeling Guy's eyes on her, she tried to take an interest in the proceedings. "What's the game called?" she asked blandly.

"Racquettes," he replied. "It evolved from a Choctaw Indian game that resembles lacrosse but is far more violent. The local athletes adore it. It's quite a spectacle. Of course, we needn't stay long. To be frank, I used it as an excuse to take you on an outing."

"Kind of you," she said distractedly.

"We can sit here on this bench, but you'll have to stand if you want a good view of the game."

She didn't mind standing. Her only problem was appearing to be interested when her thoughts were fixed on Blaine Caldwell. Somehow she must get in touch with him. Naturally, he despised her, but she had to try. How could she express the enormity of her regret over what she had done?

A cheer went up from the spectators as the two teams took the field. What followed was more like a riot than a sporting event. Each team consisted of eighty or more men, shoeless, stripped to the waist, and wearing red or blue caps. They played with a leather ball which was picked up and thrown with two spoonlike sticks toward the opponents' goal. There were no boundaries so the onlookers often found themselves in the middle of the action. Shouting and screaming, arms and legs flailing, heads cracking and bare flesh scraped and bloodied, all added to the thrill of the competition.

Rebecca stood on the bench and stared in fascination at the melee. For a moment, she forgot her aching heart. Each team had more members than the entire population of Morgan's Landing. Players seemed intent on murdering their opponents as if winning were a life-and-death matter.

The action followed the ball up and down the unmarked field of play. It went on without interruption unless a point was scored or unless, as did happen, the ball sailed past the refreshment stand and caused the structures to be upended by the athletes rushing en masse to retrieve it. Every few minutes, some hapless participant had to be carted to safety by sympathetic bystanders.

The noise was deafening. After a time Rebecca was about to suggest they leave when she heard Blaine Caldwell's name being shouted all around her.

Standing on tiptoe, her heart madly pounding, she saw that Blaine was among the players and, at the moment, he was running toward the nearest goal with the ball balanced on the racquettes. She was elated to see him so fit—apparently fully recovered from the flogging he'd endured six days ago.

It was also plain he was the favorite of the crowd as he ran full tilt through the grass, sidestepping and dodging the flying sticks of his opponents.

She found herself laughing and yelling with the others, ignoring a sulking Laurens at her side. Unfortunately, several tall men moved in front of her just as the score was attempted. A loud groan from the crowd indicated the attempt had not been successful.

Suddenly there was a hush. She tried to see what had happened but Guy grabbed her arm and roughly pulled her away from the field.

"One moment, sir," she fired. "You brought me here and I'm enjoying it." She yanked her arm from his grasp.

"Too much enjoyment, I'd say. I thought you disliked Caldwell. It appears you've gone mad for him like the rest of these fools."

"I told you some time ago that Blaine Caldwell was merely an acquaintance. If I'm mad for him as you say, why did I betray him last week?"

"You do have a point. Maybe I was hasty. I suppose we can see what's happened to him. At the moment, he's being carried from the field."

"What?" she shouted. "Carried? Where?"

"Calm yourself. He's being dumped with the others who've been injured. Generally there's a physician around who donates his assistance during the game."

Keeping a step ahead of Guy, she inched her way through the crowd. Play had resumed and soon she located the spot shaded by trees that served as a temporary shelter for the injured players. To her relief, she saw Blaine rising to his feet and brushing at his breeches. He was grinning at a teammate despite being covered with dirt and grass and a fair amount of blood. Wearing only ragged pants rolled up to his calves, with his hair clinging damply to his forehead and ears, he looked like an urchin who'd been caught in some delightfully satisfying mischief.

She started to go toward him when she was firmly stopped by Guy's hand on her shoulder. Furiously she whirled to face him. "I'll not tell you again that I intend to do as I please. If we're to continue as friends, you must try not to exert control over my life." It was time she had this out once and for all. It might as well be now.

He blazed back. "Blaine Caldwell and I have been enemies for years. He thinks his money can make up for his father's crude background. He admired your father, but he has always been condescending to me. To *me*—a member of the highest class of French Creoles. The man's a cocky young rooster with no breeding. I dislike him and all his kind—these Yankees who try to push their way into polite society. I'm telling you this so you will know where your loyalties must lie." His voice was tight with controlled rage. "I brought you to New Orleans to help you. Like any other woman, you'll do as your guardian or your husband demands. You owe me everything. If you speak to Caldwell now, you forfeit my protection. And I can assure you, he'll have no interest in the likes of you—unless it's as a plaything for his bed, to be disposed of whenever he tires of you."

She raised her hand to strike him, but he caught her wrist and cruelly twisted it.

"You may be right," she said between clenched teeth. "But I'd rather sell myself at Josie's than spend one more second as your . . . your possession."

He flung her away almost causing her to fall. "Then go the hell to Josie's! I hope you warm the bed of every river rat and sweaty field hand that can come up with a coin to buy you." Leaning over her, he shook his finger under her nose. "You'll crawl to me one day, Rebecca Gordon." His face was splotched and purple with fury.

Regaining her balance, she prayed he would leave her alone. People were staring now, and she wanted only to escape until she could decide what to do.

Abruptly Guy took hold of her arm and tried to push her toward the waiting carriage. "On second thought, you'd better go with me."

"No!" she cried. "I will not!"

She started to struggle when suddenly he released her and took a step backward. At her elbow stood Blaine Caldwell, staring at Guy with murder in his eyes.

"Let her go, Laurens."

"Stay out of this, Caldwell. I brought her to New Orleans and she's my responsibility. Mine alone."

"You want the money for her journey? It's yours, plus interest. Now get out of here. I'll take care of the lady."

"Lady?" He laughed coarsely. "A by-blow and a whore. You saw her at Josie's. You only want her because she prefers me."

Blaine turned to look at her. "Do you prefer him?"

She was frightened; she was angry; she was humiliated. How dare he even suggest such a thing? "I am not a horse at the country fair to be traded back and forth by two conceited men," she said fiercely. "You don't like each other? Fine. To be honest, I don't much like or trust either one of you. There must be one ordinary, decent man in New Orleans. I believe I'll go see if I can find him." She spun on her heels and started to walk away.

A strong hand stopped her. Blaine's eyes were crinkled in merriment belying his harsh tone. "You'll come with me, my fiery-tempered lass." When she faced him, he added gently, "We'll find a place to talk."

Over his shoulder she saw Guy marching away toward his coach. Leaving Blaine's side she walked to a broad tree and stopped to catch her breath. Her heart was pounding so hard, she thought it would fly from her chest. So Blaine had saved her from Guy; but who would save her from Blaine? He must be furious with her after what she had done to him. She had longed to apologize, but now she was merely upset and exhausted. She waited a moment, expecting him to arrive at her side. When he didn't, she turned slowly to look at him.

He was gazing at her with hands on hips, unsmiling, his look as solemn and inscrutable as a granite statue. What had happened to his former amusement, the laughter she had seen behind his eyes when he'd stopped her from leaving? He must be waiting for her to crawl to him with her apology, beg for his forgiveness, express her eternal gratitude for his saving her from Guy Laurens.

He did look extraordinarily appealing without his shirt, his beautiful body glistening with sweat. Her memory flashed to the night in the boat cabin when he'd held her against him and she'd felt the power of his taut muscles against her breasts.

She waited, holding his eyes across the distance, willing him to approach, praying he wouldn't turn away. She deserved his anger, expected it, even wanted it. Then she could explain and apologize. But his silent reproach was unendurable.

Just when she thought she couldn't bear it any longer, he walked to her and let his eyes roam over her from head to toe. "You and Mr. Laurens seem to have had a falling out," he observed coolly. "You do seem unharmed, however."

Try as she might, she could not detect a single note of friendliness or any real compassion in his voice. "You're correct on both points, Captain. But what about you? I just saw you carried from the game."

He put out one hand and leaned against the tree and crossed his ankles. She was acutely aware of his near nakedness, his broad chest with damply curling hair, the smooth caramel color of his moist flesh.

He gave her a wry smile. "I thought I was up to playing today, but my strength failed me. No doubt 'tis the result of a rather uncomfortable incident earlier this week."

"You . . . you appear recovered," she said in a small voice. "I'm naturally relieved."

"Is that so? I'm surprised at your sudden concern for my well-being."

She bit into her lower lip. This was her chance to explain her true feelings, but she couldn't find the words. She couldn't think clearly with him standing so near, looking down at her with a mirthless half-smile. "I—I'm glad you didn't go to prison." It sounded so stupid, she felt her cheeks flame in embarrassment.

His smile widened. "I'm extremely pleased to hear it, Miss Gordon. Would you care to see the results of your little victory?"

For some reason her eyes fell directly to his flat stomach where his navel was clearly visible.

"Not there," he said, still smiling. "Only really serious offenders are whipped across the belly." He moved his hand from the tree and turned his back to her. The sight of the elongated slashes and barely healed welts crisscrossing his back brought unwanted tears to her eyes.

He revolved to look back at her. His expression changed subtly. "Never mind. I doubt that your tattling caused my capture. I knew the risks. Still—I did put my trust in your discretion. You have never been particularly fond of me, so the error in judgment was mine."

She simply couldn't speak. Finally she choked, "I'm . . . truly sorry. I can explain."

He glanced around. A number of people were finding the drama beneath the spreading oak more interesting than the competition on the field. Several young ladies were openly ogling Blaine's magnificent physique.

"Come along," he suggested. "I may as well hear your explanation in private. I have a carriage near the road, but I must first locate my boots."

Did she hear a slightly more tender note in his voice? Her hopes soared. If only he would forgive her, she would stay out of his life and never, never cause him any more pain.

He pulled on his boots, slung his shirt over one shoulder and guided her to his waiting carriage. It was a slow process as he was required to acknowledge friends and fans and reassure them he was all right and would return to play another day.

They do love him, Rebecca thought as she strolled by his side. Obviously, he'd lived among these people and earned their admiration and their respect. It was an important sign, she felt, that he was a man of character as well as position. It seemed unlikely that such a popular and well-regarded man would agree to spy against the country of his birth.

He assisted her into the closed conveyance and sat down opposite her, but gave no orders to his coachman on the bench outside.

"I am truly sorry—" she began.

He waved aside her words. "Forget it happened," he said.

A moment of silence passed between them. Then she asked, "Where are we going?"

"To Dominique Hall," he said. "Unless you would rather go back to Laurens's town house—or perhaps to Josie's."

His pointed remark cut deeply. But she must remember how much pain she had caused him.

"I'm never going back to Mr. Laurens. And I see no reason to impose myself on you. I'm sure you'd like to see the last of me."

"I should feel that way, but somehow I don't. Since you've managed to extricate yourself from Laurens, I'd be more than happy to offer you the protection of my home."

For a long moment, she returned his look. She was drawn to him, wanted him, dangerously near to loving him. Suddenly her mother's words flashed into her mind: "He said he loved me, over and over, but marriage outside his class was impossible. He was a Creole and very rich." After a time, she said as firmly as she could manage, "Thank you, but I can't do that. I intend to find work—somewhere. I'll find my own place. In the meantime, there *is* a place I can go. The cottage of a friend."

"Who is this friend?" he asked with a trace of doubt in his voice.

"A lady. A Miss Morgan."

"Beatrice Morgan?"

"You . . . you know her?"

"She's been a friend of mine for years."

"Will you take me there?"

His jaw worked as he looked at her. At last he muttered, "If that's your choice. But the invitation remains open."

"I appreciate that. And I'm glad we're friends again." She tried to smile. "Do put some medicinal herbs on your back. It will help it to heal without scarring." A lump was forming in her throat.

"You're quite a talented young lady. You shoot expertly and sew beautifully. You're an excellent actress and also a physician. I'm very impressed."

"Act-actress?"

"Let me put it this way. I'm not sure exactly who you are—an innocent country sprite from Tennessee or a beauty expecting to make a fortune at Miss Josie's—or perhaps a traitor to the American cause who reveals secrets to the governor. Or are you Empress Josephine escaped from war-torn France? Who are you, Rebecca Gordon?"

14

The silence lay thick as curdled cream between Rebecca and Blaine as they traveled to Josie's secret cottage. Rebecca clutched her purse in her lap as she gazed out the window, trying to ignore Blaine's knee as it occasionally bumped against her skirts. She felt his eyes studying her from the shadows. As the carriage drew to a halt in front of Josie's, she made a decision.

"Captain Caldwell," she began in a low voice. "You've suffered on my account and I'm indebted to you for several reasons. I don't know much about political shenanigans or exactly who is guilty or who is innocent. I . . . I may not see you again and I owe you the truth. Mr. Laurens made me promise not to tell, but I no longer feel an obligation to him. I intend to find a job and pay him off for the trip money as soon as possible."

Blaine leaned forward. He had pulled on his shirt, but left it open in the front. His face still showed a smudge or two of dirt, but the breeze had cooled his perspiration and left his hair dry though unkempt around his forehead and ears. "I admire your spirit, Rebecca, but with your permission, I'd like to see you again. I'm not entirely happy to leave you here with Josie—as much as I like the lady."

"It's only for a short time, but I do want to tell you the truth. I owe you that much."

"You owe me nothing."

"The truth is . . ." She cleared her throat and faced him squarely. "The truth is I am illegitimate. My mother was a wonderful Scots woman; my father . . . my father . . ."

"Was Etienne Dufour," he said gently.

Her lips parted in surprise. After a moment, she said, "How . . . how did you know?"

"I should have guessed the minute I saw you. You are the feminine version of that very handsome man." He touched an errant curl at her cheek, then traced the outline of her jaw.

She moved away from his touch. "Then you understand why I can't see you again. It wouldn't be right."

"Etienne was a fine man. Don't ever be ashamed to carry his blood."

"Oh, I'm not ashamed. And my mother loved him, and he loved her . . . in his way. But . . ." She felt tears forming behind her eyes. She must escape before she made a fool of herself. Quickly she reached for the door handle. "Good-bye, Captain." She left the carriage and hurried up the sidewalk, praying that Josie would be there to let her in. Behind her, the coach door slammed shut. She heard the clop-clop of the horses as they pulled away.

She started to knock on the door, but it swung open and Josie greeted her with a pleasant smile.

"Come in, child. I saw the carriage. I knew who 'twas."

She felt dazed as she entered the parlor with Josie's arm around her shoulders—and as lost as a gosling on a way-ward wind.

"Sit down, honey, and I'll order tea."

"No thank you, Miss Josie. I can't stay. I've left Mr. Laurens and I must find a place to live. Captain Caldwell offered me a place to stay, but I had to get away from him."

"I'm mighty relieved about the former—but why the latter? Blaine Caldwell is a good and generous man."

"That may be so, but I want my freedom. I want to find employment, not depend on the charity of others."

Josie eased her into a comfy chair. "Understandable, but

there are two reasons you should have accepted the captain's invitation."

"And several why I could not."

"Listen to me, child." She covered her hand with her warm plump one. "If I know Guy Laurens, he won't let you go so easily. Your father's biggest mistake was to trust—"

"My father? Then you know too?" It seemed everyone knew her secret.

"I can speak freely now that you're out of Laurens's grasp. I was a close friend of your father. He set me up in business in the early days and often . . . confided in me."

"Tell me what he was like," she said with a sigh. "I know he abandoned my mother, but I don't think he was entirely bad. He didn't know she was pregnant—"

"Abandoned your mother? But that's not true. *She* left *him.* I know that for a fact. I saw her farewell letter."

Rebecca stared at Josie. "Wh-what? But *I* saw *his* farewell letter. In fact . . ." She pulled open the drawstrings of her purse. "I always keep it with me. It got a bit damp when I escaped from the *New Orleans* steamship, but at least I saved it. It's all I have of him, you see." She opened the wrinkled paper and showed it to Josie.

Josie read it quickly, then looked up in amazement. "It's a very nice letter, but Etienne didn't write it."

Rebecca felt the breath leave her body. "But . . . but my mother has kept it all these years. She only gave it to me when she was dying."

"Did Etienne himself deliver it to her?"

"No. No, Guy Laurens did. . . ." The impact of her words was like a physical blow.

"Laurens." Josie spat the name like snake venom. "Stay put a minute, child. I want to get something from my safe."

Rebecca couldn't have moved if the house had caught on fire. She sat staring numbly at the letter, frozen over the possible implications.

Josie soon returned carrying an envelope. "Etienne was brokenhearted when he got this letter. His affair with Elizabeth had been a secret from his mother, but he intended to propose to her and introduce her as his fiancée. He had a business trip, was gone two weeks. When he returned, Guy Laurens gave him *this* letter. In it, your mother completely rejected him, said she didn't love him after all and was going to her family in Tennessee."

Rebecca stared at the note, written in simple words, but in lovely script. "But . . . this isn't my mother's handwriting. She was educated, but not fancy. . . ."

"I thought that was odd too. So did Etienne. That's one reason he left the letter with me for safekeeping. He was leaving within the week to go after your mother."

Stunned, Rebecca stared again at the two letters in her lap. "Look, Miss Josie," she breathed. "The handwriting is . . . is similar."

Josie bent over to study them. "Indeed, it is. Not exact, mind you, but look at the backward flow, and the way the *t*s are crossed, and the loop on the capital *M*. They're identical in both letters." She looked up, her brow deeply furrowed. "My child, it's my opinion Guy Laurens wrote both these letters. And there's more. Before Etienne could go after your mother, he was killed. His body was found in the woods downriver. It was only Laurens who testified that Etienne was headed south to a visit a friend. But I knew differently. Etienne would not have delayed going after your mother for any reason. And I always believed Laurens knew that too."

"Are you suggesting that . . . Guy Laurens *killed* my father?" Her stomach was turning, her hands starting to shake.

"I can't say for sure, but I've always wondered. You see, Laurens took over your father's estate after that. Took full control of everything, the real estate, the money, the mortgage on my property. I knew I could never question him, or mention anything to anyone. I thought about going to Etienne's mother, but she was ailing and died soon after Etienne did. Etienne had no other family, no heirs, no one to take over his business but Guy Laurens. There's one other thing. Laurens had a comely sister. Before Elizabeth came along, it was expected Guy's sister would marry Etienne. One of those family arrangements, you know. Guy knew if Etienne married someone else, he would lose out on a fortune." She shook her head and blinked back tears. "Poor Etienne. I always suspected something. These letters are further proof I was right."

Rebecca was crying unashamedly. All she could think of was her mother's heartbreak, the way she'd made a life alone, how different things could have been, should have been for her. As for herself, she didn't mind that much. She had had a good upbringing in Tennessee, had been happy and learned skills she'd never have known if she'd grown up in New Orleans. Still, she would have had a father, Etienne Dufour. The tragedy of that loss tore through her heart.

When she collected herself and blew her nose on the hanky from her purse, she faced Josie, who was also wiping her eyes. "What can be done, Miss Josie, about Guy Laurens? And why do you think he brought me here, considering the circumstances?"

"Nothing in a court of law, I'm afraid. We don't have the power or prestige to go against a Creole gentleman in this town. And our proof is flimsy, at best. In my opinion, he brought you here to keep an eye on you until he could get you off to Scotland. As long as you were under his control, and no one knew of your relationship to Dufour, he didn't have to worry about any charges or claims you might make."

"Claims? What kind of claims?"

"Why, claims to Etienne's estate. You are, after all, his next of kin."

This thought was entirely new. She considered it momentarily, then said, "I have no intention of making any claims. I consider myself a Gordon, and I wouldn't want to take any chance on smearing my father's good name with scandal."

Josie was visibly moved. "Oh, my dear child, you are one in a million. I must say, though, that your illegitimacy would go against you in court. You'd have to prove your heritage. Laurens would fight you with money and influence gathered over a lifetime in New Orleans."

Rebecca smiled through misty eyes. "Greed is a terrible burden, Josie. Let Guy Laurens have his blood money. I'm just sorry I can't find out if he really did kill my father."

Josie straightened her spine. "One thing you can do is protect yourself, my dear. And, forgive me for saying this, but also protect me."

"From Guy?" Alarm twittered along her spine.

"As I said in the beginning, Laurens doesn't give up easily. He'll be looking for you, I'm sure. If he finds out you're here, he'll come after both of us. And if he is a murderer, he wouldn't hesitate to kill us to keep his fortune."

Rebecca half rose from her chair. "Oh dear, I'd better go. I'm sorry, Miss Josie. I wouldn't have put you in danger for anything. I—"

"I know. And I don't mind the risk if I can help Etienne's daughter. But you'd be safer somewhere else. I think you know where."

After a moment's hesitation, she said just above a whisper, "Blaine Caldwell's."

"It's the only choice. He hates Laurens as much as I do. And he keeps a large staff at Dominique Hall."

Rebecca folded the letters and handed Josie's back to her. "We'll go at once. But I don't want him in danger either."

"Blaine can take care of himself," Josie said with a wry smile. "Laurens knows that, well enough. But I'll put out the word that you're leaving for Scotland as soon as the war's over. It will help if Laurens thinks you won't make trouble for him or claim any of Etienne's money."

"Yes, do that. And it's true enough. Maybe I can do housework for the captain. He must have servants who earn their keep."

"Perhaps you can. Now come along. We'll take you straight to his home. It's quite a mansion. Right on the river."

"Oh, what about my things! My dog! I have to—"

"Not now, dear. You can get whatever you need later, when you're under the protection of the captain."

She could see Josie was eager to be out of the house. As much as she hated the thought of appearing on Blaine Caldwell's doorstep, she saw no other option. She would just have to make the best of things until she could get away from New Orleans.

15

When Josie's carriage arrived at Dominique Hall, Rebecca caught her breath at the sight of the gracious two-story house set among stately oaks and flowering shrubs. The structure took on a pale rosy glow as the late afternoon sun highlighted its buff-colored surface.

The awesome elegance of Blaine's home made her even more nervous over what she was about to do. "You will come in, won't you," she pleaded to Josephine. "I mean I can't just go to the door alone. It's so . . . so magnificent and—"

"It is magnificent. And I've never set foot on the property, nor do I plan to."

"But, Miss Josie—"

"I can't, cherie. I wouldn't think of it. I might be seen by someone, certainly by Blaine's servants. No, dear, it just isn't done. I will wait here until you're admitted, though. Then I know you'll be safe. Go along now. Blaine Caldwell is a gentleman and will be happy to see you."

"All right. I suppose I must. Thank you again, Miss Josie. This has been a very important day in my life."

"You come see me anytime, dear. But be discreet. After all, we both have our reputations to consider." Giving

Rebecca an encouraging smile, she reclined against the cushion and snapped open her fan.

Rebecca ascended the steps and crossed the broad veranda and tapped on the door. Her nerves were at the breaking point before the door opened and a silver-haired man peered out at her. "Yes'm? Oh, you must be the lady with the fresh strawberries. But why's you at the front door?"

She looked back at Josie's carriage, but got no help from that quarter. Taking a deep breath, she said, "No, I'm not bringing strawberries. I'm an acquaintance of Captain Caldwell. I have a problem I must discuss with him—right away, if you please. Is he in?"

"Who is it, George?" came a masculine voice.

"Don' know. A lady, sir, but not with the strawberries."

"Invite her in. We'll see what her problem is."

George bowed her into the foyer of the house and closed the door behind her. As he drifted away, her eyes adjusted to the soft filtered light from the transom and she saw Blaine Caldwell, a glass in his hand, standing at the foot of a sweeping staircase.

"Rebecca," he said with genuine surprise. Striding forward, he took her hand and raised it to his lips. "You are a remarkable young lady. If my memory is correct, you gave me a firm and final farewell less than an hour ago. Are you all right? I apologize for my continued state of dilapidation, but I haven't had time to change."

She interpreted his comments to imply she was rushing in pursuit of him. She saw no humor in it at all. "I'm fine," she said, cocking her head and avoiding his eyes. "Miss Josephine insisted I come, but she wouldn't accompany me inside. I really don't wish to be here, but I had no other choice."

"Not a particularly flattering greeting. Still, you're here and I consider that my good fortune. Let me get you a glass of wine. You look a bit . . . out of sorts." Slipping an arm through hers, he guided her into the spacious living room.

"You mustn't get the wrong idea, Captain. It was . . . it is . . . well, sort of an emergency. I'll leave if you'd rather—"

"Hell, Rebecca," he said lightly, "I invited you, didn't I? You said no, and now you've changed your mind."

"It's more than that. I've learned something. And I can't stay at Miss Josie's. It isn't safe."

"Why not?" A dark look crossed his eyes.

"I'd rather not say just now, but I'm afraid of Mr. Laurens. So is Miss Josephine. She thought it would be safer for both of us if I had . . . had your protection." She dropped her eyes and stared at the carpet. This was so humiliating—to stand in the home of a stranger and practically plead for assistance.

After what seemed an eternity, he cupped his hand under her chin and raised her eyes to his. His rough clothing, his shirt gaping open and his face with traces of dirt, made a strangely intriguing contrast to the opulence surrounding him. "Josie is a wise woman," he said huskily. "If she sent you here like this, she had good reason. Relax, Rebecca, and don't be so all-fired independent. Let others help you a bit. It's our pleasure—*my* pleasure, especially."

His kind tone was almost her undoing. She clamped her lips to halt any sign of weakness.

He stepped away and poured brandy from a crystal decanter into a small goblet. "Here. This is more strengthening than wine. Sip on it while I freshen up," he said gently. "Or you can explore the gardens if you like. I'm sorry I can't offer tea or dinner. My staff is away at the games and has the afternoon free in town. George has just drawn my bath and now he's gone as well. Consider my house yours, Rebecca. We'll talk whenever you feel like it."

She accepted the drink and gazed around. The difference in the decor of Blaine's home and Josie's pleasure palace was remarkable. Rather than the elaborate rococo of French Empire, his mansion was rich with polished wood floors, French country furnishings, and textured fabrics in sunset shades of cerulean blue and burnt rose.

Blaine crossed the room and drew open the brocade drapes. Sunlight flooded the area through the expansive floor-to-ceiling windows. Persian rugs graced the floor here, and cushioned chairs and a plush sofa invited comfort rather than the stiff formality of Josie's lavish parlor.

Above the gleaming white marble mantel, a portrait of an exquisite young woman dressed in the fashion of two decades past, dominated the room. One look told Rebecca that this was Blaine's mother.

"What a beautiful portrait," she said, quite spellbound by the compelling green eyes, so like Blaine's. Already the brandy was helping her to feel more relaxed.

Standing close beside her, he gazed at the picture. "Thank you. She passed away ten years ago. Both she and my father died in the yellow fever epidemic that swept through New Orleans."

"Oh, how awful."

"I had just returned from my first voyage to the Indies when I found them dying. Friends told me it was a blessing they went together—they were completely devoted. It was very difficult for me, however."

She looked up at him. "You greatly resemble your mother. She was Creole?"

"She was. My father was English to the core—red-headed, burly, smart and industrious, but not entirely refined. He worshipped her from the day he laid eyes on her. Some say he married her for her fortune, but her family cut her off completely for years—until it was plain my father had amassed wealth far exceeding theirs." He turned to her. "I'm only telling you this so you'll understand the circumstances here in New Orleans. It's still quite European. The Creoles tend to move in their own circle, like members of the nobility abroad."

Here in the late afternoon sun, she could see golden flecks in his eyes, eyes that for the moment were gentle, soft in their remembrance. She said, "I only recently learned of my own Creole blood. I haven't been quite sure what it means."

"Take pride in it—but don't let it rule you, Rebecca. The Creoles of New Orleans are descendants of the first French and Spanish settlers of the area. They hold the key to acceptance in the society of the town. Everyone else is an outsider, regardless of wealth or accomplishment."

"Even the Americans?"

"Especially the Americans."

"So that's why the Lafittes are more popular than Governor Claibourne—despite their questionable activities."

"That, plus Jean's personal charm and considerable courage."

"Captain . . ."

"Please call me Blaine. We've been friends for a good while, you know."

"Very well—Blaine. It's very kind of you to help me," she said softly. "I do want to explain why I'm here."

"But first, I want to clean up. You're welcome to explore the garden, if you like. It's prime this time of year."

As soon as he had gone upstairs, she gave the lovely room and adjoining dining room a closer inspection. She marveled at the books in several languages that filled shelves reaching to the high ceiling. Porcelain lamps sat on mahogany tables and lavish bouquets of roses and lilacs occupied an enormous china bowl in the center of the dining table. Flanking the table were armchairs for sixteen guests. A magnificent etagere held a set of dishes of ornate oriental design along with long-stemmed crystal goblets with prisms reflecting the sun's slanted rays from the windows.

Never had she imagined people lived like this. Almost reverently, she strolled through the rooms, then went outside to explore the grounds and gardens. A light breeze off the river brought moist fragrance to mingle with the scent of camellias, roses and oleander, lilacs and trumpet vines in full bloom.

"Heaven." She sighed. This was what Heaven must be like. The French settlers had made a beautiful place for themselves in Louisiana.

She agreed with Blaine that she should take pride in her Creole blood, but she was also deeply proud of the strong, pragmatic Scottish heritage of her mother. She knew she would need every ounce of strength she possessed to help her through the coming days. She had been shocked today to learn the depth of human evil, evil that had destroyed her mother's chance for happiness and damaged hers as well. She knew Blaine was trying to be helpful when he advised her to be less independent, but she couldn't take that advice. How easy, how tempting it was to rely on his strength and money and power. But she was not going to do it. She mustn't be obligated to him. He would expect something in return. She might give him her body, and if she did, she would surely give him her heart. But he wouldn't ask for her hand in marriage, and she would be left without a trace of her pride and dignity when he sent her away. Her mother had experienced that terrible pain. It was gratifying to think that Etienne Dufour had wanted to marry her mother, but then Elizabeth Gordon had had an honorable birth.

The frightening part was that when she was with Blaine, she fell under his spell. And now she would be living under his roof, for a time anyway. Yes, as soon as he returned, she would make her position perfectly clear.

Deep in thought, she strolled past a grove of acacias and came upon a delightful little pavilion created from whitewashed latticework supporting a delicate peaked roof topped by a weather vane in the shape of a peacock. The trellis served as a support for honeysuckle vines intertwined with climbing roses; the entire structure was engulfed by lush vegetation and sweet-smelling blossoms. The floor was strewn with a thick mat of fallen leaves and flower petals; a stone bench occupied one corner. Entering the secluded bower, she breathed deeply, sipped her brandy, then closed her eyes and luxuriated in the perfumed atmosphere.

Upstairs, Blaine was toweling off and having serious thoughts of his own. How adorable Rebecca had looked in her calico frock standing in his living room beneath his mother's picture. He'd told himself over and over he should forget her and get on with the serious business of war, but she was never far from his mind. Today when he'd seen that bastard Laurens manhandling her, he thought he'd surely kill him on the spot. Luckily the man was as much a coward as he was a fool and had left the scene promptly. No, it was more Laurens's style to do his dirty work slyly or against helpless women.

He buttoned a fresh shirt and put on white linen slacks. It was poor manners to leave a guest alone and unattended, but he'd had enough of the dirt of the playing field. He flinched as the cotton shirt chafed the wounds on his back. "Dammit," he cursed, and reached for his boots. He'd never forget how he had felt when Rebecca betrayed him to Laurens. That pain had been worse than the whipping which he had deserved and expected. Of course, he had tricked her into a set of circumstances which she didn't fully understand. And she had seemed truly sorry when he'd been caught and punished.

But today had been the hardest of all—letting her go at Josie's. She was so obviously confused and vulnerable, and so damned full of spirit and pride. He might have found a way to keep her by frightening her, or using bribery or even outright seduction. But he remembered once telling a woman who was doing everything to snare him, that a butterfly that lit on one's shoulder was far preferable to one trapped in a cage. He'd followed his own advice, and now the butterfly had indeed fluttered to his shoulder.

He found her in the gazebo and stopped briefly to admire her unassuming beauty. "A sight to stop a man's heart," he said at last.

She smiled a greeting. "I can't believe it's real," she said in an awed whisper. "The air smells so sweet. The only sounds are the birds and the wind in the branches, and once in a while, a boat whistle from the river. How can you leave here to go to sea?"

"A man in a free country must work for a living. My father was penniless when he arrived from Virginia. He worked hard to build up a fleet that delivered goods to far corners of the world." He refilled her glass from the decanter he had brought with him. "Sit here, if you like. It's cooler than in the house at this hour."

She relaxed on the bench. "I'll tell you the whole story now."

"All right," he said, leaning against a post.

For the next few minutes she described in detail her visit to Josie's, how they'd compared the letters, and the conclusion they had reached. She ended the telling with a firm declaration. "So I need employment, Blaine. And a safe place to live until I can leave for Scotland. If you can suggest something, I'd be much obliged."

Looking at her delicate upturned face, he felt his heart turn over beneath his ribs. "As I said before, Dominique Hall is your home, for as long as you like."

"Only if we can make arrangements for my employment, wages and a room of my own."

The proud little bird, he thought. She was in a strange land, her very life was threatened by a powerful man, and she still expected to make her own rules and fend for herself. He'd lost count of the number of women who had hinted or come right out and asked to be installed, one way or the other, at Dominique Hall. And this little chit of a country girl was making it plain she would not move into his bedroom.

Placing his foot on the bench beside her, he rested his arm on his knee. "Now, Miss Rebecca Gordon, I've had the impression from the first that you didn't quite like me. Why don't you just tell me the truth straight out and be done with it."

"I never . . . no, I won't lie. I did dislike you—or tried to after I overheard a conversation in the woods near Payton, Tennessee."

His eyebrows lifted. "Payton? You were there?"

"Yes. And I heard you talking to a man about being very secretive over your friendship with Jean Lafitte. You . . . implied you were a spy. I assumed, naturally, you were spying for the British."

"Mon Dieu." So that was it. Shaking his head, he moved to sit beside her. "But now you understand my friendship with Jean and his brother. And I assure you Jean won't betray the American cause—despite his mistreatment by Claibourne. I . . . ah . . . can't say I'm above spying. But of course, I'm loyal to the United States."

"Even after the governor had you flogged?"

"It was a fair penalty for my crime. After all, I did aid in the escape of his most valued prisoner."

"I . . . I was afraid he would hang you."

"When did your fear develop—before or after you let Laurens in on our plans?"

"But I didn't know your plans. I mean, it just appeared that you and Lafitte were plotting against the governor—and he does represent the American government. Since I suspected you were a British spy, I thought you had tricked me into some wicked plot against my country. Why, I was just too upset to consider the consequences."

"Um, yes, I can see how that could happen. You do have a short fuse on that temper of yours."

"You must believe me when I say I didn't intend for you to hang."

"Good of you," he quipped. "But Claibourne wouldn't dare hang me. We've known each other for years and have come to terms with our differences. He's pompous and straight-laced, and right now, he's madder than hell, but he knows I'm a patriot and of considerable use in the war effort."

She looked down into the goblet clasped in her hands. "But you did suffer terribly and the fine was enormous. That's why . . . why I want to apologize again."

He waited for her to continue.

She looked up when he didn't speak. "Well, do you accept my apology? I have nothing else to offer just now."

"On the contrary, I think you do. First I must insist on your pledge."

"Pledge?"

"You're not to return to Guy Laurens. If you go back to him, I may have to challenge him—and he's a hell of a good swordsman. You could yet be the death of me."

"I won't go back, except to get my dog."

"Good. There's one other requirement."

"Oh?"

"You suggested I use some herbal medicine on my back. Since you claim to have healing skills, I've brought some salve which I'd like you to apply. You can hardly refuse, since you were instrumental in placing me under the whip." He pulled a container from his shirt pocket.

"Oh, yes, I'd be happy to do that." She took the vial, uncorked it and sniffed the contents. "Aloe vera—rose water—herbs. It will burn, but it will hasten the healing."

He put aside their glasses and unbuttoned his shirt, then pulled it off and laid it aside. Turning away from her, he straddled the bench.

She poured the herbal liquid onto her fingers and began to spread it slowly over the cuts.

He flinched, then settled under her touch. It did burn, but her moist, cool fingers on his flesh soon soothed the pain; her closeness, the tenderness he felt made him forget the discomfort.

She said softly, "This should speed your recovery. Leave your shirt off till the medicine is absorbed. I . . . I'm afraid you'll have some scars. I see an old wound too."

"Put there four years ago by the shot of a British commander."

"Oh." She ran her palm over his shoulder.

Shifting around to face her, he said, "There are other kinds of wounds—some invisible." He saw extraordinary tenderness in her eyes. "I thought last week you had betrayed the American cause and betrayed me, as well," he said. "I figured you had thrown in with Laurens. I was surprised how much that hurt."

"Blaine . . . I would never . . . surely you must know I . . ."

His arms went around her; he held her close. "If it ever should happen—your betrayal, I mean—I would rather endure a thousand floggings." He brushed her parted lips with his. "You see, little Rebecca, I'm falling in love with you."

She started to rise, but he slipped his arms around her slender waist and forced her to remain. His desire was building as he pressed her to him. While touching his lips to her earlobe, he untied the ribbon of her straw bonnet and let it fall to the leafy floor beside the bench.

"Blaine . . . you can't love me. I'm . . . I'm not . . ."

He silenced her protests by covering her lips with a fierce kiss. When it ended, he spoke gently. "Look at me, cherie. I know what you are—a young woman of spirit with her feet planted firmly on the ground—yet a lady with the rare combination of intelligence and beauty and a great deal of courage." He lifted her palm to his lips, then feather-kissed her wrist.

Her hand lingered on his bare shoulder.

"I've never known a woman like you, Rebecca," he said softly. "There's a bond between us—don't deny it—whether it's our Creole blood or two souls that fate has drawn into a honeyed web. We're inescapably intertwined. I feel it. And I believe you do too."

He pulled her against his chest and kissed her forcefully, molding her to him while his fingers meshed through her hair.

She met his kiss with passion, opening her lips, accepting his teasing, exploring penetration of his tongue until there was no reality but the feel of him, his chest against her breast, the feel of his moist lips, accepting, warm and sweet, lingering. After the kiss, he moved from the bench and dropped to one knee beside her. He drew her across him and cradled her in his arms. "Ma petite cherie . . . my darling girl," he whispered, "you were created from starlight and wild flowers—born to be loved. Let me be the one. . . ." His voice trailed as he leaned near her captured breasts and flicked his tongue across the straining softness above the low-cut neckline.

A sudden breeze sent leaves swirling as the vanishing blue of twilight gave way to shadows. Petals drifted downward in a silvery, sweetly scented shower. From a distance came the low rumble of thunder.

She moved in his arms. "Blaine . . . no, please." Her voice could barely be heard, but something in its pleading softness caused him to pause, to think, and the thinking brought him to a halt.

Standing, he lifted her into his arms. "It may rain," he said huskily. "We'd better go in. I'll show you to your room where you can rest until the servants return and fix a cold supper."

For a moment, she seemed startled, as if she were awakening from a dream. Then she brushed back her hair and said, "Yes, I am tired, but I can walk just fine. Please put me down."

He did as she requested and retrieved his shirt, but kept his hand under her elbow and guided her toward the back of the house. It was sprinkling by the time they entered the kitchen. He showed her a small, charmingly furnished room adjoining it. "Will this do?" he asked, annoyed at the way his voice sounded distant and aloof. That was not at all how he felt inside. She was looking at him with pain mixed with pride. Didn't she know, he had just paid her a very great compliment? He had wanted her badly, but he'd made the sacrifice for both of them. He was certain he could have taken her there in the gazebo, been her first lover and made it wonderful for her. Had she been more sophisticated, more experienced, he might have enjoyed her body and worried about the consequences later. But Rebecca was so innocent and trusting. He hadn't lied when he'd said he loved her. He had never had such feelings for any woman. But was love enough? Their backgrounds were worlds apart. And he had no time to consider marriage, not with the English closing in on the mouth of the Mississippi. He expected to be called to help at any moment. As he watched her, he saw her struggle to regain control. He figured he was in for a barb or two before he left the room.

Sure enough, she gave him a haughty look and said, "Your moods change swiftly, Captain. At least you saved me from battling your . . . your advances once again."

"I could see your temper about to flare," he said. "I know when to beat a hasty retreat."

She glanced around. "This will do nicely. Do I have any duties this evening?"

He fought back a smile. "No. You have the evening free. I'm going into town. Tomorrow we'll discuss your employment and your wages."

"Yes, my wages. That's very important."

"Naturally. Just introduce yourself to George and Marie when you hear them in the kitchen. You'll find them a delightful couple. Au revoir, Rebecca. Welcome to Dominique Hall."

She was standing in the middle of the room, her lips set, her eyes flashing determination. He started to leave. For now, this was the best he could do for her. When he reached his favorite salon in the Vieux Carré, he'd find a way to track Guy Laurens. He didn't doubt the man murdered Etienne Dufour after being unable to dissuade him from searching for Elizabeth Gordon. When the war was over, he'd see if the case could be reopened.

Blaine's thoughts were interrupted by the sound of his name.

"Mr. Blaine . . . Mr. Blaine, sir!" George came running.

"George! I didn't know you were back. What's wrong?"

The servant related his news and Blaine turned back to speak to Rebecca. "I must leave at once," he said solemnly.

"Well, you just said—"

"No, I mean I'm leaving the city. I've just received word that Lafitte has had a terrible tragedy at Barataria."

"What happened?"

"His compound on Grande Isle has been leveled by

cannon fire. Several of his men have been killed and many taken prisoner. I'm going to offer whatever assistance I can."

"Then the English have attacked?"

"No, though that wouldn't have surprised me."

"Then who . . . ?"

"Claibourne. While Lafitte was in New Orleans warning the Americans of the British approach, the Yankees were attacking Grande Isle and destroying his home. I'd like to get my hands on our high-and-mighty governor right now. If he has no sense of honor, at least he should realize we need Lafitte's support in the coming battle."

"Oh, it's awful," she said, trailing him into the hall.

He opened a drawer in a table and removed a pistol. Checking the chamber, he said, "I'll be back as soon as possible. By tomorrow, I expect."

"Blaine, I'm going to the town house in the morning. I need to pack some things and get Pepper."

"Um. Very well. But for God's sake, be careful. Ask George to arrange for my carriage to take you there." Reaching again into the drawer, he removed a pistol not much larger than his palm and handed it to her. "'Tis a far cry from your famous long-rifle, but I'm sure you can use it if you must."

She slid it into her skirt pocket.

He looked down at her. "Get some rest now. And I repeat, please be careful when you go out. You understand the danger?"

"Yes. I do understand."

"Good. George has ordered my horse." While speaking, he had tucked in his shirttail and pulled on a jacket. "Good-bye again, Rebecca. Oh, one more thing." In a sudden movement, he crushed her to him and kissed her hard on the mouth. "I do love you, little Miss Rebecca Gordon. Don't forget that while I'm gone." Then he strode across the entry and out the front door.

16

Rebecca forced herself upward from a deep and dreamless sleep. She felt fuzzy and disoriented. Where was she? Rolling over on the tangled sheets, she peeped from beneath heavy eyelids.

She jerked awake as awareness swept over her. Dominique Hall. She was at Blaine's mansion. It all came flooding back. She remembered tossing and turning half the night, unable to relax after the emotionally charged events of yesterday. Sometime near dawn, just after she'd heard the first sleepy bird song and footsteps in the adjoining kitchen, she had fallen off to sleep. What time was it now? Drapes over the windows kept the room dark as midnight.

Quickly she left the bed and drew the drapes. When she pushed open the shutters, she was washed with sunlight and the sweet scent of flowers from the window box and moist fresh air from the river. The birds were singing their hearts out, and from the chicken house, she heard the amorous crows of a rooster. Her little room overlooked the rear of the property, a parklike expanse of grass dotted with ancient live oaks bordered by rose and azalea bushes. The stables and barns and servants' quarters were out of sight to her right. She couldn't see the gazebo, but she knew exactly where it was. The memory of how Blaine had held her, kissed her so intimately, and told her he loved her sent a tingling warmth throughout her being.

Smiling to herself she turned back into the room to freshen up and pull on her dress. She had slept in her chamise and petticoat, and knew that today she must arrange to get a change of clothing.

She washed her face with tepid water from the lavabo and tidied her hair with the ivory comb she found on the dresser. She felt wonderful today, so optimistic about everything, especially Blaine Caldwell. How could she not be happy when he'd actually declared his love and kissed her with such fierce emotion? She wouldn't worry about the dangers involved, the chance of future heartbreak, the broken dreams of her mother—at least, not on this gorgeous Indian summer day. First, she would have a cup of coffee; the delicious aroma was wafting from the kitchen. Then she'd go to the town house, pack a few personal belongings, and bring Pepper back here to Dominique Hall. She wondered what Guy Laurens would think when his trained pigeon flew from its gilded cage.

Also she'd discuss chores with Blaine's housekeeper, Marie. Perhaps she could mulch the flower beds, or dust some of those lovely things in the dining room, or even help with the cooking. The important thing was to show Blaine Caldwell that she intended to make herself useful and earn her wages. She would not be a kept woman. She was not moving into his house to become his mistress. Just because he had said he loved her didn't mean it was safe to love him back—though she knew she was dangerously close to doing so.

When she entered the kitchen, she found it deserted. She hurriedly gulped the coffee, munched a pecan roll that apparently had been left for her, then let herself out and walked briskly down the river road toward town. It was only a mile or so and she didn't need a carriage on such a lovely day. She would take a shortcut through the Vieux Carré.

Deep in thought, she was only vaguely aware she had passed into the edge of town. The streets were cobbled now and lined with shabby shops and rows of weathered warehouses.

The air was tinged with the smell of fish and rotting

garbage. Narrow alleyways were shadowed and gutters running with filthy water.

Suddenly alert, she stopped to study her surroundings. Had she taken a wrong turn? Standing quietly, she caught the sound of church bells tolling the second Mass of the day. The cathedral wasn't too far away. Royal Street must be a few blocks to her left.

She walked through an alley which seemed a shortcut to the center of town. Glancing over her shoulder, she slipped her hand in her pocket and took comfort in the feel of the derringer. Could this area be the infamous "Swamps" Mrs. Thatcher had warned her to avoid?

She quickened her steps. Her heart jumped when a huge rat scampered across the stones just beyond her slippers. Calm yourself, she chided. After all, it was daylight and she was armed.

Suddenly, shadowed figures emerged from a doorway and surrounded her. An arm went around her waist, hands clutched her ankles and others tried to pin her arms. A fist struck her jaw and she fell to her knees. None of the attackers were large—but there were so many. It was as if she had been put upon by a band of dwarfs—or children.

She screamed, but a small sweaty hand covered her mouth. She fought to free her arms.

She was more angry than frightened now. She jerked one arm free and pounded the nearest face with her fist. Then she followed that blow with several others and seemed to catch the rascals by surprise. She was no fragile town lady, after all. She kicked furiously at the nearest form, then clenched her hands and swung them like a mallet at another face looming near.

"Aggh. She's a devil!" came the cry.

"Get her purse—just get it outn' her pocket."

"Cain't, you fool—with her kicking like a mule."

"Come on, Buck, get her down, cain't you?" The voice was a childlike squawk.

The tallest boy ordered, "Oughta slice the bitch's throat. Bet she's a whore anyhow."

At that point, she drew the pistol and aimed it at the filthy urchin's head.

"Ayee!" screamed the boy draped across her ankles.

"She's got a gun!" The ragged tyke leaped up and dashed along the nearest alley, closely followed by four others—all but the largest boy.

He hesitated, cursing under his breath. Then, he too backed away and ran after the others.

Rebecca raised the gun and fired at the sky between the buildings. To her amazement, one of the children fell and was quickly abandoned by his fellow culprits.

"Oh, dear Heaven," she choked. "Surely I didn't hit him." She reached the ragamuffin just as he rose to squat on his haunches and inspect his scraped and bloody palms. When she looked closely at the dirty face, she realized it was a girl about the age of eight. The child's amber eyes were red-rimmed with unshed tears.

"Shandy!" cried Rebecca, grasping the slight shoulders.

The child's eyes widened. Tears slipped out and streaked down the smeared cheeks. "Mrs. Caldwell?" came the small, raspy voice. "Well, hellfire and glory—is it you?"

"Shannon Kildaire, I might have known. You're lucky I didn't shoot you. You're *not* shot, are you?"

"No, ma'am." The girl stood and brushed at her ragged pants. "I . . . I'm surely sorry it was you. My friends and me . . . well, we just wanted to cut a purse to get some sticky buns at the market."

"So you broke your promise to me, after all. You promised to stay out of trouble."

"No, ma'am. I promised not to cause *you* any trouble." She lowered her eyes and swiped at her tears. "Didn't know 'twas you. Surely I didn't."

"All the same, you are in trouble and likely to be in more if you don't mend your ways."

Shandy shuffled her worn sandals against a pebble.

Heaving a sigh, Rebecca replaced the pistol in her pocket and pulled out a handkerchief. Lifting the child's chin, she did her best to wipe away tears and dirt. "If I take you with me, and buy you a sticky bun, will you swear not to join that gang of trashy goblins ever again?"

The golden eyes gazed up at her with a look of skepticism and uncertainty. "Oh—maybe. But I'm not going to no orphanage."

"Orphanage? Oh, I see. Then you were in an orphanage back in Memphis."

The lips clamped tight.

"Never mind. You don't have to tell. Come along and we'll do some thinking about your future."

For a time, they walked in silence. Then Rebecca said, "Shandy, do you remember Captain Caldwell from the ship?"

"Yes'm. Your husband."

"Ah . . . Shandy, I'm not really Mrs. Caldwell. My name is Rebecca Gordon. It was sort of a trick on the ship's captain so I could keep Pepper in my cabin. Anyway, Captain Caldwell has a fine house just up the river. It's a big brown mansion with stables at the back. Now, it just might be that the captain needs some extra help in the kitchen or dusting or something like that. I'm not promising, but if you cleaned yourself up and did some honest work, you might get paid enough to buy all the sticky buns you can eat."

"Would you be there?"

"Oh . . . maybe. I'll be looking for work real soon too."

"Where're we goin' now?"

"To a house on Royal Street to get Pepper and a few other things. I'm sure you remember Pepper, don't you?"

"Oh, yes, ma'am," was the exuberant response. "I sure liked that puppy."

"Pepper's grown quite a lot. But I bet he remembers you. Look, there's Royal right there. We'll get Pepper and my things and go to the market afterward. We'll have some coffee and a bite to eat."

"That'd be nice, Miss Gordon. I'll surely be glad to see that pup . . . and . . . I'm glad you're not hurt . . . and I'm not shot."

Rebecca and Shandy arrived at Guy's Royal Street town house shortly after noon.

"Wait here, Shandy," Rebecca ordered. "I'll be as quick as I can. If a man arrives in a carriage, run as fast as you can to Captain Caldwell's house. It's the biggest house on the river road. Don't let anyone stop you from finding the captain and asking him to come. If he isn't there, wait for him and bring him here right away. Now don't worry, I don't expect Mr. Laurens to show up today. He's plenty mad at me and thinks I've run away. But, just in case . . ."

"I won't worry. But if I see a man go in there, I'll run like a buck. I'm plenty fast, you know."

Rebecca let herself in the front door and stealthily climbed the stairs. She was surprised to find her shuttered room in complete disarray—the bed stripped, the dresser drawers pulled out and emptied of their jewelry and ribbons, the wardrobe holding nothing but her simplest nightgown and robe. Everything was gone: the dresses, the shoes, the bonnets. At least she could take a few undergarments that had been left behind. In a way, it was a relief to know Mr. Laurens had already tossed her out of his life. She hoped the man would forget all about Elizabeth Gordon and her daughter.

A glance out the window revealed that Pepper was asleep in his spot in the garden. At the far end, picking the last of summer's roses, was Pearl. This would be a good time to slip into the kitchen and find a rope for Pepper and a sack to hold her belongings.

She was carrying a petticoat, several pairs of stockings and a chemise when she went downstairs to the kitchen and opened the pantry. She'd never been here before and was surprised by the large size of it and the many shelves holding silver and crystal as well as food supplies. She didn't see a rope and decided it probably wasn't needed since Pepper would follow beside her. But she did see an empty flour sack and began putting her garments inside.

The suddenness with which the door slammed shut stunned her.

She gasped as she was abruptly plunged into darkness. She heard a bolt slide into place on the outside of the door.

"No!" she cried. "Who's there? Let me out!" Dropping the bag, she pounded on the door. "Let me go—please!" She felt rising hysteria as she realized she was trapped.

"I knew you were trash," came a woman's voice.

"Pearl! Pearl, open the door. I'm leaving. I'm never coming back. Just let me out!"

"You're white trash and a thief besides. Master Laurens

came yesterday and emptied your room. Now here you are in the silver pantry filling up a sack. I'm going to fetch the master right now."

"Oh no, you're wrong, Pearl. I wasn't taking anything but my own undergarments. I was looking for a sack to carry them in, that's all. Open the door and I'll show you. I'm leaving for good." Her voice was shrill and desperate.

"You can tell that to Master Laurens. I'm going to get him right now." Pearl's footsteps on the brick floors faded as she hurried away.

Rebecca leaned her forehead against the door and fought to control her panic. She was sure there was no way to break out. How long did she have before Pearl brought Guy? It could be thirty minutes or an hour, depending on how quickly Pearl walked across town and if she found Guy at home.

Furious with herself for not obeying Blaine and coming here in the company of George, she moved back from the door and tried to think. What would Guy do with her? Could she convince him she wasn't stealing, but had just come for Pepper? She could promise to leave and never return, but would he believe her? Would he demand to know where she'd spent the night? What would he do if she told him what she knew about his forging the letters? Tarnation, he might just kill her—as he had killed her father!

She was perspiring despite the coolness. How could she defend herself? She did have the gun. Oh, but she had fired at Shandy's gang. Now the derringer was empty!

Of course, Guy wouldn't know that. She opened the purse and took out the small pistol.

A scratching on the door caused her to jump and drop the gun to the floor. "Oh drat!" She cried as she dropped to her hands and knees to look for the weapon. The scratching continued, and then a yelp.

"Pepper!" she called. "Pepper, it's me. I'm right in here."

Pepper whined and scratched furiously on the outside of the door.

Rebecca chewed her lower lip to keep from crying. This was no time for tears. "Pepper—stay," she commanded. "Stay—right there."

The dog's whining stopped. After a moment, she heard

him bump the door as he curled into a resting position just outside. It was a comfort to have him there, but could he be of any help to her? He was so gentle that she doubted if he'd even hurt a flea. Pearl had fed him and been friendly to him, so he wouldn't feel threatened by her. And more than once, she had encouraged him to make friends with Guy, though the man had no interest in the dog whatever.

She needed the gun. On hands and knees, she moved along the rough floor, feeling everywhere for the small pistol. A bit of light filtered in above the door frame, but the lower half of the pantry was lost in darkness.

Candles. She'd seen a stack of candles and some matches on a shelf at the back. Rising, she felt along the shelf and, sure enough, put her hands right on them. In a moment, she held a lighted taper and located the gun just beyond the hem of her skirt.

She put the weapon securely into her pocket and took a deep breath. There was nothing to do now but wait.

Gazing around her, she again noticed shelves laden with silver, china and crystal. An ornate silver service, much like the one she'd seen at Blaine's, glinted in the flickering light. She touched the coffeepot with one finger, then took a closer look. The letters *E.D.* were engraved on its polished rounded side.

Of course. Etienne Dufour. This had been her father's silver. A close inspection showed that the teapot and the magnificent serving tray carried the same initials. She held up the candle to light the upper shelves which held silver goblets and a large collection of bone china dishes. An elegant *D* was visible on every single piece. All of this must have been Etienne Dufour's. Naturally Guy Laurens had stored it away. It would be useless to him since it carried the initials of a family besides his own. And even Guy might have been squeamish over serving dinner on the china of a man he'd had murdered—or maybe killed himself.

Sweat trickled down her spine and she moved back near the door. "Pepper, are you there?" she called shakily.

The dog whimpered and thumped his tail in frustration.

"That's a good boy. Stay, Pepper," she ordered again. At least he might bark a warning if anyone approached.

She thought of Shandy waiting outside. Had the child

seen Pearl leave? She must be confused by now and wondering what to do. How long had it been? At least half an hour, she speculated.

After what seemed an eternity, she heard a commotion. Someone was coming. Pepper began to bark—more of a friendly alert than an angry warning.

"Good boy," came Pearl's voice.

"Yes, good boy," came the voice of Guy Laurens.

Rebecca moved away from the door toward the back of the closet. Holding up the candle, she tried to calm her runaway pulse and keep her mind alert.

The bolt grated; the door was pulled open.

"Rebecca," Guy said in a drunken tone. Without turning away from her he said, "Pearl, leave the house. I'll take care of this. In fact, don't return until tonight."

At the same moment, Pepper bounded into the pantry and tried to plant his forepaws on Rebecca's shoulders.

Taking hold of his collar, she forced him to stand at her side.

Guy entered the closet. He was unsteady on his feet and reeking of liquor. "Caught you, didn't I, my little whore."

"Your foolish maid locked me in here," she snapped, her voice firm and indignant. "I merely came looking for a sack to hold some of my personal belongings."

"Along with as much silver as you could carry, I'll warrant."

"That's not true. Look at this little flour sack. Only my intimate garments are inside."

He inched closer, but paid no attention to the sack on the floor.

Pepper growled low in his throat.

She thought about the gun in her pocket. If she let Pepper go, she could grab it. But the dog standing near offered some protection. She couldn't drop the candle for then Guy wouldn't see the gun and it would be useless.

"You never appreciated me, Rebecca."

"What . . . what are you talking about?"

"I treated you like a lady, gave you polish and manners and improved your ignorant backcountry diction. I've been patient, girl. I waited for you to care about me—to express your appreciation properly."

The pure gall of the man turned her fear into disgust. "Properly?" she asked hotly. "Was it proper for you to bring me to New Orleans to further your own purposes? Was it proper for you to send me to Miss Josie's, then *elevate* my position by making me your private possession? It would be understandable if I had been willing. But you knew I had no notion of what was going on. You intended to keep me under your thumb until you could . . . get rid of me."

"Get rid of you? Not necessarily, my dear. If you had cooperated, I would have taken care of you, given you some nice baubles. You're a pretty thing, you know. Prettier than my wife."

Dear lord, now the man was lusting after her. She could see it in his eyes. She'd have to take a chance and let Pepper loose; she must retrieve the gun. When she let go of the collar, Pepper stayed in place. At once, she drew the pistol from her pocket and aimed it at Guy's heart.

He swayed and ogled the weapon.

"Let me pass, Mr. Laurens. If I owe you for my keep, send me a bill and I'll pay every cent of it."

Guy scoured her with eyes like narrow slits. "Don't deny you slept with Caldwell—that bastard turncoat who'll likely get himself hanged before the year is out."

"That's none of your concern—not anymore. Step aside and let me out of here. You're drunk and I never want to see you again." She raised the gun toward him.

"Here now, Rebecca, don't be hasty. Mon Dieu, I wouldn't hurt you. I was your father's best friend . . . your friend too." His words were thick, his eyes glazed with liquor and lust.

"Tarnation, Mr. Laurens, I could have picked a better friend from a pigsty."

"Now, girl, you're just upset. Put down the gun and we'll have a little talk. I've never really hurt you, have I?"

She hesitated. He was right about that, she supposed. "I won't shoot you if you let me pass. I just want to take my dog and get out of this place—out of your life. I won't make any trouble for you. You have my word."

His eyes glittered. "Trouble? How could you make trouble for me?"

She kept the gun pointed at him as she eased forward. "Never mind. I'm leaving now. Step back from the door."

He took a step back, but eyed her warily. "You think that bastard will have you, but he won't. You'll come crawling back, Rebecca. And maybe it will be too late."

She hardly breathed as she inched toward him. "He doesn't own me. No one does. I'll decide my own fate, if you please. Now back up so Pepper and I can get out."

Like a striking snake, his arm shot forward, landing a blow across her wrist and knocking away the gun.

She heard him crow with glee as he grabbed her and bent her arm behind her back. "I knew you were bluffing, missy. You haven't got killer instincts, after all."

Pepper began barking furiously. He leaped and bounded and ran in circles—but he didn't attack Laurens.

Desperately she fought back, but he was far too strong for her.

He pushed her to the floor clamping her arms beneath her. He smelled rancid as he snarled near her cheek, "You had your chance, Rebecca Gordon. Now I guess I'm going to have to—"

"Kill me?" she screamed. "The way you did my father? Go ahead, but I know—and other people know. You'll never get away with it!"

His grip loosened. "What . . . what's that? What did you say?"

"I said you killed my father. You knew he would marry my mother and you'd lose your chance to control everything, lose your money, your power." She twisted and turned under his grip as she yelled at him.

He slapped her viciously across the mouth, causing tiny lights to dance behind her eyes.

Abruptly his weight lifted. She screamed again. Dizzy and gasping for air, she became aware that he was gone. It was like some force had torn him bodily from her and tossed him aside. As if from a great distance, she heard a commotion, then grunts and the sound of one solid blow after another.

Swallowing another scream, she raised to her elbows. Laurens was sprawled on his back against the kitchen table. His shirt was clutched by a man in a black cape who was throwing hard blows to his head and body. As she watched, the man released Guy's inert body to the floor and turned to face her.

Blaine! The sight of him standing there, his fists knotted in fury, left her numb with relief.

He too seemed beyond words. He drew off his cloak and moved to kneel beside her.

"Blaine," she whispered through trembling lips, "you've . . . killed him."

Brushing back her tumbled hair, he said tightly, "No, though nothing would give me greater pleasure." He moved back over the slumped figure. "Do you hear me, you craven lecher? Do you want satisfaction?" He pulled Laurens up by his bloodied shirt collar. "Say you'll meet me at Cathedral Park. Name your weapon. I'll give you two hours to recover and find a second—if anyone in New Orleans is low enough to take the job."

Laurens's face was swelling and caked with blood. His eyes were glassy as he struggled to stand. "No . . . Jesus Christ—I'll have you arrested. This is my house—my woman who—"

Blaine slapped him hard, spraying sweat and blood about both their heads. "You never owned Rebecca, and if you'd hurt her, I'd see you hanged or kill you myself." He shoved Laurens again across the table. Fighting for control, he took a step backward.

"Leave me alone." Laurens was whimpering now, wiping his hands across his face. "My wife . . . what can I tell her?"

Blaine laughed harshly. "Maybe she'll do the killing for me. I hear she inherited quite a temper from her Spanish mother. So—name the time and weapon."

"No . . . no," Laurens sputtered. "Let me go. I'll leave New Orleans for a time. I'll take my wife to France. I'll . . . I'll tell her we're escaping the war. Yes, that's it. We'll leave at once—slip past the blockade on a Spanish vessel. I don't want a duel." He moved from the table and steadied himself.

Blaine took a deep breath and for the first time gave Rebecca a long look.

Standing now, she shook her head. "Don't fight him," she whispered.

For a long moment, he gazed at her. Some of the fire left his eyes. "Do you want me to let him go?"

The thought of Blaine dueling, risking his life, frightened her more than the ordeal she'd just endured. "If he leaves New Orleans, we won't have to worry. Please, Blaine. I don't want you to fight anymore."

"Then I'll wait. If he leaves, I'll be satisfied. If not, or if I suspect any under-the-table deals, I'll kill him." He looked again at Guy. "Is that understood, Laurens? Can you get through the blockade—with or without your wife?"

Guy was leaning on the table, wiping blood from his nose with his handkerchief. "Yes, yes," he muttered. "I have connections. We can leave within the week."

From inside his coat, Blaine pulled his own pistol. He pressed it against Guy's throat. "No hired assassins. I'll watch every move you make and hound you to the coast. Is that clear?"

Guy seemed to shrivel, but he mumbled, "All this over that . . . that backwoods . . . dammit, I didn't lay a finger on her."

"You're lying. What you had in mind today would be obvious to a half-wit. And I'm no half-wit, Laurens. And neither is she."

Guy coughed blood into his handkerchief. "Just get out, Caldwell. And take her with you. I've got dinner guests at seven and I'll look like hell when they arrive. My wife . . . Sacré bleu . . . I've got to think of something."

"Think of why you're leaving Louisiana. You got that?" Blaine pulled back the hammer on his pistol.

"Yes, yes."

"All right, Laurens." Blaine eased back the pistol. "Make your arrangements and get out of the country within three days or I'm coming after you. You're lucky the lady is so merciful, or I'd fight you regardless of your pitiful pleas. I think you know what the outcome would be."

"Just leave me alone. I'll go to the Indies or France, right away—yes, at once. I have friends there—property. I don't want to live in this godforsaken swampland anyway," he mumbled, and reached for a towel and jug of wash water.

His arm around her waist, Blaine led Rebecca outside as Pepper dashed ahead of them. Once in the street, he turned to her, his brow furrowed with concern. "I should have killed him," he said gruffly.

She stroked an errant strand of hair from his forehead. "No. It's not worth the trouble. And besides, my own stupidity misled him from the start."

"Don't say that, my darling. You have never been stupid—only innocent as a young girl should be."

A child's dirty face peeped from behind Blaine's waiting horse.

"Shandy!" Rebecca cried, moving from Blaine's embrace. She held out her hands. "Shandy, you found him."

Shandy awkwardly received a hug. "Yes'm, it was easy. I ran along the river and there was this big house—jes' like you said. And there was Captain Caldwell getting off his horse at the door." She dimpled proudly. "He remembered me. We got on his horse and came flying. I never had such a ride," she said, grinning.

Blaine patted Shandy's shoulder. "A fearless young lady—and smart too. Why don't you go along to my house and tell the cook I sent you. Tell her I said to give you biscuits and ham and all the cookies you can eat. And then a bath and some clean clothes. And, if you take to horses, maybe you can help Justin, my groom, train the new pony."

Shandy's face glowed with pleasure. "Oh, yes, sir. I betcha I could do just that."

"Thank you, Blaine," murmured Rebecca. "She does need a place to live."

"She's got one. Now you, Rebecca. You need some attention too, I'd say."

Shandy disappeared as Blaine lifted her atop his horse. Then he swung up behind her.

She stiffened in his embrace. "Wait!"

"What for?"

"Pepper!"

He sighed. "Oh, yes, the dog."

The large wirey creature was cavorting in frantic circles around the horse's legs.

"Lord, I almost didn't recognize him. Is that your *puppy?*"

"He has grown a bit," she said sheepishly. "But, Blaine, I can't leave him here."

"All right. He can come with us. I just hope I can afford to feed the two of you."

"I'll take care of him," she said primly.

"Don't worry. Your pup is as welcome as you are."

She turned to smile her appreciation. For the first time she noticed dark circles under his eyes and suspected he'd had no sleep at all last night.

"Is Mr. Lafitte all right?"

"Jean's not hurt, but his compound was leveled. Two men killed."

"I'm sorry. He must hate the Americans now."

"Only Claibourne, the self-righteous bigot," he growled.

"Blaine . . . I'll never forget what you did today."

With one arm firmly around her, he put the horse into an easy gait. "Thank God your little friend found me."

"I . . . I do thank you for offering me a place to live, but . . ." She figured she'd better make her position clear, but she didn't know how to say one thing when she was feeling something so entirely different. Finally, she blurted, "I'm going to stay at Dominique Hall, but—"

"Don't worry." He made it easy for her by reading her thoughts. "I'm no Guy Laurens, you know. You'll have complete freedom while you're under my roof. I'll be away a good deal until this war is finished."

"Then you do understand. I'm glad, but there's one more thing."

"Mon Dieu, what is it?" he said, glancing at Pepper, who loped beside them, his tongue lolling happily from side to side.

"I must consider myself your employee. Honest work for honest wages." She twisted her head to look up at him.

"Oh hell, Rebecca, that again," he said with an indulgent half-smile. "What kind of work did you have in mind?"

"Anything. I'm a fair cook—and I can dust and mop and such. But you must pay me."

He looked down at her with a mixture of amusement and resignation. "You are a wonder, my girl. Very well. Marie can teach you some of her superb Louisiana recipes. But I hope my little housemaid will have occasional free hours. Is that too much to ask?"

"I suppose I can arrange that," she answered lightly, "if the work in such an enormous house doesn't take all my time."

"And what do you expect to do with your earnings, my coquette?"

After a heartbeat she said, "Save them for the voyage to Scotland—if you still intend to take me." She felt his thighs tighten as he put the horse into a canter.

"You still intend to go?" he asked, his voice turning cool.

"I really have no choice," she said, then waited for his response. If he had something else in mind, he didn't offer it. She could tell he was upset, but his silence dashed her hopes for some other suggestion.

"You do recall you offered me passage to the British Isles," she ventured.

"I recall," he said under his breath. "Naturally . . . if that's what you want."

"With my wages, I'm sure I can pay passage on some other ship." She was baiting him and could almost feel his aggravation.

"Why the hell not," he finally snapped.

It wasn't what she wanted him to say. Maybe he really didn't care if she went away. The idea of leaving him cut through to her heart. After he'd said he loved her, she had dared to hope . . . but maybe her mother was right after all. Creole gentlemen wanted blue-blooded wives. Again she turned in the saddle to glance up at him. She saw lines of exhaustion etching his solemn face. A twinge of guilt nipped at her. She had been thoughtless to try to inspire a proposal when he'd been through so much these past hours.

After riding in silence for a short time, he asked, "Oh, by the way, what happened to the pistol I gave you?"

"I used it twice."

"Twice? With only one shot?"

"It's a long story. I'll explain later. Unfortunately, I'm afraid the gun is gone, unless you want to return to Guy's to look for it."

"Not for a pistol—nor for a hundred like it. Besides we have to go to Miss Bonet's."

"Who's Miss Bonet?"

"Sit tight and you'll soon find out, my stubborn little lady." He held her to him and guided the horse into a sharp left turn.

Cradled in his arms with her head resting just below his chin, she felt hope stir to life. He had come to save her, after all, offered to fight a duel on her behalf. Maybe he loved her more than he realized. And maybe he would yet ask her to be his wife. One thing was certain, she could no longer deny her love for him.

17

By the time Rebecca reached Dominique Hall, she was weighted down with packages from Miss Bonet's House of Fashion. Blaine had watched her make her selections while he smoked a cigar and exhibited enormous patience over her indecision. She felt his pleasure like a warm caress when she modeled the two dresses she had finally chosen. They were simple frocks, one a casual at-home dress of Indian twill muslin in buttercup yellow, the other a light wool moss-green day dress with long tapered sleeves suitable for the coming winter months. In addition, she had selected a riding skirt and crisp cotton blouse, a new pair of soft leather boots, necessary nightclothes, a chemise, a petticoat and hosiery. She also ordered two bolts of cloth to be delivered later. These she would sew into additional dresses.

Blaine so obviously enjoyed buying her the clothing that she didn't insult him by offering to pay him back once she began earning her wages. She thought she would surprise him by creating a nice waistcoat from some of the fabric. Despite his fatigue, his spirits were much improved and he made her blush more than once with his glowing compliments.

They were laughing together when they arrived at the mansion, still riding double on Blaine's mount, with the boxes balanced across Rebecca's lap. George appeared on the front porch to carry in the purchases and a bright-eyed Shandy came running along the pathway from the stable, shouting and waving her arms.

Rebecca smiled warmly at Blaine as he lifted her from the saddle. To add to the din, Pepper barked loudly, first at George, then at Shandy, then at just the sheer excitement of it all.

"Come see, Miss Rebecca. Come to the barn!" cried Shandy. "There's a brand-new filly been born—just today! It's standing up already and getting its milk."

To Shandy's surprise and delight, Blaine scooped her into his arms. "Another new filly. That's two this week. You'll have to pick a name for this one, Shandy." Above the child's newly washed and braided hair, he winked at Rebecca.

Her heart turned a somersault. How handsome he was in the bright afternoon sun. His slender hips, molded into buff-colored breeches, his broad shoulders beneath a loose-flowing cotton shirt, his hair darkly curling. He'd discarded his long cloak in deference to the afternoon's unseasonable warmth. He seemed particularly taken with the precocious Shandy and was quite at ease with the child.

He reached out his free hand and she gladly grasped it as they strolled around the curving drive at the side of the house. In moments, Shandy was down and running again with Pepper galloping ahead, then doubling back to give the little girl time to catch up.

What a happy moment, Rebecca thought. It almost felt as if they were a family. She gave Blaine a sidelong glance and caught him looking at her with a tender expression. Was he having the same feelings?

He slipped an arm around her waist and leaned to brush her hair with a quick kiss. It was only a peck, but she felt it surge through her body like lightning in a summer sky.

"I'm glad you're here, Rebecca," he said near her ear. "It's been lonely at Dominique Hall for a very long time."

Smiling up at him, she said, "My mother called me 'Becca' sometimes. You may if you like."

"Becca. Nice. I'd be honored." He tightened his hold as they headed toward the barn.

Pepper had discovered the chicken house and was raising

a racket though he couldn't reach the frantically flapping creatures.

"I do hope Pepper won't be a nuisance," she said above the noise.

"He'll be fine. Should make a good watchdog."

"I doubt it," she said with a shake of her head. "He did nothing to Guy Laurens but blast his ears."

The mention of Laurens interjected a sober note. She was sorry, at once, and looked up to catch Blaine's reaction.

Before she could speak, he covered her lips with his, for a moment gently, then claiming them fiercely, pressing her to him as if with that one kiss he could save her from all the danger, the ugliness, the fear that the world had to offer.

She wrapped her arms around his shoulders, not minding his crushing power, tasting him, absorbing him, thrilling to the way her body molded against his length.

She felt a sudden sharp tug on her skirt.

"Miss Rebecca, you're gonna miss seeing the filly eat its supper."

Releasing Blaine, she felt her cheeks rouge with embarrassment. A kiss like that was hardly proper in front of an innocent child.

Blaine laughed deep in his chest and reached for Shandy's hand. "You're right, little missy. There's a time for everything in life—and this is the time for a newborn's first meal. We wouldn't miss it for anything."

Rebecca trailed the two into the barn, loving the sight of the strapping man and the feisty child skipping beside him. It could be like this forever, she thought. Everyday, through all the years. Little Shandy growing up. And someday she and Blaine would have children of their own. She could taste the joy of it as surely as she'd tasted Blaine's passionate kiss.

After a time in the barn admiring the new little Thoroughbred, she left Blaine and Shandy marveling at the pony and walked back to the house. She wanted to clean up, put on her new yellow dress, and begin helping Marie with dinner. She had promised Blaine something special, especially after he told her he couldn't stay the night but must return to Barataria with supplies of food and blankets for the homeless people of the island. She wanted to serve the two of them in the dining room, a delicious and elegant meal by candlelight using the lovely china she'd seen in the cabinet. She figured it was sort of a special occasion—her first official dinner at Dominique Hall. Of course, if Shandy would join them, that would be fine too.

It would certainly be romantic, she thought. And who could say what such a setting might inspire?

"Ah, there you are, Miss Rebecca," Marie greeted her as she arrived in the kitchen.

"Hello, Marie. I'm sorry I couldn't come sooner, but I had to freshen up a bit." She gave the light-skinned quadroon a warm smile. "Blaine . . . ah . . . Captain Caldwell has suggested I assist you in the kitchen tonight."

Marie's eyes were round with merriment beneath her fringe of inky curls tied with a silk bandanna. "Yes'm. He explained you were his guest too. He say I was to show you whatever 'tis you take to—like cooking and such. I have some mighty good recipes—some French, some Cajun, and some from my people in the Indies."

"I'd be pleased if you would, Marie. And in exchange, maybe I can show you some Tennessee stews."

Marie stood back and studied her. "My, you're gonna need an apron. Don't want to spoil that pretty dress."

"Thank you. Oh, have you seen a little girl named Shannon—or Shandy?"

"I declare, that chile is sure 'nuff full of spit and salt. She's with George at the stable. I doubt if we see hide nor hair of her from now on."

"I'm so glad she's settled. Now, show me what to do."

"Well, Master Caldwell sits down at seven sharp when he's at home. That ain't so often, you know, so this is a special do tonight. He wants two places set in the dining room. Sure seems peculiar—having a guest help in the kitchen. Mighty strange to me. But he's the boss."

"Yes, Marie, he's my boss too. He kindly offered me a room and wages until I decide about traveling to my brother's home in Scotland. I told him I could cook . . . but you'll have to help me. I've never seen the like of all these pots and pans, and sauces and spices. Why, your kitchen is like a foreign land, and I must learn to speak the language."

"Master Caldwell's tastes run toward French cooking. Tonight being special, I fixed clam bisque and lamb a la Chancelieu. Then we'll have chicken Toulouse, quail truffle and green peas. Oh, yes, baked sweet potatoes too."

Rebecca was astounded. "Lamb—chicken—and quail? All at one meal? For two people? And all the other dishes too? Why, it's enough for Washington's army."

"What's left goes to me and George and Justin—Shandy too. But of course we won't fix a big quantity like it was a party. There's wine too. And champagne. And for dessert, a nice pudding. Then the fromage de Roquefort."

"But, Marie, if I eat like this everyday, I'll be fat as an old sow."

"Well, like I say, it's a special occasion tonight. The master don' eat here hardly once or twice a month."

"Then we won't worry. We'll just enjoy it. If you'll furnish me with an apron, I'll get right to work—with your guidance, of course."

By seven the dining room was lighted by magnificent twin candelabra; china and silver place settings for two were laid at opposite ends of the table.

Rebecca had spent the past two hours concentrating on the elaborate preparations in the steamy kitchen. Although most of the cooking had been done in the summer kitchen out back, the interior cooking area was stifling with heat and humidity, and heavily scented with onion and pepper, garlic and exotic spices.

Not only had she enjoyed the effort, but she had become more eager with each passing minute for the evening that awaited her. As she placed each exquisite piece of silver beside the delicate china plates, she imagined how it was going to be to sit there in her new dress, her apron left behind in the kitchen, and gaze across the stretch of polished mahogany, beyond the blazing candles, at Blaine's handsome face. Of course, she would serve the meal herself in the beginning. But as soon as he invited her to sit, she would. And then, when they were both stuffed with food and wine, she would hop up and offer to clear the dishes. He would laugh and tease her, and then take her in his arms and kiss her until the whole world and everything in it melted into oblivion. And then . . . maybe he would ask her to be his wife. Lost in this lovely vision, she almost forgot to stir the bubbling sauce.

She was testing the quail for doneness when Blaine entered the kitchen. He was formally attired in a chocolate brown suit with white starched ruffles at his throat and wrists.

"You are an enchanting sight, Miss Gordon, in your apron with your hands busy preparing my supper. I don't know why I haven't had other lady-guests do kitchen duty before being served," he said, giving her a teasing grin. "Where is Marie?"

"Gone to the springhouse for butter. It's quite a feast we've prepared. And now it's ready. You may take your seat."

In one quick step, he was at her side and stole a kiss from her lips. "You're a delight, Becca," he said, his eyes twinkling. "Why don't you just sit at the table and let me enjoy you."

"Oh, no," she answered lightly. "I haven't yet carried out my duties as your servant."

Laughing heartily, he caressed her shoulder. "Bloody saints, I can see your mind is set. You are the most stubborn woman I've ever known. After dinner, Marie can furnish you a mop and pail and you can clean the house from top to bottom. There are only thirteen sizeable rooms including the quarters." His hand strayed along her shoulder until his fingertips found the soft skin above her collar. "And when that's done, George will let you whitewash the porches and fences. Oh, and I remember you like horses. I have four. There's plenty to do at the stable. And the silver and china—place settings for forty—always need polishing and dusting."

She grinned as she listened to his enumeration. "Don't forget the cooking," she added when he took a breath.

"Oh, yes—that."

"But I insist on working," she said, attempting to sound officious. "How can I collect my wages if I haven't properly earned them? Go along now. Ring the little bell by your plate and I'll come running."

"Very well. But remember, this was your idea." With one last disarming smile, he left the kitchen.

A short time later, she was stirring the bisque while Marie basted the chicken when she heard the tinkle of the bell. Suddenly nervous, she looked at Marie, who was not entirely happy with the chicken and was glaring at it as if it had regrown its feathers.

"Quick, Marie, what do I do first?"

Marie handed Rebecca a serving towel and said, "Jus' go out there and ask the master what kind of wine he wants. Then come back and tell me. George will be here soon to serve. Maybe by then this bird will be rightly done."

Rebecca pushed open the door, a benign smile on her lips.

Blaine was standing beside his chair. His look was indulgent and teasing. "How nice to have a fair lass come running when I call."

"Now be serious, Blaine. I want to do a proper job. Marie told me to ask you what kind of wine you want—with the first course, I guess."

"The French red. George will know."

"Well, George is still with Shandy at the stable."

"I see." His eyes were alight with amusement. "Then *you* may serve the wine."

She scurried back to the kitchen, obtained the uncorked bottle, and returned to the dining room, where she found Blaine seated and waiting. Carefully, she filled his goblet.

"Your place setting is much too far away at the end of the table. Move it here, please, madam. Then I'll pour your wine."

She hesitated and lifted her eyebrows. "Well, Captain . . . if you insist."

"I do insist. Ah, here's George now."

George bustled into the room. "Sorry, sir, to be late."

"Never mind," Blaine said pleasantly.

"Excuse me, sir, a carriage just arrived. I'll see to the door."

Blaine pushed back his chair. "Now who the hell . . ."

Rebecca was in the process of moving the place setting to Blaine's right. Now she stood still, the wine bottle in one hand, the silverware in the other.

George had reappeared escorting a woman of astonishing beauty. She was elegantly attired, her golden hair coiffed in an elaborate arrangement atop her head and intertwined with strands of diamonds and pearls. The neckline of her brocade dress was impossibly low, and at her throat she wore a necklace centered by a ruby as large as a hen's egg. Her velvet brown eyes fixed Blaine with a look as if he were a god straight from Heaven.

"Blaine, mon cher. *C'est superbe* to see you at last."

"Mon Dieu—Sonja!" Blaine replied with a stunned look. "I wasn't expecting you."

"Oh, but how fortunate I found you at home. I heard you went to see poor Mr. Lafitte." She swept to Blaine's side and passed a bejeweled hand possessively along his arm. "I've missed you, my darling." She shook her gloved finger under his nose. "You've been neglecting your little Sonja. *Ce n'est pas bon."*

He looked at Rebecca and met her confused look.

She just stared at him. He looked like a schoolboy who had been caught with a frog in his pocket.

Pain spread through her like wildfire. For a moment, she had no rational thought at all. Then when her mind began to function, the pain became anger and humiliation and disappointment. She hated herself for assuming Blaine had no other lady friends. She should have known the adventurous Captain Caldwell hadn't spent his years since puberty chastely under a rock. He was wealthy, he was single—and surely in demand by the ladies of New Orleans. He had every right to pursue another woman, perhaps one more willing than she to warm his bed. She looked again at the lady who was probably in her twenties. It was plain that *Sonja* was madly attracted to Blaine. All at once, insecurity bubbled up within her like a witch's brew. She felt certain that no country bumpkin from Tennessee could compete with such a beauty. "Excuse me," she choked. "I'll go to the kitchen."

When she started to turn, Blaine caught her arm. "No, Rebecca. We can still have our dinner. I'll have Marie lay another place. This is an old friend, Miss Sonja Delgado."

The emphasis on the word *old* caused Miss Delgado to withdraw her hand and frown.

He continued, "She has surprised me by dropping in—haven't you, Sonja?"

Rebecca watched as the woman tore her gaze from Blaine and glanced her way. The condescending look dismissed her at once.

Sonja smiled at Blaine, then tapped his cheek with the closed fan that dangled from her wrist. That certainly captured his attention. She spoke as if she and Blaine were completely alone. "My darling, I heard you misbehaved and spent the night in the Cabildo. You shouldn't antagonize our American governor, dearest. You know we must accept him as a social equal if we—and our children—are to flourish in New Orleans."

At a loss for words, Blaine stared at her, then turned back to Rebecca.

Sonja looked down at the place settings. "I suppose we could dine, but I don't have much time. I told my duenna to return here at eleven. Why, I haven't seen you in weeks." She paused. "Blaine, you're not paying attention. And why are you staring at your serving girl?"

"Sonja, this is my friend, Rebecca Gordon," said Blaine, at last finding his voice. "She's from Tennessee and is practicing her cooking skills. It's been a little game, you see."

"Well . . . I declare . . ." It was plain that Sonja had no experience in being introduced to servants. She recovered enough to wave her fan in fleeting acknowledgment. "Good evening," she murmured. Giving her attention back to Blaine, she grasped his arm. "We can stay here and visit awhile, *querido.* You know my father expects to hear from you soon."

"You didn't hear me, Sonja. Miss Gordon is my *guest.*"

Rebecca said icily, "I'm *not* your guest, Captain. I'm sure Miss Delgado is right to be upset. She obviously has first claim on your attentions."

Blaine threw down his napkin. Ignoring Sonja's shocked look, he moved toward Rebecca and clasped her arm. "I must explain, Rebecca. The lady and I are . . . close family friends. I've been so busy, I haven't had time . . . I mean, it was my intention to visit her and . . . oh, hell, Rebecca, don't look like that."

She didn't care how she looked. She was mortified beyond belief. And even a tree stump could see Blaine was fibbing. Sonja was far more than just an old family friend. Rebecca felt her dreamworld crumbling around her. One look told her that Miss Delgado was a much better match for Blaine than she would ever be. She'd been a simpleton and a fool to think she had a chance with him.

"You may as well have your dinner," she said sharply. "Marie has worked very hard—and two settings will be enough. I'm going to my room."

"No," Blaine said quickly. "Unless you agree to join us at dinner, Miss Delgado and I will leave—"

"Blaine," interjected Sonja. "My goodness, don't insist. You're embarrassing her. Besides, I wanted—"

"Miss Delgado is absolutely correct," snapped Rebecca. "Now, if you'll excuse me, George and Marie are waiting in the kitchen."

Blaine released her and shook his head. "I won't argue with you, Rebecca. Tell them I won't have dinner here after all. If you're going to be unreasonable, I don't have any choice. And I do need to have a private talk with Sonja. I owe her that much."

"You certainly don't owe me any explanation of what you do, or where you go or . . . or when you plan to return."

"On the contrary, I think I do. But I can't discuss it at this moment. Please try to understand."

"I believe I do understand. Now if you'll excuse me."

"Rebecca . . ."

She fled from the room before he could see the tears starting in her eyes. Without looking at Marie or George, she put down the wine bottle and the silver which she'd forgotten she still held, and rushed into her room. Standing in the fading light, she clenched her hands and sobbed in silent misery. She wanted to die from embarrassment and heartache. Surely Blaine would want to marry as beautiful and sophisticated a woman as Sonja Delgado. While he might have affection, even attraction for a girl from the country, he would never give up such an elegant lady to marry a simple waif. Why, she couldn't understand a word of French, even though Laurens had sent her a tutor. She sank into the chair by the window and let the evening breeze cool her fevered brow. Yes, Blaine and Sonja Delgado would make a spectacular-looking couple.

She was sorry now she had agreed to come to Dominique Hall. But she would have to make the best of it until she could leave for Scotland. At least Blaine would be gone much of the time. Wiping her cheeks, she stared out at the grounds, lovely now in the azure glow of a rising moon. She could see Pepper curled up beneath a weeping willow tree. "You're jealous, Rebecca Gordon," she said out loud. "But it can't be helped and it serves you right. Instead of learning from your mother's experience, you went right out and lost your heart. Now, how do you think you're going to get it back?"

The following day at noon, as Rebecca dusted the armchair in the living room, George brought her an envelope.

"This just arrived, Miss Rebecca. It's for you."

Dropping the cloth, she reached quickly for the letter. It must be from Blaine. He had to go back to Barataria, but maybe he wanted to explain, apologize. She couldn't yet give up hope he might somehow love her. In fact, during a sleepless night, she had reevaluated the scene with Sonja Delgado. It could be she was rationalizing, but she'd begun to see the whole event in a somewhat humorous light. Her innate self-confidence had reasserted itself and she decided she had a number of qualities to offer Blaine—if he could see past the dazzling beauty of Sonja.

But when she tore open the note her heart plummeted. She recognized at once the infamous handwriting of Guy Laurens.

Rebecca—I'm leaving the city. But I do intend to return. My hunch is Caldwell will soon tire of you and I'll have no problem reestablishing myself in New Orleans. It's obvious he has lied to you—especially about your father's death. If you repeat such a lie, I will see you imprisoned for defaming my good name. Also he has lied about himself. He is a spy for the British. If you doubt this, ask him what he was doing in the camp of the English Commander Cochrane in May of this year. If he answers you truthfully, you'll have your proof. My bet is he will lie even further to save his skin. Adieu. Guy Laurens.

Nonsense, she thought, wadding up the letter and tossing it into the fireplace. The only liar was Laurens, she told herself angrily. She would not allow herself to distrust Blaine again.

Blaine spent three days at Barataria helping Lafitte sift through the ruins of his once grand house and compound and constructing makeshift shelters for his people. Before he left Grande Isle, he wanted to help restore the dwellings to a liveable condition and split enough broken timbers into firewood to take the chill off the approaching winter nights.

Swinging an axe all day, and drinking Lafitte's rum half the night did nothing to take his mind off the tempestuous girl who had stolen his heart. The thought of her filled his every waking hour and penetrated his dreams. No woman had ever so completely captivated his mind or touched him so profoundly. If Sonja hadn't intruded on their dinner, he felt sure he and little Becca would have ended the night in each other's arms.

What a shame Sonja had chosen just that moment to pay a social call. He supposed he was partly to blame, however, for having neglected to end their stormy relationship much sooner. It was a damned awkward moment and he regretted it had happened. He never again wanted to see pain in Rebecca's beautiful and trusting eyes.

He had escorted Sonja home and said a fond good-bye, once and for all. Her vigorous condemnation of his character had been a fair enough price to pay for any hurt he had caused. Then he had gone to the waterfront to arrange for a man to keep watch on the movements of Guy Laurens until the bastard left the city.

By the time he finished his work at Lafitte's camp, he had made a decision. He would marry Rebecca Gordon as soon as the war ended—if she would have him. She was an extraordinary woman; their souls reached out to intertwine, to complement and strike sparks within each other that neither could deny. She was half Creole the same as he. As far as their different backgrounds and life experiences were concerned, he felt these would only enrich their years together. His only concern was asking her to give up her dream of living in Scotland. Maybe she would be satisfied to pay an occasional visit there.

At sunup on Sunday, the fourth morning after leaving Dominique Hall, he put his horse into a canter heading northwest along the edge of Barataria Bay. The air was crisp and his spirits were high. He was sure he could prove to Rebecca the depth of his love.

18

For three days, Rebecca worked from dawn to dark, at first in the gardens, and then indoors when cold, damp winds brought an end to autumn.

Under Marie's supervision, she began to learn some of the intricate preparations required by the French recipes. She managed to steal an hour each day to visit Shandy at the stables. The child had moved into quarters next to the new fillies and was happily caring for the variety of farm animals on the plantation.

Despite Rebecca's efforts to put Blaine out of her mind, she found it impossible. Not only was she surrounded by all his lovely possessions, but his house staff spoke his name endlessly during their workday. It was "Master Caldwell said do this," or "The captain wouldn't like that," or "Don't let Captain Caldwell catch you doing sloppy work." His presence was everywhere, filling every nook and cranny. Even when she worked in the kitchen with Marie, the woman chattered endlessly about the exploits of "Cap'n Caldwell," and how he'd increased the family fortune left him by his parents, of how well liked he was in New Orleans, and especially of how he ruled Dominique Hall with a firm, but kindly hand.

On the first Sunday of December, Rebecca found herself

alone in the great house. With the week's work completed and the master away, the servants had taken their day of rest and disappeared from the premises. Just before leaving, George had tapped on her door where she was idly thumbing through a book, and told her he had laid out a cold lunch in the kitchen and filled a tub of warm water in the master's suite upstairs.

She put aside the book and opened the door. "Is Captain Caldwell expected back today?" she asked, feeling her heart skip a beat.

"Maybe so," replied George. "Maybe not. But I always keep fresh water in the tub."

"Oh? Doesn't it get cold?"

"Master likes it cool. Anyway he never complains—unless he finds it empty. If he comes while we're out, jus' say we took off for church and we'll be back before dark."

After George had gone, she found she was too restless to settle back to her reading. She was browsing through the library in the living room, when she heard a squawking and flapping from somewhere above her. A quick inspection showed a sizable bird had become trapped in the chimney flue and was desperately trying to escape.

She ran to the kitchen and found a broom. Maybe she could give the poor thing a boost to freedom.

She realized at once that she'd tackled a messy job. It wouldn't do to have her one pretty dress ruined by falling ash and soot. Quickly she removed the dress and kicked out of her shoes. She pulled the massive brass andirons out of the hearth and found three large bricks to stand on while she forced the broom upward into the chimney. She could almost reach the bird. Standing on tiptoe, she called her encouragement: "Don't worry, little bird. Help is on the way."

It was late morning when Blaine arrived at his mansion. He swung his leg over the saddle, dropped to the ground, and tossed the reins around the hitching rail. His palms were wet with sweat. Hell, he hadn't been this nervous since he'd slipped his first love note to a dimpled darling during Mass—and had it intercepted by her dour duenna.

He didn't think Rebecca would refuse his proposal, and

he had no qualms about taking this big step in his life, so why this sudden attack of nerves. Maybe it was because of that silly business with Sonja earlier in the week. He hoped he could explain everything and regain Rebecca's trust—a trust so newly won after he'd convinced her he wasn't spying for the British. He must show her how much he loved her, and *only her;* he must tell her how much he needed her in his life, how empty it had been without her. And especially, he must convince her how deeply honored he would be to have her as his wife.

Before leaving Lafitte's camp, he had dressed with special care. He wore cream-colored linen breeches, a crisp white shirt and satin waistcoat and a black cravat at his throat. In his pocket was a pearl and sapphire ring he'd purchased from Jean's stockpile of treasures. Later, on their wedding day, he would give Rebecca the emerald and diamond ring that had belonged to his mother.

He turned the key in the lock and took a deep breath. As he entered the hall, he swept off his hat and hung it on the rack. The servants would be at church and he hoped he would have the house—and Rebecca—to himself. Hesitating, he gazed across the heavily draped rooms, aware of the stillness except for the ticking of the hall clock. He had started toward the kitchen when he heard a muffled expletive from the living room. For a moment he saw nothing, then he spotted two bare feet, two smooth well-turned calves, and one perky pantalooned bottom—of all places, in the midst of the fireplace.

Crossing his arms, he watched with growing amusement. It was Becca, all right. She was standing on several bricks balanced precariously where logs usually were laid. He noticed her yellow dress placed carefully over a chair, and beside it, her hose and slippers.

"Tarnation!" came her voice from inside the chimney. This was followed by the sound of vigorous thumping and a drifting of soot around the girl's tantalizing legs.

Grinning, he continued to watch. What an adorable sight she was. In no way could he imagine Sonja or any ladies of his acquaintance having the gumption or the desire to climb halfway into a chimney for any reason. Was she trying to clean it—or something else?

"Get outta there," she ordered. "Shoo-shoo. Do you want to roast when the fire is lit?"

So that was it, he thought chuckling deep in his throat. There was some varmint in the chimney and she was after it with the broom. What would he do with such a wife? She seemed to go from one crisis to another, in varying degrees, of course, and with the best of intentions. At least, she was handling this one with tenacity if not great skill.

He entered the room and was about to announce his arrival when suddenly the bricks beneath her toes slipped. She uttered a scream as she struggled to keep from falling.

He rushed forward and wrapped his arms around her hips, but was forced to close his eyes against a cloud of black ash that enveloped him.

Now she screamed in earnest. She fell out of the chimney like a scorched wildcat fighting for its life.

Held firmly in his grasp, she pummeled his head with one fist and whacked him as best she could with the broom handle.

Dodging, coughing, blinded by the soot, he tried to control her. Hell, if he released this blackened demon, she'd tear across the living room for sure. "Rebecca!" he shouted. "It's me—calm down."

Her screams and struggles continued unabated.

He sank to his knees in the fireplace, bringing her down beside him. Soot continued to fall like rain from above, turning the two of them into wriggling blackened forms.

"Rebecca!" he called again, and tightened his grip, forcing her to stop flailing at him.

Her screams stopped. Her eyes grew wide as she stared at him in startled silence.

"Thank you," he croaked before being overcome by another spasm of coughing. When he recovered, he looked closely at her. She was covered with ash from head to toe. Her eyes were like sapphires encased in dusky velvet. They sparkled with anger and a residue of fear.

"Are you all right?" he asked hoarsely.

She seemed too stricken to speak, but managed a nod. Even that slight gesture sent soot flying from her mass of darkened curls.

"Do you charge extra for cleaning chimneys," he asked

mildly. "My regular chimney sweep charges a dollar per stack. I will pay you even more if you'll allow me to watch—" He couldn't hold back his laughter any longer. It broke from deep inside as he gazed at her, erupting spontaneously while ashes swirled about them.

She stared at him, blinking in disbelief. "You—you're home," she sputtered.

"I'm relieved you recognized me."

Suddenly aware of her dishabille, she crossed her arms over her bosom. "There was a bird in the chimney. I only wanted—"

"I saw what happened," he said, trying to control his amusement at their disastrous appearance. "It was gallant of you to take such risk to save the thing."

"I did poke it out." She attempted to wipe her face with hands as dirty as her cheeks.

"Congratulations."

Her expression turned cold. She threw a glance toward the entry. "Are you alone, or is Miss Delgado about to appear?"

He was pleased she had asked. It gave him a chance to clear up the matter. "No, my friend Sonja will *not* appear—not today or ever, unless she has a definite invitation."

"Will that be soon? I must plan a special menu. I've learned some new recipes while you were away. I don't want to embarrass—"

He stopped her speech with a firm kiss. "Hush, Becca, and listen to what I have to say. It's true, in the past I've given Sonja Delgado my attention. Her parents promoted the relationship, and I admit I gave it serious thought. But Sonja was wrong to assume I intended to marry her. I never told her I loved her, and I explained my feelings to her after she paid her surprise visit a few nights ago. I assure you, whatever was between us is ended."

For a long moment, she merely gazed at him. He couldn't tell if she was pleased or really didn't care.

"Rebecca . . . I have told you, I'm in love with *you*. It's important that you trust me."

A softer look crossed her eyes. "I . . . I do trust you." Moving her arms from across her chest, she folded her hands in her lap and stared down at them. "Yes, I'm glad, and I *do* trust you, Blaine," she murmured.

Hell, she didn't sound glad, or look a bit pleased. She acted as if she'd just been told her favorite pet had died.

He leaned his head down to study her face. "What's wrong, darling? What must I do to win a smile?"

She glanced up at him, but her lips remained firmly set.

He reached in his pocket. "This is not exactly the location I had in mind for this, but I guess it will do." He removed the ring and reached for her left hand. "This is my pledge, cherie. I hope you will accept it—wear it with love and pride—until one day I can replace it with a wedding ring."

Her lips parted, her eyes grew wide. "A . . . a wedding ring?" she gasped.

"I wish to God the betrothal could be right away. Again I must ask for your trust." He slipped the ring over her finger, then held her eyes. "I must do something—something I can't fully explain until after the battle that's imminent. When this damnable war is over, when victory is won, then I will be able to offer you a future, security, position, everything your heart desires."

"You . . . you would marry me?" she whispered.

"If you will have me," he said, deeply moved by her obvious amazement at the idea. "I would consider myself the most fortunate man in the world to have you as my wife."

Her eyes misted as she put her hands on his shoulders. "Blaine . . . I never thought . . . I never . . ." Tears rolled down her cheeks, smearing the soot, touching the corners of her lips. She bit her lower lip, then collected herself. "Yes. Of course, Blaine . . ." She choked on the taste of ashes.

Smiling, he traced her lips with his fingers and stroked her moist cheeks.

Coughing again, she seemed caught between laughter and tears.

He hugged her to him, feeling her body tremble, then heard the happy sound of a giggle as she wrapped her smudged arms around his neck.

For several seconds, they clung to each other, sharing their laughter like two naughty children in the midst of an adventure.

He sat back and eased her onto his lap. Brushing back her hair, he said, "Lord, Rebecca, we look like a pair of dust mops. And I dressed with great care before I came to ask for your hand."

Her tears had become tears of merriment as she shook with laughter. Finally, she gained control and held up her hand to catch the light with the beautiful ring. "It's a shame Sonja doesn't pop in right now for a social call." The idea set her again into cheerful giggling.

"No, I'm satisfied to have you to myself. Of course, I didn't expect to spend the afternoon in the fireplace." He shrugged out of his waistcoat and let it fall. As he started to stand, the soot engulfed them once more. "Dammit, we're in a fine mess."

She rose to face him, her face alight with happiness. "Well, we can't sit here till Christmas."

"If we cross the room, we'll blacken everything," he noted as he stooped to keep his head from entering the chimney. His pristine attire was as soot covered as Rebecca's chemise and ruffled pantalettes.

"Don't worry, Captain, I can scrub the carpet later," she quipped. "After all, that's what I'm hired to do, is it not?"

She was irresistible standing there with her feet bare, her lovely curves scarcely covered by her undergarments. And she had accepted his proposal—or rather his promise to make an official proposal when the war was over. He knew grave danger lay ahead of him. If by some chance the British won, he could lose everything, his home, his fortune, and most probably his life. He couldn't tie her to him until it was safe to do so. But at least, now he could count on her waiting for him, and anticipate the joy they would have in the years to come. As if she were a doll, he swept her into his arms and bounded across the living room. Ignoring his own boot-prints, he marched up the stairs and kneed open his bedroom door and carried her inside.

Her lips brushed the tip of his chin as she asked, "What are you doing? Blaine . . . I think you should put me down." Her soft tone held no trace of annoyance or concern.

"I intend to," he said, placing a kiss on her forehead. He crossed his bedroom and entered the dressing area where stood the large footed tub. "Speaking of scrubbing, I know a young lady badly in need of it."

She looked down at the water. "Oh my. Well, it is inviting."

He lowered her toward the tub. "Then we are in agreement about this matter?"

"Except . . . my clothes." Her eyes glittered with excitement. And there was something warmer in their depths.

"They too could stand a good washing. Saves water this way." He placed her gently into the liquid.

"Oh, it's . . . it's cool," she cried, her hands still gripping his shoulders.

"Oh hell . . . I forgot ladies like a heated bath. Stay right there, cherie. I think I can help. He stepped away, allowing himself one quick moment to memorize the sight of her sitting upright in his grand porcelain tub, her clinging chemise outlining the fullness of her young breasts and perky nipples. Already ash was spreading across the top of the water, clouding the view of curves below. Forcing himself to go, he hurried toward the kitchen.

Rebecca sank to her chin in the tepid water. Laughter bubbled inside her. She wanted to shout her joy to the rooftops. He loved her! And he would *marry* her, after all. Laying back her head, she let her hair fan out around her releasing its burden of soot, and held up the hand bearing the ring.

It was gone. She bolted upright and gaped at the bare finger. The ring had been there moments ago. She had kept her hand closed because of the ring's looseness until she had entered the tub. She went to her knees and began feeling along the bottom. The water was so murky now, she could see nothing beneath the surface. It had to be here, she thought frantically. If she'd lost it, she would absolutely die.

Blaine returned carrying a large kettle.

"Blaine," she cried, "my ring. It fell off somewhere."

"I would bet it's in the tub," he said without undue concern. "Sit still a minute and I'll help you find it."

Sitting on her heels, she gazed up at him. A wave of love swept over her as she looked at him. He was as sooty as she had been: his hair, his face, his once beautiful white shirt and pants. She bit her lip to hold back her laughter as she watched this lordly gentleman of great wealth and power pouring hot water into the tub with hands blackened by chimney dirt.

The warm water drifted around her and she captured his eyes in one exquisite moment of mutual adoration.

He put down the kettle and sat on a nearby stool, then tugged off his boots. He tossed aside his cravat and unbuttoned his soiled shirt. With lips twitching, he carefully stepped into the tub and removed his shirt. His mind plainly on other things, he muttered, "I'll help you find the ring."

She saw the water rise as he sank to his knees carefully so he wouldn't slosh too much of the liquid over the top. His legs in once white breeches were hidden; his chest was half submerged.

She moved into the curved end of the tub behind her. "I'm sure this is . . . scandalous behavior," she offered coyly.

"You do enjoy using those new words that Laurens taught you." He cupped his hands full of water and splashed his face, cleansing it somewhat, but leaving his hair dripping in dark streams around his temples and cheeks. Running his hands through it, he asked, "Is that better?"

"I . . . I'm sure I should go." She started to stand, but a glance along her body showed that she might as well be standing naked before him. "Oh," she gasped. As she ducked back down, her feet slipped from under her and she slid under the frothy water until she was almost totally immersed between his knees.

He put his hands under her arms and lifted her upward.

Shaking her head, she blinked back droplets and grasped his bare forearms.

"Slippery little creature, aren't you," he said. "Ah, what have we here?" He held up the ring.

"Thank goodness." She sighed and reached out her hand.

Taking it, he slid the ring onto her finger, then turned her palm upward and kissed the center of it.

Delicious tingles coursed up her spine.

"It's a bit loose," he observed. "We'll have it sized by my jeweler tomorrow."

She absorbed the sight of him at that moment while his head was bent near her hand. His thick dark hair curled over his forehead and clung wet and dripping to his nape. His muscles rippled from his broad shoulders to his back where she glimpsed scars that were barely healed.

When he lifted his face to hers, she accepted his kiss with a heart brimming with love and unrestrained joy.

He encircled her back and floated her body toward him, moving his lips to her forehead, then trailing across one closed eyelid to finally return to claim her mouth in a kiss of consuming raw power. His tongue parted her lips, then withdrew to play at their delicate edge, teasing them until she could barely breathe.

Clasping his smooth shoulders, she leaned back, offering him her throat and allowing her breasts to drift above the water's surface. He placed a lingering kiss between them, then teased the buds with his tongue as if the sheer, wet fabric covering them did not exist.

Sighing in delight, she felt his hand along her waist, guiding her languidly through the water. He caressed her hips, her inner thighs, and explored the soft mound between. She lost herself in his touch, his heated closeness. She made no complaint when he untied the ribbons of her chemise and slipped it over her arms, then shifted her position slightly to enable him to remove her lower garments. The water swirled and soothed her flesh from her shoulders to her toes.

"My beautiful girl, une belle femme, ma cherie," he murmured as he moved his hands along her breasts, outlined her waist and hips and explored her secret recesses.

Gently he massaged her fragile femininity. "My precious girl, are you willing . . . do you want to go further?"

In answer, she drew his head down to receive his kiss.

"You're sure, my sweet little one? There will be some pain, I fear."

"I want you . . . want you . . ." She tried to express the aching need within her, the emptiness that was demanding to be filled.

His fingers explored her, unlocking all the latent passion of her untouched womanhood.

Writhing now under his skillful manipulation, she arched against his palm, but he moved away to loosen his own clothing.

She clung to him in a frustration of longing that was searing through her loins.

In the next moment, he was on his knees again, over her, his palm cupping her softness, his fingers teasing that magic center of desire.

Her own need was reaching the breaking point. "Please . . . please," she murmured, pleading but not hearing her words.

His fingers were replaced by something more potent, more fierce, more powerful.

A flash of sudden burning startled her.

He hesitated and embraced her, pressing his lips to the hollow of her throat.

"No. It's all right," she whispered. "Come to me, my love."

In moments, her pain was overcome by the driving force of her own passion answering the deepening possession of her body.

"Je t'aime, Rebecca. I love you . . . love you." He rocked her in rhythmical strokes, carrying her through the water, taking her on a growing tide of pleasure. Thrusting, he found her woman's core and held her for one long breath, before moving again in pulsating rhythm.

She melted before his onslaught. Like rich cream, she moved through the silver water, her body pliant, eager, holding him in a velvet vise. Her feet were planted on the inside of the tub, giving her leverage to respond to his masterful strokes.

Water spilled over the sides of the tub. His breathing was ragged. "Becca—my darling. Dear Heaven, I do adore you."

Her fingers dug into his muscular forearms. Holding him, she whimpered, on the edge, desperate for release.

With one hand under her hips, the other supporting her shoulders, he dragged her once more through the roiling water onto the sculpture of his body. Then with an anguished moan, he gave himself to her in a rush of unleashed passion.

She arched, accepting him, feeling her own release spiral

into ecstasy. Gripping him, she heard her voice crying from far away. Never had she imagined such incredible pleasure existed.

As the flow subsided, slowly he lay back in the water, carrying her with him, over him, until she rested across his chest, floating in his arms, soaked, satiated, completely serene.

Opening her eyes, she moved her hands along his shoulders. She rested her cheek against the damp, springy mat on his chest. "I love you, Blaine," she murmured, inhaling the fresh scent, listening to the low thrum of his heartbeat. "Someday you must teach me the French words."

He splayed his hands along her back and hips. "And I love you, Rebecca, now, always and forever. I never dreamed it could be like this."

"Uh-oh." She moved away and knelt in the tub.

"What is it? You're all right?"

"Of course, but I've lost my ring again." She smiled at him, reassuring, loving, tender.

He felt along the bottom of the tub and once again retrieved her ring. "Lost . . . along with other treasures," he said wryly. "Your afternoon of cleaning chimneys proved more dangerous than you expected."

Smiling at him, she stood in the tub like an emerging Venus. "I'd take the risk again," she said blithely. "Even if I knew the price."

He stepped out of the tub, sending water splashing across the floor.

Taking his hand, she let him guide her over the side.

"I love you beyond believing, Rebecca Gordon," he said solemnly, and wrapped her in a large, fluffy towel. He indulged in one more hug. "You've shared your body with me—and I treasure it more than my own." He slid his hands under her knees and carried her into the bedroom. "Rest here, my love. It will be getting dark soon. We'll see about dinner—"

A knock on the door broke into the idyllic moment.

She sat up stiffly and clutched the towel around her. She was drowsy now, heavy with contentment, but she must remember she was not yet Mrs. Blaine Caldwell.

He grabbed a towel and wrapped it around his waist. Motioning her to be silent, he cracked the door.

From the hallway, George delivered the news. "It's Jackson, sir. I didn't mean to disturb your nap, but I promised to let you know right off when he came. He's moved into the compound near town. His soldiers are riding the streets declaring martial law, so they call it. The people are scared, Cap'n. I guess I am too."

Blaine nodded. "Thank you, George. I'm glad you alerted me. Tell the staff to meet me in the kitchen in fifteen minutes. And tell them there's nothing to fear. We've all expected the general to bring troops to defend the city. This is excellent news. It means we'll soon have an end to the war. Go along now."

The moment the door closed, Rebecca left the bed, dropped her towel by the tub to soak up the water and opened his wardrobe. "I'll borrow a robe, if I may," she said over her shoulder. "Then I'll slip downstairs and dress so I can go with you to see Jackson."

"No, I'd rather you didn't," he said, while helping her into a velvet robe and tying the wide sash around her.

"But I want to see him," she insisted. "He's my general too."

"I said no, Rebecca. I need you here. And when fighting breaks out, I need to know you're safe. Now, don't let that Scottish temper flare. I'm not asking you. I'm *telling* you what must be done. You *will* remain at Dominique Hall."

Telling her? Commanding her? She was shocked and disappointed. She hadn't expected to be treated like a servant just because he'd said someday they would wed. "As your prisoner?" she snapped, feeling the magic of the afternoon quickly dissolve.

"For your own good, ma petite. A battle is no place for a woman."

Her voice was cutting. "I appreciate your concern, but I *am* from Tennessee. Jackson may have need of me."

"Don't be absurd, Rebecca. He commands the militia and a full force of volunteers. He would never permit a slip of a girl like you to enter the fray."

"I don't think you can decide that, Captain. I'll not be stashed away like a useless stick if there's something I can do. You may recall, sir, I'm the best shot in Tennessee." She faced him with hands on hips, defiant despite being swallowed by his robe.

"I do recall," he said sharply. "But there's a vast difference in a friendly shooting match and a battlefield. You'll stay here like I tell you."

"I am not yours to command, sir. I come and go as I please."

"You're acting no more sensibly than Shandy. Now go get dressed. It's possible there's no immediate danger; but you are *not* going with me today."

Without another word, she marched from the room and headed downstairs to find her dress. She loved Blaine Caldwell with every fiber of her being, but she had made up her mind and would do as she pleased. Angry and determined, she snatched up her dress and shoes and headed for her room. Only now did she notice she'd forgotten her ring. "Tarnation," she muttered. It was not the ending she would have chosen for the most profound and beautiful afternoon of her life.

19

A short time later, Rebecca joined Blaine's staff in the sunny kitchen. She faced him with the others, as if she were merely another paid servant summoned to a meeting by the master. It wasn't the role of employee that bothered her. It was his officious manner in insisting she do his bidding, in contrast to his magnificent, tender and thoughtful lovemaking. She loved him—but she had made her own decisions for years, and looked after her mother too. He had shown his love for her, but then, with the euphoric glow still surrounding them, he had ordered—*ordered*—her to stay at Dominique Hall against her express wishes to do otherwise. She wondered if there was more to it than concern for her safety. He was not a member of the militia, and yet he was rushing to report to Jackson. Whatever it was he was required to do, he had not shared that information with her. Yes, everything pointed to his desire to keep her out of his way and uninformed of his activities. He had asked for her trust, and yet he didn't seem to trust her in return.

Her hand rested on Shandy's shoulder; at her feet reclined a well-behaved Pepper. Marie, George, the kitchen girl, the upstairs and downstairs maids and the stable master made up the balance of the group listening intently as Blaine calmed their fears and gave instructions for the running of Dominique Hall in his absence.

A glance showed her that Shandy was staring with rapt adoration at her new hero, the owner of Dominique Hall. Listening to Blaine's instructions, Rebecca had the uneasy feeling he anticipated a longer absence than he was suggesting to his staff. In her annoyance at his high-handed treatment of her a short time ago, she hardened her heart and refused to consider the tragic possibilities that faced them all.

At the conclusion of his speech, Blaine dismissed the staff, but Rebecca and Shandy lingered behind.

Blaine tousled Shandy's curls. "Take care of Pepper, young lady. And see that the new filly is cared for properly."

"Yes, sir," she agreed happily.

"Rebecca, will you see me off?" he asked in a casual tone.

"If you like," she replied coolly.

She accompanied him through the front rooms and into the hall, trying not to notice how extraordinarily handsome he looked in his royal blue captain's attire, his knee boots, and his saber at his side. His hair was still slightly damp and curling just above his high stiff collar. It served to remind her of their recent incredible experience in the bath. She would have liked nothing better than to throw her arms around him and give him a passionate kiss of farewell, but her injured pride kept her silent and distant. He had said he loved her, and she returned his love in full measure. But if their relationship had any future at all, he must learn to respect her independence.

At the door, he stopped and looked down at her with an enigmatic gaze. Finally, he leaned near and kissed her cheek. "Don't be angry with me, Rebecca," he said, stroking her hair. "I'm used to giving orders when I feel something is important."

Instantly her annoyance melted. "I . . . I understand. I guess I'm not used to taking orders."

He touched his lips to her forehead. "We'll work things out, cherie. We must learn to be patient with each other."

For a moment, she held his eyes. Of course, she would forgive him, and she truly did understand his inclination to command. But what about trust? "Blaine . . . you're going to report directly to Jackson?"

"Whom did you think—the British?" he asked, cocking one eyebrow.

"Oh no . . . no, of course not. But . . . I do recall that day in Payton . . . well, I did hear you mention a British Admiral Cochrane." Watching him closely in the fading afternoon light, she saw surprise and then annoyance flit behind his eyes. She was instantly sorry she'd brought it up, but it had just popped out from somewhere deep inside her mind. "I . . . I don't mean . . ."

"What *do* you mean, Rebecca?" He didn't sound angry, only far more distant than he had a moment ago.

"It's just that . . . I don't know exactly what you're planning. I don't know what danger you'll be in . . . or when I'll next see you."

He studied her face. "I suppose you'll just have to trust me—like I requested earlier today."

She encircled his waist. "I do . . . of course, I do," she said with her cheek against his smooth coat.

"Good." He gave her a hug. "I'll return as soon as possible, darling. Wait here for me."

She didn't want him to leave while doubts plagued her heart, but she really had no right to question him further. If he was hiding something, she must accept his right to privacy. On the other hand, he must accept her right to make her own decisions. She moved out of his arms. "I will wait for you, Blaine, but *where* that will be, I can't promise."

His face clouded briefly, but then he leaned to quickly kiss her lips. "Just remember, I love you. Au revoir, ma petite Rebecca."

"Take care," she murmured. If she had said more, she would have given in to tears.

When the door was closed behind him, she turned and leaned against it and gathered her thoughts. After what they had shared today, why did she still doubt him? It must be that her mother's words still haunted her after all this time. Or maybe . . . maybe it was the letter from Guy Laurens. She had tossed it aside, but its warning was not entirely forgotten. She despised the man and hated herself for letting his note enter her mind. She jammed her hands into her skirt pockets. If only this terrible war were over, then everything would be right. She felt something in her pocket and pulled out the ring, Blaine's gift, his pledge of love. He must have placed it there when he kissed her good-bye. She spun around and opened the door. He did love her and she loved him. Nothing else in the world was more important—and she had let him go without a proper farewell. When she ran onto the porch, she saw only the dust along the river road where he'd ridden away. That settled it. She would follow him at once to Jackson's compound.

She went to her room and changed into a riding skirt and headed for the stable. Her visit to Jackson would accomplish three important things: She would offer her assistance to General Jackson, she would show Blaine she could make her own decisions, and hopefully, she would reassure him that she loved him with all her heart. Naturally, if she discovered along the way what it was he was doing for the war effort, that would set her mind at ease, once and for all.

She rode through the streets, which were now mostly deserted except for roving Louisiana militiamen. Pepper trotted along at her side. His growth had been phenomenal and his predicted role of protector was now quite plausible. "Mostly Irish wolfhound," she'd been told by dog fanciers. Whatever his breeding, he was both awesome in appearance and totally devoted to her.

It was easy to find Jackson's guarded compound on Royal Street, less easy to gain admittance.

"I'm from Tennessee," she insisted to a bearded frontiersman at the main entry. "A personal friend of General Jackson's. Tell him the girl who won the shooting match in Nashville last July fourth. He'll remember."

That information did the trick and soon she and Pepper were escorted to a wooden cabin behind the main house serving as the commander's headquarters.

Taking a deep breath, she strode inside. Would Blaine be with the general? She thought it likely since Blaine had headed here less than an hour earlier. What would his reaction be to her bold defiance of his orders?

In the rustic cabin, Jackson stepped from behind his makeshift desk and held out his hand. "Yes indeed, 'tis Miss Rebecca Gordon. Best sharpshooter in the territory—

maybe the whole United States, considerin' Tennesseans are the finest shots in the country."

The buckskin clad man who had escorted her inside coughed loudly.

"Oh, I know, Mr. Perkins. Kentucky claims a few expert marksmen too, but I'm allowed a bit of prejudice, don't you agree?"

During this exchange, Rebecca glanced around the one-room structure. To her surprise, Blaine was not with the three other men sitting near the general's desk. She wondered if he had already come and gone. She smiled at Jackson. "That's why I insisted on seeing you, sir. I want to do my part to defend my country. I've heard rumors you're a bit short of manpower."

He guffawed and led her to a rickity chair. "*Man*power! Now there's a good'n. No one could accuse you of being a man, little lady. In fact, you've become quite a fine-lookin' gal since our last meeting. I mean, you were pretty enough then . . . but . . . well, you've blossomed a good bit, I'd allow."

"Thank you. I *am* a woman, General. And I've been told once already today that I should stay safely behind closed doors during the coming battle. I hope you don't hold such a narrow view of my kind."

Jackson's expression held blatant admiration. "As a rule, I prefer ladies in their homes. I can't say I'd permit any woman to expose herself to danger on the front line of battle. But you are exceptional, Miss Gordon. If the need arises, I might allow you to take up a safe position and drop a few redcoats with your deadly skill at arms."

She guessed he was humoring her, but she responded, "I'm much obliged, sir."

He leaned near. "Now, I'm wondering if besides skill, you have the guts—yes, the guts to kill a man. It's not like a turkey shoot, you know."

She hesitated only a moment. "I've thought about that. I believe I could if my homeland is in danger . . . or for the safety of myself or my loved ones."

A loud racket outside interrupted them. The door burst open and a huge wirey animal loped into the room and took up a position by Rebecca's side.

"By the eternal!" shouted Jackson. "What monster have we here?"

Red-faced, Rebecca put her hand on the dog's massive shoulder. "I'm so sorry, General Jackson. This is my dog, Pepper. Mostly wolfhound, I'm told, but gentle, as a rule."

Jackson let the dog sniff his hand, then scratched behind his ear. "A wolfhound, for certain. A well-behaved canine is welcome here anytime." He leaned against his desk. "Where in New Orleans are you staying, Miss Gordon?"

"At . . . at a friend's house temporarily."

"Are you comfortable? I have several cottages here that are unoccupied. I'd be happy to have a fellow Tennessean on the premises."

Surprised by the invitation, she didn't respond at once. Then she said, "I'm honored, General. This may seem odd, but I do have a question."

"Speak up, miss."

"I'm acquainted with Captain Blaine Caldwell. I . . . I thought he was on his way here. Did he arrive, sir?"

"Caldwell?" Jackson's eyes blinked twice. "Haven't seen him . . . not since Nashville."

Her heart sank to her toes. Blaine had plainly said he was reporting to Jackson. That was an hour ago. Why, Jackson didn't seem to be expecting him at all. Blaine must have lied about where he was going. Had he also lied about not being a spy for the British? If he had not come here to help Jackson, he must be up to no-good somewhere else. He might even have sailed away on one of his ships. Pain thrust through to her deepest soul. She prayed she was wrong, but she decided it would be better if she stayed away from Dominique Hall until she was certain. It was all she could do to continue speaking to the general. "I believe I will accept your offer, sir. I have few belongings other than some personal items and my dog. I'll return my horse to its owner and return here before nightfall."

"Splendid. Join me for dinner in the main house. I'm having my officers in for a bite to eat after our meeting. One thing New Orleans always provides is excellent victuals."

With a false smile frozen in place, she left the cabin.

She was numb with disappointment and confusion. First Miss Josie had turned out to be a prostitute, then Guy

Laurens a lecher and maybe even a murderer. Now the man she loved with all her heart had apparently lied to her and could even be a traitor to his country. No wonder he had been so firm in ordering her to stay away from Jackson. He had said he was loyal to the United States, but now when he was needed at Jackson's side, he had completely disappeared.

She rode swiftly back to the mansion, said good-bye to Shandy, and moved her belongings into the military compound. All the while, she held out hope of seeing Blaine somewhere, prayed he might have some explanation for his delay in arriving to offer his support to his general. But Jackson had made it plain that Captain Caldwell had not been in contact with him in months. Thinking of how she had been so easily fooled, of how she had trusted him, and given herself so completely, stabbed her heart like a dozen heated lances. Laurens's accusation rose like a ghost to haunt her.

That evening, General Jackson's dinner was a lively affair, with fourteen guests at table and an abundance of spirits and native dishes. The general had introduced her as the guest of honor and a prize-winning sharpshooter from Tennessee.

She had brought toiletries and one plain frock from Dominique Hall. She wouldn't allow herself to take any of the things Blaine had given her. The dress she wore now had been Marie's and Rebecca traded her a pair of earrings for the use of it. It would allow her a change of clothing from her riding habit and later, when she had some money to provide her own clothes, she would return it to Marie. She refused to let herself think of the beautiful yellow organdy dress—and the way Blaine looked at her when she wore it. At the last moment, before she could change her mind, she had left the ring upstairs on his dressing table where he'd be sure to see it.

Picking at her plate of succulent crawfish bisque and deep-dish rice souffle, she let the conversation flow about her ears. It was a diverse group of men from all over the Louisiana territory. Talk centered on the defense of the city and grew more animated as whiskey was poured repeatedly into pewter tankards. Being the only lady present made her uncomfortable, especially knowing that the gentlemen's language was inhibited because of her. Besides, her mood was as bleak as a midnight sky in January. She vowed to leave as soon as possible.

She was suddenly made alert by a passing comment of one of Jackson's advisors.

"The Highlanders regiment is here in force—the Ninety-third Foot will lead the first charge."

"Oh?" queried Jackson. "How do you know that?"

"Our . . . ah . . . sources behind the lines sent the message."

"Well, Pakenham's a fool," snorted Jackson. "He'll send those boys to certain death."

"They did well enough against Napoleon."

"Hell, yes. The French and British fight battles as outdated as the Romans and the Greeks. This is America. Our frontiersmen will pick them off like blackbirds on a tree limb."

Rebecca cleared her throat. "Excuse me, General Jackson. What Highlanders are here?"

"The Sutherlands—a regiment from Aberdeen."

She dropped her fork noisely into her plate. For a moment she felt faint. The Sutherland Highlanders. Here? In Louisiana?

"What's wrong, Miss Gordon?"

Her emotions in a wild jumble, she stared at her plate. The Sutherland Highlanders—Gilbert's regiment from Aberdeen. He was certainly with that group if he had survived the battles in France. It must be fate that had brought him so near—just when she needed someone so desperately. She must make contact—but how—where? After all, he was bearing arms against the country she loved. But if the Highlanders led the attack, he could be killed. In fact, Jackson had said it was likely the Scots would be slaughtered.

"Oh . . . nothing," she said tightly. At all costs, she must hide her relationship to a member of the enemy forces. "I've just heard how fierce the Scots are. You say they're approaching New Orleans?"

"Cochrane's fleet is anchored off the Apalachicola River.

He's trying to recruit Creek Indians and blacks. I'm expecting a report soon from our spy who's infiltrating their command. I myself will leave tomorrow to inspect the area south of here. It's a labyrinth of canals and islands. I doubt if the British fleet could penetrate much beyond Fort St. Philip."

She couldn't sit still any longer. "Forgive me, General Jackson, I'd like to return to my cabin," she said in a strained voice. "It's been a difficult day." As she pushed back her chair, every man at the table jumped to his feet.

"Of course, dear lady," said the general.

"But I'd like to attend your next meeting, if I could, sir," she dared to add. "I might be of some service."

Chuckling at the idea, Jackson nodded. "Why, sure enough, little miss sharpshooter. I'll be back here in a few days. You'll be summoned for my next conference."

"Thank you, General Jackson," she managed, then hurried to the privacy of her quarters. As exhausted as she was after the drama of the day, she doubted if she could sleep a wink.

20

The wintry days crept by. Christmas came and went with little celebration as the citizens of New Orleans prepared for war. Every man, woman and child, regardless of ethnic background, was now united in the common cause of defense against the invading British. The presence of Andrew Jackson inspired an ardent patriotism to the United States that had never before existed in relaxed New Orleans. The streets resounded with "Yankee Doodle," and men unaccustomed to military duty refurbished their weapons and prepared to take a heroic stand at the general's side.

The first day of January 1815, Jackson's Tennessee backwoodsmen outgunned the British during a foray beyond the mud ramparts constructed along Rodriquez Canal. The imminence of a major battle heightened tension throughout the city.

During restless days and endless nights, Rebecca busied herself at the compound by preparing bandages and sitting in on strategy meetings in Jackson's headquarters. Not once did she hear Blaine Caldwell's name mentioned and she remained in an agony of indecision over whether or not to reveal her suspicions to the general. What if she were wrong—and accused Blaine falsely? There was always hope she was mistaken. She decided if General Jackson wasn't concerned about Blaine's whereabouts or activities, she would not bring up the matter.

At least she was trusted by the general and allowed to attend his conferences whenever she liked. She learned every movement of the Highlanders as the British forces pushed upriver. First the English overwhelmed Villere Plantation six miles below the city. Then they succeeded in blowing Lafitte's gunboat, the *Carolina,* out of the water near Barataria. She had to assume her brother, Gilbert, was among the enemy troops.

The night of January 4 she could no longer contain her impatience. Across the Plains of Chalmette, almost at the door of the city, the British were encamped preparing for their attack. Gilbert . . . her Gilbert . . . was likely there. So close to her after all these years. He certainly risked death. If ever she was to see him, she must do so now—or it might be too late.

She pulled on breeches she had borrowed from a stable hand and a dark shirt belted at the waist, then slid a knife beneath the belt. She bound her hair in a scarf and smeared dirt across her cheeks. Keeping in mind the muck of the swamps, she tugged on boots that reached to her knees. Finally, she put on kidskin gloves to protect her hands from brambles and briars.

She slipped out into the night. A chill overcast hid the moon, making her escape through the damp fields toward enemy lines an easy matter. What would she say to Gilbert if she found him? She had rehearsed a speech for days, hoping to persuade him to abandon the English cause—or at least take up a position at the rear of the advancing forces. She knew her effort would probably be hopeless, but at least she could try. If nothing else, she would finally look into the face of the brother she had worshipped for so long—and from so great a distance.

Blaine relaxed in a wooden chair beside British General Pakenham's desk. Outside the tent, the wind kicked up and the smell of rain mingled with the dankness of the nearby swamps. It was dark as pitch, and the English scouts had been recalled for the night.

Pakenham's mood matched the gloomy elements. "God-damn Yankee savages. Europeans would never fight with such dishonor. Chivalry is lost on these colonials," he pointed out vigorously. "It's a rule of war that sentinels are never targets of fire. We've lost every man we've placed on guard to the sharpshooting barbarians."

Blaine kept a solemn demeanor. "You're right, sir. I've never known an American with an ounce of nobility. If they'd fought with any civilized dignity, they'd never have whipped the British in '76."

"Well, we've got them outgunned, outnumbered and outsmarted. Our spies tell us the men are marching up and down the streets with muskets so outdated they're virtually worthless. Only a few militia have uniforms, and that backwoods Jackson is more concerned about his horses than his soldiers. We intercepted a letter to a Mr. Coffee in Baton Rouge in which Jackson asked about his racehorse, Pack-olett. This, in the midst of a war for America's survival. The man's a half-wit, 'tis plain to see."

"Who are our spies these days?" Blaine casually inquired. "Besides me, of course."

"You, Captain, are our best. We've appreciated your efforts for years. But we do have someone new who's offered to supply information from the bay area and the Indies, if necessary. He has a ship, is well financed, and speaks fluent French."

"Sounds ideal. I wonder if I know him."

"Normally I don't mention names, but with you, I have no worry. The man is a French Creole named Guy Laurens. He told us he had a run-in with some patriot in New Orleans. We've promised to restore his property and pay him handsomely for any information he provides."

Blaine sat in silence, his expression unchanged. After several seconds he said, "Yes, I believe I know the gentle-man. Thought he'd left the area."

"He left New Orleans. Moved his wife to Bermuda where he has relatives. I gather there was some woman in New Orleans who caused him trouble."

"A woman?"

"Whatever happened, he said it proved to him he should

support the British against the Americans. He believes European ownership of Louisiana is the only possibility for a decent future. Now that Napoleon is beaten, England is the last bastion of culture and enlightened society."

"Um . . . of course I completely agree," Blaine muttered. It was all he could do to sit nonchalantly in his chair. But he'd spent the past four weeks, ever since Jackson's arrival in New Orleans, moving among the British high command, ingratiating himself to Pakenham with gifts of small arms and a large amount of false information. This was not the time to risk his mission by registering shock at what he'd just heard. After the battle, he'd take care of Laurens, once and for all. Still, he had to pose one question. "And the woman? Did Laurens mention her name—or if she is also spying for us?"

"She's his mistress, I assume. He described her as a raving beauty but none too bright. When I was last aboard Laurens's ship in the bay, he said he was determined to rendezvous with the girl. I gather she's passing information directly from Jackson's headquarters."

"God almighty." Blaine couldn't hold back the curse. Of course Laurens was talking about Rebecca. He was certain Rebecca wouldn't spy intentionally, but maybe Laurens had reestablished some hold over her. Was it possible the bastard had frightened her into relaying information from Yankee headquarters? He remembered how annoyed she'd looked when they parted, how she'd pressed for information. He had wanted to tell her the truth, that he was spending time with Cochrane and Pakenham to get information for Jackson—but he was sworn to secrecy. It was far too risky to breathe a word about his actions, and he'd thought she'd make herself sick with worry. Now he wondered.

After leaving home that afternoon, he had stopped by Jackson's headquarters, discussed his plan and pledged the general to secrecy, then hurried to his assignment in the British camp. A few days later, he had learned about Rebecca's move to Jackson's compound. The fact she had disobeyed him was annoying, but he was sure the general could lie sufficiently to conceal his spy's clandestine activities—and would see the girl wasn't in danger. Surely it was impossible for her to pass military secrets. Laurens was lying. Ten minutes alone with him and he'd have the truth.

"What's that?" Pakenham queried, looking up from his maps.

"Oh . . . nothing. I just thought I'd like to personally meet with Laurens . . . before the battle, if possible."

"Not likely. The wheels are in motion for the attack and we'll strike on the eighth. I'm sending the Highlanders in first. Nothing better than bagpipes and tartans to inspire the troops. Laurens is waiting on his ship until the battle is won. He's a good man at sifting information, but I'm afraid he's lacking in personal courage."

"So I've noticed," Blaine muttered acidly.

Rebecca followed the river road, then slogged across a marshy field for a mile before she spotted the campfires of the British army. It had been easier to slip past the American sentries than to sneak up on a covey of quail in the woods near Morgan's Landing. She knew from General Jackson's briefings that the British sentries had been pulled close in to camp after several were killed by expert Yankee riflemen.

At last she arrived within a hundred yards of the camp and studied the area. Most of the campfires had burned low at this late hour, but she could smell the smoke and see twinkling lights extending far along the stretch of dark bayou. It reminded her of a giant reptile, not quite asleep, but waiting for the opportune moment to leap at its prey. Men were silhouetted as they milled about the fires and the tents. She picked up scattered laughter and a distant tune being played on a harmonica.

She pulled a handkerchief from her pocket and wiped some of the dirt from her face. Then she removed several pouches of tobacco and made sure they were dry. Walking boldly into the camp, she approached the nearest sentry.

"Who goes there?" he demanded, aiming his musket at her chest.

"An island boy," she responded. "I got some tobacco for sale. Want some, huh, mister?"

"'Tis a bit late to be out, lad. You could get yourself shot."

"My pap is ailin'," she explained in her best country

dialect. "I need some money tonight to pay the healer. I was afraid to ask them Yankee sentries up at Orleans. They shoot a gnat if it buzzes."

"Aye, so I've heard. Sure, give me a bag there. One thing the colonials do properly is grow good tobacco."

She gave him a pouch and took her time counting the coins he put in her hand. "Oh . . . mister, where be the Scots platoon? One of them Scotties saw me yesterday and wanted some tobacco brought over soon's I could git to it."

"The Highlanders are camped to the west. You see that light at the big tent?"

"Yes, sir."

"That's Pakenham's quarters. Over there . . . to the left . . . that's the Scots. You can see the Sutherland banner on a pole by their tent."

"Much obliged, sir," she said, her heart thudding more rapidly with every passing second.

She walked as fast as she dared toward the area the sentry had indicated. She saw a small bonfire and the pole with a bright red and blue banner fluttering in its glow. A handful of men wearing plaid trews were lounging about the fire. One minute of listening to their distinctive burred accent proved she'd found the Scots from Aberdeen.

Her heart in her throat, she approached the men. "Excuse me, do you soldiers belong to the Sutherland Highlanders?"

"Aye," came the unanimous reply as the men stared at her.

"I'm looking for Gilbert Gordon. Lieutenant Gilbert Gordon. If he's here, I have a message for him."

"He's here, laddie. That's his tent by those trees. I dinnae know if he's turned in for the night."

Her hands were clammy and her knees were shaking. So Gilbert was here—just a few steps away. "Thank you," she rasped.

Feeling the men's eyes on her back, she crossed to the tent and stood outside the open flap. A small candle inside emitted a wavering light.

"Gilbert Gordon," she called softly. "Lieutenant Gordon, are you there?"

"Who is it?" was the low reply.

"A friend. Could I . . . have a word with you?"

"Aye. Come in, then."

"You're . . . not undressed for bed?"

There was a short pause. "Undressed? What kind of a question is that, I'd like to know?" A well-built man in an open-neck shirt and plaid trousers ducked out of the tent. When he straightened up and squinted through the darkness, Rebecca caught her breath. It was as if her own mother had been reborn as a thirty-year-old man. The sight of those familiar features, the auburn hair and clear brown eyes, tore at her heart and put a lump in her throat. "Gil-Gilbert. Is it truly you?"

"Gilbert is correct. Lieutenant Gilbert Gordon. What is it, lad?"

She reached up and slid the bandanna from her hair. "Not lad, Gilbert. I'm your sister, Rebecca Jane Gordon."

His mouth dropped. He leaned near and searched her face. "Nay. It cannae be true. My sister lives in Tennessee with my mother. I'll go there after the war."

She shook her head. "I'm sorry, Gilbert. Your mother . . . *our* mother passed on seven months ago. I figured you were in France and hadn't received word."

His back stiffened. "Ye . . . ye mean she's . . ."

She longed to embrace him, to share in his grief, but he was still too much a stranger.

"What's going on, Gordon?" came a voice from nearby.

She whispered urgently, "I don't have much time. You must believe I'm your sister. I slipped across the lines to find you. Look, here's a locket that belonged to our mother. Maybe you remember it." She pulled the delicate gold necklace from beneath her shirt and displayed it on her palm.

He stared at it, then nodded silently. "Aye, she's my mother. And y-ye must be Rebecca. She wrote me . . . how bonnie . . ."

Grief etched his face. "But how . . . when did she die?"

"Last spring. She just got awful sick. I think she wanted to go."

He shook his head. "God bless her. I guess she never got over losing our dad."

Her own pain came rushing back to her, but she forced it away so she could continue. There was so little time. "I know you're grieved at my news, but what's important now is that you leave here at once. The British are going to lose. And the Highlanders will lead the first attack. You're likely to be killed." She grasped his arm. "I beg you, Gilbert. You're my brother. I need you. I've found no one else I can trust." Her voice broke as she chewed into her lower lip. She prayed he would be reasonable. "Please . . . please slip away," she whispered. "I can meet you in New Orleans."

His brow furrowed; he stared at her with sorrowful eyes. At last he said huskily, "Ye dinnae look e'en a wee bit like mother or father. But I do believe ye're tellin' the truth. Ye took a big risk coming here and I thank ye for your caring. But it changes nothing. I'm a Highlander, second in command. And ye can't know the outcome of the battle—a young lass like ye. I'm used to risking my life. I'll do as I'm ordered. But . . . afterwards I'll look for ye. Where will ye be?"

She could see he was not to be moved. If only she had more time. But already she felt eyes on her from beyond the light. "If the Americans win, I'll be at Jackson's compound. I'll find you again if it takes my last breath. If not . . . if the English prevail, I'll be somewhere in New Orleans. Gilbert . . ." Her voice caught. "Gilbert, take care." She whirled and headed back toward the outskirts of the camp. Her eyes filled as she tied the scarf once more around her head. Thank goodness, he hadn't tried to detain her. Every minute here put her more at risk.

"Who goes there?" came a shout.

After a quick swipe at her eyes, she stopped and faced the man who approached. "I—I'm selling tobacco," she began.

"You're an intruder. Come with me immediately if you don't want a hole in your gullet."

"No . . . truly I—"

Two other soldiers walked up, one carrying a torch, the second a pistol aimed at her head.

"Could be a Yankee spy," said the first.

"Take him to headquarters. Let the general decide," suggested the other.

She bolted for the nearest trees, but was grabbed from behind and thrown to her back on the ground. She kicked furiously, but was soon subdued and her wrists bound tightly before her.

A soldier jerked her to her feet and shoved her in the direction of the largest tent. "You can sell your tobacco to Pakenham," her captor snapped.

Frantically she tried to gather her wits. When it was discovered she was a girl, she could claim to be a camp follower from town. Yes, that might do. One thing for sure, she wouldn't reveal her relationship to Gilbert and thereby endanger him.

For a few moments, they were detained outside the tent. Then a guard drew back the flap and marched her inside. "We caught him coming from the Highlander camp," announced the soldier. "Don't know what he's up to."

Blinking in the light, she stared defiantly at the uniformed general seated behind his desk. It was several seconds before her gaze drifted to another man in the room, a casually dressed civilian seated close by and holding a smoking cheroot. She felt as if she'd received a physical blow when she recognized Blaine Caldwell.

21

Blaine thought he was hallucinating. One moment he was making mental notes of Pakenham's plans for the coming battle, the next he was looking into the face of a stricken Rebecca Gordon. She was never far from his mind, but he certainly hadn't expected to see her tonight—least of all in Pakenham's tent.

He stared at her, clamping his lips to conceal his shock and amazement. He barely heard the soldier's explanation of how the "boy" had been caught leaving the Scots' camp, how he had passed himself off as a vendor from town. She was dressed almost exactly the way he remembered her from the shooting match in Nashville. The sight was stunning.

She looked at him, her blue eyes suddenly wide with recognition, though her mouth was grimly set. He couldn't help admiring her coolness under duress. And she was clever enough to hold her tongue where he was concerned. She didn't appear injured, thank God, despite her hands being tied and grass and dirt clinging to her clothes. If the men had harmed her— Careful, he ordered himself. To reveal his feelings could earn him a firing squad.

Pakenham tapped his pen on the desk. "A vendor? At this hour? Unlikely," he observed. "Let's have the truth, young man. Who sent you? Are you spying for Jackson? If you cooperate, maybe we'll let your tender years save you from execution."

To Blaine's increased concern, he watched Rebecca tilt her chin in that sassy manner he had always adored, and with her bound hands tug the scarf from her hair. Despite her dirty face and rumpled boy's clothes, her feminine beauty shone through her dishevelment like moonlight infusing a cloud banked sky.

"What's this?" Pakenham asked. "A girl? Roaming through my camp? Who've you been with, missy?"

"No business of yours," she said to the commander while ignoring Blaine completely.

Blaine sat quietly as smoke curled upward from his neglected cigar. What the hell was she doing here? Had she come looking for him? He wanted to help her, but how could he if he didn't know what she was up to?

"Answer me, girl," Pakenham demanded. "Have you been selling yourself to my soldiers?"

Blaine's jaw worked in frustration. One thing he knew for sure, Rebecca was no camp follower.

"Are you a spy or a doxy?" Pakenham snorted. "Tell me who you've been with tonight—or it will go hard with you."

Watching her tight-lipped defiance, Blaine tried to untangle the mystery. He knew she wasn't a loose woman, and he was almost as certain she wasn't a British spy, no matter what Laurens had said.

Whatever she was doing here, she had put him in a dilemma—one which could cost him his life—and more important, one which could turn the delicate winds of victory toward the redcoats.

Pakenham rose and leaned across the desk, putting his weight on his knuckles. "Are you a Yankee spy?"

That question gave Blaine one clue. If she was spying for the British, Pakenham would have known her. On the other hand, she *could* be working secretly with Jackson. If so, she'd kept her secret well. Or maybe she'd just begun. After all, he hadn't seen her in a month. The idea of her being a spy seemed preposterous when he thought of the naive little imp from Morgan's Landing. But here she stood, in the middle of the night, caught in the enemy camp and refusing to explain her presence. He hid his deep concern by drawing on his cigar.

"We can't take any chances," Pakenham said. "Lock her in that shanty out back until tomorrow. No food nor water. Whatever it takes, by nightfall tomorrow, we'll have the truth out of her. Move along now. I've got work to do."

After she'd been escorted out, Blaine continued to sit in silence. Then with great nonchalance, he said to the general, "I'll speak to the girl, sir, with your permission. Sometimes a different tack will surprise the truth from a chit like that."

"Go ahead," Pakenham agreed as he returned to his chair and his maps. "But if she doesn't have a plausible explanation, or tell us who she met in the Highlander camp, I'll have her shot and be done with it. I'll not risk victory to spare a whore who could also be a spy."

As soon as possible, Blaine excused himself for the night. He had planned to go to Grande Isle, but that would have to wait until he figured out what to do about Rebecca.

He took a circuitous route and arrived at the shack. Being known to the guard, he was admitted without argument.

He found Rebecca seated on the ground in the dark, her wrists still tightly bound.

Turning up the oil lamp he carried, he squatted beside her.

For his effort, he received a look as icy as the winter Atlantic.

"Holy saints, Rebecca. What's going on? Are you all right?" He grasped her hands and found them frigid. "You've put me in a damnable spot, my little fox."

"No more than you deserve, Captain."

"Just answer one question. What are you doing here?"

"I won't tell you or anyone else."

"Control your infamous temper and listen to me. Pakenham thinks you're snooping around looking for information, or else you have a male friend among the Scottish Highlanders. If I had a choice, I'd prefer snooping. But if I'm going to rescue you, I'd like the truth."

"I'm not a spy," she said hotly, "unlike you, I might add."

Either she was lying because she assumed he was loyal to the British or it was possible she *did* love someone else.

Could she have met a man in the camp? The very thought was like a sword through his heart. "Then what the hell—"

"You needn't act so high and mighty, my fine Creole cavalier. I may be a simple girl, far beneath your class, but I would never betray my country. I'm here because . . . well . . . there's someone I had to see."

He gazed at her in the flickering light, fighting the urge to sweep her into his arms and kiss those adorable pouting lips into obedience. One other course would be to explain his own mission, but he couldn't reveal what he was doing—not as long as she was a British captive. "I don't have time to argue," he said finally. "First I've got to get you out of here. After the battle, you can take all the Scottish lovers you want. But I'll not see you placed before a firing squad."

He saw some of the starch go out of her. "They would . . . shoot me? Really?"

"Pakenham says they'll question you first."

"Oh. Torture." Fear stalked into her eyes.

He hated himself for frightening her, but it was the quickest way to gain her cooperation. Besides it was the truth. "The general gave the order a few minutes ago. I do have another question, Rebecca. You can be honest with me because whatever your answer, I intend to find a way to free you."

"What's . . . that?" she asked shakily.

"Pakenham said Guy Laurens is supplying information to him. Laurens claims you are working with him. Is it true?"

Her eyes widened. "You ask *me* that? You, who lied to me that day at Dominique Hall? You said you were loyal to the United States. You said you were reporting immediately to Jackson. But he told me he hadn't seen you. And now I find you here at Pakenham's elbow. It's proof enough that you've betrayed the United States."

He sat back on his heels. "Proof? Because I was in his tent?"

"You looked quite at home there."

"Then once again you think I'm a British spy. You suspected it before—and yet you made love to me?"

Her lashes lowered as she drew a sigh. "I wanted to believe your claims of loyalty. You surely know why. It seems my mother and I both have had a talent for loving the wrong men." She looked at him, her eyes bleak with misery. "But that's past now. I . . . I knew I couldn't love you the moment I saw you with Pakenham. I don't blame the British soldiers for doing their duty . . . for following orders. But the likes of you and . . . and Laurens . . . I'd rather be dead than be a traitor." She seemed on the verge of hysteria when she added, "They can torture me till the end of time and I will say no more."

He saw a martyr's fire blazing in her eyes. He was satisfied she was no pawn of Laurens. And she had just made a slip. "Rebecca, if you stopped loving me *just now* when you saw me with Pakenham, how could you have been in love with someone else in the meantime? Be honest, cherie, didn't you come to the camp to find *me?"*

"You flatter yourself, Captain. I had no idea you were here."

Studying her in the flickering light, he had to admit she had a point. Her surprise at seeing him in the general's tent was not pretense. And her present anger hardly indicated she loved him. Women had been known to change their minds. Fighting a sudden rush of pain, he said softly, "You do have courage, cherie." He started to rub her cold fingers, but she jerked away her hands.

"Leave me be, Blaine Caldwell. I don't want help from the likes of you."

Reluctantly he stood up. "We have a few things to settle between us, but this is not the time. Rest if you can. Pakenham is leaving at dawn, but he gave orders for you to be questioned tomorrow. I'll have to work fast to get you out of here—without compromising my own position."

"Well, don't do anything risky for my sake, Captain. You'll reap no benefits, I can promise you. In fact, if you return me to Jackson's compound where I've stayed since leaving your house, I'll more than likely tell him what I've learned about you."

He picked up the lantern. "I told you I'm a loyal American. If you suspected me of wrongdoing when you went to Jackson, why didn't you tell him then?"

"I . . . I thought about it." She shifted on the earthen floor. "But I didn't know for absolutely certain—until tonight. You must really think me a simpleton to believe you're not a traitor after what I saw with my own eyes."

He leaned over her and held up the light so he could read her expression. "I'll ask once more. Why did you come here? Were you looking for me?"

Her eyes were like blue steel as she stared up at him. "I told you once already—no. I wasn't lying when I told you I came here to find a man—someone I care deeply about. I found him and begged him not to go into battle, but he wouldn't listen. I was leaving the camp when I was captured."

"Dammit!" he snapped, his worst fears confirmed. So there was someone else—someone she'd encountered this past month—or maybe someone from her past. There were a handful of Americans fighting for the British, after all. And he admitted he really knew little about her. Only, of course, that he had grown to love her with every breath he took, with every ounce of his body and his soul. Given a choice, he'd much prefer she'd been somehow persuaded to act as a spy. A difference in loyalties was a matter that could be resolved after the war. But for her to love another, to risk her life after she had given herself so completely, declaring her love while lying in his arms only a few short weeks ago—hell, it was beyond his comprehension.

The fist grinding in the pit of his stomach made him speak harshly. "Get some sleep. I'll do what I can to save you from the consequences of your folly."

He ducked out of the shack and headed for the area where the horses were kept. He felt as if his insides were twisted into a dozen aching knots. He had been so certain of her love, certain enough to make her his wife. Even now, he couldn't believe she loved someone else. Would it have made a difference if he had told her he was spying for the Americans? Maybe, but he didn't dare let *anyone* in on his critical activities.

He found his mount and saddled it in the darkness. His plan had been to ride to the river, then canoe to Lafitte's camp, obtain another horse and report to Jackson before dawn. Now that he knew about Laurens, it was more important than ever that he warn Jackson about that bastard.

He would send word somehow, but he wouldn't let Rebecca Gordon face possible death, even if she hated him and made off with some enemy soldier. He would have to ask for Jean's help in getting her out of the camp. It was important that no suspicion fell on him because of her disappearance. She would have to stay in New Orleans until after the battle. Once that was over, he would learn the truth about how she felt. Until then, regardless of his inner turmoil, he must concentrate solely on his mission.

The packed earth felt cool beneath Rebecca's fevered cheek. She lay on her side with her knees drawn up and her numb hands tucked under her chin. Of course sleep was impossible, but she could lie in the darkness and try to rest. She would have liked a drink of water, but she had no desire for food. Her stomach was churning with nervous upset and she couldn't have eaten if she'd had a feast spread before her.

It was all so hopeless. She was sorry now she'd gone to such trouble to enter the British camp. Not only did her brother disregard her desperate warning, but Blaine Caldwell had turned up guilty as sin in Pakenham's tent. Until that moment, she had held out hope that she'd been mistaken about his character. Everything had pointed to his betrayal, but she had let her feelings rule her judgment—just as her mother had done so many years ago. Her mother had fallen deeply in love, then ended with a broken heart. It was absurd, really, that she had fallen headlong into the same fatal trap.

Lying there, her thoughts drifted to Blaine's wonderful face, his beautiful words, the way he had made her feel when he made her his own. Never again would she know such joy—and now it was forever lost. She had no one to blame but herself, and she would pay dearly for her mistake.

She was shivering and close to tears. Yes, Blaine Caldwell had made a fool of her. Seeing him so comfortable with Pakenham had not only proved his treachery, but had reinforced her feelings that he lived in a world beyond her understanding. How easily he had convinced her he was not a spy for the British. And how quickly she had fallen for his vows of love and hints at marriage. He must have found her naivete most amusing.

It was plain that Blaine would never stoop to marrying someone as foolish and lowborn as she. She had been a twit to assume that his lovemaking would lead to marriage. It didn't matter now anyway. He might rescue her to save her from pain and death—that is, if he could find the time considering his other duties. But they had no future; she must accept that fact and try to prevent misery from consuming her.

Her thoughts turned to Gilbert. What a moment it had been when she had looked into her brother's face, had beheld his eyes and realized he and she were the same flesh and blood. Maybe her gamble was worthwhile, after all. Gilbert didn't know she was illegitimate. Surely he would love her as his sister . . . someday . . . if he survived the battle and they could go to Scotland together. "Oh, dear Lord," she prayed in the silent, chill night, "let Gilbert live . . . and give me the courage to face whatever tomorrow may bring."

Her last thought before she dozed was of the strange lie told by Guy Laurens. Why would he tell anyone she was giving him secret information? It was all too much, she thought. Maybe she could figure it out if she got out of this mess alive. She finally slept despite her cold and despair.

Her next awareness was of struggling to breathe; a large hand covered her mouth and she heard a muttered curse; a gag was forced between her lips. Her first instinct was to fight her abductor, but she realized as she was tossed about with all the dignity of a trussed-up goat being hauled to market, that this was indeed a rescue.

As she was bounced across a man's stout shoulder, she became very still and concentrated on breathing. In addition to the gag, she was swathed in a blanket from head to toe.

Next came a horseback ride. Completely covered, she was held in muscular arms as the animal made its way through the cypress swamp surrounding the English camp. The only sound was the thudding of the horse's hooves in the marshy undergrowth, and its occasional snorts after it leaped a fallen log. Within a short time, she was laid gently into the bottom of a small boat, probably a canoe, and the sounds then were of insects and frogs and a paddle dipping quietly through the brackish water.

The first words she heard were "Lafitte—coming aboard." She was hoisted upward and passed from one pair of arms to another. But now, she saw a glimmer of light penetrating the blanket around her face. Dawn. A new day and she was aboard a ship setting sail. She had escaped her British captors as easily as a minnow swimming through a sieve. Efficient, silent, and no doubt the work of Jean Lafitte.

When the blanket was removed, she was lying on a bunk in a ship's cabin. Standing over her was the infamous privateer. So, Blaine Caldwell must have paid him to do his dirty work.

"Good morning, mademoiselle. I hope I wasn't too rough . . . but speed was most important." He reached down to remove her gag, then cut the ropes that bound her hands.

The sudden rush of blood set her fingers tingling. She moaned and massaged them briskly.

"Bastards," muttered Lafitte. "To damage such small and exquisite wrists."

"Thank you for saving me," she said, finding her voice. "I expect I owe you my life."

"'Tis nothing," he said, bowing. "The easiest rescue I've ever accomplished. My friend smoothed the way. All I did was waltz in—and waltz out with the prize."

"Your friend?"

"Captain Dominique Caldwell. Blaine . . . or Nikki . . . if you prefer."

"I see. He paid you well, I assume."

"Paid?" He tossed back his head and laughed, causing the golden loop in his ear to glisten in the morning light. "No, Blaine and I never pay . . . not with money. We're like brothers. I'm only repaying him for the rescue of Pierre. We take turns saving each others . . . ah . . . helping each other out of one scrape or another."

"Where is he now?"

"Gone back to the camp. His information is needed more than ever."

She pushed back her tangled mass of hair. "Of course. The information he takes to Pakenham—with your approval, it seems."

Lafitte guffawed heartily. "I can see why you and he are at odds. What has happened to honesty between lovers?"

"Honesty and love are not words Blaine Caldwell understands," she said scathingly.

His lips curling beneath his heavy mustache, he shook his head. "On the contrary, my friend Blaine is fatally attached to both. His honest nature prevents him from plying the trade which gives me such success. And love is burning up his insides, even as we speak."

She swung her feet to the floor. "He's a spy. He's a traitor, and a self-righteous snob."

His dark eyebrows shot upward. "He told me about your temper. It flares like a sunburst in the Heavens. But yes, you're right about one thing. He is a spy. But he doesn't take information to Pakenham . . . at least, nothing of value. He delivers information nightly to me. I myself deliver his messages to Jackson. Never has an American been more loyal. He risks death at every turn in the cause of freedom."

Her hands flew to her mouth.

"As for love," Lafitte continued. "He has told me how he feels about you. His heart . . . and his hand . . . were always yours to command."

She gulped and murmured, "You said *'were.'*"

"He told me last night you had a new love in the British camp. Blaine's a broken man over your rejection of his love for you."

"His . . . his love?" she choked. "But I thought . . . I mean, he said he loved me, but . . ."

"Ah, you Americans. You assume too much, and speak too little. Blaine made his intentions clear to me . . . but obviously not to you. What a shame."

She felt like bolts of lightning were crackling inside her. Putting her hand to her head, she stared up at Lafitte. Blaine loved her—and he was an *American* spy. "Excuse me, sir, but if Blaine is a spy for Jackson, why didn't he tell me tonight when he came to the hut?"

"Too risky. Remember, Laurens had just claimed you were working for *him.* Though Blaine thought that quite unlikely, you yourself swore you were meeting a Scot. He appeared a very confused and disturbed man when I last saw him."

She nodded her understanding. It was all so clear now. Her flood of joy and relief was tempered by the memory of the dreadful way she'd treated him, the things she'd said when he had come to help her, the look on his face when she'd claimed she had a Scottish lover. She had a myriad of excuses for doubting him, but looking back, they seemed weak and inadequate. If only Josie had told her everything that day . . . instead of merely saying, "Yes, he's a spy." If only she had listened to her heart instead of her mother's warning from the grave. If only she had given him the trust he had wanted and deserved. She touched Jean's sleeve. "Mr. Lafitte, I had no idea. I thought Blaine had . . . had taken advantage of me, then would toss me aside when I became inconvenient. You see, my mother . . . but no, that's another story."

He covered her hand with his. "Poor child. You imagined the worst. And then you went to another for consolation."

"But I didn't," she exclaimed. "Really, I didn't. I went to the camp to find my brother."

"Your *brother?*"

"I have to explain to Blaine. I only wanted to warn my brother . . . he's a Scots Highlander . . . to stay to the rear of battle. I don't have a lover. I've never loved anyone except . . . except Blaine."

"Ah, then all is not lost. I'm glad you told me, ma petite. I must say, I envy my friend at this moment. He's a fortunate man to have captured your heart."

"But I may have ruined everything. I have to see him. Is there any way?"

"No, my dear. He's back at the British camp by now. He asked me to take you to Jackson's compound. You're to stay there until the battle is over."

"I . . . I can't promise that. With the battle so near . . ."

"Caldwell insists you stay where you'll be safe. After your recent escapade, I would think you'd obey his demands."

"I respect him, and I love him, but I'm disinclined to obey. Of course, I will be careful; that I can promise."

"Nevertheless, I'm taking you to Jackson."

She could see there was no use arguing. Lafitte would carry out Blaine's wishes. But now, she had hope. She felt alive again. The knowledge of Blaine's love bubbled up within her like a fountain of sparkling champagne. Blaine loved her. He loved her. Her mind repeated over and over the glowing sound of it.

Lafitte shook his finger under her nose. "Don't look so smug, Mistress Gordon. If Jackson's smart, he'll keep you under lock and key until the battle's over. For your own safety."

Rebecca smiled slyly. If the general attempted such a thing, she'd find a way to escape. "May I go on deck now, sir?" she asked. "I need a bit of fresh air."

"Oui. Of course." He offered his elbow. "We'll sail to Grande Isle. Then after dining, we'll make our way into the city. The redcoats think they have it blocked, but a slick rat such as I can find a hole through any blockade."

Grinning, she took his arm. You're not the only slick rat, she thought. You can't imagine half the tricks of a woman in love.

22

Jogging her horse beside Lafitte's, Rebecca absorbed the sights and sounds of a city preparing for war. Few women were about, but armed men were everywhere, some in uniform and marching briskly, others in farmer's ragtag strolling along with long-rifles slung over their shoulders. She caught half a dozen accents, from silken French to backwoods jargon which sounded a familiar note in her ears. She even saw a band of Choctaw Indians sitting in the park being addressed by one of Jackson's regulars. She heard snatches of "Yankee Doodle" and choruses of the "Marseillaise" drifting from open windows and alleyways as she hurried along the streets. There was an undeniable expectancy in the air; the city was like a fuse that had been lit and was sparking its way toward an explosion. Jackson had fired that fuse—and Jean Lafitte had furnished the powder.

Jackson's headquarters were bustling. Lamps were blazing and men were milling about, both inside the main house and outside under the oaks dotting the landscaped private grounds.

Lafitte accompanied Rebecca through the crowded hall and opened the door to the general's office. He motioned her inside and closed the door, leaving her on her own. Obviously he had important business elsewhere.

She had left the clatter and clamor behind. Here, all was quiet and orderly, though tension filled the air like the unnatural stillness before a hurricane.

She took a deep breath and waited before Jackson's desk where his head, with its shock of shaggy gray hair, was bent over papers and maps. She felt like a naughty child waiting for a reprimand.

When at last he looked up at her, he smiled and rose to greet her. "Ah, here's Mistress Gordon." He motioned to the two men standing in one corner of the spacious room. "This is Mr. Peavy . . . and Colonel Butler. You gave us a good scare, young lady," he went on without waiting for her to acknowledge the introductions. "I should whup you good for sneaking off like that. I was relieved when I got word from Lafitte that you'd been found."

"I know, General. It was a mistake, but I longed to meet my brother after all these years. I regret to say he's marching into battle against us . . . with the Highlanders from Aberdeen."

"That's what Lafitte's message explained. I'll forgive you under the circumstances. Now, what are we to do with you?"

"Are the Tennessee sharpshooters going into battle?"

"Yes, indeed. In fact, they've been picking off British sentries for a week now. Can't miss such a handy target at three hundred yards. But then, you know all about that," he quipped.

"Then I want your permission to go to the ramparts when the battle starts."

He studied her at length. "I don't like it. I don't want a woman put in danger—even if she is a sharpshooter."

"I promise to stay behind the lines. I just . . . I just have to be there when the first attack comes."

"Oh, I see. You want to watch what happens to the Highlanders. We do expect the Scots to lead the attack with their drums and pipes. But what if you do see your brother—and see him fall?"

"Then I will at least know his fate. And maybe after the

battle, I can tend to him right away. Sometimes after the fighting, the wounded are left neglected so I've heard. I don't want that to happen to Gilbert . . . and I do have nursing skill."

"Very well, I give permission on one condition: that you swear to stay with the regulars behind the breastworks."

"Agreed. When will the battle begin?"

"It's imminent. A contingent from Tennessee will move into position as soon as we get our report from our man behind the lines. He's due here any time now."

"I . . . I wonder if that man is a special friend of mine."

"Goldurn! You're a curious creature. You *are* acquainted with the man. According to Lafitte, he helped with your escape."

Blaine. She didn't speak his name, but she felt her heart race at the thought he would soon be here. "Yes," she said with studied ease, "though I didn't know it at the time. Actually it was Jean Lafitte who carried me from the camp."

"A good man, Lafitte. Sorely misjudged by authorities here."

"With your permission, sir, I'd like to wait here to personally thank your . . . messenger when he arrives. I could sit in that chair in the corner and stay quiet as a mouse."

"Help yourself," Jackson agreed, his mind beginning to turn to more critical matters.

She took a seat in the upholstered wing chair and tucked her legs under her skirt. Watching Andrew Jackson, listening to his instructions as his aides came and went in concentrated activity, was enough to occupy her attention, except she kept one eye on the door in anticipation of Blaine's arrival. He had every right to be angry with her for the way she'd treated him. He was putting his life on the line for the Americans, had been for a long time, and she had been so uppity and insulting to him, it was a wonder he had bothered to rescue her at all. The part about Guy Laurens worried her too. She had thought he was in France or the Indies by now. Why would he return . . . and why would he take sides with the British? Either he was being well paid by them or he was seeking vengeance against Blaine. Possibly it was both. And now he'd involved her in his lies. Laurens was the only person she'd ever met who truly frightened her. His mood shifts from oily sweetness to raging tantrums were unnatural and terrifying. She could understand how such a warped person could become a murderer.

She continued to watch the door. Why didn't Blaine come? She only needed a moment with him—a moment to reassure him—and explain about Gilbert.

Sometime after ten o'clock, he strode into the room. He wore rough clothing, a wide leather belt with twin pistols encased at either side and a strap over his shoulder holding a pouch and canteen. His snug-fitting leather trousers were splattered with mud. He was bareheaded and his hair was unkempt, escaping the knot at his nape.

Looking neither left nor right, he crossed to take Jackson's outstretched hand. "I only have a short time, General. I must get back across the lines before midnight."

"Good man, Caldwell. What is your report?"

"Colonel Thornton is taking fourteen hundred men across the river tonight to launch an attack on your west bank line at dawn. This will coordinate with a frontal attack led by the Scots. Your troops at the Rodriquez Canal ramparts will be trapped between these advancing forces. You'll be forced to pull back into New Orleans if he succeeds."

"Hm." Jackson sat back into his chair and stroked his chin. "An excellent plan. If the British take the west bank, they can bombard the city from Algiers Point. What do you suggest, Caldwell?"

"Timing is the key, sir. Pakenham will send up a rocket signal at sunrise. I'm hoping to cause some delay of Thornton's men crossing to the west bank. You must concentrate every possible firearm on the central attack the minute the flare is seen. Put your batteries and your best marksmen against Pakenham, the Scots and the British regulars. If I can delay even half of Thornton's troops, we could win the day quickly. If the battle is prolonged, we're bound to be overwhelmed by their numbers."

"How do you propose to bring about this delay?"

"Thornton's men have to cross the river at night in small boats. Give me a handful of Choctaw Indians. We'll sabotage the boats before they're launched. We won't get them all, but we can cause enough confusion to slow down their movement."

"It's mighty damn risky—but just daring and foolish enough to work. Do you think you and the Indians have a chance to escape? I won't have any suicide missions under my command."

"The Indians are slippery as weasels. As for me, I don't plan to escape. I'll just drift back to Pakenham's quarters as if I'd never been away."

Jackson stood again. "You have my permission. But I want the Indians to understand the danger. You too, Captain. You'll be alone out there in the dark with more than a thousand redcoats armed for battle."

"I'm aware of that, sir. I'm counting on surprise and speed. It's worth the risk. Remember, all we need is a half-hour delay."

Jackson shook his hand again. "Then Godspeed, young man. The Choctaws should make excellent allies. They're camped in the grove just beyond the compound. Oh, and tell them they'll be well paid . . . or we'll give them some land somewhere. Fire their enthusiasm and they're the most determined fighters I've ever encountered."

"Thank you, General. I'll be off now."

Jackson stayed his arm. "Oh, hold up a minute. There's a lady waiting to see you."

During the conversation, Rebecca had scooted to the edge of her chair, barely daring to breathe.

"Lady?" Blaine swung around to face her. His first look of pleasure dissolved into a frown of wariness. "So you're here," he said in low tones. "I hope you'll stay put for a change."

Giving Jackson a quick smile of appreciation, she grasped Blaine's arm and walked with him from the room.

"Dammit, Rebecca—"

"Shh," she said with a finger over her lips. "We'll talk outside. I have to explain . . . and then you can go."

She led the way, feeling his stiff aloofness like an invisible wall between them. She stopped in a secluded garden, overgrown and fallow in the winter months and surrounded by an orchard of bare-limbed cherry and peach trees. From a distance came the song of a reed pipe playing a plaintive melody, "The Last Rose of Summer." The night air was damp and penetrating; overhead a slice of moon peeked intermittently from behind a reef of heavy clouds.

The barren tree limbs around them crackled in the breeze creating a swaying patchwork of light and shadow.

She faced him with her heart in her throat. There was so much she wanted to say. And she knew from his look, she had to undo a great amount of damage and misunderstanding in a very short time. She decided the direct approach was best. The time for playing fanciful games was past and only plain truth must exist between them. Blaine could die this night, or they could both be dead or prisoners by this time tomorrow.

Absorbing his eyes, feeling their intensity through the darkness, she began. "Blaine, I distrusted you from the beginning. It was childish, I know, but it started with that conversation I overheard in the woods at Payton. But there was something else inside me that was partly responsible. My mother on her deathbed hinted that no Creole gentleman would stoop to marry beneath his class. She had been misused by a man she had adored and loved. I found out that Etienne Dufour did truly hope to marry her, but then he was killed . . . as you know. I'm sure my mother died with a broken heart. Within a month of her death, I found myself walking that same dangerous path. It was like I was drawn on a thread of fate, and I fought my feelings like a moth being wrapped in a deadly web. When you said you loved me, I wanted to believe you, but I was afraid. I couldn't see how a man with wealth and position and power could truly love me . . . especially since I am illegitimate. But . . . I couldn't help loving you. And then when you spoke of marriage, I gave in to my deepest desires."

"Rebecca—" His voice was low, his eyes hidden in shadow.

"Please allow me to finish. Then you can go. I won't take much longer. What's most important is the part about Gilbert."

"Gilbert?"

"I told you when we first met that I was going to Scotland to find my brother. I discovered two days ago that my brother, Gilbert, was here with the English forces. He's a member of the Sutherland Highlanders, and I understand they will lead the attack tomorrow."

"My God," came the throaty response.

"You see, I had dreamed all my life of meeting him. I had to try to see him, if only for a moment before the battle. Otherwise . . . it could be too late."

His hand touched her shoulder.

She was shaking now—from the cold and from nerves at the breaking point.

"You little scamp," Blaine said with great gentleness. "I'm more guilty than you at jumping to conclusions. First of all, I assumed you loved me, expected you to love me as fiercely as I loved you. I was vain and thoughtless. And then when I thought you loved someone else . . . an English soldier you would risk your life to see . . . hell, I just cursed myself for being a crazy fool over you." His hand moved down her arm, coming to rest on her elbow. "Is it too late, Rebecca, too late to begin anew, this time with complete trust between us. I want you to be my wife . . . assuming of course, I live—"

A tiny cry escaped her lips. Reaching for him, she moved into the circle of his arms.

"My darling . . . hell, you're half-frozen." He hugged her to him, holding her against his body, his lips brushing her hair and finding their way down to the tip of one ear. "I've been an idiot," he whispered. "I'm sorry, my sweet little imp. I heaped pain upon you, adding to your worry about your brother. I didn't know, of course, and if it's any consolation, I've been in plenty of misery myself these past hours." He squeezed her, forcing her head back, then covered her lips to warm their coolness with his own heated mouth.

Her heart soared on wings of happiness. Clinging to him, for a moment she shut out all thoughts of danger and allowed her joy in his words to pulse through every part of her. He loved her; he wanted her; she would answer his need with complete faith in him, from this moment until the end of time.

Then like the folding wings of a brilliant butterfly, the moment passed.

The future with its danger seeped into her mind. "I'm

guilty too," she said. "I really believed you were a spy. Will you forgive me?"

"Only if you'll accept my proposal. This time a very official one."

Snuggling against him, she clung to the bittersweet moment. "My heart, my soul, are yours," she whispered.

"May I interpret that as a *yes?*" he asked softly.

She looked up, resting her chin on the rough fabric of his jacket. "You can, sir. Yes, yes, yes."

He placed his palm against her cheek. "Je t'aime, ma petite cherie. I will love you with my last breath." He pressed his lips to the soft widow's peak at her forehead.

She moved her hands along the back of his neck, then stood on tiptoe to again claim his lips.

After a lingering kiss, he gently eased away. "I would extend this moment through eternity, my love, but I have important work to do. Many lives, maybe even our country's freedom, depend on my success this night."

Holding back her fear, she attempted to match his courage. "I know. I heard the plan. My prayers are with you . . . and the Choctaws, and Jackson's forces. Also, I must admit, with one Scottish Highlander."

A shard of moonlight played across his eyes. "This is hard for you, my darling. I wish I could help where your Gilbert is concerned, but there's little I can do."

"I know. Where will you go after . . . after you delay Thornton's troops?"

"I'll send the Indians back and return to Pakenham's headquarters. Depending on how things go, I'll decide when to . . . ah . . . retire from this spy business. I'd much prefer to be fighting in the field. Dishonesty sticks in my throat, but it was Jackson's insistence—and I was in a unique position to do the job."

"Yes, I see that now," she said.

He crushed her in a kiss of hungry passion. Then he said huskily, "I'll come back to you as soon as I can, my love. Stay safe—for me."

"And you—for me." Her smile wavered, but she doubted he could see it in the darkness. Instead she squeezed his hand one last time, then kept her back straight as he hurried away in the direction of the Choctaw camp.

23

Despite the gloomy night, Rebecca felt like the sun had risen on her heart, engulfing it in a radiant glow that promised endless summer. She went to the cottage she had previously occupied and stretched out fully clothed on the bed. It would be good if she could sleep a bit, she told herself. Good, but almost impossible with so much happening, so much at stake in the next few hours. She covered herself with a blanket and catnapped for a time. Before dawn, she rose, nibbled on a hard biscuit left from yesterday's breakfast, and put on her only clean attire—Marie's dress. Over that, she pulled on a hooded cape she'd borrowed from one of the soldiers. Her feet were protected by soft leather boots, well-worn, but cleaned of swamp mud and ideal for whatever the day would bring.

As she headed toward the battlements, she assured herself all would go well today. Nothing could possibly happen to Blaine when they had just discovered the depth of their love, and their future beckoned with all its wonderful promise. She thought of Dominique Hall and how she'd spend her life there making Blaine happy and finding such joy in return. They would have children and live out their days in peace and love near the banks of the greatest river of their youthful country. She was sure she could make him proud of her, and in time, feel at home in the social life of New Orleans. The battle about to take place would be a turning point in the town's history, she was sure. No longer would New Orleans dwell in the exclusive isolation of its past, bound by family and tradition to Spain and France. The Americans were here to stay. Today's victory would prove that, once and for all.

She fingered the golden locket at her throat. You were wrong, Mother, she thought with a touch of bittersweet nostalgia. You meant well, and I love you for it, but you were wrong to assume all Creole gentlemen were cut from the same cloth.

A sleepy bird complained to her as she gained the main south road on the outskirts of town. Here she found Jackson's army on the move. In the chill darkness, dozens of wagons loaded with men and supplies were traveling stealthily toward the plain where the defense of the city would take place. Most of the men carried rifles and a few had muskets. Almost all were wearing woodsman garb except for the occasional band of Indians in leather and moccasins, and a number of free blacks in homespun and slouch hats. Although it was deadly quiet, there was an undercurrent of excitement and tension that electrified the atmosphere.

She found it a simple matter to hop into the rear of a wagon without being noticed. As she bumped along in the night, she considered her situation. She wasn't sure exactly what she would do at Chalmette; she had no weapon and no desire to kill anyone. But both her brother and her future husband were risking their lives. To stay away would have been impossible. Jackson had understood that, but Blaine would certainly disapprove.

Keeping her hood close around her, she arrived at the ramparts without being questioned. The barricade had been hastily constructed of mud, and extended three-quarters of a mile, from the Rodriquez Canal to a cypress swamp on the west. After studying the man-made hill, she decided its summit would offer a good view of the battle about to take place.

Gathering her skirt, she climbed to the top. The earth was soft and cool and she stretched out on her stomach and propped herself on her elbows. Before her, like a darkened stage waiting for the lamps to blaze and the curtain to part, stretched the Plains of Chalmette, empty and swathed in swirling fog off the river. Some distance away beyond the farthest line of trees, she saw the glimmer from campfires mingling with the ground fog, tinting it a pale yellow like the breath of some awakening swamp monster. The English were there preparing for the attack.

She gazed at the inky ribbon of river to the east. At this very moment, Blaine was somewhere out there, risking his life to sabotage the English boats. If he and his Indians failed, the huge British force would advance from two sides, and Jackson would have to retreat into the city to create a new line of defense.

A man dropped to his belly beside her and soundlessly primed his weapon, a long-rifle similar to the one she had left behind in Tennessee.

Other men arrived. To see them as soldiers stretched the imagination. They had no uniforms, no enlistment, no formal training, and little, if any, pay. It was more like a gathering of family members intent on protecting their land from some powerful enemy clan. Descendants of French, Spanish, Scots, English, Irish, German, African and Indian, a stew-pot of heritage and color, faced the army which had just won a sweeping victory over Europe's most powerful dictator, Napoleon Bonaparte. Was it possible, Rebecca wondered, for these first-generation Americans to come together and fight as one—to hold back the greedy monster from abroad, to prove again, as in '76, that the upstart Yankees in the New World were a power to be reckoned with?

More men clambered onto the ramparts, sprawling along its summit and preparing their weapons, watching for the first sign of dawn and for any hint that the English were on the move.

Rebecca rolled to her side at the sound of horses approaching along the road behind her. Jackson. Here at last was a man in uniform: dark blue coat with white pants, gold epaulettes at his shoulders, a satin sash and a plumed bicorne hat. He cut a dashing figure on his prancing stallion as he directed his men along the battlement.

Jackson was accompanied by two officers and a buckskin

clad frontiersman. He dismounted and conferred with his lieutenants, then disappeared along the line of waiting defenders. Did he know yet if Blaine had succeeded? Daylight was only minutes away. A distant clattering pulled her attention back to the far side of the plain. There was a stirring sound. The beast was awake and on the move.

Jackson's voice cut through the predawn chill. "Ready your weapons, men. Hold your fire until you see the *V* on the front of their uniforms. Sharpshooters may shoot at will—musketeers, wait for a sure target. Bugler boy, where are you?"

A young voice answered, "Here, General."

"Drummers!"

"Here, sir."

Streaks of opalescent blue light crept above the eastern horizon.

Jackson called, "Watch the west flank, Mr. Peavy. Alert me at once of movement there."

Rebecca took a deep breath. So much was at stake. Her fingers curled into the dried mud. If only she could do something. The waiting and watching were becoming unbearable.

Suddenly, a brilliant flare soared into the sky, followed quickly by a second and a third.

A murmur raced along the bulwarks, a rattle of last minute priming of gun barrels.

"Damned redcoats," muttered the man lying next to her. "Where's yore weapon, fella?" he asked her.

"I—I'm just observing," she answered.

He raised up and squinted at her. "What the . . . a female! Ye'd better hightail it, missy. Shootin's gonna start any minute now."

"Where are you from, mister?" she asked crisply.

"Squirrel Hill, Tennessee."

"Well, I'm from Tennessee too—Morgan's Landing. And I'm staying right here. I do have permission from the general."

"No place fer a woman . . . don't ker where you're from."

She was distracted by a shout from below. "Nothing from the west, sir. Riverbank's quiet."

"Good news, Mr. Peavy" was Jackson's response. Then he shouted, "Watch the plains, gentlemen!"

A fourth fiery flare punctuated his order. From beyond the tree line came the sound of a bugle followed by the first whining notes of a bagpipe. Drums rolled then rattled a steady beat.

"Here they come!" came the cry. "Hold your fire!"

Jackson was situated at the midpoint of the embankment, a spyglass in one hand and a pistol in the other. As the sky brightened he dropped to one knee and peered through the glass. "They're on the left in the trees," he called. "Led by the Highlanders. Send the word down. Let's hear a little "Yankee Doodle," Mr. Jones."

A *rat-a-tat-tat* of drums broke out from close by and was joined by a fife playing the rousing rebel tune.

In answer, from across the field came the skirling of bagpipes and the first clear sight of the advancing line of Scots in tartan and kilts. They marched forward with rifles and sabers ready, with more than a hundred years of tradition and pride in every step and the memory of Napoleon's defeat inspiring their confidence in easy victory over the die-hard colonials.

Jackson's men held their fire as they took a bead on the brightly colored wave moving toward them across the level plain.

Rebecca was momentarily hypnotized by the sight. It was obvious to her that the Highlanders out front were marching to their deaths. Was this the way wars were fought in Europe? Maybe, but in America, in Louisiana, on the Plains of Chalmette—it was idiocy amounting to mass suicide. In a few seconds, the Scots would be within three hundred yards; the long-rifles would cut them down like rows of cornstalks before a scythe. She could only think that her brother was there among them, maybe even carrying the bright banner up front. Why didn't they stop? Her mind screamed a warning. Go back. Go back, she pleaded silently with every yard they gained.

"Stupid fools," said her companion. "Stupid brave fools."

"Give me that," she abruptly ordered.

"What?"

"Your rifle."

"My rifle?"

"Give it to me." While he gaped openmouthed, she reached out and yanked the weapon from his grasp.

"Hey now, what the—"

She turned away and took up a kneeling position at the top of the embankment and sighted down the barrel.

"Who the hell is that?" shouted Jackson. "Get that woman down!"

She didn't hear him. Her concentration closed out her surroundings: the general, the commotion, the danger, even the competing sounds of the fife and the bagpipes swirling around her. The breeze lifted her cape and caught at her skirts. She felt nothing, saw nothing but that flag, that Highlander banner snapping in the first rays of the morning sun, a challenge moving ever closer to the American line.

She squeezed the trigger. The shot exploded, the first of the day. It cut through the air like a firebolt through a gathering storm.

The stanchion supporting the Scottish flag snapped and plunged to earth, carrying the symbol of the powerful British army fluttering into the dirt. A cheer went up from the men on the ramparts, but was quickly drowned by a massive fusillade of fire.

Rebecca had a sense of unreality, as if she were observing herself and the sound and fury of battle from some distance above and beyond her. She was only vaguely aware of the man next to her grabbing back the rifle.

"Nice shot, lady," he said grudgingly. "Couldn't have done better myself. Get down now. They's coming on."

The noise became deafening, and the plain enveloped with smoke that erupted from both sides.

She couldn't see the Highlanders anymore, but she heard the pipes still playing and knew the Scots, followed by the English troops, were continuing to advance despite heavy fire.

A sudden jolt hit her shoulder. It wasn't painful, just an intense blow that toppled her to the ground and sent her sliding down the embankment.

She felt dizzy, confused. Trying not to pass out, she felt

herself lifted by strong arms. Sounds ebbed and flowed; sounds of gunshots, shouting, a single harsh voice, then a more tender one. Now searing pain sped along her upper arm and up one side of her neck. With a moan, she clutched the rough fabric enfolding her.

"God help her," came a low, masculine voice from far away.

She was held fast; she couldn't breathe. She became aware she was traveling on horseback, cradled in someone's arms. Each jolting step sent fire through her shoulder. Gratefully she slipped into a cocoon of velvet darkness.

She awakened to pain and shadowy figures leaning over her. She felt woozy and too weak to move, but she could breathe now and the ache in her arm was endurable.

"She's conscious, Josie." The tone was hushed, the speaker invisible in the darkness.

"That's good. Here, honey, have a sip of this."

Her head was raised by a plump hand, and bitter liquid was forced between her lips.

Like a child, she did as she was told and in moments, she began to feel relaxed as the pain lessened.

"Miss Josie?" she whispered. "Is that you? What happened?"

"You took a minié ball, ma petite. But I've patched you up now. You've a nick in your pretty shoulder, but a proper sleeve will hide the scar once you've healed. Look who's here, my dear. He brought you from the field and has been hovering like a mama cat with a kitten. I told him you'd be just fine." Josie turned up the lantern's glow.

"Who? Where am I?" Rebecca touched the bandage covering her shoulder.

A man moved into the light. "You're in a tent behind the battlements. As soon as you've recovered, I'll give you a proper scolding, I do swear, Rebecca Gordon."

"Blaine," she murmured. "You're here. I . . . I . . ."

"Never mind, my darling. You're safe now. That's the important thing. And you're sure to be the heroine of the battle."

"And you're safe too," she said softly. "Oh . . . hold me."

Kneeling beside her, he gently pressed her to him. Yes, she

remembered the rough fabric of his coat against her cheek. It had been Blaine who had carried her to safety.

"Blaine." She sighed. "I'm sorry to be such trouble, truly I am. I know I was foolish—and went against your wishes. But I couldn't sit by and do nothing. I . . . I wanted to help."

He smoothed back her tangled hair and found her temple with his cool lips. "You were very brave, ma cherie. I'm just so sorry you were hurt."

"I'll be fine now. I was just dizzy for a spell. My arm feels better already."

"And you're in good hands. Miss Josie will keep a close eye on you till I return."

"Return? You're not . . . going . . ."

"Shh. I must report to Jackson, then get back to British headquarters."

"No. But why? You've done what was asked of you. I heard the general say the redcoats were delayed."

"And so they were. But the battle has just begun. The sun isn't up above the tree line. By the way, your shot was an inspiration, I must admit. Quite miraculous."

"You . . . saw it?"

Gently he massaged the nape of her neck. "I did. I had just arrived behind the lines when I saw you silhouetted in the moonlight. I didn't know it was you, of course, but I should have guessed." He chuckled near her ear. "What other woman in the world would stand alone to face the entire British army and make a shot any crack marksman would envy. Who, but my little Rebecca of Tennessee." He found her lips and covered them with a kiss aching with tenderness.

She wrapped one arm across his shoulder, feeling the dampness of his clothing, his body heat penetrating the rough cloth of his homespun shirt. His love flowed into her, lending her strength and courage.

Resting her head against his chin, she said, "What I did was nothing compared to your risk behind enemy lines. If you must go back, my prayers will be with you. And I pray this war will soon end. It breaks my heart that you . . . and my brother must fight." She looked up to search his face. "I understand now, Blaine, the way men feel when they're in battle. It has a terrible glory—excitement and fear taking hold of their insides. Why, a person's brain stops working altogether."

She saw his bitter smile in the flickering light.

"A tragic game, I agree," he said. "Why should the English want the United States back anyway? They have homes and families across the sea. They disparage the colonials and deride our desire for independence."

Josephine bent near and cleared her throat. "Pardon, but I must have another look at that bandage, cherie."

"And I must go," Blaine stated, moving away.

Sitting up, Rebecca took his hand. "Blaine, if you hear anything about the Highlanders regiment, I'd appreciate knowing . . . well, what happened."

"Your brother. I'll do what I can, my love. If possible I'll slip onto the field behind the front lines."

"Oh, do be careful." Her weakness prevented her from holding back her tears. "I . . . I . . . lo—"

The word *love* was interrupted by his quick kiss. "Au revoir, mon cher." And then he was gone.

Josie bent near and inspected Rebecca's wound.

Clearing her throat, Rebecca asked, "Have we been here long, Miss Josie?"

"Only a short while. I came an hour ago to help the ladies tend the wounded."

"Goodness, I'm such a nuisance. You must go on now and look after the soldiers."

"Only a few have arrived as yet, praise the Lord. I heard what you said about war. Such a shame, it is. I don't hold it against the men. No, it's King George I blame. If he and that upstart Napoleon want to go at each other, that's just fine. But leave us be, I say. We need our men for things besides getting blown up in some stupid war. Things like clearing land and building new towns—and making babies for the next generation."

Blaine was damp, caked with mud and grass and chilled to the bone, but he was satisfied with the way things were going. He made his way west, being careful to avoid the front lines where the noise of heated battle greeted the first light of day. Rebecca would be fine, he was sure. What an amazing little scamp she was. And his escapade with the Choctaws had been an unqualified success.

He and the Indians had had a fine time making holes in every British flatboat and canoe along the bank of the river. After the Choctaws had made short work of the sentries, they had crept along in the tall, wet grass and made certain one boat after another would sink within minutes of launching. There had been no need to damage them all—just enough to create confusion and cause delay at the critical moment. The entire operation had taken less than thirty minutes, then he had slipped back across the lines to report to Jackson. It was at that moment he had spotted the astonishing figure of his headstrong Rebecca as she coolly splintered the enemy's flagstaff. If only he had reached her sooner he might have prevented her taking that shot in the shoulder. As soon as this damnable war was over, he would hold her in his arms for endless hours and kiss away any pain she should ever endure. The very thought took the chill off his bones.

Suddenly he remembered Rebecca's concern for her brother. Stopping, he crouched in the grass and gazed toward the spot where the Highlanders had made their first approach. Even from this distance, he could see scattered bodies and the glint of useless weapons. The attack had moved forward toward the canal. If Jackson prevailed, that line could soon be in retreat back across the plain.

Running across the flat ground, he arrived at the spot where fallen men in tartan plaid lay sprawled. God, there were so many, and he had no way of knowing which one could be Rebecca's brother. Later at the command tent, lists of the dead and wounded would be posted. It was the best he could do for now.

He had started toward that area when he heard movement behind him. He drew his knife but a blow to the back of his skull sent him spinning onto the oozing earth. His head reeling, he felt strong hands grip both his arms and drag him to his feet.

"Ye're the one. I saw ye with mine own two eyes. Up to no good with them savages at the river a while back."

"You're mistaken," Blaine said as firmly as possible. "I'm Mr. Caldwell, a friend of the general's. No need to—"

"Save your breath, mister," said the second man. "Ye can explain to the commander what ye're doing using a hatchet on the boats."

Hell, they'd seen him, he thought helplessly. Rotten luck—but at least the deed was done.

He was marched to Pakenham's tent and escorted inside. It was clear at once that the British general was in a thunderous mood. And standing at his side stood an immaculately attired Guy Laurens.

"What in God's name are you doing with *him?"* Pakenham shouted at Blaine's guards. "I haven't time . . . I must leave for the field. It's nearly daylight and there's no sign of Thornton." Dressed in full military uniform, he frowned at the sight of the captive Caldwell. Solemn-faced orderlies stood at attention like ramrods driven into the ground.

"We saw him down by the river," one Scot explained. "He had worked over Thornton's boats."

Pakenham moved closer and stared hard at Blaine. "God almighty—what were you doing, Caldwell?"

An officer ducked into the tent. "Excuse me, sir, but we don't have the ladders."

"Ladders?" Pakenham snapped.

"Yes, sir. The ladders to scale the ramparts. Someone was supposed to furnish them . . . but—"

"Holy Christ!" The commander seemed about to explode.

Another head poked inside the tent. "Excuse me, General, it's nearly dawn. The Highlanders are ready to move out."

"I'm coming. I'm coming. Too late now—too late . . ." Pakenham sputtered in his anger. Turning to Laurens he said, "Our meeting is at an end. I appreciate your information." Then he glared at Blaine. "I'm deeply disappointed, Mr. Caldwell. I trusted you and this is what I get for it. A bloody spy—and a saboteur, as well."

Laurens stepped forward to give Blaine a look of utter disdain. "The man's a bastard. I could have told you, General, if I'd known he was skulking about." His lip curled with sardonic pleasure. "But he's caught now. It's quite ironic—and satisfying."

"Satisfying?" asked Pakenham while pulling on his gloves. "How so?"

"I'm well acquainted with Blaine Caldwell. I can attest to his duplicitous nature."

Silently cursing, Blaine kept his tongue in check. His fortunes on this new day had reached an all-time low.

"Too bad," observed Pakenham without real interest. "Well, I'll have to deal with you after the battle, Caldwell." He shook his quirt under Blaine's nose. "But you'll be shot for your treachery, sir. Whichever way the battle goes, you can count on facing a firing squad. I guarantee it." He turned to Blaine's captor. "If anything happens to me, Lieutenant, see that this man has the fastest trial on record—and is executed for spying. That's an order."

"Yes, sir," the lieutenant said crisply.

"Laurens, I suggest you return to your ship. You'll be informed of the outcome of the battle."

"Thank you, General," Laurens said, still smiling at Blaine. "I'll just have one final word with your prisoner. I don't expect to see him again."

Pakenham swept from the tent.

Blaine heard the British commander ride away just as daylight seeped into the sky.

Chains were promptly produced and the Scottish guards began securing Blaine's ankles and wrists. During the process, he kept his gaze fixed on the smirking Laurens, who was lounging against the edge of Pakenham's desk.

Finally Laurens said, "So we meet in different circumstances, Captain."

"Entirely. You've betrayed your country, Laurens, and dishonored your word."

Laurens laughed. "You're one to throw stones—you who are about to be executed for spying. A disgraceful end, I'd say, to the Caldwell family ambitions in Louisiana."

"And what of the Laurenses' reputation . . . after the Americans win the battle."

"An unlikely event. But I'll not be at risk and you'll be dead. I'll merely return to the city and claim what is rightfully mine."

A new dread crept along Blaine's spine. "What do you

mean?" he asked, just barely aware of the irons being tightened around his ankles.

"With you dead, your lands will be sold at auction—perhaps to me. That may prove attractive to our friend, Miss Gordon."

"Forget it. Rebecca isn't the naive young woman you expected to control. And I assure you, she would swim to Scotland before she would allow you in her bed."

"Allow? Since when do illegitimate droppings presume to allow anything. She's merely the windblown seed of a man I once did business with—a man, I might add, whom you told her I murdered."

"On the contrary, *she* gave me that bit of information."

"But how . . . then who told . . ."

"You admit it's true?"

He cocked an eyebrow. "Did I kill Etienne Dufour? I don't mind revealing the truth to a dying man. Yes. With one well-placed shot, I secured my family a fortune."

"You bastard," Blaine growled.

"The only bastard is Rebecca Gordon. If she decides to be more cooperative, I might yet keep her for a time as my mistress. Her looks do stir a man's blood. If not, I may have to force her—"

"You'll pay hell, Laurens." Blaine strained at his bonds. "She'll kill you first."

"I was about to say, once I've enjoyed her bounty, I'll arrange for her to join her father. It wouldn't do to have such a loose-tongued wench ruining my reputation in New Orleans."

"You'll never get away with it," he said, fury and disgust churning through his insides.

"Oh, I think I will. If the English win the war, they will be grateful when I turn over their little Yankee spy to them for execution. If the Americans win, which I doubt, I'll just take matters into my own hands."

"You'll roast in hell, Laurens."

Laurens laughed again. "This is a most amusing conversation." He removed his gloves from his vest pocket. "And I'm wasting my time. Look at you, Caldwell. You look like a varmint who crawled from the swamp. You're helpless and soon to be shot." He slapped the gloves against his palm.

"No one deserves it more. I'm just delighted I was here to see you like this. If testimony is needed at your trial, I'll gladly provide it. When you face the gun barrels, I hope your last vision behind your blindfold will be of Rebecca Gordon —naked in my arms."

Blaine was tugged by the guard toward the tent door. He knew it was useless to struggle, but at that moment he would gladly have given his life if he could have taken Guy Laurens down with him.

24

After Josie took away the light, Rebecca lay still for quite some time listening to the distant roar of the cannon like an invisible storm on the far horizon. Drifting in and out of sleep, she heard the groans of injured men arriving at the tent, and of the muffled voices of the women and occasionally a physician's barked command.

Gradually she realized that morning light was dappling the canvas enclosure. She made an effort to rise and was pleased with her returning strength. All around her, wounded soldiers were being carried in and placed on pallets and cots to await the doctor's attention.

Josie hurried to her side and steadied her.

"I'm really much better, Miss Josie. Truly, I feel fine, just a tad hungry."

"That's a good sign. There's hot coffee and biscuits just outside."

She glanced around. "But look at these poor men. Some are bound to die."

"A few, most likely. To be honest, I'd expected more casualties. There are only a dozen American dead, so far."

"I'm going to view the battlefield, Josie."

"What?"

"I'm worried about my brother. The Highlanders were

leading the attack. I saw their plaids and heard their bagpipes."

"You'll do no such thing. You're going straight to New Orleans, missy. And no arguments." She shook her finger under Rebecca's nose. "You gave us a fine scare, young lady. And I promised Captain Caldwell I'd look after you."

A man in uniform ran into the room. "It's over! We won! The damned redcoats are in retreat! Hallelujah! It's a great victory! Whoopee!"

From beyond the bulwark came the sound of gunfire and a cannon firing a victory salute.

"Over?" Rebecca gasped, staring at Josie. "So quickly? Why, it's still early morning." She hurried outside. The first thing she saw was Andrew Jackson approaching on his magnificent steed, cantering easily, doffing his hat from time to time to acknowledge the cheers of bystanders, his face alight with a broad smile.

Gripping her shoulder against renewed pain, she ran toward him.

When he saw her, he reined up and waved his hat in her direction. "By the Eternal," he thundered. "There's that scrappy lass. How you be, Miss Gordon? I thought we'd lost you, for certain."

She stood beside the high-strung horse and gazed up at the general. "I'm fine, sir. Just a nick on my arm."

"Good to hear that. I spoke a while back with your friend, Captain Caldwell. He saved our hide, I can tell you. Thornton's men got across the river, but an hour late. We were ready for 'em and drove 'em back—just like we did the regulars at our front. We'll have a parting skirmish or two, but we've won the day."

"I'm so pleased, General Jackson."

"And you, little lady, were quite a sight. Your superb shot was an inspiration to all the troops. Our shooters picked off the infantry before they got within fifty yards of the bulwarks. Like shooting pigs in a pen, I'll swear. Only"—his brow furrowed briefly—"the Brits showed plenty of courage. They took terrible losses and kept on coming."

A lieutenant came running along the road from the battleground. "General! General Jackson!" he shouted.

Jackson spun his horse. "What is it, sir?"

"We just got word. Pakenham is dead. Shot off his horse at the height of the battle. The army has retired to their camp carrying most of their wounded."

"They won't be back," said Jackson. "After the whupping they took today, I expect total retreat from Louisiana. But keep the guard posted. I'll be at headquarters." He tipped his hat toward Rebecca. "Stop by, Miss Gordon. We should soon hear from your captain."

"Congratulations, General," she called as he galloped in the direction of New Orleans.

Josie arrived on the scene. "Go home now, Rebecca, to my house. Rest a spell. I'm going to the battlefield with the ladies who have volunteered to help. We don't make any distinction between Yankees and redcoats—not when a man is hurt."

"I'm going with you."

"No, you're not. You've lost a good deal of blood and besides . . . you're an unmarried lady. It isn't proper. Now me . . . well, that's a different story. There are plenty to help. Marie Leveau and some of her people have volunteered."

"I feel fine, Josie. I'm not a sheltered city girl who might faint at the sight of a little blood. And . . . I must look for someone."

"Well, come along. But if you feel sick, promise you'll come right back and lie down. I don't have time to waste hauling a swooning girl back from the plains."

A few minutes later, Rebecca stood on the ramparts and wondered if she would have to swallow her pride and go home after all. Bodies in uniform lay across the Plains of Chalmette as far as she could see. Redcoats and tartan plaids, colorful, torn, and eerily motionless, intermingled in the field of brown grass. Limbs were twisted at grotesque angles and there seemed no sign of life.

With weak knees and sweaty palms, Rebecca followed Josie onto the battleground. Summoning her courage, she headed directly to the area where she could see bodies with the tattered tartan of the Sutherland Highlanders. Gritting her teeth, she scanned the youthful, tortured faces with gaping mouths and stunned eyes—faces whose features and coloring reminded her of her neighbors and friends in Tennessee.

Gilbert was not among the fallen.

Overwhelmed with relief, she rejoined Josie and the other women who were searching for survivors. Members of the militia had also joined the effort and stretchers were being brought to the area. At the far end of the field, English wagons were moving among the dead and wounded.

She wanted to help, but her head began to feel peculiar and her stomach unsettled. Wary of Josie's warning, she decided to return to New Orleans and wait for news of her brother—and for Blaine's return.

The day after the battle, Rebecca moved her belongings from Jackson's headquarters to Josie's small cottage. She had no appetite and spent much of her time sleeping. Loss of blood and exhaustion, Josie had said. While all of New Orleans was in the throes of wild celebration, Rebecca remained in quiet seclusion—waiting, watching, and wondering.

One week after the great victory at Chalmette, she packed a picnic in preparation for a stroll to Dominique Hall. She longed to visit Shandy and Pepper and see the house once again. The happiest moments of her life had been spent there. It was Blaine's home, and she hoped a visit might ease her loneliness and worry.

During Shandy's single visit to Josie's, the child had been full of news from Blaine's mansion. In a most adult fashion, she had given a detailed description of the activities there, of how Marie and George were managing, of how the new foal was growing bigger every day, and of how the entire staff was sprucing things up in anticipation of the master's return.

If he returned, Rebecca thought. The English were making an orderly retreat down the Mississippi, but not even Jackson had received any word regarding Blaine Caldwell. The staff at Dominique Hall didn't know the risk he had taken, nor of his promise to return as soon as the battle was over, nor that he had asked her to be his wife. She could hardly think of that night in the garden of Jackson's compound without breaking down in tears. What if he just disappeared and she never knew what had happened to him? She wouldn't be the first woman to wait a lonely lifetime for a soldier to return from war.

She packed the basket with cheese, thick slices of bread and some oatmeal cookies Josie had baked before leaving for her "hotel." Her ears perked up when she heard the front door open and someone walk into the parlor.

"Josie?" she called.

There was no answer.

Her heart jumped. "Blaine?" She dropped the cookies and threw open the kitchen door. Striding toward her with a look of satisfaction on his face was Guy Laurens.

She tried to slam the door, but it was too late. He shoved it open and grabbed her wrist.

"My little whore," he said under his breath. "You've found a mentor in Josephine Laclair. What has she taught you, cherie? She was good once . . . knew all the tricks. She's an old hag now with nothing to offer—not even for free. But you . . . now that's quite another matter."

Desperately she fought to free her arm, but pain scorched her shoulder. "Leave me alone," she said fiercely. "You promised Blaine—"

His laugh stalled her words. "I promised Blaine," he echoed sarcastically. "You may recall, I had no choice at the time. But everything is different now. He may even be dead . . . or soon will be. While I—"

"Dead!" she choked. "How . . . how would *you* know that."

"I saw him during the battle. He was caught by the British when he tried to sabotage their boats. Guess it worked too, which is all the more reason for him to be shot."

His words tore through her, leaving her appalled and speechless.

"Oh. You grow pale, dear. Too bad. And I see blood seeping through your sleeve. Oh, yes, I've heard the story. Everyone is calling you the heroine of the battle. You've got quite a reputation. Someday that may earn you an extra coin or two at the bawdy houses along the river. I can hear it now: *Lay with the heroine of the Battle of New Orleans. She'll spread her legs and show you the source of her courage. Come one, come all.*"

She aimed her fist at his smirking face, but he stopped the blow and twisted her arm behind her.

"Ah, my dear, you shouldn't have cheated me of my rightful place." He lifted her bodily to the butcher-block table in the middle of the kitchen.

"Cheated you?" she said hoarsely. "What are you doing?" Fear numbed her brain. She realized he was insane and she couldn't reason with a madman.

He pressed her against the block.

She fought back, kicking and twisting, but failed to break his hold on her.

He laughed. With one hand, he encircled her throat, squeezing it just enough to start a pounding in her ears and blurring her vision.

Leaning across her breasts, he moved his other hand downward. With one violent motion, he ripped the fabric of her skirt and fumbled with her delicate undergarments. "Lovely. Young. Virginal," he muttered with eyes narrowed with lust. "Caldwell is out of my way and now all will be mine." It was as if he talked to himself, as if she were an inanimate object existing for his pleasure.

She couldn't see them, but she felt his hands on her thighs. "He'll kill you," she whispered through a throat nearly compressed by his brute strength.

"He'll kill no one. He'll be executed as a spy. I'll take my rightful place in New Orleans society. I'll buy Dominique Hall. My wife will like it for a summer home by the river. And you, my girl, might like to be my mistress, after all."

"I will die first."

"He said you'd say that. Very well, it's your choice. Probably safer anyway." When she struggled, he slapped her viciously. "You'll just disappear; no one will know the difference."

"Josie . . . Josie will know," she choked.

He laughed. "That whore? She wouldn't dare make trouble. If she did I would take care of her in the same way. You're mine, not his," she heard him mutter from just above her.

She shrank against the table and tried to scream. One arm was trapped behind her back; the other had no feeling. She was vulnerable to his violation; there was nothing she could do.

The hand crushing her windpipe loosened. "No, don't faint, Rebecca. I want you awake to enjoy this. I hope you scream, fight, suffer. All the more pleasure to me."

He was struggling with his trousers. His sweat dripped across her bare breasts.

She never heard the shot. She lay tense, waiting, helpless against the agony and degradation he would force upon her. Her eyes were tightly closed and she was biting her lip and tasting blood. If her screams pleased him, she would at least deny him that small satisfaction.

Something hot and wet was running along her cheek. Opening her eyes, she looked into his face. He was staring at her, his mouth open, surprise etched in every line. The wetness was a stream of red liquid, dripping steadily from a wound above his right eye. He fell forward, crushing her with dead weight.

She screamed then, but it sounded weak and far away.

With one hand, she shoved against him. He rolled over and toppled to the floor.

She sat up on the table and looked across the room at Josephine, who still held the pistol. Circles of pink rouged Josie's cheeks and her eyes were set and staring like enormous bronze coins.

"Josie . . ." Rebecca whispered. "He . . . he was . . ."

"I know attempted rape when I see it," Josie said in a leaden voice. "Your father would have wanted me to kill him. I did it for Etienne—and for his daughter."

Rebecca moved off the table and leaned dizzily against it. "You were right to do it, Josie. Thank God . . . Thank God." For a moment, she stood there, trembling and faint. Then she went into Josie's arms and wept on the woman's broad bosom until her tears were spent.

Josie let her cry, then guided her to a chair in the parlor. "I'm so glad I came home when I did," she said, sitting on the arm of the chair. "Lucky. So lucky."

Wiping her eyes, Rebecca looked up at her. "Why . . . why *did* you come home so early?"

"I had news."

Her heavy look sent a warning to Rebecca's heart. "What . . . news? Blaine?"

"He's been captured. Found guilty of spying and sabotage. I'm sorry, child. He's to be executed in two days. Jackson got word an hour ago and sent a message to me. There was a trial of sorts at the British camp. Blaine was questioned—refused to confess, found guilty, partly because of testimony by Laurens—and he will be legally shot. As soon as I knew Laurens was in New Orleans, I hurried right home."

Rebecca felt herself grow cold as she listened, like a frigid blanket was lowering over her. "But . . . can't Jackson . . . do anything?"

"Nothing. He said he knows Blaine is guilty. And the British are bitter over their terrible losses. They're moving south now, shelling as they go. They want this withdrawal done quickly and to get on their way. General Jackson was deeply sorrowed, but he said there was no time to negotiate or to do anything to save him."

For a time, Rebecca sat in silence, her hand clutching her torn bodice, oblivious to the fresh blood, hers and Laurens's. Only the sound of the grandfather clock bonging three times broke the stillness.

Finally Josie spoke softly. "Lie down, cherie. I'll bring you some brandy. Then I'll go to the church and fetch a priest to take Laurens away. There may be an inquiry, but I don't think I'll be arrested."

Rebecca looked up. "Oh, Miss Josie, I wasn't thinking of your danger. You've killed a man to save me. I'll testify, of course. Surely after what he tried to do—"

"Don't you worry, honey. I have plenty of power in this city. And Laurens was thoroughly despised. Besides, if you explain what happened, no one will doubt you." She stroked back hair from Rebecca's moist brow. Smiling slightly, she said, "After all, you are the heroine of the battle. Every man, woman and child in New Orleans is singing your praises."

25

"Amazing woman—absolutely amazing." Jean Lafitte rose from his chair and greeted Rebecca with a rakish smile. "You came alone to Grand Isle? In a boat at night? Caldwell made no secret of your beauty and wit, but it appears he underestimated your courage. Still, such behavior should be expected from the woman who has become a legend in Louisiana since shooting down the English standard at the battle."

Rebecca knew by his relaxed and pleasant demeanor that he hadn't heard the news. Skipping polite conversation, she went right to the point of her visit. She told him about Blaine's capture and scheduled execution. "You're the only person who can help me," she concluded. "I would have traveled through hell to reach you."

His eyes no longer sparkled. "Mon Dieu, he's gotten into a fine fix, it appears. And there's little time to extricate him. Are you certain Jackson can do nothing?"

"I spoke with him yesterday as soon as I heard. He is deeply distressed, but says spies are traditionally shot—and Blaine knew the risks from the beginning."

For a time, Lafitte paced in front of his desk. His once grand house was little more than a ruin, but enough of it had been salvaged to make it habitable.

Rebecca waited silently for the privateer to consider the options.

At last he turned to her. "First we must find out where he's being held. A midnight raid might be a possibility. If not that, I have contact with some British officers. Perhaps a well-placed bribe—"

"Excuse me, Mr. Lafitte," she interjected.

"Please call me Jean," he said, attempting a smile. "I feel we're well acquainted."

"Yes . . . Jean. I was going to explain about my brother. I've met him only once. He's an officer in the Sutherland Highlanders . . . if he still lives. I searched the battlefield for his body, but didn't find him. Maybe we could reach him. Maybe he would help."

Lafitte gazed at her with blatant admiration. "Even I underestimated your courage, my lady. If Caldwell dies tomorrow, he can still consider himself a lucky man to have gained your love. Hmm." His brow creased. "We must work quickly. What's your brother's name and regiment."

"Lieutenant Gilbert Gordon of the Ninety-third Foot."

He thought a moment. "We need to contact him right away. You can write a letter to him—carefully worded and ask for a meeting. I'll send it with Mangas, one of the island men who's been trading with the British troops."

"Yes. I'll do it at once."

"Come along. We'll get Mangas on his way and then you must be my guest for breakfast. I'm sorry I have nothing more elegant to offer. As you know, my home was razed and thus my accommodations are limited."

"You don't need to apologize, Jean. You've given me the first bit of hope I've had since yesterday."

The next hours were the longest and most agonizing of her life. Every minute that passed was a minute of Blaine's life ticking away.

Shortly after two P.M., Lafitte's envoy returned to Grand Isle with a message from the English.

In Rebecca's presence, Lafitte tore open the envelope and scanned it quickly, then smiled up at her.

"What? What is it?" she asked breathlessly.

"It's from a certain Major Ellis Blanton. He's in charge of

Caldwell's execution, and I gather he's not too happy about the assignment."

"Will he help us?"

"Don't know yet. But there's more. A meeting has been arranged for us later today at the British encampment below Fort St. Philip. Only a small force remains there with one frigate loading supplies. Both you and I will be allowed to attend—as well as your brother, Lieutenant Gilbert Gordon."

"Then Gilbert's alive!" she cried. "Thank God. And will we see Blaine?"

He nodded. "That also has been granted since he is a condemned man."

She thought her heart would burst. She would see him; surely somehow he could yet be saved. "When do we go?"

"We'll leave right away. The camp is just over an hour's journey by boat. On the way, we'll think of a plan. And I'll take a sack of gold in case I can arrange a bribe."

She reached out her hand to clasp his. "Thank you, Jean Lafitte. I'll never forget this—and if Blaine survives, you'll be repaid in full. You know . . . we're to be married," she added softly.

"Then he finally worked up the courage to propose." He put his arm around her shoulder. "I'll do all I can, I swear, to see that your wedding takes place."

At midafternoon, under a white flag of truce, Rebecca and Jean Lafitte entered the tent of Major Ellis Blanton. The major rose from behind a plank desk to greet them. Beyond his tent, in the broad main channel of the Mississippi, an English frigate rode at anchor.

At Blanton's side stood Lieutenant Gordon, clad in his Highlander tartan and trews and with a sizeable bandage wrapped around his forehead.

As the major and Lafitte shook hands, Gilbert crossed to Rebecca and drew her into his arms. The gesture came as a complete surprise and caused her eyes to mist.

"My dear sister," Gilbert said in a low voice. "I didnae know if our first meeting was something I imagined. Come outside. We'll speak privately while the major discusses matters with Lafitte."

Arm in arm, they left the tent. She looked up at him,

seeing him clearly in the light of day. Again she was struck by his features, so similar to her Mother's. "Is your wound serious?" she asked.

"Nay. Actually it saved my life by rendering me unconscious during the first advance. So many of my comrades were killed. 'Twill be a sad day when our regiment returns to Aberdeen."

"But you're alive. And soon the war will be over. I'm so thankful you were spared."

He looked down at her with great tenderness. "Rebecca Gordon, my own sister. With Mother gone, I hope ye'll come soon to Scotland. I want to make a home for ye. Ye'll love my darlin' wife and the bairns. I have three, ye know."

"I know. And I had planned to do just that, Gilbert. But now everything has changed. I'm pledged to marry a man from New Orleans." She intertwined her fingers. "And I do love him so. Only . . ."

"What is it?"

"That's why I've come with Mr. Lafitte. My fiancé is Blaine Caldwell, an accused spy."

"The man who's to die tomorrow?"

"Yes. Unless somehow I can find a way to save him."

"Oh, Jesus, how sad this is." He took her hand. "I'd heard a spy was captured. The man sabotaged Thornton's boats and changed the outcome of the battle. We all admire his bravery, but, my dearest Rebecca, he cost English lives—and a spy must pay for his crimes. I'm afraid there's no savin' the man."

She studied his ruddy cheeks, his auburn hair peeking from beneath the bandage. Should she trust him? A mistake could cost Blaine's life. She decided she must. There was no other way the plan she'd proposed could possibly succeed.

"Gilbert, if . . . if I could save Blaine, with no risk to you, would you be willing to help?"

He thought a moment. "You say this lad is your betrothed?"

"Yes. Oh, he's a good man too. Not only brave, but a man of character and of property. Before the war, he ran a shipping business he inherited from his family. He's half-English, you see. Half-English and half-Creole. He agreed to spy only at General Jackson's insistence. That was after one of his own ships was boarded and his crew impressed into the British navy. You must agree, that was a terrible thing."

"I dinnae always agree with English methods. But still . . . spying . . ."

"We're to marry as soon as he's free. We'll live at his fine home in New Orleans." Her voice rose. "Oh, Gilbert, we're deeply in love. I know he spied for Jackson, but he was a patriot, after all. He risked his life for what he believed in. He mustn't die for that. I beg you to help us."

"No, lass, no need for begging . . . or tears, either. If I can help ye, I will. But dinnae ask me to betray my country. That I willnae do—not even for my own kin."

"Oh, I won't do that. All I'm asking is for you not to betray *me* when the time comes. And to help Mr. Lafitte influence the major. Oh, yes, there's a little playacting involved. It won't be difficult, I promise."

"Ye'd better tell me all about it."

It took several minutes to describe her plan. Gilbert shook his head in amazement, then finally arched his brows. "It's just mad enough to work, Rebecca. And my part is simple. But if ye get yourself into deep trouble, I'll be hard put to save ye, I fear."

"No, if it doesn't work, you mustn't reveal your part. I would be heartbroken if I lost Blaine *and* brought harm to you as well. Promise me, Gilbert. Give me your oath."

"I swear," he said solemnly. "Aye, on our mother's grave."

"Thank you from the bottom of my heart. And when this is over, I will come to Aberdeen. And I'll bring Blaine with me. Who knows, we may have babes of our own by then."

Lafitte, followed by Major Blanton, approached them.

"We can see Captain Caldwell now," Lafitte announced. "He's being held in a shack beyond the marsh." He gave Rebecca a hard look, holding her eyes, sending her a secret message with his stern expression. "You'll be pleased to have your revenge, Mademoiselle Gordon. I understand my friend has been brought to a lowly state."

"He may be *your* friend, Mr. Lafitte, but he's no friend of mine." She was relieved at the strength and brittleness of her voice. So the play was on. And Blaine's life depended on how well each participant acted out his part.

The four walked single file along a narrow, overgrown path winding its way beneath towering cypresses draped with gray-green moss. Lafitte followed Major Blanton, Rebecca followed Lafitte, and Gilbert Gordon walked last. The air was moist and cool, pungent with the smells of stagnant water and rotting vegetation.

Keeping her back straight and her eyes on Lafitte's cranberry red jacket, Rebecca steeled herself for the scene she must play. The most difficult part was knowing she must hurt Blaine purposely, and of course he would have no idea what was happening. She had hoped for a moment alone with him—or even that Lafitte might be able to give him a signal, but with the major hovering near, that would be impossible.

They arrived at a windowless shack, its rickety frame door held fast by a rusty padlock.

Rebecca's first thought was that a strong and clever man like Blaine might be able to break out of such a ramshackle enclosure. And there were no guards in the area.

But when she entered the prison whose only light was oblique shafts of sun seeping between cracks in the logs and penetrating downward from a rotting roof, she saw to her horror why nothing more sturdy and secure was necessary.

Blaine was chained across the top of a plank table that was inches too short for his long frame. He was shirtless and his arms were fastened with ropes to the table legs.

Her breath left her at the sight of his prone body, the scars along his bare chest, his wretched condition. But most frightening of all was his still face with closed eyes, the growth of beard along his chin, and dried blood mingling with strands of hair across his forehead. Was he conscious? Was he even alive? She almost betrayed her true feelings when she looked down at him. Quickly, she covered her face with her hands as if she were repelled rather than stricken with anguish at seeing him like this.

Lafitte was not required to be so inhibited. He leaned over Blaine and cursed. "Dammit to hell. Caldwell, mon ami . . . what have they done to you?" His voice was scalding.

Clenching her fists at her side, she prayed for control. She was able to draw a breath when she saw his eyes open and his head turn toward Jean. Leaning against the wall in the shadows, she struggled to hide her emotions.

"He was questioned a bit," said the major. "But all that's over now."

"Questioned?" shouted Lafitte. "Looks more like torture. Didn't he have a trial?"

"Yes . . . a rather quick one. But the legalities were observed. He was caught in the act of sabotage, after all. And our army is on the move. This war isn't over, you know."

His face tight with fury, Jean faced Blanton. "The war for *Louisiana* is over. The American victory was decisive and the English are skulking downstream like angry schoolboys, taking potshots as they retreat."

"The bombardment continues at Fort St. Philip. If the fort surrenders, we move north again to attack the city."

"The fort will never be taken. You're wasting your cannon on a foe inspired by the victory at New Orleans. Now tell me why this man, a captain in the Louisiana militia, is being treated like this?"

"He's a spy. I was present at his questioning and I can tell you he's as hotheaded and stubborn as they come. They wanted information on Jackson's forces and the chance of Yankee reinforcements arriving from Virginia. Caldwell declined to cooperate. Of course he knew he would be shot, but he could have saved himself a good deal of suffering."

All this time, Rebecca kept her eyes fixed on Blaine's face, watching him change from a state of semiconsciousness to agonizing awareness.

He moved on the table, his jaw clenched against the pain.

Lafitte reached out to touch his shoulder. Blaine's skin was gleaming with sweat despite the damp coolness of the hut.

The jaded privateer was visibly affected by the sight of his friend's misery. "Tell me, Blanton, when will he be released from this . . . this god-awful condition? I thought a condemned man was allowed some dignity before the end."

"He'll be fed tonight . . . something. Probably allowed a cup of wine. Tomorrow he'll be cleaned up and made ready for the execution. He requested a military uniform so we stripped one from a dead Yankee."

Rebecca felt weak, but knew she must begin her part or

time might run out. Stepping forward, she spoke loftily. "Let me see the villain," she said, and moved near to stare down at him.

Blaine raised his head with effort and looked at her. His face was drawn, his eyes sunken and confused. "Who . . . Rebecca . . . no," he whispered, then dropped back to the table.

She bit her lip. Could she go through with it? His magnificent body which she had embraced, his arms which had held her close, his hands, strong with tapered fingers which had so tenderly caressed her and guided her along the path of womanhood—that he should be subjected to this—it was almost more than she could bear. Silently she prayed for strength.

"Captain Caldwell," she said sharply. "I'd prefer to see you hanged, but at least I'll have my revenge."

He lifted his head. The chains across his chest and binding his ankles rattled as he moved. "Is . . . is that really you . . . Rebecca?"

"It is, you two-faced devil. I'd like to see you hanged for . . . for rape. But I suppose shooting will do just as well to rid the earth of you."

Lafitte grabbed her arm and spun her to face him. "Shut up, woman. It's enough he's accused of spying without adding that nonsense about rape. Besides, you agreed to keep your mouth shut if I brought you along."

"After what I paid you, you have no right to complain. I'll have my say—and my revenge."

At this point, Gilbert stepped forward. "Mr. Lafitte, if my sister says she was raped, she's telling the truth. If Caldwell were not about to die, I'd kill him myself. As it is, Rebecca has asked for that honor—and I'm inclined to give it to her."

"What's all this?" Major Blanton interjected.

Lafitte gave Rebecca a vicious stare. "This wench claims Caldwell raped her. She's convinced her brother it's true, but not me. Why would a man rape such as her when he has his choice of any lady he wants, either blue blood or gypsy."

"Doesn't matter a hell of a lot," said Blanton. "He'll be dead this time tomorrow."

"It matters to me," snapped Rebecca. She pulled a

derringer from her pocket and pressed it against Blaine's temple.

He continued to gaze up at her, his confusion deepening.

"Wait!" commanded Blanton. "Don't do that. Why kill a man who's already doomed?"

She didn't dare meet Blaine's eyes. "Because I hate him—I despise him. I'm a ruined woman because of him. I had a marriage proposal from a landed gentleman. He withdrew it when this captain bragged about how he . . . he'd taken me to bed."

"Then witness his execution tomorrow. I've given permission for Lafitte to claim the body. You can witness it all, but don't blow out his brains today. Give him time to think about his death. You can see for yourself he's none too comfortable at the moment."

"Rebecca . . . what are you saying?" Blaine asked just above a whisper. "You can't—"

"I'm saying shut up, Blaine Caldwell. I've a gun at your head and I'm likely to pull the trigger."

"Then do it," he said bitterly. "I'd rather you kill me than the British."

She swallowed the knot in her throat. "Just—hush," she insisted, wondering if she could survive the next few minutes.

Lafitte helped her by saying, "You little bitch. He paid you, didn't he? You know what that makes you!"

Gilbert thumped Lafitte's arm. "Watch your tongue, you bloody pirate."

Blanton moved between them. "Enough, Gordon. You and I will handle the execution—noon, tomorrow. Bring your rifle and two rounds. You can salvage your sister's honor, if that's your intention. Now you, Miss Gordon, put away that pistol."

In response, she cocked the weapon. "Maybe I will. But on one condition."

"What's that?"

"*I* will be the executioner tomorrow. I'll kill him, legally and without help from anyone."

"Ridiculous."

She reached into the purse at her waist and pulled out a velvet pouch full of coins, then tossed it to Blanton.

"I'll make it worth your while, sir. You can supervise, of course, and my brother will also stand by with his weapon. But *I* will fire the shot—and I promise you it will be a fatal one."

"With that delicate lady's handgun?" Blanton asked.

"No, sir. I'm expert with a rifle—a long-rifle, actually. I'll put a bullet through his black heart."

"You murdering whore," Lafitte snarled. "I always knew women were more bloodthirsty than men."

Blanton weighed the pouch in his palm. "It's . . . it's quite out of the ordinary. If my superiors hear of it—"

"No one need know," she said. "I want the satisfaction. I demand it," she said fiercely, pressing the pistol against Blaine's flesh. He didn't flinch, but just looked up at her with confusion in his eyes.

The major shook his head. "No . . . I don't think—"

She removed several more gold coins and held them out to him. "Choose at once. If you take the money, we'll be on our way and return before noon tomorrow. If not—my brother will retrieve my pouch and I, Major, will pull this trigger."

Her glance swept to Blaine who now closed his eyes and seemed to relax. His calm resignation, his acceptance of death at her hands tore through her heart and made her adore him more desperately than she believed possible. If only she could explain. Love and fear enveloped her simultaneously, causing the pistol to shake in her hand.

"Let the lass do it tomorrow," Gordon urged. "If she hesitates or misses I'll finish him off."

"Oh hell, why not," Blanton suddenly agreed. He stuffed the pouch in his coat and took the coins from her hand. "Dead is dead. If it's so important to you to take your revenge, I suppose the order of the court will be carried out. I'd like to get *something* out of this ill-fated trip to America. Gordon, be at my headquarters before noon. If your sister and Lafitte show up, we'll give her the first shot. If not, you and I will perform the execution as planned. Now all of you, get out of here. Someone will be along soon to see to his last meal."

With a trembling hand, Rebecca replaced her pistol and forced her eyes away from Blaine's ravaged face. He hadn't defended himself—nor had he shown anger at her cruel threat. Did he actually believe she would kill him—or was he too weak to care? Whichever, he would have to wait until tomorrow to find out the truth. As for her, she would die a thousand deaths during the long hours ahead. At least so far, the plan was working to perfection. As she followed the path out of the swamp, she kept her head high, her mouth firm, and a fixed angry stare aimed at the back of Jean Lafitte's head.

26

Blaine sat on the end of the table where for much of the past three days he had been chained and half-conscious. He could take some pride in the fact that the torture he'd endured had not caused him to betray his country nor beg for mercy. He had prayed for death a few times; death he didn't fear. But it hadn't come, so today he would face a spy's execution—and be done with all life's pain and futility.

Only one thing confused him. Why had Rebecca come to the hut with Lafitte? If he hadn't been so acutely aware of her presence, he would have sworn he was having some fever-ridden fantasy. But she had been real: her rich dark beauty, her eyes laced with passion, and the cold steel of her pistol pressed against his head. He had expected her to shoot. Hell, she'd be doing him a favor. Maybe that's why she had come—to more quickly end his suffering. A mercy killing was the only reason that made any sense.

But Jean and Rebecca had seemed to be arguing. Had Jean prevented Rebecca from killing him? Someone had intervened; he wasn't sure who. If Jean had thought he was doing his old comrade a favor by extending his life a few days, he was mistaken. In fact, it would have made more sense for Jean to put a bullet in his brain rather than expecting Rebecca to do it. Maybe that was the cause of the argument. He'd been too fuzzy-headed to know what was going on. But if Jean and Rebecca had been trying to help him, they were poor partners in the task. The least they could have done was figure out in advance who would pull the trigger.

He shifted uncomfortably, rattling his wrist and ankle chains in the process. He was clean now and dressed—dressed for death. The blue woolsey jacket of the Louisiana militia chafed the cuts and bruises on his back and chest. But the stiff knee boots felt good, adding support to his weakened ankles and leg muscles. He hoped to God he could walk to the place of execution without stumbling in his steps.

It seemed a long wait before his guards returned to escort him to the clearing near the river. The two men were from Liverpool, just young lads, and appeared more nervous and upset by the proceedings than he was. They had slipped him an extra biscuit for breakfast and even a cup of brandy. True, they had kept a gun on him while he was unchained, but they had apologized profusely when they had fastened the irons over the raw wounds on his wrists.

He walked along the narrow path, his feet dragging a bit with the weight, but his head up and his mind clear. The first moment of dizziness had passed, and he was certain now he would not make a fool of himself by showing any weakness. He breathed deeply of the fresh pungent air, even noticed a snake slither into the brackish water beside the path.

He was relatively sure Jean would be there at the end, his good friend to the last. Some time ago, he had asked Jean to place him in the family crypt at Dominique Hall if anything should happen to him. Hopefully those wishes would be carried out. Would the United States take note of his sacrifice? Maybe—maybe not. Spies were usually expendable and soon forgotten. Possibly Jackson would have a kind thought for him. After all, Blaine thought, he'd done a damn good job of this spying business—and given his life to save New Orleans. Jackson would be the hero, of course—go on to fame and glory. That's all right, he decided. Jackson was a good man. A man well suited for the times.

Rebecca. The thought of her filled his heart with bittersweet longing. He supposed she was grief stricken. Poor little girl hadn't had much of life's pleasures. His deepest regret was that he hadn't married her before the battle. At least then she would have inherited Dominique Hall—and someday make some incredibly lucky man an adorable, rich wife. On the positive side, she was evidently under Jean Lafitte's wing. Jean would protect her from the likes of Guy Laurens. Who knows, if Lafitte had a lick of sense, he'd marry the girl himself. The moment Blaine had the thought, he was sorry. Somehow, he couldn't bring himself to the point of relinquishing Rebecca to Jean—not even from the grave.

Outside Major Blanton's quarters, Rebecca stood near Jean Lafitte. Close by her side, she clutched a Tennessee long-rifle, primed and ready.

She had spent last night at Grande Isle, alone and pacing the floor of her room at Lafitte's house. He had provided her with a sumptuous meal, but she couldn't swallow a bite. Nor could she sleep in the bed with its mounded feather mattress and satin sheets. How could she, when Blaine lay in agony in the hut in the swamp—not knowing she held his life in her hands. She felt that everything she had ever done, or ever been, had led her to this moment in time. From her secretive and humble birth, her young days spent practicing marksmanship in the woods near her home, her first meeting with Blaine, events had carried her like the powerful flow of the Mississippi toward her fate, hers and Blaine's. If only he knew, if only she could explain before . . . before . . .

Waiting now for Blaine to be brought forth, she tried to remain calm, but it was impossible. This morning she had practiced with the gun. Only five out of eight times had she been as accurate as was required. Jean Lafitte had doubts. She saw it in his eyes. But he had agreed since it seemed Blaine's only hope. He had provided the gold for Blanton, and played his part to perfection. Even Gilbert had done well, taking a risk though he was barely acquainted with the people involved.

Gilbert appeared now. He was in formal dress of plaid jacket and kilt—appropriate for the solemn formality of a spy's execution.

Rebecca joined him beneath the trees to whisper a private

word. It still felt strange to speak to him like a brother. But she admired him, and would never forget how he had come to her aid.

"I see ye brought your weapon," he observed grimly. "They say 'twas ye who shot down the Scottish banner at Chalmette."

"Would it make a difference today if I admitted to it?"

Reaching out, he touched her shoulder. "Nay, lass. I'm guessing anyone who could do that could easily have killed the flag bearer. Ye didnae do that. I'm . . . I'm just glad ye're a crack shot . . . for the sake of your young man."

"I pray I'm doing the right thing. If all goes well, we'll be leaving quickly. Lafitte has a boat on the canal waiting to take us to one of Blaine's ships near Barataria. I . . . I wanted to say good-bye now . . . and thank you."

"I see . . . and I understand. But ye know, if ye miss . . . I'm duty bound to kill him myself. And whichever way it goes, I must administer the coup de grace—a single shot to his head."

"But we discussed that."

"Aye. You must not miss."

"I won't. I can't. It's just that I'm so nervous. I'm . . . terrified."

He slipped a finger under her chin. "Here now, Miss Rebecca Gordon of the Aberdeen Gordons. Ye have good Scots blood in your veins. Ye won't fail. I'm certain of it." His smile carried reassurance.

"Then I'll say good-bye, Gilbert. And God be with you—till we meet again."

He leaned over and kissed her lightly on her forehead. "I'll soon be back in the Highlands," he said, leading her back to the tent. "I'm finished with war for good. Come see me one day, little sister. I'll be watching for ye—and for your bonnie smile."

Major Blanton exited the tent. Before Rebecca could speak to him, two guards appeared coming along the pathway from the swamp. Between them, walking straight and tall, strode Blaine, as if he'd just arrived to take command of his ship.

The sight of him almost buckled her knees. Never had he

looked more handsome or more confident. In military uniform though bareheaded, he was as dashing a figure as Jackson had ever been, only more youthfully handsome. He was actually smiling and chatting with his guards as they unlocked his shackles. The change in his appearance since yesterday was stunning. He was well-groomed, clean-shaven, clear-eyed and almost jovial. He nodded to Major Blanton and shook hands with Lafitte.

She watched closely from her secluded spot in the trees, hoping beyond hope that Jean would find a way to let Blaine in on the plan. Somehow Blaine must be warned to appear to die at the proper time, otherwise he could actually cause his own death.

"I've brought a flag," Lafitte was explaining to Blanton. "An *American* flag," he said pointedly.

"Naturally," answered the major. "You may remove the body once the coup de grace is administered by Lieutenant Gordon."

Blaine stood casually by, listening to this exchange as if the weather were under discussion.

Blanton turned without meeting Blaine's eyes and took up a spot on a small rise. Drawing his sword, he ordered, "The condemned man will stand against that tree. Guards, prepare him."

One of the guards approached with a blindfold.

"No, that isn't needed," said Blaine.

Lafitte stepped forward. "Caldwell, put the damned thing on."

Startled, Blaine looked at him. After a moment, he said with some sign of weakening, "It isn't necessary, Jean."

"I say it is!"

Still in the shadows, Rebecca gnawed her lip. Silently she pleaded for him to accept the blindfold. Then, at least he wouldn't see her when she . . .

The guard produced ropes.

"No," said Blaine firmly. "No ropes." He stood stiffly before the tree where he'd been placed. Looking at Jean, he said, "I won't embarrass my friend by trying to escape."

The sight of the half-smile she loved so well stabbed at her heart. His courage took her breath.

Lafitte waved aside the guards. "Forget the ropes. I myself will tie the blindfold." Before Blaine could protest, Lafitte grabbed the cloth from the guard and moved near his face.

Although everyone was watching closely, only Rebecca knew the importance of this moment. At last Jean had a chance to whisper in Blaine's ear. It was critical that Blaine know what to do after he was shot and before the coup de grace was administered.

Jean fumbled, cursed, made a new attempt to tie the cloth. Leaning close to Blaine's head, he struggled with the knot for several seconds, muttering in French as he fastened the blindfold in place.

Blaine no longer objected, but waited calmly for his friend to complete the task.

Finally Jean stepped away.

Rebecca moved away from the trees and stood in front of Blaine—not too close, not too far. She was relieved he couldn't see her, but more than that, she was certain Jean had told him what was going to happen. The question burning in her mind was whether or not Blaine now knew that *she* would do the shooting.

She looked at Lafitte, being careful to keep an angry expression fixed in place.

His response was a cocked eyebrow and slight nod. It was a very good sign.

Her hands were clammy. With her gun resting on her side, she wiped her palms along her skirt.

Suddenly Blaine spoke. "One moment. It's customary in England, I've heard, at beheadings and the like, for the victim to offer a coin and grant forgiveness to the executioner. Though I am Creole, I am also English. In honor of my father, I request this privilege." He reached in his coat pocket and removed a coin.

Lafitte tried to intervene, but Major Blanton snapped, "It's a tradition, pirate. Let your friend have his way. Come here, madam. Get your Judas coin."

She was going to faint. She just knew it. But from somewhere deep inside, she summoned every ounce of inner strength. She walked forward, her rifle balanced on her hip. When she stood directly in front of Blaine, she mumbled, "So . . . hurry up and forgive me."

He smiled ever so slightly. "Rebecca." It was so soft, it was lost in the rustle of the tree leaves.

She was paralyzed. So now he knew *she* was going to shoot him. Would he be willing to trust her skill? Would he understand how desperate she was at this moment—how terrified?

"Are you there?" he asked for all to hear.

Her lips were frozen.

"Hold out your hand. The coin of death is for you."

Slowly she raised her free hand.

"I forgive you," he said rather dramatically, "for taking my life."

He reached out, grasped her hand and pressed the coin into her palm. "What's this?" he demanded. "A woman? I protest!"

She could have strangled him. Staring at his face, she saw his lip twitch with amusement. She must keep her wits and play out the farce. "Tarnation—shut up," she hissed between clamped teeth. Then loudly, "Unhand me, you villain," she cried. "I'll have my revenge!"

"Fair enough, Rebecca Gordon. But I claim one thing more before you send me to Hell." In a swift movement, he wrapped one arm around her waist and dragged her against him, entwined his fingers through her hair and found her lips, then kissed her with all the fire and passion of a man possessed.

"Stop that!" came a shout from behind them. "Get her away!"

At Blanton's command, the guards jumped forward and tugged her out of Blaine's arms, then shoved him against the tree trunk.

He laughed. "I'm satisfied," he said firmly. "I'm glad to die with that treacherous woman's taste on my lips."

She rushed back to her position and whirled to face him, raising the rifle as she turned. "Get out of my way," she cried to the guards. "Just let me kill the arrogant bastard before he further insults me!" If she hadn't screamed something, she would have collapsed. How could he take such a risk—rattle her nerves, *kiss her,* when she needed all her concentration to put a bullet through his body? Dear Heaven, he was turning the whole thing into a joke.

Sighting along the barrel, she saw he was now standing quietly, waiting, his arms relaxed at his side. His smile was gone, but he showed no trace of fear.

Lafitte moved close, closer than was necessary or even safe if the shooter had been anyone but Rebecca.

The two guards moved to stand behind the major, who raised his sword.

Gilbert slid his pistol from his belt and held it ready.

"Take your position, Miss Gordon. I'll lower my weapon as a signal." Blanton was pale and the tip of his sword shook in the noontime sun.

Something clicked in Rebecca's head. She heard the official at the fair in Nashville order her to step up and take her best shot. Her nerves settled into deadly calm; nothing existed but her target.

Her future, and Blaine's life, depended on this one shot. It was easy, close, the blue fabric, the button on the pocket below his heart—down a bit—right a bit. The fleshy spot along his side. The wound must be there. She sighted and inhaled deeply—then sighted once more. Her hands were steady. Be still, Blaine. For God's sake, be still.

The sword swept downward.

Slowly she squeezed the trigger. The rifle exploded, recoiling against her shoulder. Down the glistening barrel, she saw Blaine knocked hard against the tree, his arms out, his head back, then tumbling forward to land heavily on the ground at its base.

Dropping the gun, she swayed where she stood. Her brain hammered. Don't move, Blaine . . . oh my love, don't move.

He drew up one knee.

"Oh hell," uttered the major, his sword forgotten in his hand. "Hurry up, Gordon, get the job done."

Rebecca knew her cheeks were streaked with tears, but she ignored them and stayed rooted in place. She was sure she had hit the exact spot where she'd aimed. Now it was up to Gilbert—and Lafitte—and Blaine himself.

Jean knelt by Blaine, his flag unrolled and trailing the ground. He said something near Blaine's ear.

Gilbert's arm moved forward, the pistol pointed at Blaine's temple.

"Holy Jesus," she whispered, clenching her fists.

The pistol cracked. Blaine's body arched once, then fell limp to the grassy earth and remained perfectly still.

Lafitte threw the flag over the body. Standing over it, he made the sign of the cross. Then he looked at Rebecca. "God curse you to eternal hell, woman. You've done your deed—had your revenge. Now get to the boat. I want to take my friend's body out of here and prepare it for Christian burial."

She felt her breath return in ragged gasps. She knew Jean Lafitte, and he looked more concerned than heartbroken. Surely, this meant Blaine was alive.

Hope gave her strength. "I doubt if Christ would receive such a lecher," she said loudly—too loudly perhaps, but shouting released her tension.

Lafitte lifted the figure draped with the red, white and blue.

"Wait a minute," ordered Blanton. "I say, Lieutenant Gordon, is he dead?"

"I wouldnae miss, would I?" answered Gilbert. "I'll sign the papers, if ye like."

"No, no, I'll sign. Just get him out of here. If Pakenham were alive, he'd have my hide for allowing such an execution."

Rebecca hurried to Gilbert and pecked him on the cheek. "Thank you, my darling Scot," she whispered. "Good-bye, brother," she said for all to hear. "Between the two of us, my honor is avenged."

She rushed after a retreating Lafitte. The pirate carried the body slung over his shoulder, none too gently, she thought. Already the back of Jean's forest green jacket was beginning to darken with Blaine's blood. It seemed a great deal of blood if she'd hit the spot where she'd aimed. New fear crept into her heart. She prayed silently: Please be all right, my darling, my love. Oh, dear Lord, let him live.

27

"Hell, Jean. I'm not a sack of potatoes."

Lafitte had just laid Blaine on the mattress of his bed on Grande Isle.

"So you're awake, mon ami. You slept like a babe all the way."

Blaine grunted and tried to sit up. The pain in his side sent him dizzily back to the pillow.

"Here—I'll help you get out of those bloody things. No sense in ruining fine linen sheets."

He allowed Jean to remove his coat and shirt and check the bandage at his side. "You make a tolerable nurse, Lafitte, but I'd much prefer Rebecca. Where's my lady?"

"Gone for medicine and bandages at Doc's cabin. She'll be here shortly, I expect."

"I suppose she's in a devilish mood after all this."

"She is a bit on edge. I told her you were too tough to die—especially at the hands of a woman."

Blaine chuckled at the thought. "I said she was special, didn't I?"

"*Special* is hardly sufficient praise for that little lady. If I'm ever attacked by Barbary pirates, I'll send for her at once."

Blaine laughed, but it ended in a moan as he pressed his side.

"Careful," said Jean.

"It hurts like blazes."

"Of course. But it's only a flesh wound. Won't even need stitching."

An idea formed in his head. "Does Rebecca know that?"

"Oh, she's fussing and stewing—thinks she's nearly killed you."

"I might have some fun with that twinge of guilt."

"Now, Caldwell, haven't you caused her enough misery for one day?"

"Don't worry. She can stand a little teasing."

The door opened to admit a bright-eyed tyke followed by a huge, lumbering black dog.

"What is it, young lady?" Jean queried.

"Well, hello, Shandy," Blaine said, plumping his pillow. "What brings you here?"

"I came on the packet from New Orleans. 'Scuse me for barging in, but I had to get here as fast as I could, sir. I heard you was being executed, and I couldn't find Miss Rebecca. But here you are, Cap'n, so it cain't be true you're dead."

"No. I'm very much alive. But you mustn't tell anyone. It's a secret from the British."

"Wouldn't matter no more. The war's over."

"I'm not so sure," Blaine noted.

"But 'tis. We got word in town this morning. Bells ringing and horns tooting. A treaty was signed a long time ago—before Christmas even. Why, the war's been over for weeks. 'Twas over before the battle at New Orleans was fought."

"Sacre coeur!" Lafitte snapped. "This is the truth?"

"Yes, sir. Guess the Yankees won."

"That's great news, Shandy. Oh, this is Mr. Jean Lafitte. Jean, this is Shannon Kildaire, an old friend of mine. And this is Rebecca's dog, Pepper."

Jean swept into a bow. "I'm honored to have such guests."

Shandy crossed to the bed and Pepper crawled underneath it. "I have a letter for Miss Rebecca. And this too. Is she here?"

"She'll be here soon," Blaine said, taking a small item from Shandy's hand.

"I see her coming now," said Jean, glancing out the window.

Shandy squatted and spoke to the dog. "Stay, Pepper! Stay right there, till me or Miss Rebecca says to come out."

Blaine smiled fondly at the child as she hurried out the door.

Shandy greeted Rebecca outside. "Hi, Miss Rebecca. I brought you a letter."

Her arms laden with bandages, Rebecca stepped onto the porch. "Why, Shandy, I'm surprised to see you."

"I brought you a letter from Miss Josie. She said it was real urgent you got it."

Rebecca hated any delay in returning to Blaine's side, but she sat in a wooden chair and smiled at the little girl. "Very well. I'll read it quickly, then see to my patient. The captain's . . . well, been shot, you see."

"But he's not dead. I'm sure happy he's all right."

"Yes. I am too," she agreed, keeping worry and fatigue from her voice. "Now, let's see what Miss Josie has to say." She opened the letter and rested it on the bandages in her lap. She read it through twice before its contents registered. It said that Josie had been found justified in the killing of Guy Laurens. It said the war was over, and things were returning to normal in New Orleans. But the stunning news was that a claim had been filed for Rebecca as the only living heir of Etienne Dufour. Two days ago, the court had found in favor of Rebecca. She would inherit the entire Dufour fortune and his estate property in the new Garden District. In short, Josie's lawyers, armed with old letters and new information, had made Rebecca a very wealthy woman.

She was staring in amazement at the letter when Jean came onto the porch. His worried tone belied the merriment behind his eyes. "Rebecca, Blaine's awake and asking for you. I'm afraid he's suffering quite a lot."

Jumping from her chair, she stuffed the note in her pocket. "I'll go right in."

Jean reached for Shandy's hand. "Are you hungry, Mademoiselle Kildaire?"

"Yes, sir."

"Then come along and we'll get you some gumbo. While you eat, I'll tell you a tale you won't soon forget."

Rebecca pushed open the door and hurried to the bed. Blaine was lying quietly, his face pale against the pillow. He opened his eyes as she bent over him.

For an instant, she absorbed his look, then let her gaze flow across his bare chest above the sheet and drop to his hand resting over the bandage on his side. Her long rehearsed speech of apology fled.

Looking into his face, seeing the dark circles under his eyes, achingly aware of his smooth bronze skin and dark hair across his well-muscled chest—and of the scars he bore, both old and new, and of the wound she herself had inflicted, she could only stand in silence, overcome by love and remorse. His expression was serious, his lips firmly set. The thought prowled through her mind that he might be angry with her, that he thought her plan of rescue absurd, despite the fact that it had succeeded. She said at last, "I'm so sorry, Blaine. I didn't want to hurt you, but I couldn't think of any other way. Are you in great pain?"

"I believe you did this to me, while I was blindfolded and helpless." He lifted his hand from the bandage.

She was struck again by the gracefulness of his hands, his strong fingers. They had stroked her to the heights of ecstasy. Now, resting on the white sheet, they seemed remote and disembodied.

"Did you miss your primary target?" he asked.

She studied him. His voice was strong. He might be in pain, but she was certain now he was not seriously hurt. "Miss my target? What do you mean?"

"I thought you might have taken off a larger piece of my hide than you intended."

"Umph. I haven't missed at that distance since I was four. I aimed at the fleshy part of your right side. I expected blood and pain—but hardly death. You'll notice that's exactly what happened."

His brow furrowed. "So the joke was on me. Cooked up by you and Lafitte."

"At least Jean was able to warn you. But that business with the coin—and that kiss—you could have ruined everything."

"I was confident you could manage." The corner of his lip

twitched. "It was certainly the bright point of *my* experience."

"Well, it was just awful for me," she said, sudden exasperation replacing sympathy. "If you hadn't done your part, Gilbert would have had to really shoot you to save the rest of us. The coup de grace, you know."

"I know. My right ear is still deafened by the blast."

She put her hands on her hips. "I do want to compliment you on appearing to be dead."

"Thanks to the American flag."

"That was Jean's idea."

"An excellent one."

This conversation was not going as she had wanted. "I'm sure I must apologize for shooting you. But it was better me than Major Blanton or one of his officers. You owe my brother, Gilbert, your thanks for his cooperation—and Jean Lafitte about three hundred gold dollars."

"And you? What do I owe you for blasting this hole in my side?"

"Only your life, I suppose."

"I thank you, then. But you've caused me more pain than any man ought to endure."

Her heart melted. "Oh, Blaine, I know . . ."

"Here I lie—shattered by a woman—brought low by her cunning and her strong will. And there you stand, exhibiting not the slightest sympathy, compassion or guilt."

"But . . . I am sorry. Truly."

He pulled the sheet up over his chest and closed his eyes.

"Oh, my goodness," she said, her worry erupting again. She placed a hand on his forehead. It did feel very warm.

"I'm so cold," he said without opening his eyes.

"You may have a chill. I'll get a blanket."

"No. No. I've got a better idea." He raised the sheet and motioned her to climb in beside him.

Without hesitating, she stepped out of her slippers and moved into the bed. Putting her arm across his chest she nuzzled against his shoulder.

He took her hand and placed it over the bandage.

"Oh, my poor darling, it must hurt so."

"Yes," he said with a large sigh. "Here too."

"But—over your heart? I didn't . . . Oh," she said, grasping his meaning.

"And here."

"Blaine!" She was shocked when he moved her hand below his waist.

"Later," he said with a sly smile. "Don't move now." He grasped her hand and placed something over her finger.

She pulled out her hand and saw the pearl ring she had left behind on his dresser. "Oh," she cried. "Where did you get it?"

"Shandy brought it just now," he answered, running his fingers along her neck, tracing the delicate curve revealed above her bodice. "She found it in my room. Thought you had lost it and might like to have it back. Thoughtful child, that Shannon Kildaire." He was murmuring, raising to touch his lips to her wrist, the back of her hand, the tips of her fingers.

"Yes," she said, turning toward him. She lightly kissed the rise of his shoulder. His flesh was hot on her lips. "Blaine, I love the ring—and I love *you*—more than life."

"There'll be other rings, my darling. You'll have a magnificent wedding ring, and necklaces, and dresses, and travel, all the things I want to give you—things you've never had. Surprises, lots of surprises."

She cuddled against him. Smiling into his chest, she murmured. "I'll have some surprises for you too, my darling."

He stroked her hair. "Like what, my little sharpshooter?"

"Oh, I'll tell you later. Just some news from Josie."

"All good, I hope."

"All very, very good." She stroked his forearm. "I do hope no one thinks I have to shoot a man to get him to marry me."

"Hm. That should make for interesting speculation in New Orleans."

"Are you feeling warmer?" she whispered.

"Much—merci beaucoup, cherie."

"I like it here—beside you."

He pulled her close. "It's your place always—in my bed or at the marriage altar—on my ship or at Dominique Hall.

Stay, lass, and fill my arms with your fiery, dangerous beauty." His lips claimed hers, teasing, lingering, then forcing and devouring.

A scratching noise came from beneath them.

Ending the kiss, he smiled down at her. "Oh, I almost forgot," he said, pushing to one elbow. "Shandy brought you something else. Look under the bed."

She rotated and leaned over the side, acutely aware of how Blaine had wrapped one arm about her lower body. She lifted the trailing blanket and peered into the darkness.

A large wet tongue swept across her nose and cheek.

Jumping back, she clung to the sheet to keep from falling. "Pepper!" she cried. Her delighted laughter mingled with Blaine's as her Creole cavalier drew her into the shelter of his arms.

Author's Historical Notes

In 1812 the fledgling United States of America entered a war against England that has often been described as unpopular and unnecessary. Variously referred to as "Mr. Madison's War," "The Second War of Independence" or "The War of 1812," it began largely over England's high-handed practice of stopping and boarding American ships at sea, then impressing Yankee seamen into the British navy. The proud young country, recently enlarged by the immense Louisiana Purchase, was flexing its muscles after winning the *first* War of Independence against the imperial British. The war hawks in the new capital of Washington were not about to take such insults without a fight.

Whether justified or not, this final confrontation against our Mother Country had its share of tragedy and glory. Britain's sea power was at an all-time high. England had just scored a decisive victory over Napoleon, and then turned its attention to the upstart teenage United States, which was refusing to recognize the authority of its powerful former parent. The war lasted over two years and ended in a twist of irony. Its most famous battle, "The Battle of New Orleans," was fought weeks after a peace treaty was signed in Belgium on Christmas Eve 1814. The battle would catapult Andrew Jackson toward the White House and create a new American legendary hero. Instrumental in Jackson's victory were the dashing French privateer, Jean Lafitte, and the backwoods sharpshooters of Tennessee and Kentucky with their deadly long-rifles.

I owe a debt of thanks to my son, Brent, and his lady, Angela, for taking time to research in New Orleans for details of the sinking of the steamship *New Orleans.* Though controversy exists over whether the *New Orleans* was a stern-wheeler or a side-wheeler, she was indeed the first Queen of the Mississippi, a heroine in her own right. She proved the Mississippi could be navigated by steam power, and amazingly she survived the catastrophic New Madrid earthquake while en route to New Orleans in December of 1811. But in July of 1814, she sank near Baton Rouge after becoming impaled on a hidden tree stump.

In New Orleans, on November 30, 1803, at the Place d'Armes, the flag of Bourbon Spain was lowered and replaced by the flag of the French republic. Less than one month later on December 20, a small group of fashionable citizens gathered again for a ceremony. The French flag was lowered; the American flag raised. It was reported that "a few Americans in one corner cheered the new flag."